It All Started with My Neighbor

RONELLE HERRICK

Fulton Books
Meadville, PA

Published by Fulton Books 2022

ISBN 978-1-63985-592-6 (paperback)
ISBN 978-1-63985-593-3 (digital)

Printed in the United States of America

I would like to dedicate this book to my grandson
Zachary Summers, who inspired me to write
it. May he one day find his own path.

Chapter *1*

Mick opened one eye to glare at the clock, although he already knew that it wasn't really necessary. He had already hit the Snooze button three times. He usually tried to get out of bed on the second alarm shrilling "Panda" by Designer, but last night he overdid his stay at the Marine Bar and he felt a little bit groggy this morning. So with one eye open, he smashed his hand down on the alarm, swore, and threw his legs over the side of the bed. He sat there with elbows on knees, head in his hands, trying to remember the name of that cute little brunette talking to him last night.

"Shit, I need to get to work!" he said out loud. "That she-witch Sheelya Conklin is supposed to be at the office at nine thirty this morning." People that knew of her called her the Viper of Rockaway. "I know she comes to me because no one else will have anything to do with her." Although, as he stood up, scratched his balls, and walked toward the bathroom, he knew he was the only PI for miles around also. So there was not a lot of choices in this rural area.

The water was running for his shower, and this being an old house, it took a good five minutes to get hot. He literally could take a dump and brush his teeth before the water got warm enough to shower under. He rummaged for some clean clothes in his closet while he waited for the water to get hot. *A little problematic,* he thought. *The clean clothes, anyway.* If memory served him right, you had to wash clothes in order to have clean clothes, and he couldn't remember when he had last done any laundry. He knew the ones on the floor were not clean enough to wear, or the ones on the chair or the bed, for that matter. That left very few choices hanging in the closet. He started to rummage through what was left on the few hangers there were. *Good God,* he thought. *I have not seen that gray cowboy shirt in ten years or more!* As he stood there, noting his poor clothing choices, he considered again the thought that he really should hire a housekeeper. One about thirty-five, cute, petite, and no additional baggage. She need not have a high IQ or anything either. He smiled wryly as he found a suitable blue polo shirt with the words *Drugs Kill* on the front. His last girlfriend had given it to him. *Well, guess this will have to do. At least it's clean.* It wasn't like Sheelya would care what he wore; she never looked higher than his crotch, anyway. He set the shirt on the bathroom counter, next to the jeans he had worn the past three days. *Another day and they will be able to stand up by themselves,* he thought. He stepped into the shower and let the hot water take over.

As he soaped and washed his hair, he remembered back to when he first bought the house. It was an old 1950s bungalow style, and they had installed the hot-water heater in the garage, so the water had a good distance to travel before it reached his bathroom in the back of the small house. He had fallen in love with it as soon as he had walked through the first time. It suited him just fine. It had been well-preserved, and a lot of work had gone into its upkeep. It had been a two-bedroom, one-bath, but he had had another small three-quarter bath installed after his old Army buddy had come to visit and they had to share the same bathroom for a week. He wasn't going to let that happen again. It had cost a little over ten grand, but it had been worth it. He happened to like the older, vintage-style homes as opposed to the newer craftsman or saltbox style. His house was only a two-block walk to the beach. Well, the main highway was in between his house and the beach, but for marketing purposes, he could say it was two blocks. Worked on him when he bought it, anyway, he thought.

When he stepped out of the shower, he wiped the steam from the bathroom mirror. *One of these days, I should fix that fan,* he thought as he eyed himself critically in the mirror. He stood just slightly over six foot two, with perfectly even, stark white teeth. *Thanks to my dad. The only thing he really did for me was to make sure I got braces when*

I was twelve years old. That was only because his teeth were so bad he didn't want me to go through what he went through as a teenager. He remembered his dad telling him the kids had called him Big Ed, named after the show *Mister Ed* "Ed the talking horse." His dad had also been a big kid. Mick had seen a couple of pictures of him in his mom's old photo album. There was a couple that she hadn't ripped up, anyway. He remembered that picture; his dad had a big smile on his face, showing a set of big pearly whites. That was about the only picture he could remember his mom having of his dad. She had told him he had just received a promotion and then that was it; he disappeared for years without letting them know where he was.

"Quit your goddamn reminiscing this morning!" he said angrily to himself. He looked closer at his reflection in the steamy mirror. "Kind of disappointing you are, ole man. Not so sure your mother would be proud of you today." He critically eyed his red eyes and the gray that was creeping into his dark hair and beard. Seemed like it was just yesterday he was thirty, married, considered good-looking, and buff from working out almost every day. He walked out of the bathroom and over to his dresser to find a clean pair of socks. *Of course not!* he thought as he pulled out socks, none of which had a match. *Well, one black and one navy would have to do for now. At least I have a decent pair of Nike's. The high-top ones will cover the mismatched socks.* He cursed under his breath as he sat heavily on the side of the bed and tied his shoes.

It didn't take long to have a cup of coffee in hand, and as he stood at the kitchen sink, he drank from his favorite cup. A man's cup. Deep-blue color with a whale's tail for a handle. Another thing his last girlfriend had given him. He sighed a little wistfully, thinking about her. She had been sweet. She had always had some little gift for him, and what did he give her in return? Well, yes, that, but anything meaningful? No, not really. He put a piece of bread in the toaster, surveying what was left in the bread bin. *Hmm, only a couple of days past the expiration date. That's not so bad, but I had better think about getting a few groceries before I come home tonight, or I won't even have a piece of bread for tomorrow.* He looked in the coffee bag again. *Almost out of that too,* he thought. He hated going to the grocery store. Most times he stopped at the little mini-mart just down the street if he ran out of milk or beer, but it seemed he was almost out of everything and it would mean the big-box grocery run after work. He wondered, if he got Colin's sister to do housekeeping, would she be willing to do some grocery shopping as well? He felt better as he thought about bringing someone home to a clean house that actually had food in it. He was pretty sure she would do it for him. She cleaned other people's houses, and he knew she had a little bit of a crush on him.

He stood over the kitchen sink, drinking his coffee and eating his toast. More than a messy house, he hated when things got out of order. A little OCD there, which he was sure came from his mom's side. He remembered how meticulously she had kept the house when he was growing up. He smiled sadly, thinking about his mom. She had been one hell of a strong woman. He looked up at the ceiling and said out loud, "Don't give up on me yet, Mom. I got a few good years left to make you proud."

The sink, where he stood, was underneath the window on the side of the house facing one of his neighbors. He noticed her porch screen door was just a little ajar. He stood here every morning he was home and looked out this same window and never noticed her screen door open before. His neighbor was a meticulous woman. That much he did know about her. He had only met her a few times even though they had lived next door to each other for at least three years. She was the type of woman who never left her house dressed in anything but a matched ensemble. The times he had seen her, he remembered, because she always looked like someone who had stepped out of a senior fashion magazine. Her shoes and purse matched the color of her clothes. Her jewelry and even her glasses matched what she wore too. Her hair was pure white, but he thought it was natural, and she was very attractive. He figured she had to be sixty-five or almost that. They happened to be at the mailboxes at the same time one evening, and she commented about getting something from Medicare. They had discussed a few age-related things and how time seemed to fly by as you got older. She said she couldn't believe she was almost eligible for Medicare and she

IT ALL STARTED WITH MY NEIGHBOR

just wasn't ready for that yet. He thought her not only attractive but intelligent also. He had enjoyed chatting with her about the latest current events. They even touched on politics, which he normally never did with anyone, but it seemed they were basically on the same playing field in that respect.

Her name was Carla Hardcastle. He got a slight chuckle out of that because she looked anything but hard. They discussed origins of names, and he introduced himself as Mick Meade—Irish, of course. When he was in school, he was known as Mick the Prick. His dad was pure Irish, he explained, and she laughed. In fact, his dad was still alive and "living the dream" in La Jolla, California, with his second wife. He usually went down to see them at least once a year. He remembered telling her that they were aging well, with a nice group of active friends in their senior community. They played pickleball, did lawn bowling, went to the pool for water aerobics, and had a group of friends that they switched out the entertaining with. He had met most of them on different trips down there. They all worried about him more then he worried about them, despite the fact that all of them were in their late seventies and eighties now. You know, the old cliché. "Mick, when are you going to find a nice woman and settle down? You are almost too old now to give us grandchildren before we kick the bucket." How many times had he heard that question? Although there was one older gal there that had actually hit on him. Talk about uncomfortable.

He had spent a good half an hour at the mailboxes that evening, talking to Carla. He had told her how he had hated his dad for leaving his mom, but as he grew older and his dad had remarried, they had reconnected, and since neither one had any other family, why not try to get along? It seemed to work for them. He went on to say that he tried to get down to see him a couple of times a year, but he had been so busy this year he hadn't made it once yet.

He then went on to say that they had gotten hopeful when he introduced them to his last girlfriend, Connie. Connie Taylor was her name, and she was a gorgeous forty-two-year-old that he had dated for about two years. She had been the assistant of one of the most prominent criminal attorneys in town, when in actuality there

9

were only two attorneys of any kind in the whole town. They had met quite by accident while they were both investigating the death of one of his best friends. Connie had been gathering information for her boss, and he was investigating because he had become suspicious about how his friend had died. A boating "accident" just didn't sit well with Mick since he knew his friend knew boats up, down, and sideways. There was just no way he could have had a boating accident. They both had grown up around boats and had been out fishing together when they were ten years old.

Anyway, he looked at Carla and wondered why he was rambling on like he was. She was looking at him with body language that indicated she had all the time in the world, and her eyes just seemed to encourage conversation. Either that or he was just desperate to talk to someone. She didn't interrupt, just listened, unlike most women he had met.

At that moment, a fairly brisk breeze rustled the hedges between his yard and Carla's. He heard her screen door slam shut, breaking his train of thought. He looked over at her back porch. Kind of odd, he thought. He set his coffee cup in the sink and started out the back door to go and check to see if everything was okay over there. Carla would smile and wave at him whenever she saw him looking out the window or if they happened to be in the backyard together. They weren't close neighbors, but they were neighborly. He would have to say he knew her better than he did any of his other neighbors, which was pretty sad actually, he thought.

Carla kept the hedge between their two houses trimmed herself. She appeared to enjoy yard work, so he certainly wasn't going to discourage the trimming, although he would have preferred more of a privacy hedge. He could easily jump the low hedge, which he now did, and was on her back porch in seconds, knocking on her screen door. She did not come to the door or call out a "Come in." He knocked again, louder this time. Odd, he thought. He knew she was usually home on Wednesday mornings. She had told him she had a "standing" appointment with an old friend who came by about ten o'clock for coffee and whatever new pastry she had whipped up. They had invited him in for coffee one time, and at that time, he had a slow week so decided to join them. If for nothing else, he figured it would be mildly interesting, and he remembered how heavenly the smell was coming from under the cloth of the basket she held.

Her friend was named Evelyn, and she was almost as meticulous as Carla, if that were possible. They had told him that every week they took turns with a new recipe and made either coffee cake or muffins. This particular Wednesday, it was orange-blueberry muffins with a cinnamon sugar topping. He could still remember them. He couldn't even make brownies from a mix, he thought with chagrin. He remembered he had thoroughly enjoyed himself and got a kick out of listening to the two gals reminisce about their younger, wilder days.

Mick went to the window and peered in where there happened to be a small gap between the two curtain panels. He rapped on the window but then stopped when he saw what he thought was part of a shoe lying sideways, leaning up against the bottom of the cupboard. Mick gave a little start and went back up on the porch. This time he turned the knob on the door, not expecting it to open, but it opened up into the laundry room. Being a private investigator, Mick usually carried a handgun. Actually, he wore a discreet shoulder holster and, often, an ankle one as well. Right now, however, they were both on his kitchen counter, since he had not gone out the door to officially start his day.

He opened the door wider, calling Carla's name as he did. Walking through the laundry room into the kitchen, he steadily kept his eyes open and his brain tuned for anything amiss. Although he knew by this time that something wasn't right. He had investigated his fair share of crimes, and he always got this feeling of cold awareness when he knew something was not how it should be. He felt like that right now. He slowly made his way toward the kitchen from the laundry room, then stopped short just a few steps into the kitchen. There he saw Carla lying on the floor in a pool of congealed blood, with a knife protruding from her back. Mick looked around the clean, tidy kitchen. He noticed an open drawer, a kitchen towel on the floor by Carla's right hand, and another, smaller paring knife on the counter on top of a wooden cutting board. On top of the cutting board, there was also a sliced lime and a half-full margarita glass. Somehow, that didn't fit with the image Mick had of Carla. Who would have thought she liked margaritas?

Chapter 2

Mick looked around for any indication of some type of scuffle, or even something out of place. Even after three years of living no more than twenty feet from her, he really hadn't known Carla that well. *What the hell!* he thought and walked around the kitchen, looking for any kind of clue as to what really happened. *This is not how I planned my day to start.* Who in the world would want to kill his nice neighbor? He looked down at Carla and the pool of blood. *No sense in calling 911,* he thought. He could tell she had been gone for a few hours. Most likely since last evening, by the looks of the half-full margarita glass. Rigor mortis had set in, and her mouth was in the set shape of an O, like she had been taken totally by surprise.

He looked more critically around the kitchen but couldn't find a thing out of place. Every cabinet door and drawer was closed. She didn't have much of anything on the clean granite counters either. Even the coffeepot looked like it was never used. That was the only appliance on the counter. Nothing else was left out anywhere.

He gingerly walked around the body to the living area. No sign of any disturbance there. He checked the front door, and that wasn't locked either, so Carla obviously must have known who she was letting in the door, or she wouldn't have let him/her in. Most likely, it was a he, he thought, based on his experience. Women usually did not like knives—harder to kill someone with. Maybe she had been expecting someone, although there was only one margarita glass on the counter. She must have opened the door for whoever it was, because one thing he did know about Carla was that she was adamant about going around and checking to ensure that all her windows and doors were locked up at night. She had lived alone for almost four years since her husband, Robert, had died. He remembered she had also told him one time that she had been broken into after he had died, so she was doubly cautious all the time. She had thought about getting a dog but then decided against the added responsibility.

Carla had had Mick over for coffee a couple of times after he had met Evelyn, but his work kept him so busy at all hours of the day and night she stopped asking him after he turned down a couple of other invitations. Now he felt guilty for not taking the time to pay more attention and visit once in a while. She was probably just lonely and had wanted someone to talk to. He actually knew how that felt himself.

He certainly couldn't find any worthwhile clues down here. There might be fingerprints left somewhere, but everything sure looked neat, clean, and tidy. He decided to check upstairs before he called the police or EMTs. As a PI, he was just too curious to not see if there were any clues. At this point, what did a few more minutes make, anyway? It certainly wouldn't bring her back. Sometimes he found he could be more thorough than the police in an investigation. They were always so busy, even in this little burg. But then again, there was all the bureaucracy and bullshit they had to go through to get the simplest things done.

Mick thought back to when he was a police officer. Actually, a detective on a narcotic squad that had worked out of Oakland, California, but after fifteen years working on narcotic cases, he had had enough of the scum of the earth. He also grew to hate the dis-respect that came from citizens they were trying to help protect in Oakland. After a while, it seemed like no one really appreciated how hard they all worked or how many times they had risked their own lives to protect the public. It had come down to his wife leaving him before he quit, and by then it was too late for them. His late hours and having to leave in the middle of dinners, movies, and the night had finally worn her down. She left him for someone that was more stable, with a quieter lifestyle. Someone that had a three-figure income and wasn't afraid to have children. He was grateful she hadn't fallen in love with one of his friends or neighbors; he didn't think he could have lived that down. No, apparently, she met someone at the library, of all places, and they ended up sharing more than their love for a good story. Served him right, he thought. She had been a sweet woman and had deserved to be treated better than he had done. As far as he knew, she still lived in the suburbs near Oakland and had had two kids. Thank God they had not had any children together. He might have had to stay in that hellhole, and that would have really worn him down in the end. As far as he knew, she had moved out to the suburbs with her husband and kids and they all lived happily ever after. At least he hoped so. She had been a nice woman and certainly had deserved a better husband than he would ever be.

He had left her the house and moved north, and the only reason he ended up in the small coastal town that he had was an old friend of his, someone he had met at the police academy. His name was Randy Delaney, and he had always kept in touch with him. Randy was the kind of guy that you could always depend on to watch your back. Boy, had they seen some heavy shit when they worked together, especially on the night shift! Randy had always been the better of both of them at keeping in touch. Mick thought the reason they had hit it off so well was that they both had the ole Irish in them. Although Randy's dad had not upped and left them to fend for themselves. He had always felt that they were like cousins or something. About ten years into that and there just happened to be an opening on the small police force in Rockaway. That had been a godsend since, at that time, Mick had hit about his lowest point in life. He figured a small coastal town would be a great place to start over in. His friend described it as a quiet, peaceful little town with the beach a stone's throw away at any time.

Even though his dad had left his mom when he was about ten years old, his mother had persevered and managed to make a great life for the two of them. When she had passed, she had left Mick enough money to quit Oakland and start up his own private investigative business. If only he could make enough money to make a real living, he thought wryly. "Oh, what the hell, I can get by!" he said out loud when he should have been thinking about poor, dead Carla lying on the kitchen floor. *What is the matter with me?* He shook his head and looked around the tidy living room one more time. *Get on with it, man!*

Mick had always loved the beach in a small town back when he used to visit his aunt years ago as a child. He thought it would be a great place where he could settle down and start over. The one thing his friend had not let him in on was the politics and pettiness of a small-town police force. It was brutal, and he only lasted a couple of years before quitting and starting his own private investigative practice. He only had himself and his clients to worry about at that time.

Thankfully, his mom had left him a little money when she died, and he had just left it in an account to gain the little interest that it did. He actually thought it would go to a son he would have one day; that was what his mom's last request had been to him, anyway. His mother had worked hard her whole life. When his dad had left, Mick thought he must have been about ten years old, maybe a little older, but he didn't think so. His dad had always sent his child support payments to his mom, she never told Mick she sent them back Mick himself had rarely seen him while he was growing up. His mother remained so hurt and angry for so many years she always managed to put the kibosh on any arranged visit they might have had. Finally, his dad had given up, remarried, and had a couple more kids himself. Mick had never really blamed him, though. He knew how his mom felt, and he had always stood by her decisions.

His mom had been a wonderful person, but many times he remembered coming home from school to an empty house. He would fix himself a bologna sandwich and watch reruns of *The Sopranos* until she got home. His mom had had to make her living as a housekeeper for other wealthier people. He remembered her telling him that since his dad was gone, he was the only man in her life and he was enough for her. He could not remember her ever dating or having any other kind of relationship with any men. And she died shortly after he had graduated from the police academy. How she held her cancer at bay until then was beyond him, but she did and she was so proud of him then. He smiled to himself, thinking about her.

He shook his head sharply again. *What in the hell? Why do I keep reminiscing all this stuff now? Things that happened years ago, I can't do a damn thing about, especially not right now.* He had been a PI for the past nine years; he needed to concentrate and think like one now.

He took the stairs two at a time and found himself standing in Carla's bedroom. He looked around at the feminine surroundings. Like the downstairs, it was all clean and as neat as a pin. Her bed was made up with a beautiful, handmade quilt and matching shams. Nothing appeared out of place. There were no clothes on the floor, no female toiletries left on the dresser. He looked in the closet, then the bathroom. All appeared neat, clean, and tidy. Everything looked like something out of a women's magazine. *Wish I could be half this tidy,* he thought to himself. He looked in the closet. All her clothes were lined up in coordinating colors, as were her shoes and her necklaces. There wasn't so much as a sleeve out of place. He opened the bathroom door and wasn't surprised at how clean that was also. No washcloth on the sink. No toothbrush on the counter. Not so much as a spittle of toothpaste in the sink either. Was this how normal people really lived? he thought with chagrin. *No way could I live this neatly.*

He had only been upstairs in Carla's house once before, and that was because she had lost an earring down the drain in her sink and she had tried a couple of plumbers but since it was late at night, they wouldn't come, and she didn't know who else to call at that time of night, so she had called him. Two hours later, after taking the drain apart, he had retrieved a diamond stud earring. It must have been almost a whole carat. She said her husband had given it to her on their fifth wedding anniversary and she would have been devastated if it had been lost for good. She couldn't even stand the thought of it sitting in the sink muck overnight. He told her he would get a replacement elbow for the sink and replace it tomorrow when he got home from work. She was so grateful to him that she gave him an expensive bottle of red wine and told him to share it with someone special. He told her he really didn't have anyone special, so why not just share it together? She thought that was a great idea; since she had worked up some anxiety about the ring, she wouldn't be able to sleep right now, anyway. Mick had enjoyed the wine and the conversation.

Again, he felt bad he hadn't paid more attention to her when she was alive.

His mom would have loved Carla's house, he thought. Even though they never had a lot of money, his mom always had things looking classy. He remembered she was always working on some pillow or needle project or something that would make their house more upscale. She had been someone else's housekeeper for most of the time while he was growing up, and sometimes she took an occasional evening job when he got older so she could afford to pay for more things she felt a teenager needed. He looked up at the ceiling then and closed his eyes for a few seconds. She had died shortly after he had married, but at least she had seen him graduate from the police academy, and then she was not only proud but had also had a huge neighborhood party for him. He smiled to himself at that thought. *Here I go again,* he thought. *I am losing it.*

Mick went down the short hallway to a second bedroom. It looked more like a craft room than a bedroom, however. There was a twin bed in the corner under a mountain of material. *Wow!* He felt like he had stepped into a quilt shop. The only reason he would have even recognized all that stuff as quilting material was that his wife had made him go to a quilt show one time. She actually had bribed him. He remembered her whispering in his ear, "You go to this quilt show with me and I will have a nice surprise for you later." Well, he was surprised—she could really pull off that slinky, sexy black negligee! It made the whole quilt thing worth it, although it had cost him a pretty penny for the king-size quilt he had ended up buying.

As he stood looking around the small bedroom, he noticed the closet door was open and what appeared to be a scarf lying on the floor in the crack of the open doorway. He walked across the room, which really was about three long strides. The room was probably only twelve by twelve. He opened the closet door further and caught the scarf as it fell to the floor. It was more of a serape-type thing than a scarf. It was made of a flimsy kind of silk with pink flowers on a lime-green background. He actually put it up to his face and could smell a jasmine perfume. He knelt down to untangle the material and noticed a small wall safe behind the other clothes and scarves hanging in the closet. He pushed everything aside to take a closer look and noted that the safe was not fully closed. Mick reached in his pocket to retrieve a pair of vinyl gloves; since he hadn't touched anything, he hadn't felt the need to put them on, but now he felt he had better. *No sense in contaminating a crime scene,* he thought to himself. The safe opened easily, but as he leaned in to get a better look, the only thing in it was a silver dollar. He picked it up to examine it closer. Ben Franklin's face was on the coin, as it should be, and it was dated 1954. He figured that would be about Carla's birth year. Maybe she had a lot of coins and someone left one behind by accident. She could have had anything in the safe; however, it was only about twelve by twelve, so more than likely it was for money or jewelry she kept in safekeeping.

He looked around the room again. Well, Carla had never talked about how she stood financially. For all he knew, she could be living in a modest house with substantial savings tucked away. He tried to remember if she had mentioned relatives or other friends besides Evelyn. He rarely saw anyone coming or going at her house. He always felt she was a little reclusive, as he was. Some people just liked things that way. For about the tenth time, he wished he had paid more attention to her when she was alive. Hindsight was always kicking him in the butt.

Chapter 3

Mick stood there with the silver dollar in his hand. If Carla had something worth stealing, why not just take this silver dollar too? What was the point in leaving it there? Maybe the killer just got scared and didn't realize it was left behind? Did Carla have a stash of silver dollars' worth some real money and the killer took the rest of them? Was there something more valuable in the safe, and was it just an accident that one dollar got left behind? Mick picked up the coin and turned it over and over between his thumb and index finger. His mind was a jumble of thoughts, but he wondered if there was more to the coin than one might think. As far as he knew, a Ben Franklin silver dollar was only worth between six and eighty dollars maximum, unless there was some mint he was unaware of. He was no expert on coins, but his dad had given him a small collection before he had left his mom and he used to spend a lot of time poring over the coin books, looking up their worth. He kept hoping he would find something authenticating their value, but to this day they were only worth about five to ten dollars.

Mick put the coin down and took out his cell phone. He figured he might as well take a picture of both sides of the coin to look up later. He did know that there were some that were worth some money; he just hadn't been lucky enough to have one. He put the coin back exactly as he had found it. He then left the safe a little bit ajar and walked down the stairs deep in thought.

When he got to the bottom, he looked in the kitchen at poor, dead Carla lying on the floor in a pool of her own blood. *Damn, that shouldn't happen to such a nice lady, stabbed to death in her kitchen while having a margarita. She probably hadn't died instantly either,* he thought, *by the position of the knife in her back.*

Just as he took out his cell again to call the police, the front doorbell rang. *Oh, great. Now what?* He went to the window and peeked out through the mini blinds. He saw a tall slim woman about Carla's age, he surmised. She had whitish-colored long curly hair, and she was stacked for an older gal. What really caught his eye, though, was her jewelry. That was some big jewelry to be carting around on one's body. Her necklace was a huge geometric silver design with inlaid turquoise and some other stone he couldn't identify. They just happened to fall into an ample cleavage. And how could a pair of earlobes support such huge turquoise earrings?

He opened the door a crack and said, "Hi, I'm Mick, Carla's neighbor. And you are?"

With that question, the gal turned toward Mick and smiled, and then he recognized her from when they had all had coffee together. *Damn.* He couldn't remember her name. She, on the other hand, looked him up and down, somewhat with disdain, he thought. *Hey, I combed my hair, at least! It was a rough night, and I didn't expect all this drama so early in the morning.* Although he knew it wasn't that early for most people; 10:00 a.m. was more like midmorning, and she did not look like most people. He gulped as she held out her hand and said, "Mick, I believe it is? My name is Evelyn Bridges. I think we met a year or so ago here at Carla's. She and I have been having coffee and pastry for the past two years or so every Wednesday. Although, I must admit, neither one of us can come up with any new recipes anymore. How are you?" She held out her hand to shake his, and he took it, saying, "I'm sorry, Evelyn. I didn't recognize you. You've done something different with your hair." *That always works,* he thought.

"Yeah, well, it grew, and it has a rinse. One gets tired of the same old thing, especially at this age," she said. "Where is Carla, by the way?"

Mick stepped out onto the porch and closed the door behind him. *Man, she is a looker,* he thought, and when he got closer, he could smell her perfume, which was intoxicating. *Stop it,* he silently told himself. *Stick to business.* He looked Evelyn in the eyes and told her there had been an accident. "I came over to check on Carla this morning because I was worried about her. I know how careful she is, and when I looked out my kitchen window, I could see her screen door was opening and closing with the wind, so I went in to check and make sure everything was all right."

Evelyn immediately became pale and put her hand to her mouth. *Wow!* Roger thought her lips were a luscious-looking lavender. He looked away from her and down the porch to keep his imagination from wandering. "Evelyn, I am so sorry to be the one to tell you this—in fact, I don't know how to sugarcoat it—but Carla is dead," he said. "When I got here this morning to check on her, I found her on the kitchen floor." Mick was unable to say any more as Evelyn immediately became tearful and said, "Was it a heart attack? Just last week we both sat here and vowed we needed to make doctor's appointments for complete checkups."

She started to say something else, but Mick interrupted with, "No, it wasn't her heart, and I hate to even say this, but it looks pretty clear that she was murdered."

Evelyn stepped back away from him and looked at him skeptically, with a shocked look on her face. One hand went to her ample bosom, and the other to her mouth. He really thought she looked like she might faint. He held out both arms to steady her. In so doing, she fell into his arms and started to cry. What was a man to do? He just held her against him and let her cry silently.

Evelyn told him between sobs how she and Carla had met in a support group when both their husbands had cancer. They both had been reluctant caregivers and had bonded after sharing stories of some of their experiences. They had helped each other get through some of the terrible things that happen when someone you love has cancer. Both husbands had passed within a month of each other, and they had been meeting on Wednesdays ever since. It wasn't just Wednesdays they would meet, though; sometimes they met out for lunch or an early dinner. Neither one of them liked driving at night anymore.

Evelyn gave a small hiccup as her tears started to subside a little. She reached into her purse for a Kleenex with which to blow her nose. She looked away from Mick as she did so.

"Evelyn," Mick said as he stepped away from her and held her at arm's length, "I have not called the police yet. I need to do that now. Why don't you go over to my house and sit and have a cup of coffee? And we can talk when I am through here. The door is open. There is still coffee, which hopefully is still drinkable, and I will be there as soon as I get done with the police."

Evelyn looked at him with sad, teary eyes and nodded. "I think I will take you up on that offer. I am way too upset to drive right now, and I would like to wait and see what the police think. I just can't imagine who would want to hurt Carla. She wouldn't have hurt a fly!"

Mick gave her an encouraging smile and told her he didn't think it would be a good idea to try to drive right now either. He didn't expect her to jump the hedge, so he walked down the porch and over to his house and told her he would see her as soon as he could and to make herself at home. He called the precinct's number as he walked back to Carla's house.

Mick knew most of the officers at the police station. After all, this was a small town, so there were only about five officers and one hot secretary, who would not give Mick the time of day even when he poured on all his charm. Probably better for him, he thought. Her boyfriend was about six foot five and all muscle. He had played football until he injured his knee and had to come back home with his tail between his legs. Mick had seen him work out at the gym a couple of times; he could bench-press three times more than what Mick could.

He held his phone up to his ear and heard, "Rockaway Police Department, Debra speaking. What can I do for you?"

"Hey, Deb, how ya doing? This is Mick."

"Not bad," she replied. "Haven't seen you in a while, though. How are you?"

"Oh, can't complain. I have a little problem, though. Is Officer Delaney around?"

"He's in the back," she said. "Do you want to talk to him?"

"No, don't need him to come to the phone, but tell him to come to South 1031 Coral Street. I am at my neighbor's house, and she's been murdered."

"No, no," he then interjected. "She's been dead for quite some time, at least ten hours. Can you let Randy know? And then he will probably want forensics and the medical examiner to come also. I will wait at the house for him. Thanks, Deb." He clicked off and went back into Carla's house to wait for Randy.

It didn't take Delaney more than eight to ten minutes to arrive. The precinct was on the other side of town, but the town was only about a whole mile long. Mick spent the next fifteen minutes or so bringing Delaney up-to-date on what Mick himself knew or had observed. He neglected to tell him anything about Evelyn, though. He wasn't quite ready for her to have to go through an interrogation at this point. He knew she was still in a state of semishock and wasn't ready herself. After he filled Officer Delaney in on everything, he left him and the other officer, who Mick did not know, to do the real police work.

He hopped the hedge again back into his own yard and took his back steps two at a time. He called Evelyn's name as he went in the back door. And as the door slammed behind him, he saw Evelyn jump up from the chair she had been sitting in, nearly toppling her cup of coffee. Mick said sorry, that he hadn't meant to startle her, and then he sat down to tell her what he knew, which was a little to nothing more than what he knew half an hour ago. He told her that even though he had lived next door to Carla for three years, he hadn't really known her very well. He told her that he was a private investigator himself and he would be looking into what had happened, along with the police department. He might be able to find things out quicker, since he didn't have all the bureaucracy and red tape to deal with that they had.

Evelyn said that she and Carla had become quite close in the past few years, but recently, Evelyn had felt Carla had pulled back a little bit from that closeness. Nothing that Evelyn could really put a finger on but that she didn't seem to be as forthcoming in conversations as she once was. Not that they discussed their most intimate secrets, because they really didn't have any, but Evelyn felt that Carla had wanted to discuss something a couple of times but either the timing wasn't right or she didn't know how to start the conversation. Either way, now that Carla was gone, so was whatever the message was. Evelyn said she couldn't help but think it had something to do with Carla's stepson.

Evelyn went on to explain to Mick that she had met Carla's stepson once. "If you could call it that," she said. "He practically knocked me off the porch one morning." She went on to explain that it had been months ago. He had been at Carla's when she had arrived at her usual time. She could have sworn she could hear them arguing when she went to knock on the door. She tried to eavesdrop before knocking, but the only thing she could clearly make out was, "Where is Dad's collection, you bitch?" Evelyn said she was unable to hear Carla's reply when, all of a sudden, the door was thrown open, taking her by surprise with the force of it. He had sent her to her knees, barely giving her a sideways glance, let alone an apology for knocking her down. He had stomped down the stairs and gotten into his car and screeched away.

Mick asked her to describe whatever she could remember about him. She said that he was about six feet tall. Shorter than Mick, she thought. He had black hair sprinkled with a little bit of gray, from what she could see. He had worn a black baseball cap, and he had been wearing all-black clothes. Evelyn said she remembered getting up and examining her knees, which were both reddened and scraped from the force of her landing on them. She went on to say that Carla had come out of the house and helped her brush off, and then they both went inside. "I had asked her what that was all about, but she was very evasive. It was then I noticed her eyes were red, like she had been crying. She did tell me then that the man that had so unceremoniously knocked me down was her stepson, Mark, who she hadn't seen for about three years. He had been in prison on some drug charges, apparently, and that when she and Paul were married, they rarely saw him then either. He was pretty much estranged from his dad, and Paul had told her that he felt he was to blame for that. It seemed that Mark blamed Paul for his mother's death and that Mark had never totally been the same since she had died. It seemed like when Paul did hear from Mark, he always had some sob story and wanted a handout of some kind. Carla made it sound like she had only seen him once since her husband had died, and he had asked her for a loan. Sounded like she scoffed at the term *loan*, knowing he would never pay her back. She had also told me that she knew that Mark had inherited a couple hundred thousand dollars from Paul, but Mark had never been able to hang on to money due to a slight gambling problem he had. Carla had been annoyed that Mark was even included in his will, knowing that giving the 'kid' money was like pissing in the wind."

Mick couldn't help but smile at her description.

Mick asked her if she could describe the car he had been driving. Evelyn told him that her husband had been a bit of an auto enthusiast, and whenever they went somewhere, he would drive her crazy making out makes and models of vehicles as they drove down the road. He was mostly interested in older models, but he loved sports cars and had been on the lookout for an expensive old Mustang before he got cancer. "So in answer to your question, it was an all-black Mustang, around 1975, with fancy, highly polished chrome wheels. I even remember the license plate had an *M* before any of the numbers, but I don't remember them," Evelyn told Mick. "I probably paid attention instinctively because he looked so angry, even scary, when he left. I was thinking that I hoped he hadn't hurt Carla while he was there. Oh yeah, I remember he had a small dent on the passenger-side rear bumper. That's about all I can remember."

Mick wasn't done probing her for answers, though. He knew there were always other things people could remember if the right questions were asked to jar their brain. "Did Carla ever mention where this Mark lived?" he asked. He could see Evelyn bite at her lower lip, concentrating on what she might have heard. She thought she remembered Carla saying something about a day's drive away, Idaho maybe. She looked at Mick and asked, "Do you think maybe Carla's stepson had something to do with her death? Who else could it be?" She went on to say that Carla had told her that she and her husband, Paul, hadn't had a lot of friends and the ones they had were all couples, and after Paul's lengthy illness and then his death, the couples didn't come around anymore and she hadn't bothered keeping in touch since she always felt like the third wheel.

Evelyn said that both she and Carla had remained in their respective small beach towns because they liked it once they had gotten adjusted to the winters. Evelyn told Mick that Carla had been writing a book on the life of the harbor seal and she would often just go and sit on the jetty, waiting to spot some. "Wow, who knew?" That was more of a statement than a question, he told Evelyn. Evelyn went on to say that she was never one to invade someone's private space and she felt that Carla was a lot like her in that respect. They both respected each other's privacy. "That was one of the reasons we got along so well," she explained. They thought a like politically, they didn't believe in gossip, and they were both working on their own projects, which kept them pretty busy. "Unlike a lot of the other women who live around here. But you probably already are aware of that." And she smiled at Mick. "Right now, I feel so helpless and sad."

Mick was afraid she was going to cry again, so he took both of her hands in his and said, "I will find this guy. I promise."

Chapter *4*

"Evelyn, I know how difficult this must be for you, what with your planning on a nice chat and a simple cup of coffee this morning. And instead, you find out your friend has been murdered. I have dealt with these kinds of things in the past, and so it is not as hard on me. I am not unsympathetic to your grief, but if you think of anything else, please let me know immediately. No matter how insignificant you think it is, it might truly be helpful. I am going to have to tell the police that you showed up this morning to have your coffee klatch with Carla. I just wanted you to have a little time to process this whole thing before you got harangued by the police department. Trust me, I know how unsympathetic they can be," Mick said. "How about if I drop you off at your house? You can leave your car here for now, and I will stop by later this evening with your car. I can have my assistant give me a ride home, or if you are up to it, you can give me a ride back home in your car. We could even have dinner together if you feel like you'd like someone to talk to." He did look at Evelyn sympathetically, although in the back of his mind his idea of consoling might be a little different from her idea. "Right now, I have some work I have to do. My nine thirty client has tried to call and text me, and I haven't been available. I can picture her smoldering as we speak. I can give you a ride home now if you'd like."

Evelyn looked at him, her eyes still brimming with tears. "I would really appreciate that," she said. "I can't imagine trying to concentrate on driving right now." She gave him a timid smile and walked toward his truck.

On the drive to Evelyn's, which was only fifteen miles away, they were both lost in their own thoughts and conversation was limited. When they arrived at her house, Mick played the gentleman and got out to open the door for her. He walked her up the sidewalk to the front door. He was impressed with the style of her house and the landscaping she had in the front. It was a cute, beachy-style cottage with a great front porch, complete with a two-seater swing, overlooking a waterfall and koi pond. Everything was landscaped beautifully. He could see into the backyard and noticed she also had a peekaboo view of the ocean from the back deck. *Wow, nice,* he thought. He asked if she did the landscaping or if she had it done. She explained how much her husband enjoyed yard work and that when he retired, he experimented with some more professional landscaping. He had had fun with it, and it was all easy for her to maintain, she told him. Then she further told him she had thought about moving after her husband died, but she just couldn't imagine giving up the little house after all the work they had put into the yard and the house itself.

Mick took her hand and said again how sorry he was about her friend's death and asked her to try to not think about the recent events and just take it easy the rest of the day. He would see her later. He held her hand longer than he should have, thinking how beautiful and vulnerable she looked right then. She eased her hand out from his and smiled up at him. "Let me know if you hear anything new, please. Otherwise, I will just see you later. Thank you so much for taking me home." She let herself into the house with a wave of her hand but did not look back at him.

Mick got back in his truck and sat there for a few minutes before driving away.

He called Sheelya as soon as he was on the road again. Man, he really did not want to deal with whatever bullshit she was going to give him today. She had always been right on time with money when it came time to pay him, though, and he didn't have the resources to turn her down as yet. *Better get it over with,* he thought. "Hey, Sheelya! Hi, it's—"

"I know who this is, you dumb son of a bitch! Your number comes up on the screen. Where the hell have you been all morning?

We were supposed to meet here three hours ago. I have been calling and texting, with no response! Whose bed did you drag your sorry ass out of this morning, anyway? How dare you stand me up!"

Mick looked at the screen on his phone and felt like throwing it out the window, but he knew he couldn't do that, so he started over. "Sheelya, my affairs are really none of your business, but my next-door neighbor was murdered last night and I had to talk to the police before I left the house this morning. Plus—"

Again, Sheelya cut him off midsentence. "I really don't give a flying fuck about your neighbor! You need to get to your office in ten minutes, or you can kiss me and my money goodbye!" She added a few more choice words before his phone was quiet.

Mick swore as she clicked off. Personally, he didn't care two hoots for her, but he sure did appreciate her money, and he was a little limited on that right now. God, she was a pain in his ass. She had a lucrative interior design business, which was not easy to maintain here on the coast, but she was also on her fourth wealthy husband. She really didn't need her business, but she enjoyed sticking her nose into other people's business and she got to do that with her decorating. She did once tell him it was the only thing that gratified her self-worth, but he only half believed that. He had heard some of her stories related to the people who hired her. A sleazier lot, some of whom he knew.

Despite her snarly attitude and foul mouth, she was one hot, wild number under the covers. He had met her in a bar one night, and she was bad-mouthing her then second husband. He had moved her to the beach and the godforsaken town she was complaining about while he traveled all over the continent. She had had a little too much to drink that night, but then so had he, and one thing led to another and they ended up tangled in the sheets at one of the local hotels in the next small town down the coast. When he said *tangled*, he meant it. He hadn't been prepared for the gymnastic workout she provided him. He hadn't met anyone like it before or after. It was a onetime event, but she was always willing to go at it again. He was thinking of that event when, out of the corner of his eye, he saw a small, furry, brown critter run across the road in front of his car. He slammed on the brakes, swearing and shouting that this just was not his day. He'd had enough to deal with thus far.

Mick got to his office in exactly ten minutes, and damned if the bitch wasn't parked in two whole parking spots. He only had three spots in front of his office, as it was, and there was a blue Volkswagen parked in one of them. Her damn oversize Cadillac Deville straddled the white line of the other two spots. He knew she had done it on purpose. His small office was on the second floor of a redbrick building on Main Street in Rockaway, but there was never any parking out front, so the city allowed him three parking spots on the side of the building. They even had made a sign for him designating those as Meade's parking only; all others would be towed. After all, he did pay rent. Right under Mick's office was a large salon that included just about anything a woman could want. They did hair, nails, feet, facials, even massages. He had taken advantage of a free massage more than once since they moved in. The owner of the salon was a really nice gal, although rather homely, and she liked the idea of a PI being on the second floor. It worked for him, and on his downtime he got a nice view of all the boobs—whoops, *babes*, he meant—who came into the salon. Not a bad gig, he thought to himself with a shrug and a little smile.

He had to drive his car around the corner and park a block away from the building. All the other spots were taken. He was thinking about Evelyn as he hurried up the sidewalk and then let himself into his office. "Sheelya," he said as he held out his hand.

She snarled something unintelligible and slapped his hand away. "I need to talk to you about Smutty," she said. "I think the bastard is cheating on me—*me*, of all people! If he thinks he is going to get away with that, he has another thing coming." Her arms were crossed around her ample bosom, and she was pacing back and forth in his small office.

Mick tried again. "Sheelya, let's sit down and you can tell me all about it." He called to his assistant. "Hey, Colin, sorry I was late this morning. I will fill you in later. For now, will you bring me two cups of coffee? One black and one with cream and sugar, please. I owe you. Thanks!" He looked at Colin and rolled his eyes as he shut the door to his office.

Chapter 5

Well, Sheelya did sit, but there was literally nothing Mick could say or do to calm her down. She was like a snarling hellcat. How ironic, he thought. It wasn't like she hadn't slept around a time or two.

Colin brought the coffee in and handed them both a cup. He didn't stick around; he just gave Mick one of his "I'm sorry" looks.

Mick tried to ask Sheelya questions in a rational manner, hoping to be able to make some sense out of what she was going on about. What he could surmise of her lengthy diatribe was that her now fourth husband, Smutty, was seeing one of the young ladies in his office. Sheelya was not quite ready to give up on him yet; she had not managed to pigeonhole enough of his money for her own future endeavors. Not to say, the least, was for her rather-expensive lifestyle. She told him that one of his partners had let her in on their dirty little secret and she figured out why he had told her after he had asked her to meet him for a drink then tried to feel her up while sitting at the table. "You men are all alike!" She looked at Mick and scowled.

As she went on, Mick thought about the time he had met her at the Martini Bar at the golf course. She didn't drink unless it was top-shelf. He recalled a thin etched glass at twenty-five dollars a pop with a virgin olive in it, no less. Who knew you could even order a virgin olive? He sighed. *I digress,* he thought and looked back at Sheelya, wondering how someone could have the stamina she did to rant on and on. Personally, he couldn't give a hoot about her and Smutty and whomever Smutty wanted to bed. If he wasn't so in need of a paycheck right then, he would not even be having a conversation with her. Smutty's real name happened to be Smitty, which was also a nickname, but Sheelya had always called him Smutty, so it stuck. Seemed to fit him in any case.

Finally, Mick raised his voice an octave above hers to be heard, telling her he would help her prove Smutty was seeing someone. He could do a little investigative work, snap some photos, and it probably wouldn't take him more than a couple of weeks to get whatever she thought she needed. "Yes!" she said and started walking toward him. "That's exactly what I want." She put her arms around his neck and smiled up at him. *Here we go,* Mick thought. *I knew I should have gotten a couch for this office instead of two chairs.*

An hour later, Mick was finally able to send her on her way, but not before he pocketed a healthy retainer for his "work," thus far, anyway. Shaking his head, he thought, somewhat sadly, *A man's gotta do what a man's gotta do.* He sat down at his computer and started Googling away. He would let Colin handle the Sheelya crap, he thought. He hollered out through the closed door, and in two seconds, Colin was standing by his desk.

"Yes, boss," he said with a grin.

"Well, you probably already know what I am going to ask, but I will ask anyway. Sheelya needs to catch her husband red-handed with his new little lovemate. So I am passing that off to you, as bosses are allowed to do. Good luck, though. I am knee-deep in something else right now."

Colin gave him a little salute, with a "Yes, boss," and had turned to go back out the door when Mick stopped him. "Hey, Colin, remember my neighbor Carla? You fixed the lock on her door about six months or so ago," he said. "Well, I found her dead on her kitchen floor this morning, with a knife in her back. That was why I was late." He started to say more, but Colin made a gasping sound and put his hand over his mouth. Mick needed to remember that Colin was a little green to be given graphic information without a little more finesse. "Sorry, Colin," Mick said. "Didn't mean to drop that on you so suddenly. It took me by surprise also. She was a really nice neighbor, although I am guilty of not paying enough attention."

Colin started to ask him questions, but Mick had to put his hand up and stop him.

"Colin, I would like nothing better than to fill you in on what I know, but I have to get a couple of things done first. I promise I will fill you in later, okay? Your taking care of the Sheelya situation will be a huge load off my mind. Thanks, buddy."

Colin knew when to quit, so he left and quietly closed the door to Mick's office.

Mick put Sheelya's little issues in the back of his mind and started looking for information on Mark Hardcastle. He spent about half an hour and was not finding anything useful. He smacked the side of his head with the flat of his hand. "Ouch, but duh!" came out of his mouth. He probably wasn't a Hardcastle; maybe Carla had kept her maiden name. So he searched for Carla Hardcastle and would work slightly backward.

He had just remembered that when he and Carla were at the mailboxes, discussing Medicare, among other things. She had told him she had retained her family name when she got married to Paul. She had been thirty-seven at that time and didn't want to go through the hassle of changing everything; plus she thought it was a ridiculous practice that a woman was supposed to change her name just because she got married. You were the same person, whether married or not, she had said, so why go through all that?

He was dumbfounded by all the information that did come up under "Carla Hardcastle." She seemed to have enjoyed somewhat of a reclusive lifestyle even though he discovered she had actually written several books under the alias of Joan Brewster. She was the author of six romance fiction novels that had earned her a sizable income. Who would have known? he thought. She sure lived conservatively for someone that must have had some money. Apparently, after the romance series, she was interviewed by CBS as Carla Hardcastle, giving away the pseudonym. She had stated that she was tired of writing nonsense and wanted to write something that had more substance. She had written a nonfiction book about marine wildlife. Her husband, Paul, had been a marine biologist, and some of his stories and findings had fascinated her. Mick thought back to what Evelyn had said about Carla studying the harbor seals and doing some research for a book. How could he have lived next door to someone and not know that? That was not only his problem but also part of today's society's woes. No one got involved with their neighbors anymore. They were so consumed with their own lives they didn't take the time to notice what was going on in someone else's. How sad was that? he thought.

As Mick continued with his Google search, he found out Carla's husband's name was DeGuard. Looked like Paul had been previously married to a woman by the name of Cynthia McCall and they had had two children, a son, Mark, and a daughter, JoAnn. After another fifteen minutes or so, he could find no further information on Carla. He began a search to see if he could uncover any more information on her husband, Paul DeGuard.

Paul had had somewhat of a prominent career as a marine biologist. His first wife, Cynthia, had been killed in a tragic head-on collision by a drunk driver, and the family had taken her death pretty hard. The newspaper article stated that the family had moved away from the small town in Idaho. Mick wasn't able to find much information after that. Seemed like Paul had ended up "licking his wounds," so to speak, before he found Carla.

He then searched for Mark DeGuard, who sadly had not fared so well. He had been in a juvenile detention center in Washington State at the age of fourteen for theft and underage drinking. From there he was in and out of detention, mostly for minor infractions, until the age of nineteen. The he got more adventuresome. He had stolen a car and driven 1,200 miles and did not get caught until he ran a red light in a small town in Ohio. The local boys were just sitting, having a cup of coffee and a doughnut (of course, the news media had to throw that in there) at the local village café. The light was at the only intersection in town, so it wasn't like law enforcement had a lot to do. Mark spent a year in prison after that little episode.

When he got out of prison, it seemed like he listed his address as Rockaway. The prison required an address on record when anyone was released. They wanted assurance that you had someplace to go. It didn't mean you had to stay there, but you had to list something on your release paperwork. Maybe he did end up at his dad's for a while, Mick thought. It would appear that he had trouble holding on to any one job for very long. Looked like he had several labor-type jobs after release, but then there was nothing to be found for the last ten years, off the grid, or just hadn't gotten caught. Mick had a hard time imagining someone with that kind of background actually going clean after that many years. He had seen it happen, of course, but not often.

He reappeared at about age forty-two, when he was arrested for driving under the influence. He had run over someone's dog and left the scene, but someone had spotted him and turned it in. He had been picked up two days later on his way out of town. He got sentenced to three years but only had to spend one. He probably wouldn't have even served that much time except he had a court-appointed attorney that probably didn't do the best job for him.

His last known address was listed as Pine Lake, Idaho. Mick had never heard of Pine Lake, so it must be a relatively small town, he surmised. He put "Pine Lake" into Google, and lo and behold, a bunch of information came forward. *What did we ever do before the internet?* he thought. It sure made it easier to get information. Pine Lake, Idaho: population, 1,210; located about sixty miles northeast of Boise; elevation, 4,500 feet. So pretty mountainous, Mick thought. This Google search did bring up a little more information on Mark, so he must have an address or a post office box or something. According to this, he very well could live there still, because his name showed up at the Pine Lake Furniture factory on Route 42. No longer there, however. Mick calculated that he could probably drive to Pine Lake in about fifteen hours. *Hmmmmm,* he thought, *I might have to take a little road trip.*

Mick decided, while he was hot on the Google trail, he might as well look and see what he could find out about the rest of the family. JoAnn was born in 1974. That would make her a couple of years older than Mark. She married an architect who was responsible for developing sustainable log-type cabins in Montana. They were small one-bedroom cabins complete with water towers that collected rainwater, wind-generated electricity, and solar power. Mostly for young people who could afford to live off the grid. *Interesting,* thought Mick. *Just what I thought I wanted to do after I left the narcotic division in Oakland. It still sounds like a great idea, but not so realistic anymore. Who would not love getting away from the hassle and bullshit, though?*

Mick sat up straighter in his chair. "What the heck?" he exclaimed. He leaned in to read the newspaper article. It appeared that JoAnn's husband had also been killed in a car accident. The newspaper clipping was dated June 10, 2006. Douglas Benson was on his way home after picking up his children from choir practice. He was driving a Ford Explorer and swerved to avoid hitting an elk that had wandered onto the road. Instead, while avoiding the elk in the road, he lost control of the car, veering off the road into two elk standing in the field by the side of the road. His children were killed instantly. While veering off the road, he nearly collided with a second vehicle, a small Dodge pickup, which ended up in the ditch, but without any damage to the vehicle. Whoever was driving that vehicle did not stay around to assist at the scene but did call 911 and gave the whereabouts of the accident. In a later article, there was mention of Douglas being on life support for three weeks before it was decided he would probably never regain consciousness.

JoAnn went into a severe depression with the loss of her whole family and was hospitalized at Bethany Psychiatric Institute. The small town of Bishop, Montana, mourned the loss of the Benson family. They had been involved in several civic events throughout the years. Mark had coached the girls Little League games, and JoAnn had volunteered at the school library. Many friends and colleagues were devastated. A later article stated that the town would miss JoAnn as she had moved to a town in Idaho to live with family.

Mick searched further but could find no mention of any other family but Mark DeGuard, so he figured that maybe she had gone to live with her brother. That didn't add up, though. It appeared that even though JoAnn had probably needed psychiatric help— who wouldn't after a terrible accident like that?—why would she go and live with a brother who, in all appearances, had been a loser his whole life? How awful for her, if that was the case. Mick glanced at his watch. *Crap, again?* he thought. It was already six o'clock, and he should have been at Evelyn's by then. He quickly shut down the computer, grabbed his jacket, and headed for the door.

Chapter 6

Mick got his cell phone out of his pocket and quickly hit Evelyn's number. "Hello, Evelyn. It's Mick. I am so sorry, but I am running late. I have been on the dang internet, researching everything I can find on Carla and her family, and the time got away from me. Are you still up for dinner?" He didn't wait for an answer and just plowed on ahead. "I can pick you up in about fifteen minutes. They opened a new restaurant in Netarts. I have been wanting to try them out. They specialize in a variety of oyster dishes, and they make cocktails infused with lavender, ginger, and other natural things." He finally stopped for a second and asked, "Evelyn, are you there?" He waited to hear her reply before he asked anything else.

"Mick, that does sound wonderful, but I really don't think I am up to getting dressed to go out. I have been in a funk all day, and one of the things I find that relieves stress for me is to cook. I check out new recipes, and then I cook them. Thank God that doesn't happen very often, or I would weigh two hundred pounds!" she said. "I experimented today, making a crab ravioli with a lemon cream sauce, a spinach arugula salad, and an almond crème brûlée for dessert. I have a wonderful pinot gris chilling, and I just set the table. So you see, no need to go out. I was just assuming you would come here. How does that sound?" Evelyn paused and then said, "I have been racking my brain all afternoon trying to come up with some more information that might help in your investigation. I thought of a couple of incidental things but don't know if they will be very helpful or not. I would really like you to come by so we can discuss further."

Mick looked pleased. "I will be there in about twenty minutes," he said and disconnected his phone.

Mick looked at the clock as he locked his office door. *Should I pick up another bottle of wine?* he thought. *Or would that seem like I have ulterior motives? Oh, what the hell!* he surmised. There was a small market on the way to her house that actually stocked some decent wines at an affordable price. It couldn't hurt to bring a bottle as a gift; didn't mean it had to be drunk the same night, right? *But then again, we could.* And he smiled slyly as he got in his car to head up the street to the local market.

Evelyn met him at the door before he had a chance to even ring the doorbell. *Damn, she's a nice-looking woman,* he thought again. Her hair was pulled back casually, which showed off the pair of dia-mond-and-ruby earrings she was wearing. She had on a clingy, but in all the right places, maroon-colored one-piece slacks outfit that looked stunning on her. Right in the middle of that ample cleav-age rested a large diamond-and-ruby pendant. *Wow,* thought Mick. *I could eat her up from where I stand!* He couldn't remember when he had been with someone that was this attractive and put together, so to speak. He shook his head, took a breath, and handed her the wine he had just bought. "I thought a Malbec would go good with the crème brûlée you mentioned. You look delicious—I mean, some-thing smells delicious." And Mick turned a couple of shades of red to match the wine he had brought. He gave her a boyish grin as she led him into her living room.

"Have a seat," she said. "I have a pinot gris chilling. I just need to take a peek at the ravioli. It's a recipe I have never tried before, and it's a bit challenging to get it just right." He watched as she went back into the kitchen, and he surveyed the rest of her house. *Nice,* he thought. From the outside it was a pretty typical beach-type bungalow, but the inside was quite modern. It had obviously been remodeled with expensive taste. A large open-concept living room with beautiful hickory floors, modern off-white Danish-style furniture, with dark-stained coffee and end tables, all appearing to be custom-made. She had vibrant, colored abstract canvases on the walls and some infused glass pieces that seemed to be paired with the canvases. *Interesting,* he thought. *I've never seen anything quite like that.* He got up to take a closer look at one of the canvases. In the smallest possible writing, he could make out the name Evelyn Bridges in the right-hand corner of the canvas. "Well, I'll be damned!" he said under his breath.

Just then, Evelyn came into the room with two glasses of wine. She said, "What do you think?"

Mick made a jump, startled out of his reverie. "Wow!" he exclaimed as he turned to take the wineglass. "These are magnificent! The colors all weave together incredibly. So you are an artist, and Carla was an author. How amazing. My abilities in either of those would fit into a thimble. I have always admired people that can create beautiful things just from their imagination."

Evelyn gave him a rather-humble smile and thanked him. "Let's sit down for a few minutes and enjoy the wine before we eat. The ravioli is going to take another fifteen minutes or so." She gave him a big, sweet smile as she patted the seat next to her on the couch. He couldn't help but admire her necklace and the cleavage it sat in as he told her so. "Oh, a very dear friend gave me this before she passed away. It had been in her family for two generations, and she had no one to give it to. It is lovely, isn't it?" she said as she patted the piece of jewelry.

Mick sat down beside her on the sofa, and she looked up at him with moist eyes. "I have really been trying to think of anything else that might be of some help to you related to Carla. I still can't believe she's gone, and been murdered no less. I have been reliving conversations we have had and trying to put together anything that she might have said that would be helpful."

"Well, I can tell you one thing that might carry some weight," Mick told Evelyn. "That is, I know she had a small safe in her spare bedroom. When I checked through the house, the safe was slightly ajar, like someone had just forgotten to shut it all the way. There was nothing in the safe but a silver half dollar dated 1954. I don't know anything about old coins, rare or otherwise. Did Carla ever mention anything about collecting coins or having old coins that might be worth something?"

Evelyn sat for a minute or two, racking her brain for something she might have heard but didn't pay much heed to. "Well, I seem to remember she once said her husband, Paul, had inherited a coin collection from his grandfather, and she indicated that there were a few coins that she thought were worth several thousands of dollars but that she had put them away, and because she didn't need any money, they were just in a safe place. I just assumed she meant they were in a safe-deposit box someplace. Do you think she actually had them in that house safe?"

"Well, she certainly could have had them there," Mick told her. "The safe was big enough for some type of collection, and I would not have seen it because it was hidden behind the clothes hanging in that closet. But I happened to spot a scarf that was a really vibrant color, so I went to take a closer look. I pushed all the clothes aside and discovered the safe. But it just seems odd that there would be one lone silver dollar left in it. So if her husband had a coin collection with some coins that were worth something, would that really be enough to murder her?" He really wasn't expecting any answer from Evelyn; he was more or less just talking out loud at that point. "Although I have known criminals that would murder for a lot less than a coin collection," Mick said.

"Well, I think her stepson would be a prime suspect, in my opinion," Evelyn said and looked at Mick. "I can tell you, he scared the living daylights out of me when he knocked me down on the porch. If you could have seen his face, there was an intense anger about him. It was almost like seeing the devil or something else equally as evil. I'm not kidding. That's the only way I can describe him. Pretty dire straits if he would murder his stepmother for a coin collection, though."

Mick turned toward Evelyn. "Do you know if Carla drank margaritas? There was a margarita glass half-full on the counter and a cutting board with a lime on it. Not that that means a hill of beans, but I just wondered if you ever had seen her drink a margarita."

"Well," Evelyn looked thoughtful for a second, "we usually met in the morning for coffee, as you know, but we did occasionally meet for dinner. Carla, kind of like me, was rather of a recluse, probably our more artistic-type nature. I do remember, she usually drank white wine. I don't ever remember her drinking a margarita when I was with her, but again, it was seldom we met in the evening."

"I am going to pay this Mark DeGuard a visit next week, provided I can find him," Mick said. "He lives only a little over a day's drive away in Idaho. At least that's the last address I could find for him. So I am going to do a little private investigation myself. See what I can find out. Did Carla ever mention a stepdaughter by the name of JoAnn?"

Evelyn thought for a bit and said she couldn't remember anything. "There might have been a mention, but it had to have been insignificant so as not to be remembered. I just can't say at this time."

Evelyn put her empty glass on the coffee table and put her hand on Mick's knee, saying, "Let's eat dinner before it turns into mush." She gave him a gracious smile, causing him to have an audible intake of breath.

"Sounds great," he said and followed her into the small dining room.

As she went to get the food, he noted the table was set with china, crystal, a vase of flowers, and candles. It was all very tastefully done. It had been a long time since anyone had set such an attractive table for him. He felt rather sheepish since class was not what was on his mind when he came over this evening. Evelyn poured them another glass of wine and told Mick to have a seat. She then went into the kitchen to dish up the plates. When she returned with two steaming, delicious-smelling plates, Mick looked at her and said, "I have to tell you, Evelyn, I have not had this nice a meal, in this nice a surrounding, in… I really can't remember when. So I want to thank you for doing all this." He took another bite of the ravioli and just sighed; it was so good. "Heavenly!" he said. "I usually get a burger to go or eat over my kitchen sink. This is quite a treat for me." Evelyn told him she enjoyed cooking, and since her husband had passed, she rarely cooked that much because it was no fun cooking for just one person. Nevertheless, she found cooking therapeutic; it had helped her stay calm and focused on more than one occasion. "It kept my mind occupied this afternoon, thank goodness."

She went on to tell Mick a little about her husband, David. He had always had a saying when anyone came over for dinner: he had married her so he would never have to eat out again. He was sort of kidding, but it was mostly true. They rarely went out for dinner. They went to the theater a lot, but that sort of petered out when they moved to the coast. He loved a good movie, and they would go to every play that they had at the playhouse in Tillamook. In fact, they had gone to a play the night before he had died. *Man on the Mountain* had been playing at that time. She told Mick that David hadn't been feeling very well, but that night he seemed to perk up a bit, maybe with just the thought of getting dressed up and getting out of the house. He died the next day when he lay down to take a nap and never woke up. She thought that all the medications finally took a toll on his heart. It was for the best at that point, though. He had lost at least fifty pounds, his body looked like that of an eighty-year-old, and he was so tired in the end.

"Wait a minute!" Evelyn said. "I just remembered something. Don't ask me what made me think of it now, but Carla had said that one time she and Paul had taken a road trip through parts of Northern United States and one of their stops was in Colorado. She said they had had a horrible time. They had stopped in to see a relative. I can't actually remember who or what kind of relative, but it was one of her husband's, and the wife wasn't very nice to the husband while they were there. I really was only half listening, to be honest, but I remember Carla getting kind of worked up while she was talking about it. It upset her that the wife was treating the husband so badly in front of her and her husband. Apparently, the wife had some prior engagement at her club and clearly didn't have time for visitors. She had made it very clear. Carla was surprised at how disappointed her husband had been. He hadn't spoken much the rest of the day, so she figured the relative must have had more significance to him than he had let on. I guess the whole thing was just very disappointing. Carla had never met any of Paul's other relatives, so she was disappointed herself. Anyway, this may not mean anything."

"Or it might," said Mick. "Like I said, you never know when something, no matter how insignificant it may seem at the time, makes more sense later on down the road."

Mick was quiet, thinking about the whole situation. Evelyn reminded him that Mark could very well be dangerous and perhaps Mick should just let the police take care of the whole thing. Mick said he was very prepared to let the police get involved but that due to all the loopholes they were required to jump through, he might have better luck if he continued to carry on himself. "I will be careful," he told Evelyn, "but I worked for the police department and I know how bogged down in bureaucracy they can get."

Mick looked at his crème brûlée dish, empty. Then he glanced at the bottle of Malbec he had brought. That was empty too. What time was it, anyway? They had been so wrapped up in their conversation he hadn't realized how much time had gone by. He looked at his watch: eleven o'clock. Evelyn stood up and took Mick's hand as she did. "I know it's getting late and you probably want to get an early start on your day tomorrow, but I haven't shown you the rest of my house yet. I have some other artwork upstairs that is even more interesting than the ones down here. Why don't I show you?" She gave him a coy little smile as she turned off the kitchen lights. "This mess will still be here in the morning."

Well, what could he do but follow her upstairs?

Chapter 7

Mick woke up and rolled over, almost falling out of bed. He sat up on one elbow, trying to get his bearings. This obviously wasn't his bed, because he always slept on the right-hand side of the bed. He was lying on the left-hand side, and his right hand was painfully asleep and tingling. He looked over and noted Evelyn's head was on the pillow, but her neck was on the crook of his arm. He slowly and quietly started to slide it out from under her, trying very hard not to awaken her. Although as he watched her sleep, he had the urge to wake her. *Wow, that was some night!* he thought. He had not expected that at all. "Down, boy," he quietly said and eased himself off the bed. He had a busy day ahead and no time to think of other things, no matter how pleasant those thoughts might be.

He found his socks and boxers in a heap at the end of the bed, but his shirt and jeans were in two different spots down the hallway. He figured he had better go home and shower. He needed to pack a bag for his imminent road trip.

He walked down the hall into the kitchen to leave Evelyn a note. He noticed she had the coffeepot ready to turn on in the morning and had two coffee cups already out on the counter. *Well, couldn't be helped,* he thought. He jotted a quick note and left it under one of the coffee cups. He hoped she would understand that if he was going to make it to Pine Lake before the end of the day tomorrow, he needed to get an early start. After last night, he hoped she didn't have any expectations of a relationship or anything remotely like a commitment. That was not in the cards for him. He jotted a quick thank-you for the great evening and that he would leave her car keys at the sheriff's office. He would ask his assistant, Colin, to drive her car to her later today. Colin was always willing to take on any odd job that Mick offered him. Thank God for that.

Back at his house, it only took him another forty-five minutes to shower, shave, and throw some clothes in his old Army bag. *Man, this bag has seen some rough roads,* he thought to himself. *Hope this won't be another one.* It was still only 6:00 a.m. by the time he locked his front door and got into his truck. The police station was on the way out of town, and it would only take a minute to stop by there and drop off Evelyn's keys. He would give Colin a call from the road and fill him in on what was going on. Well, not everything, or Mick would never hear the end of it. It seemed like everyone wanted to see him settled down, married with kids. He sure had met his share of unhappy married people, so there sure didn't seem to be any rush.

Looks like it will be a nice day for a road trip. The sun was on the rise, but it was a little overcast, so easier on the eyes, he thought. He checked all the mirrors and adjusted his seat belt. He eased his truck out onto the street and headed toward the police station.

He walked in the door of the police station but did not know the officer on duty. So he didn't have to worry about making small talk. He told the officer to give the keys to Randy and to tell him that he would call Randy later and explain. *Looks like they hired another rookie,* he thought as he got back into his truck. It wasn't like there was a lot of crime in Rockaway. It was a very small town, and most of the arrests were of drug- and alcohol-related crimes, that and domestic violence charges. He had seen his fair share of those while a police officer. Winters could be long and gloomy on the coast, and there were not enough activities to keep people busy. They had five officers now, and to Mick that seemed like two to many. Oh well, not his problem. He got back into the truck and on the road.

Coffee, black and strong, was what was needed now. He hadn't taken time for his usual morning routine. Wake up, take a shower, dress, have coffee, then take a crap. In that order, the day went well. He wasn't superstitious or anything like that, but he had noticed that when he veered off that schedule, things just seemed to go awry.

Thank God for Colin. Even though he had to keep after him on occasion, he really had lucked out when the kid came to him looking for work. Mick had known Colin's sister, Bethany, just by bumping into her at the grocery store and post office. He couldn't help but notice her. She was very attractive and had a perfect 10 figure. He found out she was in her early forties, a single parent of two, and worked at the cheese factory in Tillamook. Along with half the population, he thought. He had talked to her on several occasions and learned that she had a younger brother who was moving to Rockaway to be closer to her and to help her with the kids. She was grateful he was doing that, but he would need a job when he got here. He was going to start taking classes in business at the local college so would only need something part-time. Mick had tried to get a little closer to Bethany, but she indicated that was not at all possible at this time, so he hired Colin instead and Bethany became a friend of his. Might come in handy someday, he thought to himself. Turned out Colin was very handy with a lot of things and a likable guy, so it was working for all of them.

Mick stopped at the coffee shack in Garibaldi for a large almond latte with whipped cream and a little coffee bean on top. Not exactly his strong and black normal coffee, but he figured after last night, he could use a little treat. He wasn't exactly thinking of Evelyn, though that had been a treat in itself, but of his now-dead neighbor, Carla. He shook his head. He couldn't get the picture of her lying on her clean floor in a pool of blood, out of his head.

Next stop, the Shell station in Tillamook, the bathroom, then he could be safely on the road. He would be good to go for quite a few miles after that. It had been years since he had been any farther east than Hood River. He was actually looking forward to the drive. He allowed himself an extra minute to grab a breakfast burrito at the gas station, and then in no time he was burning up the pavement, which was very hard to do on Highway 6 toward Portland. It must be the worst road in the state, he thought to himself. It certainly had its share of accidents. The most recent one, he was thinking, was a fatal accident involving a large bull elk in the middle of the road. The one just before that had involved a small Toyota flying over the guardrails and into the ravine. People drove too fast and then didn't pay attention, and it was not a road to fool around on. He liked to drive fast, but even he would not take a chance on Highway 6. There were fatal accidents every time you turned around.

The sun was just cresting over the mountain, and he could see a pink sky ahead. He fiddled with the radio, trying to find the one station with any music that would come in, until he got over the mountain. He didn't mind top 40 for an hour or so. He usually drove too fast, so when he got over the mountain, he put the cruise control on. He had gotten pulled over six months ago on his way into Portland, and the officer had not cared to hear his story of when he was a police officer. He tried to be a little conciliatory and mentioned he knew how hard their jobs were, what with all the homeless alcohol and drug addicts they had to deal with. The ticket cost him $280 along with the fact that his insurance had gone up $50 a month. Mick was glad he didn't have to deal with the bureaucracy of a police department anymore. Portland used to be one of the cleanest cities he had ever seen. *Boy, that sure has changed!* he thought. That was one of the reasons he had wanted to move to the Oregon coast. He was sick of cities, the number of people, and their trash. He lived at the beach, but the city was only a two-hour drive away. He felt he had the best of both worlds. Although, since he had moved to the beach, he rarely drove into Portland anymore. He was always disappointed when he did.

He drove along the Columbia River, enjoying the scenery. Lots of wind turbines in the area. He watched some windsurfers and parasailors as he drove down the highway. Today was exceptionally windy. He had always wanted to try windsurfing, but now at this age, it wasn't on his bucket list any longer. Those guys had to be really strong to hold on to those sails in these winds. He would need to choose a little less physical activity at this age, he thought. Back in the day, maybe skydiving. That made him smile wryly, remembering the woman that had talked him into going up on the plane, only to end up parachuting without him, when he had chickened out at the last minute. *I had better get back to the gym, sooner rather than later. At least that's a safe bet to getting into shape.* He looked at himself in the rearview mirror with a slight smile. *Just think of the ladies you could pick up if you were in better shape. Remember that brunette? What was her name? Annette? Yeah, how could I forget that one. Her name rhymed with the color of her hair.* He mouthed an obscenity at his reflection. *Man, you need to pay attention.* He shook his head at himself for at least the third time today and tried to find another radio station that would give him some news.

He drove along for another five hours and decided it was time to take a little break. He saw a road sign announcing the exit for Douglas Springs, five miles ahead. Good time to pull off for a few minutes. It was more a village than a town. Fine with him, as long as there was something he could grab to go. He found a taco wagon and decided on the chicken quesadilla for only $6.50. He marveled at the fact that you could find something this tasty for that cheap. He walked to the quick mart next door and picked up the few toiletries he needed. How he hated paying the inflated prices that the quick mart offered, but he also hated the big chain grocery stores that had aisles and aisles of useless stuff. Truth be told, he hated any kind of shopping in general. He was still about two hours from being able to stop for the night. Once he got on the road, he realized he could make it to Pine Lake in one long day of driving. Since he started at six, he could make it there about that time, but at night.

Back on the road, he thought about this Mark DeGuard and tried to strategize how he could meet up with him. At least he hoped he could make that happen. He was pretty good at finding out what he needed to. He thought of himself as a detail-oriented investigator who didn't mind taking a few chances to find or get what he needed. He was so lost in his slightly narcissistic thoughts that he almost passed the exit for Pine Lake. He quickly turned the steering wheel to the right. He ended up overcompensating and almost ran off the side of the road into the Big Pine Lake sign, announcing, "Population, 700," in small letters, written under the black bear.

He hadn't really found out much about the town itself before he got in the car and left Rockaway, but he was glad it was a small place. It shouldn't be too hard to run this DeGuard guy down. *No pun intended,* he thought. He had spotted a sign that had listed two hotels, one being a Motel 8, and the other one called Dotty's Ranch House. He chose Dotty's. He never could stand those large cheap hotel chains. They were all basically the same. He pulled up in front of what looked like a large bungalow with a faded sign announcing "Dotty's Ranch House." *Looks like Dotty could use a handyman*, he thought as he walked up the steps of the large porch. The porch had one broken step, and the handrail appeared to be held to a post with one nail only. *Can't be many people coming through here*, he guessed.

He opened the door, and a small bell tinkled over the top of the door. He entered a small quaint lobby with a stone fireplace that actually had real wood burning in it. He took a big whiff and enjoyed the smell of the pine logs burning.

"Well, hey, there," someone said as he closed the door and walked up to the counter.

"Well, hey, yourself," Mick said and added, "Tammy," as he looked at the name tag on her ample bosom. "I wish all women would wear name tags. It sure would make it easier for feebleminded men like myself." He gave her a wink and his friendliest smile. "I need a room for at least two nights, not sure how much longer after that. Do you have something available?" He looked at her luscious, full pink lips and her piled-high, bleach-blond hair and thought to himself, *Now there is my kind of gal!* She was really adorable and petite, except for her breasts, which were far from petite. He loved petite women. They were so much cuddlier than taller or bigger women.

She looked directly at him and said, "Well, as a matter of fact, hon, we do. Do ya all want a king or queen? The king is $102, and the queen is $92." She smiled at him. He loved a gal with a Southern accent. He asked where she was from, and she answered, "Yeah, this drawl did not originate in these parts." She gave him a deliciously bigger smile. "I was born and raised my first eighteen years in Nashville, Tennessee. My daddy took a fishing trip here a few years back, and he liked it so much he never left. I was just out of high school back then and had no plans so decided to come and be near him. Been here almost twenty years now. I love it. You can't find any cleaner air than what's in these mountains."

Mick handed her his driver's license and credit card. She became all businesslike as she entered everything into the computer. "This here is a pretty small town. We don't get a lot of tourists this time of year. It's between the ski season and the summer tourist season. What brings you here, hon?"

He started to explain that he was looking for an old friend by the name of Mark DeGuard. He went on to tell her that he hadn't seen Mark in years but he was passing through on business and thought that if Mark still lived here, he would surprise him. He tried the last number he had for him, but it had been changed.

Tammy pursed her lips and concentrated. She finally said, "Most people don't take well to surprises, but it's your friend, not mine, and I think there must be a DeGuard in town. I saw that name on a mailbox out on Hidden Valley Road. Never seen a body or nothing, but my dad lives off'a that road, and DeGuard is kind of a different name, so I remembered seeing it. Ya cain't see the house at all from the road. It's surrounded by a huge wrought iron fence with a locked gate at the entrance. Maybe they have one of those call boxes or somethin' where you can announce yourself. I have never seen the gate open, and I have driven by there tons of times visiting my dad."

He smiled while listening to her talk. Then he shook his head slightly. "Tammy, thank you. You have been more than helpful." He put his credit card and license back in his wallet and took the key she handed him. He looked at the key. "Oh, 10, my lucky number. How did you know that?"

This time she looked at him and winked. "You all have a good night's sleep," she said as he started for the door.

He turned back as he reached for the doorknob. "Where is the closest pub where I can get a beer and a sandwich?"

Tammy turned back around and said, "Well, there is a pub within walking distance, actually. It's pretty near the only game in town. The only one open at night, anyway. It's just down the street about four blocks from here. I am headed that way as soon as ole Wayne comes in to relieve me. I always stop for a Manhattan before I head for home. Sometimes I get talked into a second one, if ya know what I mean?" She gave him a coy smile this time.

Uh-oh, he thought to himself. *I really better watch out for this one. She is just a little too cute for me!*

He tried to get out the door, but she went on to tell him the place was called the Caribou on account of the caribou that had broken away from the herd that was running down the middle of the street back in 1904. Apparently, the caribou had run head-on into the door of the pub. Scared the beejezus out of the customers back then. Broke its neck so they had it mounted and its head hangs over the entrance of the door, changed the name to the Caribou. "At least that's what I've been told," she said. "You see a lot of old locals in the joint, but most of 'em go home before it gets too late. We get the tourists on their way to Yellowstone in the spring and summer, along with fishermen and campers." She broke off as a young man came in the back door. "Oh, hey, Wayne. Glad ya finally got here. You're only thirty minutes late, ya know? Remember what Dotty said the last time you were late?"

Wayne looked like a scared little rabbit. "I remember," he said. "She said she would shitcan me. Please don't tell her, Tammy. I really need this job, and my car broke down on the way home this morning, so I had to ride my bike here, and when I went to get it out of the shed, it had a flat tire."

Tammy looked at him and smiled. "Hell, Wayne, I ain't gonna tell her. I'm no snitch! But ya know Dotty will find out anyway when she looks at your time card."

Wayne smacked his head. "Oh, shit. Well, will you vouch for me?"

"'Course I will, sugar. I know how much you need this job."

Mick watched as she picked up her purse and gave Wayne a pat on the head, like a beloved dog, he thought as he watched her. She flounced out the door that Mick still held open and said, "Keeps him a little beholden to me." She whispered and winked. She then waved and walked toward the glow of lights from a few blocks away. *Nice ass,* Mick thought as he watched her saunter down the street. He was thinking how nice it would be to crawl into bed with that on a cold night. He sighed as he closed the door behind him. *What in the hell is wrong with me? Keep to the business at hand, man!* he wordlessly scolded himself. *It's only been about fourteen hours since you crawled out of a bed that contained a beautiful, soft, openhearted woman, and here you are thinking about getting into bed with another one. No wonder you can't find a steady relationship!*

He unlocked room number 10 and threw his duffel bag on the chair. He unwrapped his toiletries so he could brush his teeth. Dog breath was not one of his favorite things. Equally so, it was not impressive with the ladies. *Yuck.* He looked at himself in the mirror and grinned. *Well, there is no business like the business at hand.* He looked at his hand and laughed out loud. *Okay, no pun intended. Not exactly what I had in mind.* He washed his hands and flattened down the top of his hair. Damn colic stood up like a stick. He pictured Tammy sitting on a barstool just down the street. He knew a little walk wouldn't hurt him.

Chapter 8

It didn't take any time to find the Caribou; not only was it the only building that looked like it was a bar, but it was also the only one that had any lights on, and there were cars parked out front. Mick walked into the dimly lit interior. He spotted Tammy right away. She was sitting with her legs crossed at the end of the bar. Nicely shaped legs she had too, he thought. *Wonder who the old geezer is.* He looked old enough to be her father, but then she had mentioned a dad, so it very well could be him. Mick picked a barstool in the middle of the bar and ordered a PBR from the bartender. It was his down-home beer and they just happened to carry them here. He had tried other beers—what other self-respecting man had not?—but PBR was his favorite, light, cheap beer. He liked some IPAs and ales but PBR was like an old friend that had stood by him for many years. Mick wasn't really too keen on trying new things. Except maybe women. He didn't mind trying new ones of those. It kept him young. He shifted himself on the barstool with a grin.

"Hey, there," Tammy said. "I didn't see you come in the door. I see ya decided to check the place out, huh?"

Mick looked at her as she walked by him, and said, "Well, it did appear to be the closest place to the hotel. I never have more than three beers, or drinks, for that matter, if I have to drive anywhere. This also looks like the only game in town, like you said."

"Ya got that right," Tammy answered him. "Kind of hard for a single gal to hook up sometimes."

He found her eyes were looking him up and down instead of the other way around. Him eyeing her, anyway. *Wow,* he thought. *This is a new experience. I don't get out of town enough, I guess.* He watched Tammy's tight ass as she turned back and headed to the ladies' room.

Mick motioned the bartender over to where he was sitting and asked him what was good on the menu. The bartender looked at him a little warily. He didn't often see new people in the bar at this time of year, and he was especially protective of Tammy. She was a nice gal and a good customer. He told Mick that the special was a tritip chili with corn bread. He just happened to have some left. He told Mick it packed a bit of a wallop, though. "Well, so do I," Mick told him as he looked down the bar to where Tammy was sitting. "I guess I'll try some." Tammy did not turn back around or even give him a glance. She seemed totally engrossed in what the old guy was saying. He tried to eavesdrop on their conversation, but the music was just loud enough that he couldn't hear what they were saying. He couldn't help but think what a cute gal like that was doing in a place like this. An old cliché, he knew, but he did wonder. It didn't seem like there was much to do in this little burg but maybe hunt and fish, and she didn't look like she would really like either. However, looks are deceiving, as Mick well knew.

Just then, the bartender set the chili and corn bread in front of him. "Don't say I didn't warn you, though." Mick took three big bites before he realized his lips were on fire. *Sets a wallop, all right!* he thought as he gasped for air. He ended up drinking his beer in three big swigs to cut the fire in his mouth and throat, but added a shot of Jack Daniel's, just for good measure. After all, it had been a long day. When he had finished eating, he asked for his bill louder than necessary and paid the bartender. He turned toward Tammy's way one more time, but she still didn't turn around and acknowledge him. *Just as well,* he thought. *I need a good night's sleep, anyway.* He paid his bill, leaving a sizable tip, and thanked the bartender as he put on his hat on his way out the door.

As he walked back to the hotel, he couldn't help but admire how the sky was filled with stars. Very rarely did he have the opportunity to see such a clear sky literally filled with light from the stars. Living on the coast, one had to get up in the middle of the night to see any stars at all. It was often foggy and overcast, especially this time of year. He let himself into number 10. The place was what he would call shabby chic, even by his standards. Everything looked and smelled clean, however, and there was coffee for the morning, and a small refrigerator and microwave. Really, what more could a bachelor ask for, anyway? He didn't feel especially tired, more wound up, he thought, even though it was almost eleven. He decided to put on the TV, and he started to channel-surf for something worth watching. Not many channels, so he ended up with an older episode of *NCIS*, probably one he had seen before. He had semireclined on the bed with a small Jack Daniel's on ice when he heard a knock on the door. *What the hell?* he thought. He looked at his watch: 11:20.

He went to the window and opened the curtain a crack. *Well, damn,* he thought to himself and smiled. He opened the door and met Tammy's smile, which was even bigger than his. His glance fell to the wine she was removing from her bag. "Well, hey, there. I couldn't talk at the bar. My dad was so upset. He is having problems with his girlfriend, and he hasn't been feeling that well. He finally moved out and is renting a studio apartment just outside of town. The other side from where he was living. It's a good move for him because it's over the garage of a friend of his, but I am worried about the both of them. They are both in their seventies. My dad is seventy-seven, and he can't drive that well at night anymore, and Polly, his girlfriend, doesn't drive at all now. I finally told him to go home and we would talk some more tomorrow. So here I am."

Mick wasn't sure if she was out of breath or out of conversation, so he said, "Come on in." He took the wine from her and took the plastic off the only two cups in the room. Didn't seem right to drink red wine out of plastic, but that was all there was. Fortunately, it was a twist-off cap, because he surely did not carry a wine opener. He poured them two healthy cups. They then sat on the edge of the bed, side by side, and nudged the two cups together. "Cheers." They both said at the same time and took swallows.

Tammy woke up at six the next morning. She said she didn't want either Wayne or Dotty to catch her leaving someone's room. She explained that Dotty was a really nice person and great to work for, but she took over in the office at seven sharp and she worked until noon, when Tammy came in to work. The hotel was small, and there were only the three of them and a part-time housekeeper. Dotty covered all the shifts on their days off, and pretty much anything else that came up. She told Mick she would have to get home, take a shower, and still stop and check up on her dad. She gave Mick a quick peck on the cheek and took off before he could even say so much as a thank-you. And he did want to thank her. That had been an unexpected, most pleasant surprise, he thought as he closed the door with a Cheshire cat's grin on his face.

There was a small continental breakfast in the lobby, so Mick was able to grab a bagel and cream cheese and a cup of coffee before he left the hotel. He quickly introduced himself to Dotty, who appeared to be doing some paperwork, so no need for small talk. He bade her a "Have a nice day" and was in and out in ten minutes. He had a plan for a little stakeout down the street from the DeGuard house. He drove to the address that Tammy had given him. She didn't remember the exact number but said it was close enough, and there weren't many houses in the vicinity, so it was easy to find. There was the name DeGuard on the mailbox, which was a little odd because it didn't include any house number. *They must not have many postal patrons in this little burg,* he thought. He peered at the gate, parked his truck on the shoulder, and got out to walk around a bit. He looked for security cameras or something that might indicate that there was some type of security. He saw the gate had some type of lockbox or coded box. He assumed that if someone came down the drive, the gate would open from the inside, but one might need an opener to get in from the outside. He figured he would just move his car back down the road a little bit and wait to see what, if anything, would happen.

He got into his truck and planned on settling in for a bit with a book. He reached around into the back seat for a copy of *East of Eden* by John Steinbeck. Not exactly what Mick would call light reading, but a good book for a stakeout. It was long and full of detail. He didn't figure he would get so involved with reading it that he would miss something important. He hadn't graduated to a Kindle yet; he much preferred a book. Pick up, put down, simple. He didn't have to worry about a battery or the expense if he left it someplace. Especially since it turned out he was pretty good at misplacing things. He had read the book in high school but had always wanted to read it again. There was so much detail to grasp, but as a teenager, all he wanted to do was get enough out of it to pass the test the teacher had given them. Now that he took more time to read, he found he enjoyed books with a lot of detail.

He was only about twenty pages into the fifth chapter when a black Mustang came down the drive. He could not make out the license plate; he was too far away to see from the angle the car was at. The driver waited for the gate to open, then pointed the car away from Mick. He could make out the license plate at that angle: D-1774. And it looked like an Idaho plate. The windows on the car were so darkly tinted he could not make out if the driver was a male or a female. The Mustang was driven slowly out the gate, but as soon as the wheels hit the pavement, it took off like a bat out of hell, throwing bits of gravel behind. Man, if he didn't hurry up, he wouldn't be able to follow it. Fortunately for him, he didn't have to follow it for very long, though. The car was driven into Pine Lake and was parked in front of a US bank. The driver got out with a package under his arm. Mick squinted to see if he could get a look at the guy. He went to take his binoculars out of the glove compartment to get a closer look. It sure looked like Mark DeGuard. It was a medium-built man wearing all-black clothes, including his baseball cap, which was pulled low over his eyes. He had a slightly stooped appearance, along with a slight limp. Mick watched him walk into the bank and decided to just sit and observe things. After about fifteen minutes, however, he started getting a little antsy. Obviously, Mark was taking longer than necessary for a deposit or withdrawal, and there wasn't anyone else coming or going in the bank. *Although since so many people do their banking online instead, you don't see as many people as you once did coming or going from a bank. Mostly just older folks who can't get used to a computer,* he thought.

It was at least another ten minutes before he emerged from the front door. He appeared to be whistling, and his gait was a little livelier. He had something different under his arm than when he went into the bank. It looked heavier with the way he was holding it. Mick watched as Mark got back in the Mustang and squealed away from the curb. Mick sat for a moment, debating what to do. Follow the Mustang or go into the bank to see if he could find out anything useful? *Oh, hell,* he thought, *let him go. I would be better off finding out any information I can. Maybe I can turn on the charm and get lucky.* He got out of his truck and started up the walk into the bank.

He stepped into the front entrance and looked around. He was the only one in there, and there was only one teller at the window. She was fairly young, tall, and slim, with dark-brown hair. Cute, he thought. He was preparing to turn on the charm when she said, "Good afternoon. May I help you?"

"Hello, there. Was that Mark DeGuard I just saw leaving?" Before she could answer, he continued, "He's my brother-in-law, and I was supposed to meet him here, but I was running late. I am pretty sure that was his car I saw pulling away as I pulled up." He held out his hand to the teller. "My name is Mick Meade." The small-town bank was all one big open space with a teller counter, no security windows. He did note a security camera on the ceiling pointing in his direction, though.

The teller looked up at him and said, "Hello, Mr. Meade. Yes, that was Mark who just left."

"Did he say if he was coming back or anything about meeting me here? I can't believe he couldn't have waited a few more minutes for me. I drove all the way from the coast in Oregon and couldn't get here until late last night. I left him a voice mail, but I think service here could be a little sketchy. I wasn't really sure if he got my message or not. Just like him not to wait for me. We've certainly had our ups and downs, and ins and outs, if you know what I mean." He looked crestfallen as he glanced at the teller's name badge. "Did he, by any chance, get something out of the safe-deposit box, Jennie?"

She looked up at him and smiled when he said her name. "Well, as a matter of fact, he did. I can take you back there if I can see your ID first."

Mick looked down at her and answered, "No, that's okay. I will catch up with him later. Did you, by any chance, notice what he was carrying under his arm when he left? Mom would roll over in her grave if he took everything out of the box without me being here."

He saw Jennie hesitate. Then she gave him a big toothy smile. "Well, I really wasn't paying a whole lot of attention. He didn't want me back there with him, and since no one else is here right now, I just left him alone in the vault. We can do that since everything else in there is locked up. I do recall seeing him carry a canvas bag when he left. The kind you carry money and coins in. It even could have been one of our US Bank canvas bags. We let customers use them."

Mick thought for a moment, then said, "Well, thanks for your help, Jennie. I will just see if I can catch up with him. You have a great day now." Mick walked out the door and got back in his pickup, thinking about Mark. He most likely did get something out of a safe-deposit box, but what?

He sat mulling things over in his mind, in particular, *How do I use my uncanny abilities as an investigator? I need to get a closer look inside that gate. That might give me a better idea of who Mark really is and if Mark had anything to do with Carla's death.* Mick was almost certain he was involved somehow. He was thinking he could probably scale the fence. It wouldn't be that difficult. *Hopefully, there is not a trained-to-kill German shepherd or some other large dog to protect the place. That could be a problem. Though I could always go get a hunk of meat, just in case.* He headed back the way he had come. The bank was only a few blocks from the hotel. Instead of going back to the hotel to pick up a few things, he pulled into the parking lot of the Caribou Bar and Grill. *Just a little sustenance to boost my courage,* he thought.

The sustenance ended up being two PBAs backed with two shots of Crown Royal and a large cheeseburger, no fries. Had to watch his figure, ya know? Although he thought that his burger was more in line with taking a nap than scaling a wall. When he left the bar an hour later, he walked to his truck lost in thought. He looked at his cell phone. *Crap.* He had two missed calls and three unread texts. *Damn, must have had the ringer turned down.* When he checked the settings, he found out the ringer was completely turned off. Probably after Tammy turned up last night. Although he didn't remember turning it off.

He checked the numbers, but there were no messages. He checked the texts, and the first one was a scathing text from Sheelya. Hell, it had only been a couple of days since he had seen her. The woman was such a witch. There was a text from Evelyn wishing him safe travels and whatnot. *That's sweet,* he thought, *considering the way I left her.* The third text was from Tammy. It included a thumbs-up and a smiley face. *How in the hell did she get my number? She must have looked at my phone when I was in the bathroom. I really should have better security.* He looked at his phone again. The numbers listed were both from Sheelya, but no messages.

He put the phone on the console, started his truck, and eased out onto the street. He looked in his rearview mirror into the back seat. He had stored a knife, rope, flashlight, and an apple, just in case this took a while. He had some extra water, but as he looked around for his book, he didn't see it. Damn, where was his book? He reached under the seat and felt it lodged against something soft. He pulled his hand away. *Yuck.* What the hell was that? Whatever it was, some of it was squished against the binder of the book. *Good God,* he thought, *I need a housekeeper for not only my house but my truck as well!*

Chapter 9

Mick drove the truck onto the shoulder of the road and parked about one hundred feet from the gate of the house. There just happened to be a big oak tree with lower branches hanging over the road, providing some needed shade. He turned off the engine and was prepared to sit and see what happened. Maybe Mark would leave again. He knew he should return a couple of phone calls, but he hated to break stride with what he was doing. He noticed a new number on the call log yesterday but figured that could wait until later to return; the caller hadn't bothered to leave a voice message, so it couldn't have been too important.

Just when he was looking for an adequate bush or tree he could take a leak behind, the gate opened and a car emerged from the middle of the trees. He looked at his watch, four o'clock. He looked at the car. It was not the black Mustang but a nondescript-looking, gray-colored car. He thought it was either a Hyundai or a Subaru, but he wasn't sure. Just like the Mustang, though, its windows were tinted so dark he could not make out the driver. But it was not Mark; he was pretty sure of that. Mark sat up taller on the driver's side, and this person sat low in the seat, barely seeing over the steering wheel. He started the truck and waited until the small car was down the road about a quarter of a mile before he pulled out onto the highway. He had followed the car for about twenty miles when he noticed a road sign that listed, "Boredom, Idaho: 5 miles." *Funny name,* he thought. He wondered how some towns got their names. He knew of a town called Boring in Oregon—almost the same thing. "Well, I think I will just see where this little car is going," he said to himself.

In his business, he found that talking to himself helped him think a little clearer. Most of the time, there was no one else to talk to, anyway, so it was a habit he had picked up. Didn't always make him sound normal, though, when he found he was talking to himself over the vegetables in the grocery store.

The small car, which he could tell now was an older-model Hyundai, had stopped in front of a Wells Fargo bank. He parked about six car lengths away on the opposite side of the street and watched as a petite middle-aged redhead got out of the car. She had a huge black patent leather purse hanging over her shoulder. For all Mick knew, this could be Mark's cleaning lady, or maybe just a friend. He thought back to the pictures he had viewed on the internet, but he could not recall anyone with red hair. Not that that in itself meant anything. Lots of women changed their hair color as often as they changed their underwear. Well, maybe as often as he changed his underwear. His ex-wife had changed the color of her hair every time she went to the salon. It used to drive him nuts. Just when he got used to one color, she came home with a different color.

He watched as the redhead went into the bank. Kind of a déjà vu, really, he thought, since he had just observed Mark do the same thing not that long ago.

Mick got out of his truck and crossed the street and went into the bank himself. He stood at the counter and fiddled with a deposit slip. Another small local bank that had open teller windows. He could only see one teller. He was hoping he would be able to hear what the woman and the teller said to each other. He heard the teller greet the redhead as Mrs. DeGuard. They were engaged in some type of small talk, and he noticed Mrs. DeGuard had greeted the teller by name but she did not have a name badge on. They seemed to be on friendly terms. He couldn't get close enough to hear exactly what they were saying, but he could catch little snippets of the conversation. The redhead wanted to put something in a safe-deposit box. He heard her say that it was some type of a surprise for her husband, so she couldn't leave it at home. "I don't want him to find it or find out," he heard her say.

While they walked to the back of the bank, Mick quickly walked back outside to his truck. He sat in the driver's seat a few minutes, mulling over the situation. It was now almost five o'clock. He couldn't recall anyone, by the description of the redhead, that he had seen on the internet. He really did not think that Mark had a wife, or something would have been listed for him to follow up on. Either Mark had recently married or "Mrs. DeGuard" was not really Mrs. DeGuard. The only female he could bring to mind that might be in the picture was Mark's sister, JoAnn. Just then, the redhead came out of the door of the bank. The way she was carrying the purse, it was obviously lighter than when she went in. She opened the back door of the car and threw the purse on the back seat. Mick watched her make a U-turn and head the car back the way she had come. He figured he might as well just follow her back.

He kept the Hyundai in view but stayed a good distance back so he wouldn't be seen. Not that it would probably make a difference. The woman driving the car didn't appear to be paying much attention. She looked like she was bobbing her head to some music or something. He followed her back into town and into the parking lot of the Towne Market. He pulled into the rear of the parking lot while she went into the store. He got out of the pickup and followed her in. She grabbed a basket. He grabbed a basket. "Well, let's see what happens," he said to himself as he started to follow her through the store, picking up a piece of fruit as he went. It was certainly a clean little market specializing in organic foods and natural products. *Kind of spendy, though,* he thought as he looked around. *Wouldn't want to depend on buying everything here.* He watched as she got some cereal off a high shelf and lost her hold on it, the boxing falling on the floor. She bent to pick it up, and he couldn't help but admire what a nice ass she had. She stood up, flinging her hair back over her shoulder. She was cute, but he never did like redheads. Any redhead he had ever met was covered in freckles, and then they had to stay out of the sun. So it just seemed they were not outdoorsy at all, because they had to be so careful when they were in the sun. This gal had a great tan, and it didn't appear to be from a salon, but a nice, natural light-brown look. Her legs were muscular looking, so he figured her for a jogger or walker. *Nice,* he thought. His mind wandered, and he lost track of where she went down the aisle. *Get a grip, man!* He chastised himself for the thought and went to see in which direction she had gone.

He nonchalantly sidled up to her as she was picking up a lemon. "I am terrible at picking out fruit," he told her. "My late wife always did the grocery shopping. Do you know how to tell if a melon is ripe or not?"

She glanced in his direction and must have decided he wasn't some kind of a pervert, because she gave him a slight smile. "Well, I am not so good with cantaloupe, but I think you press your thumb in slightly on the bottom and there shouldn't be a lip around the stem." She demonstrated what she meant. Then she lifted the cantaloupe to smell it. "It should smell sweet and slightly musky. Like a woman." Then she looked at him, licked her lips, and winked.

Whoever said that the best place to meet women was in a grocery store had the right idea. *Why didn't I think of this before?* he wondered. He introduced himself to her as Colin Watkins, new in town. They stood chatting about the town and the surrounding area. She had not actually said where she was from; she did say that her name was Wanda and she had come to town to take care of an elderly aunt and that she was bored silly. "There is a canyon near here the gal at my hotel told me about that is supposed to have a great trail that isn't too difficult a hike," Mick said to her. "I was thinking about checking it out tomorrow. Would you like to check it out with me? Or am I being too forward? I have been accused of that before." He gave her his boyish smile. "Also, of being arrogant, bold, conceited. You name it, I have probably been called it."

She actually laughed and said she would like to go on a hike. She hadn't been anywhere but the grocery store and the café since she had arrived. A hike would do her good, she said. Wanda went to take his hand and to say thanks. He felt what he thought was her finger rubbing on his inner palm. *This could prove interesting,* he thought. She was obviously flirting with him now. They walked together to the checkout counter. Mick had picked up a six-pack of beer along the way, and Wanda waited for him outside on the sidewalk. He asked her if she wanted to pick him up or just meet back here in the parking lot and he would drive. She told him she wouldn't be able to leave before ten o'clock in the morning. She always had a few things that her aunt needed before she went anywhere. He told her she had better wear more comfortable shoes than what she had on now, or she wouldn't be walking very far. She gave a little nod as she got into the Hyundai and waved a goodbye in her window. *Hmmm, interesting,* he thought. He stood there at least five minutes while he watched her drive down the road.

Mick thought about going back to the Caribou bar for dinner but decided against it. He didn't want to run into Tammy tonight due to having to get up early in the morning. He had picked up a few things to nibble on, along with the six-pack of beer, so he was good for tonight. He decided the best thing for him to do was to go back to the hotel and get a good night's sleep. He parked his truck around the block instead of the parking lot at the hotel. He was attempting to exhibit a little more cautious behavior, although tonight he was more worried about Tammy stopping by.

He remembered two years ago, when he had walked into his hotel room and got hit in the back of the head with a baseball bat. He had sustained a concussion and was literally blind for more than a week. Turned out that the attack had nothing to do with the case he had been working on, as he had thought, but had actually been the boyfriend of a woman he had spent the previous night with. *Doesn't pay to be too nice,* he thought. He found out later that the woman had actually told her boyfriend about him and of the night, wanting to see how jealous he got. Well, Mick was the one who found out how jealous he got. He never saw the woman again. The incident made him a little overcautious when he had to stay in a hotel.

Mick got a beer from the little refrigerator and sat down with the open IPA and a ham and cheese sandwich he had picked up while in the market. He put his feet up on the chair opposite the bed and let out a small sigh. *Now, I could get used to this quiet, clean room,* he thought. The bed was made. The room smelled clean. Just then, his phone gave a little pinging noise. He looked at the name. *Oh, Christ, Sheelya.* He debated in his head, *Answer, not answer? Oh, hell.* She would only hound him until he did talk to her. He gritted his teeth and said, "Sheelya, hello. What can I do for you?" How he managed the positive, upbeat lilt to his voice, he wasn't sure. The woman was a tyrant.

What he heard, with the phone an arm's length from his ear, was, "Mick! You miserable turd! I have been trying to get ahold of you since yesterday!" He just let her tirade go on until she seemed to run out of breath.

"Sheelya, I have not left town without giving your situation considerable thought," he told her. "I had to leave town on another case, but I have my assistant, Colin, watching your husband and his so-called girlfriend. If there is anything going on, trust me, Colin will find out. He already managed to obtain some compromising pictures, but nothing is concrete yet. When he gets more information, you will be the first to know." His even tone and quiet voice seemed to placate her a little, because her voice was quieter and more relaxed sounding when she spoke again. He went on to tell her that he would be back home in about a week or so, and by then he was sure Colin would have something worth waiting for.

When next she spoke, her tone had taken on a soft, seductive quality. "Well, Mick, I think I can find something to hold against you."

He didn't hear the rest of the conversation since he clicked off his phone. He turned the volume down so he wouldn't hear the damn ping during the night and went into the bathroom to brush his teeth.

Chapter 10

Mick woke up at about 6:00 a.m. and checked his phone for any messages before he even got out of bed. He returned a couple of emails and texts and then went to get ready for the day. He headed into the bathroom for a shower, glancing at himself in the mirror as he went. *Clearheaded this morning, big guy. Not bad.* And he gave his reflection a big grin and scratched at his head. He had agreed to meet Wanda at ten o'clock, so he figured he would go find a substantial breakfast and run his truck through the car wash. It was covered with dried, dead bugs and bird crap from the drive here. *I wish I could be as particular about my house as I am about my truck,* he thought wryly. He remembered he had passed a small café yesterday, Grannies, or something like that. He would hate to have someone think he would drive a vehicle as dirty as his had gotten. It just didn't fit his image. *Yeah, right,* he thought. *Like I really have an image anymore.*

He opened the door of Grannies Café and a bell tinkled. He looked around and saw there were only a couple of people seated at two tables. The waitress told him to sit anywhere he wanted, so he chose a small table by the window. When she came over to take his order, he noticed she wrote everything slowly and meticulously on a small tablet. He ordered his standard restaurant breakfast of, three-egg Western omelet, hash browns, and rye toast. She had just set down a whole carafe of coffee on the table, and he looked closely at her when she leaned down to do so. No wonder the place was called Grannies, he thought. The old gal must be in her eighties. She waddled away with his order, and he looked out the window as the morning was waking up outside.

It was only about ten minutes when his breakfast was set in front of him. "Do you know any DeGuards that live around here?" he asked the elderly waitress. "I am an old friend of Mark DeGuard, and last time I talked to him, he gave me an address near here, but I went by there and that wasn't his house. The people there had no idea who I was talking about."

The waitress looked at him up and down and said, "Well, sonny, why don't you just give him a call? You young people are always on those dang cell phones. Purt near ever'body's got one in these parts. Cell service ain't so good, though."

She had started to walk away when Mick said, "Well, I would do that, except I dropped my phone in the lake about two weeks ago and I lost all the contact numbers I had stored in the phone. Do you know who he is?" Mick gave her a look and smile a mother would love.

She looked at him a little suspiciously but must have decided he was okay to talk to, for she said, "I see that Mark ever' once in a while. Not so much as I used to. He used to come in here at least twice a week, but I have not seen him in a couple of months. He never was sociable like ever'one else around. He would come in for coffee and pie and never talked to anybody, but ya know, this is a small town, and pretty much ever'one knows ever'one else. Lately, I have only seen him going into the post office, and the postmaster is a good friend of mine. She says he comes in weekly to pick up packages wrapped in black plastic. Now, I didn't get to be no eighty-three years old 'out knowing somethin' about sneaky folks. There is somethin' not quite right about that guy. He don't fool me with his hanky-panky. Like he's up to no good, in my opinion." She gave him a wrinkled smile and told him her postmaster friend's name was Ethel and she might be more helpful.

In the meantime, Mick had finished his breakfast while she was talking. He got up from the table and glanced at her name tag. "Well, Henrietta, I thank you kindly." He tipped his ball cap at her and laid money on the table for his breakfast, including a generous tip, thinking that packages wrapped in black plastic didn't necessarily mean "hanky-panky."

Mick walked across the street to the post office. Maybe he could learn a little more about Mark from the postmaster, he decided. A little bell tinkled when he opened the door. He looked up, thinking, *Jeez, is this the only security they have in this burg?* It seemed that every place he had been to had had a little bell of some sort over the door. A wizened tiny hunchbacked old woman came up to the counter. She could barely see over the top of it—she was so short. She looked like a dwarf in a long dark flowered dress. She had disheveled long gray hair and a pointy nose, with an actual brown wart on her chin. If he didn't know any better, he would have thought he had stepped into one of the Grimms' fairy tales. She offered him a little wrinkled smile and said, "Well, what can I do for you, young man?"

He looked over the counter at her and said, "Well, I would like to buy ten stamps. I know the postmaster knows a lot of people in town, and this is a small town at that, so I was wondering if you would know a Mark DeGuard? Henrietta said she knew who he was but that you might be able to tell me more about him. I lost his phone number and I went to the address he had given me, but I must have written it down wrong, because he doesn't live there and the people in the house had never heard of him. By the way, my name is Mick Meade, and I just met your friend Henrietta at the café when I had breakfast."

With the mention of Henrietta's name, her little mouth turned up at the corners. "Oh, honey, Henrietta and I go way back. Longer than before you were a thought in your daddy's head! Are you a friend of Henrietta's?"

"No, not a friend. I just met her while I was having breakfast. But we did get to talking, and she said that you might be able to help me. I am looking for an old friend by the name of Mark DeGuard. We went to college together. Have you seen him lately?" Again, he gave his most genuine, irresistible smile.

"Well, sonny, let me tell you something," she said, and her mouth turned into a thin line. It was hard to make out a mouth at all through all the wrinkles on her face. He wanted to reach down and pet her. She lowered her voice even more and stepped up to the counter. "I think that man is up to no good. Ya know how you can sometimes just tell on a person that they don't mean well?"

Mick looked her in the eyes and said, "Well, yes, I suppose I do, but what do you mean?"

She looked him up and down a couple of times, as best as she could in her diminutive stature, before she said, "You look like a pretty sharp young man. Educated, ain't ya?"

He was thinking to himself, *Thank God I put on clean underwear this morning. It feels like she can see right through me!* "Yes, I went to Cal State, but that was a long time ago. That's where I met Mark."

"Well, that man is not a nice man, I can tell you that," Ethel said.

Mick was hoping she would get to the point pretty soon. He didn't have all morning. Instead, he smiled encouragingly. "You don't say. How do you mean?"

"Well, I know some stuff he gets in the mail is pornographic, and that is just plain wrong. I seen some of that nasty stuff myself."

Mick was thinking, *Well, pornography does not a murderer make, but it does prove interesting.* "How do you know it is of that nature?" he asked her with a look of innocence on his face.

"Well, 'cause one time a package came and it had gotten mangled and I was going to fix it. Ya know, we always get our mail through at the post office. I just happened to get a peek at the contents, and there were little girls in those pictures. They was naked, mind you. Stark naked! And they couldn't have been more than ten or twelve years old! It was disgusting." He was worried she might have a heart attack right in front of him, as agitated as she was getting while talking. She started to get a little short of breath before Mick put a reassuring hand on her shoulder and asked her if she had notified the police of what she had found. She leaned over and whispered that she had been afraid to. "I can't do that now," she said. "You aren't from around here, honey, but I got myself a bit of a reputation." She took her finger and circled the side of her head. "Like, some folks think I am a little squirrelly and all. Ya know what I mean? They probably wouldn't've believed me. So I kept it to myself and started to watch him closer."

Mick couldn't help but smile at her as he took her wrinkled little hand in his and said, "Well, you seem right as rain to me," thinking that in his business he had come into contact with some real perverts that would probably curl that hair of hers.

She let out a big cackle and went back into the back of the post office without another word. He stood for a few seconds, thinking she was going to come back, but it appeared she had disappeared among the large post office bags.

Mick looked at his watch. *Oh, great.* That took longer than he had planned. It was already two minutes before ten. He didn't want to be late for his little adventure with Wanda. She might not stick around and wait for him. He hollered a thank-you at the little dwarf postmaster and hurried out the door. He couldn't help but think about what she had told him about Mark. Maybe he was a pedophile and a murderer; that was the worst kind of criminal in his book. Even after all the years spent in law enforcement, he never could understand how someone could coldly or deliberately murder another human being, or anything, for that matter. He had never been much of a hunter himself. He remembered his dad had encouraged him and even taken him on a couple of hunting trips, but it had been anything he could get used to. He had enjoyed the time with his dad, but that had been about it.

Mick opened his glove compartment as he was headed down the street to the market. He took out a small 9mm handgun he kept stored there. He checked the clip and then put it between his belt and the band of his jeans. When he got to the parking lot, he could see Wanda standing outside of her car with her arms crossed on her chest. Whoo boy, she did not look very happy.

Mick opened the truck door and hurried over to where Wanda was standing. He pasted his best smile on his face and said, "I am sorry I am a little late. I had to mail something at the post office, and the postmaster was very chatty, not to say she wasn't interesting, but I had trouble getting out of there. Have you ever seen her? She looks like a little dwarf." Mick felt like if she didn't uncross her arms and say something, he would end up babbling and feeling stupid.

"Hello, Colin," she said tightly. "I have been here ten minutes. Since I had the time, I took the liberty of picking up a couple of waters, beers, and something for lunch, but I don't like to be kept waiting."

"Well, let's get on the road, then, shall we? My vehicle or yours?" He smiled, trying to sound sincere.

"Your truck," she said. "It's not like the trailhead is way off the beaten track, but the road to get to it is full of potholes, my aunt said. She also said that the trail isn't very well maintained either. I actually did go up there once since I have been here, but the road was such that I didn't dare take my car any farther. It might be better at this time of year."

"I did go online and check out the trail," Mick said as he fiddled with the buttons on his radio. "There is a waterfall at the end of the trail, and somewhere along the way, there are a couple of caves, but I can't remember what it said about how long the hike itself is."

Wanda set the cooler on the floor in the back of the truck and then got in the passenger seat.

"It's about six miles round trip if you take the whole hike to the top of the mountain and back down, but it looked like the hike to the waterfall and back was only about four miles. Did you bring a sweatshirt?" he asked her. She still hadn't said much. "I read that it can get about ten degrees cooler down in the canyon." He pulled a dirty sweatshirt off the back seat and handed it to her. "You can always wear this if you need something warmer. It's only a little dirty."

She looked sideways at him. "No, thank you," she finally said. Then added, "It's about a twelve-mile drive out the north side of town."

"Sounds good. Let's go," Mick said as he backed the truck out of the parking lot and onto Main Street.

Chapter 11

He attempted small talk, but it seemed to fall on deaf ears. She wasn't the chatty type, that was for sure. He tried, "Where were you born?" "Go to school?" "Get married?" the typical stuff you discussed with people you had just met. She finally said that she had been married once but that was a long time ago and she wasn't looking for any relationship at this time. She did go on to say that she had been in Pine Lake about six months or so, looking after an elderly aunt that had contracted hepatitis C and that she had become quite ill with it. "I could tell she wasn't thrilled with Pine Lake. She had mentioned that a couple of times." She went on to say that now that her aunt had been treated for about six months, she was much better, and Wanda was trying to decide what to do next. Mick had started to ask her another question when she looked at him and said, "Do you mind if we just put some music on? My aunt can't tolerate anything but quiet, classical music, and I really would like to hear some top 40, if you don't mind." She turned her head to look back out the window.

"No problem," he said. "I will see what I can find." He fiddled with the buttons some more. "I don't have Sirius or anything, but the radio has some solid speakers." Just then, an old song by Hank Williams crooning, "Your Cheating Heart," came on the radio. "Wow, I haven't heard this song in years!" he said. "My mom loved country/ Western music, until my dad cheated on her, then she wouldn't listen to any kind of music after that." He looked over at Wanda, but she wasn't paying any attention to what he said. She didn't look away from the window until it was time to pull off the main road.

"There is the turnoff, right after that forty-five-mile road sign. The trees tend to cover up the sign for the park. You need to slow down, though. It's pretty rough off the main road." She had finally opened her mouth. Which was a good thing, because Mick had not seen the sign for the park at all. It was pretty faded, and the top right corner was gone altogether. He made a left-hand turn onto a rutty gravel road and saw the park sign up ahead. "Green Springs Canyon, no ATVs allowed." *Well, that's good at least,* Mick thought. He hated those noisy things, and they were usually a bunch of idiots trying to show off for one another. He drove a little farther and stopped the truck in a small parking lot surrounded by huge sequoia trees. He got out and stood in awe as he looked up at the huge rugged trees. He couldn't resist snapping a couple of pictures, capturing one of Wanda while she wasn't looking. She had knelt down to tie her shoe, and when she straightened up, she had ahold of the backpack. She handed it toward him. "Will you carry the cooler? It's not heavy, but it's too heavy for me to carry. I put in four cans of beer, two waters, and a couple of sandwiches."

"No problem," he said to her as he took the backpack from her. He then started walking toward the trail. He noted only one car in the parking lot. It was a small rust-colored Fiat with a license plate that stated, "HOT#1." *Ha ha,* he thought. He wondered if the driver was a man or a woman. "Thanks for thinking of the food and drinks. I have been known to never turn down a cold beer. It's a beautiful morning for a hike, and I am looking forward to a little exercise." Wanda at least had a smile on her face. She seemed to enjoy the antic-ipation of a hike. She was taking big gulps of fresh air as she started up the trail behind him. "If I remember correctly, the path is steep in some places, and there are no safety rails anywhere. See the sign on the fence?" She pointed to an aged, barely legible poster. Mick had to get up right in front of it to see what it said: "Beware! Hike at your own risk. Trail maintenance done yearly only. Watch for fallen logs and loose rocks."

"Well, at least they give everyone a fair warning," Mick said. He looked closer at the sign, and in smaller print at the bottom were the words "No cell service available." *Great place for an accident to happen,* he thought. He looked sideways at Wanda, who seemed to be concentrating on her footing. It wasn't even steep yet. He sure hoped she was up for this. *She must think I am kind of odd. There is absolutely no way she would have any idea why I would be interested in her,* he thought.

The path turned out to be just as rugged as the pamphlet had said. Wanda seemed able to keep up with him, though, with no problem. She didn't even need to stop and catch her breath; therefore, he couldn't either. He really did not want a petite woman showing him up. After all, she probably was able to get regular exercise. He made up some chitchat shit, but she offered no response. He walked carefully on the parts of the trail that had the most severe drop-offs. He was rattling off nonsense when a deer ran across the trail about twenty feet in front of him. "Holy crap!" he said. "That scared the bejesus out of me!" He turned to check on Wanda's reaction, and she didn't seem the least bit perturbed. Maybe she hadn't even seen the deer, what with concentrating on her footing and all. The trail got more rugged and steeper, if that were possible. When they said there was little maintenance, they were not kidding.

After about an hour and half of mostly silent walking, with some heavy breathing on Mick's part, they came to the end of the first part of the trail. Now they were down in the canyon. The trees opened up to a large open green space. There were mountains on all sides of them. Just ahead, another hundred feet or so, there was a huge pool of crystal clear water. He could see the sun reflecting off it. A waterfall about thirty feet high dumped into the clear water. It wasn't a huge cascade but enough trickling down the rock face, with splashes here and there. More rocks jutted out from the face of the cliff. He was mesmerized by the sparkle and beauty of the whole place. It was like a fairy land, making him wish he could slow down and smell the roses once in a while. Life was too short to miss out on the beauty of Mother Nature. He looked up at the sun in the deep blue sky and calculated it must be about high noon. He could just imagine elves hiding under bushes and fairies behind rocks. He couldn't remember when he had seen a more mesmerizing place.

He looked at his watch. Well, he was almost right: it was twelve thirty. And just then, his stomach growled. He looked over at Wanda and saw that she had sat on a rock by the water. She was staring into it, lost in thought herself. *Wonder what she is thinking.* He sat down on a rock himself and put his hands in the pristine water. He could see his reflection and clear to the bottom. He could see little minnows swimming around and a fish jumping to capture a bug in the middle of the lake. The water was freezing cold, reminding him of the Metolius River in Central Oregon. *Another beautiful place,* he thought. *Peaceful, quiet, scenic, and not many people around.* The way the water rippled slightly when bugs dipped down for some water was hypnotic. "This certainly is a beautiful spot. Well worth the hike when you get here."

Wanda looked over at him briefly and said, "This is one of the prettiest waterfalls I think I have ever seen."

Well, at least she hadn't fallen asleep, he noted. "Hey, Wanda, just out of curiosity—"

She cut him off midsentence. "No more questions, Colin. I just want to enjoy the solitude and sounds of the water for a bit, okay?"

"No problem," he said, and he took the backpack off his shoulders and set it down on the ground. "Well, in that case, how about one of those beers you picked up?" He took out two Sierra Nevada IPAs and popped the tabs. He took a long draw on the beer before he handed her one. "What a coincidence," he said. "My favorite beer. Nice and cold too. Thank you for bringing them."

"Well, I am a wine drinker myself, but every once in a while, when it's really warm, I like a cold beer, and the clerk at the market said they just started carrying this brand, so I thought I might as well try one. I also picked up a couple of turkey sandwiches. I hope they are all right. Can you pass me the one without the cheese, please?" She held out her hand toward him.

"You don't eat cheese? Or have a lactose problem?" Mick asked her.

"No, I do eat some, but since I have been here, staying with my aunt, who is a vegetarian, there hasn't been anything like that in her house. So since I have not had any in about six months, I have just kind of gotten used to going without so much dairy, which can't hurt me, I guess. I have lost a few pounds, anyway. I think I feel better because of it also." She started eating her sandwich and didn't say another word.

Mick glanced over at her, wondering what her game was, anyway. She seemed nice enough, although not very friendly, or maybe more *reserved* was the word. He wondered what her relationship was with Mark. He was certain she was hiding something, and he was going to find out what it was. The whole story of living and taking care of an aunt just did not ring true to him. She never looked at him when she was talking either.

Chapter 12

He hadn't realized how long he had sat there, lost in thought. He was plotting in his mind how to get both Wanda and Mark out of the house at the same time so he could get in and get a closer look. He had enough gear to scale a fence and pick a lock if need be. Knowing they were both there, though, did make it a little trickier.

Just then, Wanda said, "It's after two o'clock. We'd better head back. Half the way back is uphill, and it gets dark about four thirty. And you mentioned wanting to take a peek in one of those caves on the way back. I sure don't want to be on this trail in the dark. I read in the local paper last week that a hiker was attacked by a cougar on this very trail not more than a couple of weeks ago. The hiker got away from the cougar only because there ended up being another hiker in the same general area who had the balls to scare the cougar away. The other guy was pretty banged up in the process." She gave a little shudder. "I don't want to see one myself."

They packed up what trash they had and headed up the trail. It was actually easier going up than down. He felt more sure-footed going up, and the backpack wasn't as heavy since they had drunk and eaten everything Wanda had brought. There were just the two waters that were left. Just then, a magpie screeched and startled him into moving a little faster himself. They reached the first cave in about forty-five minutes, and Wanda plopped down on a rock just off the side of the trail. She said there was no way she was going in that dark hole, so he went in by himself.

The entrance of the cave, Mick knew, was just barely six feet high, because he had to duck to get under the entranceway, and once

79

in the cave, he was not able to stand all the way up. He took out a small flashlight and scanned the light around the interior of the cave. He wished he had brought his larger flashlight, but he hadn't thought of it at that time. *Wow,* he thought. There were a few very small stalactites in the corner. He was surprised that a stalactite could grow in the drier climate that the cave seemed to have, but he did not know much about their growth, anyway. It didn't seem damp to him, and the weather was still pretty warm. There was a rock with a flat top that could have been used for a table. It had two smaller rocks sitting next to it that looked like someone had set them there for chairs. He would have loved to have something like this in his backyard when he was growing up, he thought. Someone had carved something on the side of one of the rock walls, but it looked more like a "B + J" and then something indecipherable. Probably some young couple marking their territory. He had started back out of the cave when something shiny caught his eye. He leaned down to pick it up. It was a bright-blue cigarette lighter. He also noted a couple of cigarette butts in the corner. They looked like Marlboros, and they weren't that old. They still maintained a clean-looking filter. *Well, maybe the Marlboro man had been here.* Smiled at his stupid thought.

As he walked back out into the light, he said to Wanda, "I think someone had been in there recently. I could see where some outlaw type could use it as a hideaway back in the day. If they weren't over five foot nine, anyway." He chuckled. "I have always wondered what it would be like to travel by horse, finding shelter and food along the way. I think I would have liked living back then."

Wanda didn't even look at him as they had resumed their hike. Her eyes were on the path, and she seemed to be concentrating on her footing again, his small talk falling on deaf ears like before. He looked at the trail. It was steeper and narrower than the one they had taken on the way in. He had wanted to do a loop rather than go back the way they had come, but it might not have been the best idea. The trail through this part couldn't even be two feet across, with the rock face on one side and an abyss on the other. He looked down. *Not sure anyone could survive a fall from here,* he thought. Just then, Wanda let out a little shriek and he watched as some loose rock tumbled over the side of the cliff along with Wanda's left leg. She had lost her footing, and her arms were starting to circle as she tried to catch her balance. There just happened to be a small fir tree rooted in an outcropping on the side of the cliff, and as her leg went over, Mick grabbed the bottom of the fir tree and reached out to grab Wanda and pull her back toward the side of the cliff. She fell against him, clinging to the front of his shirt. He could feel her heart racing against his chest, and she started to cry as they stood there a moment, catching their breath.

Well, that was enough to rattle her cage, he thought.

"Wow, that was close," he said. "Let's get the hell out of here. It looks easier about thirty or so feet ahead. I can see a little clearing at the end of this rock cliff."

"I can't get down soon enough for me," she said and then didn't say another word the rest of the way back to the parking lot.

When they returned to the parking lot, the first thing he noticed was, the little rust-colored car was gone. When he stepped from around behind the park sign, he didn't see his truck parked where he had left it. It was gone too. "What the hell?" He smacked the front of his head as he swore again. He hadn't had the truck very long, and it was the first time he had ever bought one brand new. It was a Ford Super Duty F-150. He had spent over $50,000 on it just last year. He had debated about having an extra security alarm installed and then had decided not to spend the extra money. *What a jackass.* Beauty before brains—that was him all right. He looked over at Wanda, who looked equally stricken. "Oh, for God's sake. You must be kidding me? I left my cell phone on your console because I knew we wouldn't have service in the canyon. Now what do we do?" She sounded close to hysterical. Besides the near fall off the cliff, she actually showed some true emotion.

"Well, I rarely don't have mine." He reached around to his back pocket and took his cell phone out and tried the internet to see if a local tow company would come up on the screen. Nothing came up on the screen, and he swore loudly. "I guess we will just have to walk out to the main road. I know I had cell service before we took the road into the park. It's only about a mile from here."

Wanda looked rather grim when she looked at him. "I can't take another step until I relieve my bladder. Another reason I seldom drink beer. They go right through you."

Mick pointed to a honey bucket off to his left. You could actually smell it before you could see it. Having it hidden behind a tree did little to disguise where it was.

Wanda looked at him, exasperated. "I can't go in that," she said.

"Well, it is what it is. Either that or the woods. And watch out for cougars, in that case." Mick looked at her and chuckled. She turned quickly around and headed back into the woods toward the beginning of the trail. *What a bitch,* he thought as he waited for her to come back. He had always wondered why they were called honey buckets.

She returned in five minutes, saying, "I can't use those damn outdoor toilets. All I can imagine is something down in that hole. They give me the heebie-jeebies, and they usually all smell horrible. I'm ready. Let's get the hell out of here before it gets dark."

They both took off at a fast pace while the sun started to set behind them.

When they got to the main road, Mick was able to call the local police station and explain their situation. They told him that normally they were not able to provide transportation, but due to the extenuating circumstances, they said someone would come out and offer them a lift into town. "After all, it's not like we can send a taxi or an Uber," the officer had told him. "This is a small rural town. You'd have to go at least fifty miles to get to a town big enough to provide any public transportation."

Mick had a look of impatience on his face. "If it's all the same to you, Officer, can you just send someone as quickly as possible? It's getting dark and cold while I stand here chatting. I would really appreciate it."

The officer said he had already dispatched someone to get them, but while he was waiting, could Mick just answer some basic questions? Mick gave him the make and model of the vehicle. He explained that his insurance card was in the glove box, so he did not have the VIN number on hand, but he could call his insurance company in the morning. He offered the license plate number and the color. The officer asked if he knew of anyone that might steal the truck, or could a relative or someone have come and borrowed it? Mick was getting really impatient at this point and had to take a deep breath before continuing. "Look, Officer, I am just in town visiting friends. I live on the Oregon coast. I have no family here, wasn't planning on staying, just planned on a quick visit and passing through." The officer asked him to please come into the station to fill out some paperwork as soon as he was able.

While he and Wanda waited, Mick tried to figure out how someone could have stolen the truck way out here. He swore to himself for not getting the extra security. Although way out here, there was little chance anyone would have heard an alarm going off, anyway. Most times those alarms were so loud they scared someone out of stealing. While he was lost in thought, Wanda was pacing back and forth on the side of the road. He tried a reassuring tone while relaying what the officer said, but she seemed more interested in kicking at the gravel on the shoulder. *Oh well,* he thought, *it might be good for her mental health.* And she wasn't berating him for something he had no control over, anyway.

Just then, he saw a black-and-white car coming into view. Mick told Wanda that she could be dropped off at her car and he would go to the station to fill out paperwork. He doubted that she would be needed for anything, but just in case, would she mind giving him her phone number? She looked at him with a sour expression and said, that's if I even get my phone back and reluctantly gave it to him. The officer stopped the patrol car and got out to introduce himself. Wanda refused to look at him, just climbed into the back seat before Mick even introduced himself. If Wanda was trying to avoid conversation, she was out of luck. She didn't say two words, and Mick just explained what he had already told the other officer on the phone. The officer was persistent in trying to gain more information, though. He looked in his rearview mirror at Wanda sulking in the back seat.

"I know most of the people that live in Pine Lake, but I haven't seen you before, miss. Are you just visiting also?"

She looked at him in the mirror but quickly looked away. "I have only been here about six months," she slowly said. "I have been taking care of my aunt, who was ill but is now recovered, so I won't be staying much longer."

"Oh well, who is your aunt? I bet I know her. I have lived here most of my whole life, except when I went to Boise to go to the police academy. I stayed with my granny there for a little over a year. As soon as I graduated, though, I hightailed it back home. They just happened to have an opening in the police department right here in Pine Lake. I sure lucked out on that!" He looked at Wanda again in the mirror.

She rolled her eyes and bit her lip before she said, "Oh, you wouldn't know her." Then she continued, "She actually lives in the next town over, and she's been a bit of a recluse the past ten years or so. She hardly ever leaves her house anymore."

The officer tried again, but just then, Wanda started coughing like she was unable to stop. She reached over for the water bottle that she had laid on the seat and started drinking like she couldn't stop. Mick watched as the officer studied her in the mirror. *Hmmmm,* Mick thought. Maybe he wasn't the only one that found her to be a little suspicious.

It didn't take as long to drive into town as Mick thought it had taken to drive out there, but maybe Wanda's attitude had something to do with that. As they drove into the parking lot of the Towne Market, Mick watched as Wanda literally bounded from the back seat, practically before the car had come to a complete stop. The officer got out and called after her, but she didn't give him so much as a backward glance. He shouted, "I may need to ask you a few questions later! Can you leave your phone number?" She either did not hear him or chose not to; she just got into her car and took off. He turned and looked at Mick. "What's her problem?" he asked. "She couldn't wait to get away from us."

Mick was still sitting in the front seat and turned to look at the officer. "Not really sure," he said. "I just met her in the market yesterday, and we got talking. She was bored, and I didn't hook up with my friend, so we decided to go on a hike together. I had never seen her before yesterday. She did give me her phone number reluctantly, but I have no idea if it's really hers or not might be a moot point anyway if the phone got left in the truck."

The officer was watching her until she turned the corner and was out of sight.

"Well, let's head to the station and get some paperwork filled out. I will take the number then. I may want to ask her a few questions. Especially if we find out your truck was stolen. She seemed pretty evasive to me. Kind of an odd duck, don't you think?" the officer said and glanced at Mick.

"Yeah, pretty odd," Mick said. "Let's get this over with. Do you think there is any chance you will get the truck back in one piece?" he asked.

The officer looked at him and shrugged. "Your guess is as good as mine, but in my experience, it's not very likely. What is more than likely, we will find the chassis on some old logging road and it will be stripped. We have had several car thefts in the past six months, and they are all pretty much the same MO. We get a call from some logger or someone trying to find a place to target shoot and they tell us there is the hull of a car or truck left on the side of the road. Those calls come from the guys who are responsible enough to give us a call. Most of the ones we find are within a fifty-mile radius of Pine Lake, so we think it is some local guy down on his luck and we just have not been able to catch him or them yet. We think it's more than likely not just one single person. Unfortunately, whoever it is, is good. We haven't been able to get any leads yet."

"Well, crap," Mick said. "That's just my luck. I am about seven hundred or so miles from home. Is there any place in this little burg where I could find a car or truck to rent?"

The officer looked at Mick with raised eyebrows. "Yes, there is, but I have to warn you, you will be taking your life in your hands. Joe's Auto is in back of the Shell station at the end of Main Street. He always has a couple of wrecks he will rent out in an emergency. I wouldn't trust them to go very far, though. Joe isn't known for being the most reliable person. So his vehicles are not either."

"Well, damn," Mick swore. "I don't have much choice at this point. I will have to go and see what he's got to offer tomorrow." He shrugged. "Let's get this paperwork over with. I can walk back to the hotel from here."

The two men got out of the car and walked into the police station.

Chapter 13

When Mick got back to his hotel room, it was almost seven o'clock, so he figured he would give Joe's Auto a call tonight instead of wait for tomorrow. *Maybe someone will still be there,* he thought. *After all, what do people have to do around here in their spare time? What a pain in the ass this is! Only game in town, though, so doesn't give me any choices.* He was sick thinking about someone dismantling his truck. Thank God he had taken his handgun out of the glove box. He didn't need a stolen handgun on his conscience too.

Joe answered the phone and told him gruffly that he was just on his way out the door. "Don't know why I answered the damn phone anyway." Mick told him that he was glad that he had, and he made arrangements with Joe to pick up one of the only two cars he had available to rent. It was either the 2010 Ford Focus or a 2009 Subaru Forester. He figured he had better go with the Subaru. It was a year older, but they had more room in them than a Ford Focus.

He then went back to his hotel room to call his insurance company to leave a voice message. He had known his agent for years, so he knew there would be no problem with getting things covered, but again, a pain in the ass he just didn't want to deal with right now. He heard the voice of his agent, Linda, his agent's assistant come on the line. He was surprised to hear her actual voice instead of a recording. He had expected by this time of day that she had already left the office, and he had been prepared to leave her a voice message. It was then that he remembered the hour time difference. They exchanged a few pleasantries, then he explained everything that had happened. She assured him that there probably would not be any problem, but if anything came up, she would be sure to let him know. She said she was just finishing up for the day and needed to lock up, but she was certain that he was covered for rental car insurance for up to ninety days. By then, either his truck would be found or gone for good, and he would need to get a new vehicle, anyway. He thanked her and breathed a little sigh of relief. He was glad to have stayed with the same insurance agent all these years. In the whole time, he had only had to turn in a simple fender bender, which had not been his fault. He had rear-ended the ass who had stopped to avoid hitting a gray squirrel. Linda had been with the agency even longer than he had been a client. In fact, he had dated her a couple of times. She had been a damn good piece of ass, but other than that, they found they hadn't had much in common. It had ended amicably, though, which was better than some of his other relationships. He still couldn't believe this was happening while he was so far from home. "Damn it!" he swore to himself.

He got a beer out of the little refrigerator and sat on the edge of the bed, pondering the day's events in his head. The more he thought about what had happened, the more suspicious he became that things just didn't add up. Why would car thieves even be in a place as remote as the park was? The next vehicle he would get, he would have better security—that was a given. He couldn't help but think, somehow, the theft was not just a coincidence but a personal attempt to get at him for something. Even though the police chief had told him there had been several recent vehicle thefts, it just didn't add up. It just seemed like it was odd that he took Wanda out there and he came back and his truck was gone. She could have checked his license plate numbers and found out what his real name was. He would have done that if he were a woman going on a hike with a stranger. She could have Googled information about him, just as he had done about her. It was not easy to remain anonymous in today's world. Maybe she had someone steal the truck just to slow him down.

Too much thinking was giving him one major headache.

He got up to use the bathroom and planned on going out to get something to eat. He finished his beer and went to open the hotel room door. Just as he pulled the door toward him, he practically knocked over Tammy, who had her hand up to knock on the door at the same time it opened. "Wow! Well, hey," she said. "I didn't see your truck in the parking lot, so I thought I would find out if you were here or not. The housekeeper said you had been gone all morning, and then I didn't see you come back this afternoon." She gave him a Cheshire cat's grin. "I thought I would check to see if you had gotten back before I went home."

Mick looked at her. She sure was sexy. "Well, aren't I in luck?" he said as his stomach emitted a low growl. He took her by the elbow, and she stepped into the room toward him. She held up a brown bag and handed it him. He took it and looked inside. "Smells like Mexican," he told her.

"It is leftover tacos, chips, and salsa. Dotty treated us today, and neither of us could finish what she bought, so she said I could take the rest home. Which I was going to do, but I decided to check up and see what you have been doing."

"Well, I sure am grateful you did," Mick said, and he got her a beer from the refrigerator.

When Mick woke up the next day, it was just getting light outside. He groped through the tangled sheets, but the bed was empty, save for himself. *Just as well,* he thought. *I need to get a vehicle and figure out what the hell is going on here.* He hoped the owner of Joe's Auto would not be as surly as he had been on the phone. He was about ready to knock out someone's lights. His mood was foul, and it shouldn't have been, what with the entertainment Tammy had provided. He didn't suppose there were too many people wanting to rent vehicles in this little burg. One of the two cars would be there, he figured.

He untangled himself from the sheets and stood up. *Whew,* he thought. *I need a shower.* He glanced at himself in the bigger-than-life vanity mirror as he passed it on the way to the toilet. "Yuck, Mick, you look like hell!" he said to himself as he noted his five o'clock shadow, unkempt hair, and slightly bloodshot eyes. Had they really polished off his beer, then the red wine that she just happened to have in her car, and then ridden each other like a couple of rutting animals? What happened to calling it an early night and getting a good night's sleep? As he stood with one foot on the bathtub, trying to get the water adjusted to a decent temperature, he couldn't help but smile to himself. At least there were benefits here, and he chuckled as he got into the shower.

Forty-five minutes later, he closed the door behind him and started down the street to Grannies Café. He was clean-shaven. Visine did the trick on the red eyes. If anyone would observe his jaunty walk, they would think he did not have a care in the world.

The little bell over the door of the café jingled as he opened it. The old lady, Henrietta, was not in sight, however. A young gal in a short pink skirt, sporting pink pigtails, no less, and wearing a black apron, literally bounced up to him, beaming. "Hello, there," she said loudly. "You all sit anywhere you like and I'll be with ya in just a short shake of the hand." She handed Mick a menu, which he took, and he went to sit at the table by the window that he had sat at yesterday. When he sat down, he looked around the small café. He wondered why there seemed to be so many people from the South here. He figured out of the few people he had met, half had Southern accents. What would pull them to northern Idaho? he wondered.

The waitress bounced up to him with a coffee carafe and said, "Coffee?" He noticed she had two little diamond blings on her teeth when she smiled.

"Well, yes, thank you. And can you just leave the carafe?" Mick asked her.

"Why, sure thing," she said and then went to take the order of an elderly couple in the back booth.

He noticed that Henrietta was behind the grill in the kitchen area. She must be the chief cook today, he figured. With that, she looked up and gave him a nod of recognition. He waved and smiled a greeting at her. Just then, he was startled by the young waitress, who had come up behind him to take his order. He glanced at her name tag: Candy. Well, that seemed appropriate, since her hair clearly resembled the cotton candy he remembered of his youth. She didn't look more than sixteen years old. *Young Candy*, he thought.

"Would you all like cream and sugar?" she asked him.

"No, thanks," he said. "I will have two eggs over easy, a slice of ham, hash browns, and rye toast, no butter, please." He handed the menu to her, but she had the tip of her tongue between her two front teeth, concentrating on writing his order.

"Was that sourdough toast ya said?"

Mick sighed. "No. Rye, please."

She looked at him then and grinned. "It will be out here faster than you can say, 'I love a good cuppa coffee and have a nice day.'" She winked at him as she turned and flounced away.

There were three men sitting at the counter, lingering over their coffee. They were bantering back and forth and trying to flirt with the young waitress. Definitely local guys who probably came in here every morning. He knew of some of the same type of guys that had coffee in the Cow Bell in Rockaway every morning. Hardly ever had breakfast, but they sure took advantage of those refills.

The older couple in the back must have been in their late eighties or so. They blended in with the high backs of the booth and were engrossed in their own conversation.

Mick glanced at his watch. It was only eight thirty. He looked back out the window, and as he did, he saw a man with a ball cap, pulled low over his face, enter the post office. Mick squinted at the guy. *Is that Mark?* he wondered. He sure looked like the same guy he had seen the day before yesterday. About his height and build. Mick looked up and down Main Street but didn't see the black Mustang. He wasn't sure what he was going to say, but he jumped up from his seat and hollered at the waitress that he would be back in just a minute. She was just picking up his plate of ham and eggs to deliver to him, but she shrugged and put it under the warming lights. Mick opened the door and scurried across the street.

He had just gotten to the post office when the man with the ball cap practically knocked him over in his haste getting out the door. Mick noted that he had a couple of black packages in his arms. One of the packages flew out of his hands as he collided with Mick on the steps. Mick quickly leaned over to pick up the package to hand it back to the guy. As he did so, he got a better look at his face. It was Mark DeGuard, he thought to himself. It had to be. *Man, I thought I looked bad this morning! This guy beats me hands down. And his breath!* Mick had to turn away and almost gagged. Mark briefly looked at him, grabbed the package out of Mick's hands, gave a curt nod, and started to walk down the street. Mick watched him as he quickly turned the corner off Main Street. Mick couldn't believe the difference in the looks of the man he had seen on the internet and who he had just seen two days ago. Although he hadn't seen him as close up as he had now. Man, this guy looked sick. His complexion was wan, his skin a slightly grayish tinge, and his clothes seemed to hang on him. Mick stood watching as the black Mustang careened around the corner as it headed up the street. Mick actually scratched his head as he watched it disappear. He turned around to go back to the café.

The tinkle of the bell on the door made everyone's eyes turn toward him. He just gave a little wave as he sat back in his seat. Candy brought him his breakfast and poured him some coffee from the carafe. He smiled at her, but she didn't say anything as another couple had come into the café and she busied herself waiting on them. Mick sat deep in thought as he ate his breakfast, barely tasting his food. How could Mark look so different in just about a forty-eight-hour period? He hadn't smelled right either, Mick thought. It had been a sweet, sickly kind of odor, more than just old alcohol breath. He thought for a moment. He had smelled that kind of a smell before, but he could not pinpoint where he had smelled it.

He finished his breakfast before he had even realized he had started it.

Candy had put his tab on the table, while he was lost in thought. He glanced at it, then pulled out several bills from his wallet and left them on the table too. He left the restaurant with a nod and a wave to Henrietta in the back.

Chapter 14

Mick walked down the street to Joe's Auto. The man behind the counter looked up as he entered the door, and introduced himself as Joe Williams, owner of the auto body shop. Mick looked around the shop. There was junk and car parts everywhere. The counter was littered with papers, file folders, candy wrappers, tools, and at least a half-inch of dust and grime in some places. Joe himself seemed to fit right in with the general unkempt atmosphere. He was small in stature, with a long scraggly gray beard halfway down his chest. His T-shirt had a few holes in it, and by the brown color added to his facial hair, the holes were most likely from cigarette burns. Although at the moment he had a mouth full of chewing tobacco that he spat as he talked. Mick did not want to shake this man's hand. Who knew where it was last! So he just introduced himself as Mick Meade, the man who had called last night to inquire about a rental car. Mick smiled a little slyly to himself, thinking about the previous evening, while a picture of Tammy popped into his head.

"Oh, no problem," said Joe. "The little Subaru sits right outside there. I got some paperwork you have to fill out before you can drive it away, though."

Mick took out his wallet and laid his driver's license and insurance card on the counter. Joe looked at them but said, "I don't do nothing with the insurance companies. You can pay by credit card or cash. I don't take no checks either."

Mick just started signing where he was supposed to and kept his mouth shut. He reached back in his wallet and slid his credit card across the counter. Joe kept on talking. "I get my money pretty darn quick from the credit card companies, even though they get their dang percentage. It still works for me."

"Yeah, yeah," Mick said. "Anything odd or particular I need to be aware of?"

Joe looked at him with a grin, showing a mouthful of nicotine-soaked teeth, with a gap in the middle. "Right foot on the gas and she goes. Left foot on the brake and she stops. Pretty simple."

Joe took Mick out the side door, and they stepped outside into the back lot while they were exchanging the few words they had. Mick looked around the lot. It didn't look any better than the littered office had. Broken-down cars appeared to be everywhere. He spotted a greenish Subaru with a gray-colored passenger door about twenty feet away. It had a small crack in the windshield on the passenger side also.

"I suppose that's the car I just rented?" Mick said with disgust.

Joe looked at the car and said, "Well, there ain't nothing wrong with the way she runs. Someone brought her in after they had a slight accident with a deer. They sorta felt like the car was unlucky after that, seeing the deer died and all. She runs fine, though." Joe handed Mick the keys, and Mick took out his cell phone and snapped some pictures of the sorry-looking car. Not that any more damage could possibly hurt the appearance of the little wreck, he thought.

Mick got in the little Subaru and spent a couple of minutes adjusting the seat and the mirrors before turning the car on. After starting the car, he checked the gauges and swore. The gaslight came on. He looked at Joe and angrily asked, "Do you suppose there is enough gas in this bucket to make it to a gas station?"

"Oh, sure. No problem!" Joe huffed. "You can go another thirty miles after the gaslight comes on. Besides, the Shell station is only two miles from here." After he said that, he walked away to go answer the phone, which had begun to ring in the office. Mick just shook his head in disgust and drove the car out of the lot.

How embarrassing is this? he thought. *I never even drove a beater car when I was a teenager!* He pulled out onto Main Street and headed for the gas station. He remembered seeing the Shell when he had driven into town. "Damn!" he said out loud as he slapped the steering wheel. "All my gear was in the back of the truck also. Now I will have to find somewhere I can replace at least some of it." He cursed out loud again as he drove down the street. *Every small town has an Ace or True Value,* he thought. *Guess that will have to be my next stop.*

By the time he got the gas, stopped at the hardware store, and replaced most of his gear, it was noon. The sun had come out, and it was about seventy degrees. Pretty warm for this time of year, he surmised. The Shell station just happened to have a little market, so he picked himself up a six-pack of beer and some munchies. He wanted to stop at the hotel and let them know he was going to stay another night. He kind of hoped that Tammy would not be there; he didn't need any more distractions at this point.

He was in luck, he noticed, when he walked in the door. It was Dotty, the owner, sitting behind the counter. "Tammy not here today?" he asked.

Dotty looked up at him, rolled her eyes, and said, "No. She called in sick. Some female thing."

Mick looked away and cleared his throat. "Well, I just wanted to let you know that I will be staying another day or two." He then relayed the story of the theft of his truck and that he wanted to stick around to see if it was found or where it ended up.

Dotty immediately sympathized with him and knocked off twenty dollars for the next couple of nights. Not that twenty dollars was a big deal to him, but he appreciated her gesture just the same.

"Thanks, Dotty. That is very nice of you. And don't worry about room service. All I need is a couple of clean towels."

She was busy checking her computer but told him she had already taken care of the room and the towels. She looked up and said, "Oh, and I took the liberty of dumping the empty beer and wine bottles in the trash." She gave him a wink as he walked out the door.

What the hell! he thought. That was the third female that had winked at him in the last twenty-four hours. That was a record even for him. He smiled and shook his head as he quietly closed the door behind him.

He got in the little Subaru and started back toward the DeGuard house. He was glad he hadn't left his book in the truck; he wouldn't have been able to find another one on short notice, and he had this anal habit of not starting a new book before he had finished the last one he was reading. He parked under the same tree as he had the day before. He looked at the clock on the dash. *Hmmm, twelve thirty.* Well, that obviously didn't work either. He knew it must be after two o'clock. *Might as well make myself comfortable,* he thought.

He was almost halfway through *East of Eden* when he looked up. It was now almost five o'clock, and the gate started to open. It wasn't the black Mustang, but it wasn't the car that Wanda had driven when she met him the other day either. *Or was that just yesterday?* he thought wryly. *Seems like a long time ago.* This car was an older Chevy Camaro, silver in color, with the same dark-tinted windows, of course. He was not able to make out anything inside the car. He rolled his eyes upward. He could tell whoever was driving turned their head to check for traffic, but he couldn't make out if it was a male or female. If it was Wanda, she wouldn't recognize this car, anyway, he thought. Whoever it was had on big sunglasses and a scarf around their neck. He made an assumption it was a female, unless the male was disguised like a female.

He pulled out onto the highway after the car was a reasonable distance down the road. He knew now that there were not many places to go, so he need not follow too close. He followed the car to the next town. The same one he had been to the other day. He followed the car as it was driven through the ATM, and he busied himself looking through the console, but with one eye always on the driver. He was almost certain it was Wanda. She had been wearing the same style of bracelet when they had gone on their hike as was on the arm that she had crooked out the window. He had even commented on it, trying to get her to make conversation. He had told her that the ruby was his mother's birth stone and he had once given his mom a bracelet like the one she was wearing. It looked like a rather-expensive gold-and-ruby bracelet. He watched her as she seemed to retrieve an awful lot of bills from the ATM. He only ever took out two hundred dollars at a time. He wasn't even sure how much money a person could withdraw from an ATM. He followed the car at a good twenty car lengths and expected it to turn back toward Pine Lake, but instead the car went north, and as soon as it cleared the last forty-five-mile road sign, it sped up to at least ninety miles an hour, and Mick could barely get the piece-of-shit Subaru up to sixty. So he ended up turning the car around and headed back to the DeGuard house.

By now it was almost dark outside.

Chapter 15

Mick had already decided he would scale the wall and hope he was lucky enough to see what was going on without being detected. He wanted not only to see inside the house but also to find out what Mark was really up to. Maybe he could come up with some reasonable story that Mark would believe. He could say the gate happened to be open and that he was looking for Wanda, who he had seen drive through the gate before he could catch her. Of course, Mark probably would not have any idea who Wanda was, since more than likely she hadn't given him her real name. He could say that they had had a date and she had left her scarf in his car. But then, he remembered that he didn't have a scarf in this car. It had been left in his truck by a gal that he knew had left it on purpose so that she had an excuse to call him and hoped to see him again. She had called, but he had ended up telling her he hadn't seen the scarf and then he had just stuffed it in the console. He could be pretty mean when he wanted, he thought. But that gal had driven him nuts with her constant nonsensical chatter.

He drove to the same spot by the same tree. *Damn!* He missed his truck. No self-respecting man should be seen driving one of these hippie mobiles. His phone beeped, indicating he had a text. Sure enough, it was Sheelya, and then two missed phone calls. One call came from Colin, and the other was an unknown number. He would give Colin a call later after he got back to the hotel. There was no moon, and it was cloudy enough that there were very little stars out either.

He decided to move the car a little closer to the entrance of the property. He reached around to the back seat for the rope, flashlight, and jackknife. At least that was easier done than from his truck. *What a piece of crap,* he thought for about the tenth time that day. He checked for the 9mm, which was still secure in the back of his jeans. He tightened his belt one notch just for safer keeping. He looked around and cautiously started to walk toward the gate. Well, what do you know? It really wasn't locked. Maybe it hadn't been all along but it just looked like it was. The whole gate itself was pretty darn rusty. He looked around again before slowly opening it. *No dog* was the first thing he thought of. He started walking cautiously up the driveway. He took his gun out and held it in front of him, just in case he needed it in a hurry.

The house itself wasn't set back as far down the driveway as it seemed from the road. The arborvitae was set so close together it grew as one and obliterated the house from any view. He stood in front of the dark house amid the sound of crickets and the occasional tree frog as background noise. There didn't seem to be anything going on from inside the house. He could detect a small light filter through a crack in the heavy drapes at the side of the house. *Nice,* he thought as his eyes adjusted to the light. A few stars had managed to pop out through the cloud cover. He looked up at the rooflines. It was a Tudor style, complete with stained glass windows in the turrets of each roof peak. There was a huge ornate oak door set in an arched opening that contained stained glass windows on each side of the door. It wasn't a large house, but you could imagine some royalty housekeeper opening the door when you knocked on the door knocker, which just happened to look like a knight on a horse. Back in its day, the house must have been luxurious. You could tell it was built to withstand whatever weather came its way. *Mark must have gotten the house from a rich relative,* Mick thought. *No way he could have obtained it on his own, unless he inherited someone's money.*

Mick walked stealthily toward the side of the house. Everything looked deserted from his perspective. Even though the curtains were closed, there seemed to be no light shining anywhere. He walked around the perimeter of the whole house, and it all looked dark and rather sinister, he thought. There also was not a star in the sky, and the moon was almost completely obliterated by a large dark cloud. Mick gave a small shiver as he walked up the cobblestone pathway to the back door. He stepped up onto the back deck and almost put his foot through a rotted board. The sliding glass door on the back deck had vertical panel blinds on the inside, and one was cracked about an inch. He put his head against the glass and saw a small ray of light that, as near as he could make out, was probably just a night-light. It seemed to be in the hallway off the kitchen. He couldn't see very far into the kitchen, but he presumed that was what it was from its proximity in the house. Plus, he could make out the silhouette of a counter.

He carefully tried the slider and was amazed to find it wasn't even locked. He took his flashlight and shone the beam as far as it would go into the dark room. Definitely the kitchen, and it all looked pretty tidy. There were a few dirty dishes left in the sink, a pot on the stove, a towel left on the counter. Much cleaner than his place, he thought wryly. To the left of the kitchen was a large fairly formal dining room with a table and chairs that could easily seat ten people. It was littered with packing boxes, post office boxes, and assorted types of papers. He stepped closer to get a look at what was in the boxes. They were filled with different things, from what he could see. Some had file folders, and some had things wrapped in newspapers and tissue paper.

He stepped in closer with his flashlight and pulled out one of the files. It was an old income tax return. He filtered quickly through the rest and saw old medical bills, invoices, bank statements, etc. He looked in another box and lifted out a small clay figure that was partially wrapped in tissue paper. There appeared to be other figures in the box of the same type of medium, all small clay figurines of some sort. He fingered through another box, and the name DeGuard caught his eye. He lifted out some forms with an illegible name on it that appeared to have gotten wet. The print on the paper was barely legible. He lifted out a file with some old newspaper clippings in it. Some loose papers fell out of the file onto the table. He peered closer, but the clippings were pretty old and weathered, and his flashlight was not the best source of light in the dark room. One clipping contained a picture and an article that was a little easier to make out. He read what he could in the dim light. It appeared to be a clipping of the accident that Mark's parents died in. It was deemed a tragic accident. *Hmmm, aren't they all when death is involved?* Mick thought to himself. He continued reading the article. It seemed his mom was killed instantly due to a head-on collision with a pickup truck operated by a twenty-seven-year-old man. Here he had to squint to make out the man's name, but it looked like Thomas Hardcastle. That startled him. He remembered the name *Hardcastle* had come up when he was browsing the internet for information on the DeGuards. *Hardcastle* certainly was not a common name. Could this guy in the article be a relation to his neighbor Carla? That would be quite a coincidence if he was.

He focused what light was left on the flashlight battery and just tried to pick out the highlights of the article. He read that the driver of the pickup drifted over the center yellow line on the narrow road and ran the other vehicle off the road. The driver of the pickup had told the sheriff that he had tried to avoid hitting a dog that had run onto the middle of the road. The sheriff had detected the smell of alcohol on Mr. Hardcastle and had him perform a sobriety test. Mick was thinking that back in the nineties, it wasn't uncommon to have a drink and drive, especially in Montana, where the accident had happened. He remembered a time he had stopped at a small pub in northern Montana in the nineties. He had ordered a whiskey sour in the middle of the summer because the temperature had reached ninety degrees and his air conditioner hadn't been working. He was only going to have one with his lunch, but the barmaid had asked him if he wanted one to go. Well, that was a novelty he couldn't turn down, so a to-go whiskey sour it was. The law was pretty lenient in that little burg. He even remembered what the barmaid looked like. Although he found out he could usually dredge up the looks of most of the women he had come into contact with, even the homely ones. He sighed.

"What the hell am I doing dredging up the past at this time. Get on with it, man!"

He read a little more and thought, with two people dead, Thomas should have had a hefty prison sentence, but he was found not guilty by a trial of his "peers." The whole incident was deemed an accident, and the jury claimed that Thomas had tried to avoid a dog on the highway. The newspaper article included some history on Thomas himself. He had been born and raised in Liberty, Montana, and his parents had owned the general store that had been in the family since before the turn of the century. Douglas McCall just happened to be in the wrong place at the wrong time. He had been on his way to pick up his kids from a school function. Douglas had been on life support for a few days before it was decided upon that he had permanent brain damage and would never recover from the accident. In fact, it was noted that Thomas himself had been injured, but nothing that was life-threating. He had shattered his right femur, received various contusions, and had a broken collarbone. *Hmmm*, Mick thought. *How does all this tie in with Mark DeGuard? I know there is a connection, and I am going to find out what it is, if for nothing else than Carla's sake. Especially since I was such a sack-of-shit neighbor.*

Mick picked up another article that was lying on the stack. In 2000, Thomas had been arrested for stalking a woman he had previously dated a few times. The woman had tried to break off from the relationship, but Thomas wasn't about to give up that easily. He had broken into her apartment, and she had awakened to find him standing over her while she lay in bed. He hadn't woken her up; she woke up because she had heard what sounded like a gunshot. She screamed when she saw him looking down at her. She could tell he was intoxicated by the way he was weaving, trying to keep his balance, so she gave him a hard kick and knocked him reeling backward into her dresser. He ended up hitting his head on the corner, stunning him for a few seconds. It was long enough for her to run outside and get to the house of the neighbor, who called the police for her. He was arrested for breaking and entering, but they couldn't pin anything else on him, so he didn't spend long in jail that time either.

Suddenly, Mick's flashlight flickered. *Damn it,* he thought and hit it against the side of his hand. The flashlight was new, as were the batteries, but maybe the batteries were not any good. Maybe people did not buy that many batteries in the little market. He realized after looking at his phone that he had been standing there for almost half an hour. The house was eerily quiet in all that time. He had forgotten where he was. The articles had made him even forget the mission he had set himself on.

He put down the last article. He didn't want to waste what light he had left on the flashlight. He wanted to go and explore the interior of the house while he had the chance. His flashlight would have very little light in a short time.

He shone the dim beam down the hallway. *Darker than that cave in the park,* he thought. There was no sound coming from anything but an old grandfather clock that sat in the corner of the huge living room. It had a prominent *ticktock ticktock* that sounded especially loud in the quiet darkness. Evidently, the room was not used much. The books in the bookcases were covered with dust. There was one lone ashtray on a huge oak coffee table that was covered in dust also. The chairs in the room were covered in sheets, which were covered in dust. Apparently, no one in the house cared about this room, because it obviously hadn't been used in a very long time.

Chapter 16

He started slowly down the hall, pausing at a small half bath on the way, what would have been called a powder room back in the day. Just barely big enough to house a toilet and sink. *Wow, outdated. The thirties or forties,* he thought at a glance. Farther along the hallway, he stopped at a small bedroom and shone the beam of flashlight around the room and into the corners. Nothing unusual to be seen. Looked like the living room, dusty and unlived in. It contained a small twin bed, a bedside table, and a small desk. *Nothing out of place here,* he thought. There was a closed door at the end of the hallway, which Mick proceeded to walk toward. Instinctively, he went to hit the light switch at the end of the hallway wall but drew his hand back quickly. That would not be a good idea, he thought. He maintained that there was no one in the house, but still, no sense taking any huge risks. Perhaps someone was just sleeping off a drunk. He didn't want anyone waking up scared and having a gun at their side, or something along those lines.

He hadn't seen Mark's car in the driveway or anywhere on the grounds, although he remembered seeing a small carriage house set back in the woods. It might have been big enough to house the Mustang. He tried to open the door when he got to the end of the hall, but the doorknob twisted in his hand without opening. He tried twisting the knob back and forth a few times, but it still didn't give. *Well, what do I have to lose?* he thought. He stood back a foot from the front of the door and slammed his left shoulder against the door while turning the knob at the same time. It made a loud creaking noise, and Mick about flew into the room. "Jesus Christ!" he said out loud and looked around. "Why don't I just wake the dead?" He held himself upright by holding onto an office chair, and he shifted his weight to get his feet underneath him again. He blinked and looked around, trying to get his eyes adjusted to the dark interior. His flashlight had taken a leave somewhere in the room when the door crashed open. He bent over and started groping about for the light. By edging and feeling his way, he was able to locate the flashlight, wedged between the office chair and the leg of the desk. He stood up and turned the light on, surprised that the beam was as bright as it was. He shone the light around the small dark room, stopping near the ceiling. *Holy shit, what is that?* he wondered.

He took a few steps so he was right under a line of pictures spread out across the length of the room. He was shocked by what he saw, and he was not one to be shocked very easily. There were pictures of young girls in various stages of undress, posed in various suggestive ways. All the young girls had makeup on, making it difficult to tell their ages, but by the looks of their youthful figures, some of them could not have been more than nine or ten years old. Most of the girls appeared to be Asian, but Mick couldn't tell if that was the effects of the makeup or if they really were Asian. He got to the end of the line and saw little toddlers dressed about the same way, but their bodies had a waxy sheen to them, appearing to resemble those of porcelain dolls. *What kind of sick, twisted degenerate keeps these kinds of pictures around their house?* Just looking at them gave him a sick feeling in his stomach. He made a hasty retreat back out of the room, thinking about the type of person that would want to have those kinds of pictures in their house, let alone on some kind of display. The guy was obviously some kind of pervert. He felt totally disgusted and angry, as he closed the door on the dark room.

There was a staircase that went up from the end of the long hallway, and then there appeared to be a door at the top of the stairs. The house was structured to look like a small castle, but it looked bigger from the outside than when you were here on the inside. Probably due to the turrets housed on all sides of the house, Mick guessed. The main living space seemed to be a pretty big size, though. Mick figured he could fit at least four of his house in the size of this one.

Mick decided to head gingerly up the stairs. The rest of this stuff wasn't going anywhere at this point. He paused on each step, straining his ears to hear what even he wasn't sure of. It was like a tomb—it was so quiet. When he reached the top of the landing, he could see a small neat bedroom on the right. It did not look like it had been lived in, though. There didn't appear to be as much dust in here, so obviously someone had been here and cleaned it. It definitely looked like a young woman or a girl had been in here last. It was very feminine and tidy. Neatly made bed covered with a handmade quilt. Small vanity with a few toiletries on top. There was a small old dresser and a bedside table with a lamp and two books. One book was titled *Tell Me about Old Coins*. The other was *How to Get Out of the Country Almost Free*. Both were labeled nonfiction. *Interesting titles,* he thought. *Where can you do anything almost free?* That made him think about the time he had taken his wife to Mexico. They went to a small town called Laredo, before Laredo became more popular. They were sitting on the beach, and a young gal approached them with a felt box of silver jewelry, and her catchphrase was, "You buy for senorita, senor?" *When I asked how much, she said, "Well, almost free." At that time, I thought it was hilarious! She was so darn cute I ended up buying a matching set of earrings, necklace, and bracelet. But I have to say, they were not almost free. They were a good deal, if I remember correctly, though. She had loved the set at that time.* He wondered if she still had them. He also remembered how she had rewarded him the night they returned to their hotel. He couldn't help a small smile as he looked around.

There was another small room up on this level also, but this one did not look like it had seen any type of cleaning for weeks. It was also very minimalist. There was a double-size bed, a small dresser, and a rocking chair. It did not appear like anyone had done anything in here for a very long time. The upstairs was built in the shape of a T, with doors at each end. Mick walked to the last door he hadn't looked into yet. He reached for the knob and slowly started to turn it toward the right. This one turned easily enough, so he opened the door into another dark room that smelled horrible. He gagged at the stench. He shone what little light he had left on his flashlight around the room. It was a jumbled mess of clothes, magazines, papers, and food detritus. There was a broken vase lying in the middle of the floor, and a picture frame had apparently shattered next to it.

Mick continued to shine what light he had and stopped at the bed. There appeared to be someone lying in it or on it—he couldn't tell which, what with all the crap on the bed and the body. He edged closer to the body to get a better look. He put his hand out to feel for a pulse in the neck and couldn't feel a thing but cool, slightly damp skin. He pulled his hand quickly away. It was definitely a male; its torso was covered in thick kinky black hair. Mick could tell he wasn't breathing, but he knew to check for a pulse anyway. He put his face down close to the mouth of the body and could not feel any breaths. He moved his light up to the face of the body, and sure enough, it was Mark DeGuard. He backed up and covered his mouth, even though he was well aware he couldn't catch what Mark had.

Chapter 17

Mick stood stock-still, with his flashlight flickering eerily on the face of Mark DeGuard. His mouth was agape, with a line of thick, dried gray spittle pooled on his pillowcase. His skin had a sick, yellowish sheen, and he was curled in the fetal position, like he had been in extreme pain or distress.

Just then, Mick's flashlight flickered out and there was no light in the room. "Shit," he said under his breath. He stood there a few seconds, trying to get his bearings in the pitch blackness of the fetid room. He was aware that most wall switches are located on the open side of doors. He figured he would just have to find his way to the light switch. He put his arm out, hand extended, and gingerly made his way back the way he had come into the room. He groped his way toward where he knew the doorway was. He ran his hand down the side of the wall but couldn't feel any switch there. He let his hand extend farther away from the door as he inched his body forward. As he did so, his foot hit something solid but soft. He almost fell over whatever it was, but he was able to catch his balance by holding on to the doorframe.

"There," he muttered under his breath.

He flipped on the light switch, and the room was filled with a dull, grayish light. He looked up at the ceiling fixture, which contained only one low-wattage bulb that was lit. He looked down at his feet and said, "Well, no wonder there was no barking dog." His right foot was pushed up against a big ball of black fur that was in a position not unlike Mark's body was in on the bed. The dog's tongue was hanging out onto the floor, and there was a puddle of dried saliva and some kind of nasty-looking barf beneath it. Mick was not a dog lover, but the sight of the sorry-looking animal gave his stomach a little lurch in respect for the dog. He found he had more sympathy for the dog than for the sick, perverted man who was lying on the bed. Poor dog had no control over who owned him.

Mick looked around the crowded bedroom and thought that between this room and the room with all the pornography, it must have been where Mark spent most of his time. The room was more than lived in. There was a coffee table next to the bed, and it was littered with beer bottles, whiskey bottles, Coke cans, an empty pizza box, and what looked like a dried-up ham and cheese sandwich. He saw what looked like a half glass of milk on the floor under the coffee table. He bent down to look closer. It stood out among the other discarded beverage containers because it looked an odd color of gray. Mick found a dirty sock and picked up the glass. It was a watery, grayish color, with a few flecks of something floating on the top. He sniffed at the contents in the glass and noted a slightly sweet odor that caused him to remember just the other day, when he had run into Mark outside the post office. He had gotten close enough to him to smell an odd, sweet odor that, at that time, he thought was alcohol.

Now that Mick knew there was no threat from the dog or its owner, he started to take in the other contents of the room. He surmised that Mark had been dead for quite a few hours, by the look of the rigor mortis that had set in, although Mick knew that could happen in as little as two hours in some cases. There was a wallet lying open on the coffee table. Mick reached in his pocket for vinyl gloves. The last ones he had on him. He was grateful the wallet was lying out. He really hadn't relished the thought of reaching into the dead man's pocket. The driver's license identified the dead man as one Mark DeGuard, five foot ten, 185 pounds, brown hair, hazel eyes, and the date of birth, February 10, 1972. *Well, got that about right,* Mick thought to himself. *He sure was healthier looking when this picture was taken.* The man on the bed couldn't have been more than 150 pounds soaking wet. He looked at the date on the license. The picture had been taken almost three years before. Mick looked back at Mark. His unhealthy pallor and sunken cheeks indicated he must have been sick for a while, anyway. Something had happened to him, and from the description that Evelyn had given him, it must have been fairly recent.

Mick went over to the dresser and started to open drawers. Nothing but a jumbled mess of clothes. He checked the bedside table and rummaged through a bunch of old receipts, keys, books, and then he felt a piece of glass, which he lifted out of the drawer. It was an old picture that had been lying under a dirty plaid handkerchief. It looked like a younger Mark DeGuard with his arm around an older woman. The picture must have gotten wet at some time, because the upper edge was discolored and the picture itself was of poor quality. Mick squinted at the woman in the picture. Half of the face was discolored from where it had gotten wet, but it sure looked like his deceased neighbor Carla. A younger one, with wavy black hair and a smile on her face. So apparently the relationship between Carla and Mark had had some meaning in the past. They both appeared happy in the picture. In the background, there was a lake with a dock and what looked like part of a tablecloth on the ground. It was hard to pinpoint how old they were in the picture, what with the water damage and general discoloration. There was a mountain in the background, and the sun had been shining. Could have been a nice family outing, by the smiles on their faces.

Mick sat on the only chair in the room, on top of the dirty clothes that covered the chair. He studied the picture, then looked at both Mark and the dog. The dog seemed to be even stiffer than Mark, but that could be because the dog didn't weigh as much as the dead man. Mick figured both of them had been poisoned, by the way they appeared, and it did not look like it was a painless poisoning. Mick thought back to a poisoning case he had been involved with when he was on the police force. A lot of similarities in that and what he was looking at now. Most poisonings are painful. Your guts usually dry up or bleed out, and then your internal organs break down. Not a pretty way to go, by any means.

So if Wanda, or whoever she was, had poisoned Mark and the dog, what did she stand to gain from that? Mark must have trusted her at some point; she had lived here for who knew how long. She must be his sister, although Mick hadn't seen much similarities in the two of them. Lots of siblings did not look alike, though, and maybe they hadn't had both the same parents. How could a woman live in the same house with that kind of pornography hanging up? It would sicken him if he had to look at anything like that, and he could not imagine living in the house and not knowing what was going on. Only twisted, sick people looked at stuff like that. Mick thought he would go back and look at the newspaper articles and the papers he had left on the table. Maybe he could find out more information in the articles. He stood there debating about calling the police. *Sooner or later?* he pondered. If he waited too long, he would only be in trouble himself. He couldn't just leave the dead man and the dog without calling the police. Who knew how long they might lie there and rigor mortis turned to soft and ripe before too long?

Mick stood up and stretched and figured he would have a look in the closet before he made any momentous decisions. He opened the door, but the contents appeared to be another jumble of clothes and shoes. He pawed through a few things on the floor, but he didn't find anything out of the ordinary or incriminating. He walked into the tiny bathroom and rummaged through the drawers. Nothing but dried-up toothpaste, a bar of soap, a nasty-looking toothbrush, and hair. *Yuck,* he thought. *Guess I am not the only male with no housekeeping skills.* He opened the medicine cabinet. It contained Band-Aids, shaving equipment, a couple of tubes of half-used cream, Neosporin, and some prescription containers. He picked up the containers one by one and read their labels. Amlodipine for high blood pressure, Prednisone for gout, Methotrexate for psoriasis, and one labeled Revlimid, which he had never heard of, and the label did not state what it was for either. There was also the hugest bottle of Tylenol he had ever seen. *Must be from Costco,* he thought. He picked up a small container that had no lid on it and looked inside. There were only six pills left. He glanced at the label, and it read, "Oxycontin 20mg, 1 every 12 hours for pain." The prescription was for sixty tablets. Mick wondered if maybe Mark had ingested too many, but if he had, it wasn't from this container. The label read that it was dated the appropriate time line from how many pills were missing. He put it back on the shelf and took out his cell phone to Google "Revlimid." *Hmm,* he thought. It was a type of chemotherapy drug for someone suffering from myeloma or lymphoma. Well, that sounded like Mark had a bit of a problem. Mick thought of a friend of his who had told him he had received a diagnosis of lymphoma, and he hadn't lived a year after that.

Mick made sure he put everything back where he had found it. He left the bathroom and walked back into the dirty bedroom, which had an odd, sickly, sweet smell to it. He knew he should be able to identify that smell, but right now it totally eluded him. This whole mess was starting to really bug him. He walked gingerly around the dog and out of the room, wishing he could have just minded his own business and let the police find whoever killed Carla. Why he felt he had to stick his nose in where it really didn't belong was beyond his reasoning. *Although it's hard to untrain the trained or teach an old dog new tricks. Something like that,* he thought. He turned and looked at the dead man and his dog again. He leaned down to take a whiff of the dog and could detect the same sickly, sweet smell on it also.

He stopped in front of the closed door he hadn't opened on his way to Mark's room. He gingerly turned the doorknob, hoping there would be nothing dead in this room. He found the light switch, and the room was illuminated in bright white light. He detected the faint smell of perfume, and the room was clean, although somewhat disheveled. *Definitely a woman's room,* he thought. The dresser drawers were open, and there were clothes half-in and half-out of the drawers. There were lace panties, along with a filmy lace negligee on the floor and hangers lying on the bed. The bed was neatly made, though, and there were slippers half-under the bed, neatly placed by the footrail. *Looks like someone was in a hurry to get the hell out of Dodge,* Mick thought. He went to look in the drawers, but they were mostly empty. Nothing but an old sweatshirt and pair of sweatpants that certainly did not go with the lacy stuff lying on the floor. He walked over to one of the nightstands and opened up the bottom drawer. There was nothing but some wadded-up tissues and then a book in the top drawer. He glanced at the title, *Men Are from Mars,*

Women Are from Venus. Oh, good grief, if that doesn't date oneself, he thought.

He noticed a small narrow door to his left, and he went to go open that. There was a bathrobe hanging on the inside of the door. The bathroom was even smaller than the one in Mark's bedroom, if that were even possible, he thought. Something someone thought about after the house was built. You couldn't even bend over in a shower that size without hitting your ass and head at the same time. There were only two small drawers on each side of the miniscule vanity. They didn't contain anything but a couple of bobby pins and some loose brown hair. *Hmm,* he thought. He was pretty sure that Wanda had not been a true redhead. Probably died her own hair. He could smell the same cologne in the bathroom. *Jasmine,* he surmised. Although Wanda had not seemed the type to wear a flowery perfume. Mick sniffed at the air. He rather liked the smell of jasmine. It reminded him of his mother. She had always liked the flowery, sweet-smelling perfumes. The bathroom was sparkling clean. It had a fresh smell to it also. Whatever else Wanda was, she had good house-keeping skills. All the more reason for Mick to wonder how she could have stood to live in the same house as Mark.

What could she have gained by his death? he wondered. He thought back to when he saw her going into the bank with the over-size purse. She could have left before Mark died, but that didn't seem very likely, since he was pretty sure that was her he had seen leaving the house. She was probably getting her stuff put together while Mark was lying there dead. *Pretty gruesome pair. More than likely deserved each other,* he thought. *If Wanda had poisoned Mark, wonder why she hadn't removed some of the incriminating newspaper articles. And then why poison the dog too? Unless it just made it cleaner and easier for her to take off without looking back. If Mark had been the one to do himself in rather than wait for the lymphoma to take him, why do it in such a painful way? He probably could have gotten enough drugs from his physician. And then again, why the dog?* He wasn't getting anywhere by going over and over the same information. Wanda would be long gone by now, but her fingerprints were bound to be all over in the house, so there would be questions that would certainly involve her.

"Oh crap!" he said out loud. "What a frigging mess this is, and I really don't need to be in the middle of it. All because I felt sorry that I didn't do more for my neighbor when she was alive." He started walking out into the hallway and back down the stairs, thinking how he should just call the police and stay the hell out of everything. He knew he couldn't stay out now, though. His motto had always been to finish what he started. He couldn't change his habits. He really was an old dog in that respect.

Now that he knew he could turn the light on, he wanted to go back and check some more of the clippings and files that were on the dining room table. Mick thought about the picture he had seen in Mark's room of a younger Carla standing by Mark, with his arm around her. That had obviously been from a happier time. Or at least better than what Evelyn told Mick she had witnessed. Or what she thought she had witnessed. She wasn't actually sure that had been Mark DeGuard; she just more or less assumed it had been. Maybe it had been someone else entirely. She admitted she had not gotten a good look at his face. She had been certain the car he left in had been a black Mustang, and Mark had owned a black Mustang.

Carla had talked a couple of times about her deceased husband, and always with kindness and compassion. Maybe he had taken the picture and they were all on an innocent family vacation. Whatever it had been, anything or anyone can change with time. Mark was obviously into some pretty kinky stuff, what with his graphic pornography collection. Anyone that could derive any pleasure out of seeing underage girls in that type of environment was one big sicko in his book, maybe even a psychopath.

Mick walked back into the dining room and flipped on the light switch. A chandelier lit the room up brighter than he was prepared for. He blinked and rubbed his eyes several times to try to get acclimated to the bright white lights. He picked up one of the newspaper articles again. This one was dated April 10, 2010. It contained another article about Thomas Hardcastle. This one referenced a woman who had accused Thomas of a sexual assault. The article went on to state that a Julie McCalister had dated Thomas a few times, but when she had tried to break off the relationship, it had proved to be a little harder than she thought. She had been a dancer in a strip club, with a reputation for dating the customers. She was adamant that everything was all aboveboard, meaning just regular dates with normal sexual appetites. Thomas, on the other hand, had other ideas in mind, and she had told him that she was not into any kind of bondage or aggressive sex. She went on to explain that Thomas had tried to force her into doing something she didn't want to do and she had become afraid of him. He was mean and intimidating. (Her words.) He had had too much to drink one night, and when he came at her, she had given him a forceful shove with her foot that knocked him against the television, which fell over and knocked him out cold. She hadn't waited around to see what kind of shape he was in, just took off and skipped town. Thomas had ended up having to go to the ER with a head injury, but there were no consequences from the altercation. He probably would have gotten off with a slap on the hand, anyway, Mick thought. A lot of small Midwestern towns were that way. If women chose that type of career, then men just figured they had to take their chances, anyway. *Piece of shit,* Mick thought. Mick had always had respect for women, and he also knew how to treat them.

He rifled through another box that contained file folders, and he pulled out a couple of older bank statements. They just looked like ordinary statements with checks and balances. There were old checks that contained Mark DeGuard's name on them, but no address. Mick looked around the room again. He spied one manila folder lying on the seat of a dining room chair. It looked like it had fallen off the table. It was half-open, and Mick reached down to pick it up. The folder had another envelope inside, which he opened up, and then he took out a couple of legal-looking papers or forms. He spread them out on the table. They appeared to be some type of certificates authenticating some old coins. He looked closer at the writing on the certificates. The document stated that the coins were very old, in very good shape, and the collection was worth over two hundred thousand dollars. It all looked pretty official. There was one penny alone that was very rare and worth about eighty-five thousand dollars. Then there were several rare quarters, Indian nickels, and a couple of dimes that weren't included in the list of coins, for over the two hundred thousand dollars. All told, that was a significant chunk of change right there. *So where is that coin collection now?* Mick wondered.

He thought back to the old 1954 dollar he had found in Carla's safe. If one was desperate enough, a collection like that would be worth stealing, but killing for? *That's a tough one to swallow,* Mick thought. Of course, when he was a police officer, they put people away for a lot less than that. Especially those that needed narcotics to feed their filthy drug habits. Maybe Mark just got desperate enough to need that kind of money. *Where do Wanda and Thomas Hardcastle fit into the ugly picture?* Mick wondered. It sure seemed like Mark was well aware of who Thomas was, by all the articles that presented him as an unsavory character.

Mick took out his cell phone and proceeded to snap some pictures of the various news articles. In the meantime, he was trying to think of what he was going to tell the police when he called them. How to explain being in the house with a dead man and his dead dog. It didn't take him long to figure it out. He was going to get the hell out of the place and call anonymously from a pay phone or landline. Something not as easy to trace as his cell phone.

Chapter 18

Mick took his cell phone out to dial 911, which seemed the best option for him at this time. He could just say he went to visit his old college roommate and when his friend didn't answer the door, he was worried about him, especially since he was expected to visit. He could say he just let himself in and this was what he had found. Although, he considered, he might be better off leaving an anonymous tip from a different cell phone number. He looked around the area before leaving. He had worn gloves, he hadn't touched anything without gloves on, so no one would ever know he had been in the house. He opted for the latter and went out to his car for an old phone he had had registered in Colin's name. If and when they questioned Colin, he could say the phone had been stolen. Which probably would never happen because there were so many "burner" phones that could never be traced.

Mick gave the 911 dispatcher the name and address of Mark's house, said it appeared there had been some foul play, and left it at that. When the dispatcher tried the "twenty questions" routine, he signed off and got into his car. No sooner had he started the engine and turned the car around on the highway to head back into town than he could hear the sirens. *Christ,* he thought, *they must have been close by.* He stepped on the accelerator, shaking his head in disgust. *No real suspect to avenge Carla's death, no truck, no Wanda, and who the hell killed Mark? Am I losing my touch or what?* he thought. *I need to just pack it up and get out of Dodge. Better head back and get a decent night's sleep first,* he thought with disgust at himself.

He parked in front of the hotel, thinking about his next steps. He needed to call the grimy auto parts guy and let him know he would get his piece-of-crap car back to him in a week or so. He needed to make a couple of phone calls to catch up on business that he had been neglecting. He opened the door to his hotel room. It smelled like Pine Sol, which he appreciated. He still could not get that sickly, sweet stench from Mark's bedroom out of his nostrils. *Maybe a hot shower would help,* he thought. Clear his head too. He couldn't help but think that somehow this Thomas Hardcastle was involved in all this. He had been sure the most likely suspect was Mark, but now in light of the other information he had discovered, he wasn't sure. He did not think that Mark had done himself in; he was too much of a weasel to do that. *Man, I am beat.* Mick thought and went into the bathroom to take the needed ten minutes to adjust the shower to the right temperature.

When he got out of the shower, he felt 90 percent better. He went to the little refrigerator and got out one of the beers he had left in there. He popped the tab and took a long pull. Man, he thought, that did taste good, especially after the day he had. No sooner had he sat down in a chair and put his feet up on the other chair than there was a knock on his door. He looked down at himself, still wrapped only in the towel he had used after his shower. He looked at the little clock on the bedside table, which showed "9:00" in blue lettering. He peeked out of the slats of the blinds. Lo and behold, there was Tammy standing on the steps. *Is there no stopping that girl?* he thought. He opened the door a crack and started to tell her how beat he was and that he had to get up early in the morning. He had gotten the first sentence out when she stuck the toe of her cowboy boot in the crack of the door and held up a bottle of wine in one hand and a bag in the other. The bag had to have Chinese food in it, by the unmistakable fried smell wafting from it. He continued his protest, but just then her jacket fell away, exposing the nicest two to three inches of cleavage on top of a tight little maroon number she was wearing. He found himself swallowing hard, and he looked down at her smiling up at him and said, "Oh, hell, girl, come on in. I guess I didn't realize how hungry I was." He pulled her into the room as he shut the door with his bare foot.

When Mick woke up the following morning, Tammy was already gone. *Wow! Well, so much for small talk,* he thought. *Seems like I am living the dream, or wet dream, so to speak.* He stretched out on the bed and sighed, luxuriating in his thoughts of last night. *Man, that girl must be double-jointed!* He smiled and swung his legs over the side of the bed and stood up. "Ow!" he said out loud as he gingerly rubbed his balls. They were slightly red and a little swollen. *Whew, good thing I am headed home,* he thought. *I am not sure I could handle another night of what Tammy has to offer.* He shook his head a little sadly as he headed in to take a shower for the second time in twelve hours. He couldn't get the water temperature to lower his body temperature, it seemed. *Probably don't have enough hot water for the number of hotel rooms they have,* he thought. *Oh well, a cold shower couldn't hurt me this morning.* He chuckled to himself. He thought about the past couple of evenings. He had had the best sex ever, with a beautiful, warm, sensual woman and no commitment involved. How did that happen? he wondered. Seemed like a dream, and hopefully that was true.

As he packed up his sparse belongings, he noticed a note propped up against the empty wine bottle on top of the refrigerator. He couldn't help but smile as he opened it. It read, "Thanks for a great night, sugar." Followed by a little smiley face. "I know you can't stay, but please keep in touch." *Well, she couldn't have been much over thirty-five,* he thought, so that really put a smile on his face. Who knew? Maybe there was a little stud left in him, after all. He gave himself the ole once-over in the mirror before he shut the door on the little hotel room. He would not be able to forget this little place for quite some time, he thought.

The doorbell tinkled as he opened it and walked into the small hotel office. He thanked Dotty, telling her it was a great place to stay and that he appreciated her hospitality. He went on to say that he would probably be coming back when he returned the car to Joe's Auto, but for now he would be checking out. She got his invoice off the printer and handed it over to him, telling him he would be more than welcome to come back any time. He slid a small folded piece of paper across the counter and asked her if she wouldn't mind seeing that Tammy got the note. Dotty looked up at him and winked. "Sure, no problem," she said. He smiled sheepishly as he gave her a wave of his hand and walked out the door.

He got into the driver's seat of the Subaru and tried three times, all unsuccessfully, to get the car to start. He hit the steering wheel with the flat of his hand and swore, refusing to believe it was just the cold morning. "Piece of shit!" he shouted childishly. On the fourth try, the engine managed to sputter and turn over. He fiddled with the heater buttons, thinking it must have gotten down to below freezing during the night. There was a thick layer of frost on the windshield. He let the car run a few minutes before returning to Joe's Auto. He wanted to check one more time before he left, to see if there was any sign of his truck. The police officer had told him that Joe's Auto would be the one towing it back to the yard if it was not able to be driven on its own.

Sure enough, when he pulled into the auto yard, he spotted his truck right away. Or what was left of it, he thought. "Good God almighty!" he swore under his breath. He let out a big sigh as he got out of the little car. The windshield was intact, but the truck had pretty much been gutted. The seats had been removed. The expensive sound system was nonexistent. He opened the top glove compartment—nothing was left in there but a Kleenex. He opened the bottom glove compartment, which he was more concerned about. He had installed a hidden compartment in that one, and you could not detect the latch unless you knew it was there. There was a small lever under the dash, which he hit with his finger, and the back compartment was revealed. *Thank goodness the thieves hadn't discovered it!* he thought. He reached in and pulled out his hammerless .38 Smith & Wesson, which was always hidden there in case of an emergency. He was never without his 9mm, but this little .38 meant a lot more to him. His mom had given it to him when he had graduated from the police academy. Originally, she had bought if for herself, as a means of protection, but she discovered she was not even comfortable having it in the house, so she ended up giving it to him. Mick had gotten her a dog instead. Not only was the dog protective, but he had also become her best companion until the end.

He pocketed the little pistol, then jumped off the bed of the tow truck. "Sons of bitches!" he snarled as Joe came out of the office door.

"Purt a near picked it clean, they did," Joe said, with a toothpick hanging out of his front tooth. "I will let you notify your insurance company, and then someone can call me for damages. Nothing left worthwhile, though, I can tell you that much."

Mick shook his head disgustedly. "Well, I am not sure that piece of crap will even get me home," he told Joe. "It took me four tries this morning to try to get it started."

Joe gave Mick a look and a leer. "Oh, no problem. That baby will get you wherever you need to go. Just pretend it's an ice queen and give it more foreplay." With that, the old buzzard snickered, waved his hand, and walked away. "Give me a holler when you get back in town!"

Mick thought maybe he would be better off getting a ride to the airport and just flying back to Oregon, but he hated to fly. It wasn't the flying itself that he didn't like; it was all the germs you subjected yourself to in the airport and on the plane. The last time he had flown anywhere, it had been to Cancún, and he had brought every disinfectant he could think of. He still had caught a cold when he got back home.

He got back in the Subaru, and this time it started right up. *Well, here goes nothing,* Mick thought as he drove out of the parking lot. He tapped the dash and said, "Baby, don't fail me now." He shook his head and fiddled with the radio, thinking he might just try to drive straight through till he hit his hometown street. He had had enough of this burg for a while.

Chapter 19

Mick was glad to see the sign for Rockaway. It was 8:00 p.m., and he had been driving the last three hours in the dark. He noted the sky was full of stars as he pulled into his driveway. *Man, it feels good to be home.* He got out of the car with a yawn and a big stretch. He managed to talk to Sheelya but was unable to reach Evelyn on the drive, and he had made a connection with three other people who were inquiring about his services. So all in all, that was a good sign. He needed to get back to some real work, which would help take his mind off his dismal failure at not finding out who had killed Carla. On top of that now was the death of Mark, and he might never find out any details on that particular story. His mind was set on a murder theory, just not clear who the murderer could be. He was almost 100 percent sure it was not a suicide. Most slimeballs like Mark were just too chicken to give society a break and commit suicide.

He got his duffel bag out of the cramped back seat and bent over. Damn little car had given him a kink in his lower back that had been riding him the last two hours of the drive. He had not called his assistant yet, and he would have to do that after he got settled back in the house. Sheelya, in her usual Sheelya way, had informed him that she had tried to get ahold of Colin and had been unable to do so. Of course, she was more than annoyed with him. He let out a sigh of resignation. Some things you just couldn't change. He was beat, and tomorrow was another day. He would deal with it then. He was looking forward to sitting in his own recliner with his feet up and enjoying an ice-cold brewski. His own haven, where he wasn't required to perform.

He walked up onto his deck in the dark and looked at the sensor light by the door. The light had not come on when he hit the bottom step. *Hmmm, must have burned out,* he thought. He remembered that he had changed the bulb less than six months ago. *The crap you buy nowadays,* he thought as he opened the front door and fumbled with the light switch. He found the switch, but the ceiling light did not illuminate anything. *Jeez, it's flipping dark in here,* he thought. He always kept a night-light on in the hallway going into the kitchen. Then there was another one usually on in the kitchen. He often got up in the night and came down to get something to drink, or even to sit in his recliner. Everything was pitch-black now. He groped his way to the desk that sat outside the kitchen door. He opened one of the drawers to retrieve a flashlight. Once the flashlight was on, he pointed it into the living room. He stood there stock-still and couldn't believe what he saw.

"Jesus H. Christ!" he said in a shocked voice. "You have got to be kidding me."

His living room was a torn-up, shambled mess. His couch cushions were slashed, his coffee table was overturned, his magazines and books were strewn all over the place. Some of his artwork was smashed on the floor. Papers, pens, envelopes, and even placemats were scattered everywhere. He was afraid to look further into the house. He took his 9mm out of the back of his waistband and stood at the ready, with it loaded and cocked. He started to make his way into the kitchen, where he hit that light switch and at least the kitchen lit up with a light fluorescent glow.

He looked around the kitchen. The kitchen was in the same shambles as the living room was in. Food containers were ripped open, and contents were all over the floor. Fortunately, he never had much food in the house, but his cabinet drawers and cupboards were all wide open. Dishes, cutlery, pots, pans, towels, and cleaning supplies were scattered all over the floor. "What a freaking mess," he said with total exasperation. It appeared that whoever had broken in was looking for something that he couldn't find. Mick could not even think of what the heck that could be. It wasn't like he had a lot of valuables or anything. Even the refrigerator had not gone unscathed.

The door was hanging open by a head of lettuce and an overturned jar of dill pickles that were in the way of its closure. The smell of vinegar filled his nostrils. *Who goes through someone's refrigerator?* he thought as he sat down with a thump on a kitchen chair. He was certain whoever had done the destruction was no longer in the house. There was chocolate ice cream melted at the bottom of the refrigerator, a few small pools of water that were probably melted ice cubes, and the milk had run down the floor and traveled into his heating vent. *Oh, Christ, that will smell good when the heat goes on!* he thought.

Someone must have been really pissed to go through and cause such a mess. Spilled cereal mixed with Ajax mixed with orange juice mixed with alcohol. It just didn't make any sense to him. He tried to recall if any one woman he had recently been with could have possibly had a pissed-off boyfriend or husband. None came to mind. The last pissed-off boyfriend had gotten the licking he deserved. He had treated his last girlfriend terribly, and she had been very happy when Mick had gotten done with him. Their relationship never amounted to anything but a few laughs and a couple of dinners. She had shown her appreciation of his taking down the boyfriend a peg or two.

He went out into the hallway and started down the hall to his bedroom. His house was more like a cottage than a full-size house. He had had it remodeled to add a bath and a walk-in closet to his bedroom. It was still small, but quite comfortable for him. He had another small bedroom he used as an office-slash-guest-room. It was usually tidy because it rarely got used, since he seldom had any visitors.

He was feeling pretty intimidated to open either bedroom door at this point, afraid of what he might find. He tentatively opened the first door, which was his office. "Oh, Christ, could it get any worse?" It looked like the rest of the house. The same type of nonsensical shambles everywhere. He looked at the top of his desk, where his computer was supposed to be, but it wasn't. The drawers to his small desk were open and empty, most of the papers and contents appearing to be strewn all over the room. Thank God he had backed up everything that was of importance just before he had left town. That little flash drive was safely locked in his gun safe in the garage.

His bookcase was overturned, and books and the few knickknacks he did have were smashed into bits on the floor. The room contained one small twin bed, the mattress of which was half off and half on the bed. Coats, boots, and what hunting gear he had were scattered everywhere. The small nightstand was overturned, with its contents scattered about. What money he did have, which had been left to him by his mom, was in the gun safe also. He did not want to think about anyone destroying that or being able to get into it. He was afraid to go into the garage. Better just suck it up and check his bedroom next, he figured.

He stepped over the detritus and walked the few steps to his bedroom door. He took a deep breath and then gingerly opened the door. *Could it be any worse?* he thought disgustedly. His stomach gave a little turn. His bedroom looked even worse than the rest of the house. He was beginning to think this was a personal vendetta, not just a drive-by robbery. There was one difference he noticed immediately. There were a few dark-red blood spots caked on the sheet of his bed. As he stepped further into the room, he noticed a few small spots of what looked like blood also on the carpet leading into the bathroom. He looked around at the clothes on the floor, at his bed with the blood, and at a split down the side of his mattress. More clothes and shoes scattered everywhere. It was not unlike the scene he had discovered at Mark DeGuard's house, minus the dead dog, he thought.

All of a sudden, a whiff of something nasty hit his nostrils. He walked over to the pile of bed linens in one corner of the bedroom and discovered a soft brown mound in the middle of the pile. He peered closer and backed away, gagging. There was a huge pile of shit among the linen. He did not think it looked or smelled like dog shit either. "How disgusting!" he mouthed as he backed away from the mess.

The whole thing was mind-boggling to him. His truck, and now his house, totally trashed. It couldn't just be a coincidence. He walked into the bathroom and noticed a small dried spot of blood on the corner of the bathroom vanity. When he looked up at his mirror, he noted a small speck of rust color on the edge of the vanity mirror.

He reached up slowly and opened the medicine cabinet. He stepped away with a slight gasp. Where his small first aid kit had sat neatly on the shelf now lay a small finger caked in blood. He looked closer at the finger, mostly to assure himself it was real, not just a fake, leftover Halloween decoration. The finger appeared to be a woman's, not just by its size, but that there was a little bit of red nail polish left in the nail bed and cuticle. He plopped down on the top of his toilet seat in disgust. He was not only distraught by the whole mess but was also really pissed off now.

He looked around and said, "What the hell is going on around here?"

Chapter 20

He looked around his bedroom again and back into the bathroom. He shook his head in disbelief. He considered himself a strong man with a strong stomach, able to take things in stride, but this was different. Of course, he had never been on the receiving end of a vendetta of some sort. His neighbor, his truck, his house—what next? He took his cell phone out of his back pocket and dialed the local precinct number again. *They are going to think there is something wrong with me,* he thought.

He looked at the time and hoped that Randy Delaney was still on duty. He would much rather give him a report than the idiot that called himself the chief of police. God only knew how he was voted in three terms in a row. Maxwell Marker had been the chief of police for the past ten years. Mick had known his father, who had also been the chief of police before that. That was pretty common in a small town like this one, but Marker Sr. had been a nice guy, a smart and thorough investigator, a pillar of the community, civic-minded, helped his neighbors. His son, however, was a lazy sleazeball, practically the opposite of his dad, and Mick could not understand how he had been re-elected so many times. Mick was pretty sure he sat in someone's pocket, and the fact that his uncle was the mayor in the next neighboring town didn't hurt him either.

Mick himself had had more than one run-in with the asshole. Marker thought he was the town's gift to the police department. There had been a time when Mick would have given him information that actually would have helped solve a crime, but the guy was so arrogant he wouldn't listen to what Mick had to offer, anyway, so

Mick had given the info to Randy, and Randy had managed to solve the crime but, even so, received little credit for it. The last time Mick gave Marker some valid information on a drug-related crime, he was treated with such disdain and his lead was completely disregarded that Mick decided not to bother anymore. As it turned out, Mick had been correct on the lead, but Marker took the credit for solving the crime. He couldn't put two and two together if he actually did see a hand in the cookie jar. All his brothers had the same cocky attitude. Big fish in a small pond, throwing their weight around. Which couldn't have been easy, since they all weighed in at about three hundred pounds.

That wasn't Mick's biggest problem at this time, though. He knew he could rely on Randy to look into the situation.

"Rockaway Beach Police Department," said the female voice on the other end. "This is Melody. How may I help you?"

Mick couldn't help but smile at the sound of her voice. He liked Melody. She wasn't the brightest, but she was always cheerful and a real sweetheart. Best thing was, she always flirted with him when he called or dropped by the station, when he knew Randy was working. "Hi, there, Melody. It's Mick here. Is Randy around?"

There was a pause, and then Melody said, "I will transfer you to his phone. How ya doing, anyway? I haven't seen you around in a while. Is Everything okay?"

"Well, actually, no, Melody. Things pretty much suck right now," Mick said. "That's why I need to talk to Randy."

"Oh, I am sorry, hon. You are lucky you caught him still here. Oh, we both had some paperwork to catch up on. Ya know that old wino that camps out across from 101 by the jetty? He up and decided to walk across the highway just as it was getting dark, and he got hit by a car." Mick rolled his eyes toward the ceiling. When Melody got on a roll, there was no stopping her. "He actually lived and then had to be life-flighted into Portland. The poor guy that hit him was beside himself and practically inconsolable. Even my charm didn't get through to him. In fact, he is still here with Randy. He's going to get the guy some coffee so he can talk to you. Well, here he is now. Come around when you can. I have been saving something for you."

And on that note, she hung up. He wondered what the heck she had saved for him.

Randy came on the line with, "Hey, Mick, what's up? I only have a minute. Poor guy in the back is in pretty rough shape. Not worth the old wino, that's for sure, but so far there is no news if the guy will make it or not. So I feel sorry for him."

Mick said he understood and then paused. He wasn't sure exactly where to start. "Well, Randy, it's like this. Some maniac broke into my house and completely vandalized it. It's not like I really have much that's worth anything, but it sure seems like whoever it was, was looking for something. I have been gone for a few days, and while I was gone, my truck was stolen and vandalized too. Kind of a coincidence, if you ask me. My truck chassis was found, and that was about it. Now my house is a shambles also. Drawers were opened, and contents were all over the place. Cupboards were ajar, and dishes were thrown and lying broken everywhere. Closet doors were pulled off, and clothes were strewn all over. My bed linens were on the floor, and someone actually shit on them! No kidding—a big stinking dump in the middle of my sheets! My mattress was slashed. It wasn't some kind of normal robbery. I don't think…" Mick paused to take a breath. Randy didn't say anything until the part about someone taking a dump in the sheets.

"Wow, that's nasty. Are you sure it's not an angry boyfriend or something?" Randy was well aware of Mick's fondness for the ladies.

"Ha ha," Mick said. "Trust me, that is the first thing I thought of, but I have been so busy lately I haven't had time for any affairs, let alone illicit liaisons."

This wasn't the time or place to mention Pine Lake, Mick figured.

"So…that's not the end of the story, though," Mick continued. "I found a spot of blood on the carpet, and another one on my sink in the bathroom. The bathroom had broken glass lying on the floor, so I figured the guy must have cut himself throwing my shit around, but when I opened the medicine cabinet, I found a small woman's finger lying on the bottom shelf. I assumed it was a ring finger, by its size and because there was a white line where a ring must have been, before the finger was cut off. Holy hell, who does shit like that but the Mafia on TV? Whose finger could it be? I know I have pissed people off in the past, but believe me, I have racked my brain for anyone recently, and I just can't come up with anyone. Even an angry boyfriend in the past doesn't make sense for that kind of destruction." He sighed. "And someone's finger? I didn't touch anything but the finger, and I picked that up with vinyl gloves."

"Whoa there, Mick. You said you found a severed finger in your medicine cabinet?"

"That's exactly what I said, Randy," Mick interrupted him. "I thought if I gave you the finger, no pun intended, you would be able to trace where it came from." he chuckled to himself.

"That maybe you could put a rush on it getting identified."

Mick finally ran out of steam. "No problem," he said to Mick. "The little woman is visiting her mom in Seattle right now, and she took the kids with her. I was going to try to get some stuff done around the house, but then McGuire said he had to take a couple of days off, so that plan went down the toilet. I will come by in about half an hour. I just need to finish some paperwork, and then I was planning on taking this guy"—and he gestured with his head to the back office—"to a hotel also. His car is not drivable, but his wife will come and get him tomorrow. So I can stop by after that." He told Mick not to worry; at least he hadn't been home when whoever it was broke in.

"Thanks, Randy," Mick said and hung up the phone.

Mick figured he might as well make a couple of phone calls while he waited for Randy to come by. He would have to make them at some time, anyway. Now would help take his mind off his situation. He called Sheelya first. He waited for her voice mail to finish. "Hello, there, whoever you are." *Man, she needs to give up those cigarettes,* Mick thought. *Her voice sounds like its coming across a gravel road!* "I am currently unavailable at the moment, so please leave your name and number and I might call you back." She snickered.

Mick had heard the message before.

"Sheelya, Mick here. I have some information that you might find interesting. So give me a call when you can." His phone went dark. *I don't have jack shit,* he thought, but maybe that would buy him some time. *Hopefully, Colin is true to his word and does really have something.*

His next call was answered on the first ring. "God, Mick, where the hell have you been? I thought you said you would be here this morning!" Before Mick got to say anything, though, Colin continued, "That damn Sheelya somehow got my number, and she has been doing nothing but hammering away at me. Seriously, man, how can you cope with her? She's, like, some kind of python and wants to suffocate you. Christ!" Colin sighed. "I do have some good news, though. I managed to take some pictures of her husband going into a hotel with a young lady who, if I am not mistaken, is the one who works in his office. They were there for a few hours, and he looked a little worse for wear when he walked out of the hotel. At least he didn't look as perky as when he went into the hotel, I can tell you that. I also caught up with them in a dive bar in downtown Tillamook, and she was practically straddling him at the table! Can't say she has very good taste. He looks like an overfed weasel." He chuckled.

"So when can we meet up? Are you coming into the office tomorrow? I want you to check out these pictures, and I sure could use some pocket money, if you get my meaning."

Mick rolled his eyes. "Yes, Colin. Good job. I know exactly what you mean. How about if I try to make it into the office around ten? I just got back this afternoon but had a little surprise waiting for me. My house was ransacked while I was gone, and I mean *totally* vandalized. So right now, it's hard for me to concentrate on much else but my own problems. I will have some money for you tomorrow, and I will probably have to ask your help with my house. I appreciate everything you do, and you know I am not much of a carpenter, so there is probably some extra money in this whole mess for you."

"Wow!" Colin said. "That's a tough break. I won't keep you. You can tell me all about it tomorrow. I can help with just about anything. I took this next semester off school to help my sister. Her deadbeat husband stopped paying his child support, and right now she does not even know where he is. So I am helping her with the kids and with some general repairs around the house. It works for both of us right now. I will see you tomorrow, and hey, hang in there. I am sure you will get things figured out. You always do, man." Colin hung up the phone.

Mick wasn't exactly motivated to move, but he knew he had to. He was still shell-shocked by the latest events that had just happened. At least this should get Sheelya off his back, and he knew Colin had worked on a couple of other little cases for him, so that was good too. He would need to concentrate for a while to see if he could find out who had destroyed his house. He went into the kitchen to see if there was a beer that had gone unscathed in the wreckage. *Ah, an unharmed IPA in the very back.* He popped the tab and went to sit on a kitchen chair to wait for Randy.

Chapter 21

Mick opened the door before Randy even made it to the doorbell. "Man, thanks for coming over tonight," Mick said as he held out his hand for what he knew would be a ball-busting handshake. Randy was six foot four, and probably 240 pounds of solid muscle. They had remained friends from the time they had graduated the police academy. They had gone their separate ways for a few years but had always kept in touch. Randy had gone back to his hometown, and Mick wanted to try to gain his fame and fortune in the big city. A lot of luck that had done him, he thought. Brought up short by a very complicated case that had gone sideways and got his partner shot in the deal.

Randy took Mick's hand. "Good to see you again, Mick." He looked into the living room. "Sorry it's under this kind of circumstance." He whistled. "It looks like someone set a bomb off in here! Jesus, what a freaking mess."

Mick led Randy into the kitchen, where the chairs could actually be sat on, while Mick went out into the garage. He came back with two Coors, knowing Randy, while off duty, would never turn down a beer, and opened them before he sat back down. "Can you believe this mess?" he asked Randy.

Mick sat down with Randy and went on to tell him the whole story of his trip to Pine Lake after he had found Carla dead. "I really don't have a clue of anyone holding that big of a grudge against me, and this looks more like someone just out to cause destruction, not a robbery. And why all this vandalism? Doesn't make sense to me,"

Mick said. "I keep coming back to Carla's death and then what I found while I was in Pine Lake. I think they are connected somehow."

They sipped on their beers, which for Mick was more of a chugging, before Randy said, "Well, walk me around and let's see if we can find any likely fingerprints anywhere."

"I kind of doubt you will," said Mick. "I took that approach too, but the guy had to have been wearing gloves. Maybe we can pick up some DNA from the big dump he left in the bedroom."

"Yuck," said Randy. "I'll let you bag it. I can handle blood, but not shit. It will take a while to find out anything, I'm afraid. The lab we use in Portland actually caught on fire last week, and since we haven't had to send anything to it, we haven't found another one yet. I will get on it first thing in the morning, though. If there was a murder involved, they work a little faster, but a robbery or even this mess, your guess is as good as mine."

Mick led Randy through the rest of the house, all the while exclaiming, bewildered, how he did not understand what was going on. He showed him where the feces ended up in the middle of his bed linen. At that point, Randy took out a special bag for Mick to pick it up with and put some in. "Gross," he said. He put the bag down on the floor before taking him into the bathroom. "This is where it gets even more bizarre," Mick told him. He opened the medicine cabinet to show Randy where the finger had been lying in the dried blood. "I don't know if this was taken off someone before they died or after and it's just meant to scare me."

"Wow," said Randy. "Is there a body lying around someplace we don't know about? Maybe one that the finger belongs to."

Mick looked at him with chagrin and said, "Trust me, I thought of that but have looked under and over everything, even in my bait freezer in the garage, and there is nothing. Doesn't it look like a woman's finger? It's awfully small."

Randy took another small bag out of his vest and gingerly picked up the finger and dropped it into the bag. Mick's stomach did a little flip-flop as the finger made a faint plop when it landed in the bottom of the bag. "Well, this certainly isn't something we see every day around here now. I haven't dealt with any severed body parts in months, and Carla's murder is still pretty fresh in our minds. Haven't got any leads on that yet either. Now drunks and domestic violence, I see all the time. The occasional fatal car accident or the drunk driver not quite making it home, those are norms around this part. This should prove to be pretty interesting. Leave it to you, Mick, to drop this little mystery in our laps. Ya know, I came back home to live a nice, quiet little hometown life, but you just couldn't leave it alone, could you?"

Mick knew Randy was kidding him, but with a little side of truth. Sending the finger in with the feces might get quicker results.

"Hard to say, though. Depends on where we find a lab that's available and how backed up they are. Sometimes it's weeks before we get results," Randy said. "I think I got all the information I need for tonight. I am going to wait until tomorrow to fill out a report, but I will need to go back into the station to get these bags in the freezer. I'm beat. I have been working overtime every night since that asshole of a chief has been off with his pseudosickness." He sighed. "We'll talk again tomorrow, buddy. You look like you could use some sleep too. Where are you going to stay tonight? You are welcome to come to the house. Since Vickie is away with the kids, I have an extra bed."

"Nah, thanks, man," said Mick. "I am going to stay at the Little Salmon in Tillamook. I need to check on a couple of things there tomorrow. My financial guy called me while I was out of town and said I better come in and talk to him when I got back. I sure as hell hope something is not wrong with my finances too. That would be the icing on the cake at this point."

"Oh, hey, I know what I forgot to mention." Mick stopped Randy from getting into the patrol car. "Tomorrow, see what you can find out about a Thomas Hardcastle. I am pretty sure that is Carla's brother. Kind of a badass dude, been in and out of prison. Something shady about him and their relationship. I will keep you posted if I find out anything myself."

Randy got into the patrol car as he said to Mick, "Ya know I will have to let the chief know what is going on. I can leave out the messiest details, but it is a crime scene, and I can't get away with not telling him, or he will have my head when he finally comes back to work."

135

"Yeah, I know," said Mick. "Just so long as I don't have to deal with the son of a bitch. Lazy, good-for-nothing sorry excuse for a cop I ever came across!" Mick sighed. "Thanks, Randy." He shut the patrol car door, and Randy waved as he drove back toward the police station.

Mick went back into the house to retrieve a clean shirt and jeans. *If I even have any,* he thought. *Man, Randy's right. I probably look as bad as I feel. Hopefully, this mess is not too daunting for even Colin.* He looked around one more time, shaking his head, before he turned the light off and went to lock the door. Kind of like locking a barn door after the cows got out.

He got in the car and drove toward Tillamook. He would have to talk to his insurance agent again. He hadn't talked to him but twice in a whole year, and now it was twice in one week. He was going to shit when he got the report on the damages in his house. His mind was running through a whole gamut of different scenarios that just didn't match up.

He hoped the Little Salmon wasn't full. It was a small but clean and reasonable hotel. The best part being, there was a little bar and grill a block away. You could get a great burger or soup and salad, and they hadn't changed their drink prices, probably in the last five years. The insurance company would probably reimburse him for the night or how many other nights he needed at the hotel. All depending on his house situation, Mick thought. Mick had always prided himself on being as thrifty as possible. It was the way he had been brought up, and it was a hard habit to change. His poor mom had always been thrifty, but it was because she had to be, in order to make ends meet. Her ways had been ingrained into the way he was brought up since a small child, and he had never had a problem with being thrifty, but staying at a hotel, no matter the circumstances, seemed like an unnecessary, problematic situation in his mind.

He drove the piece-of-shit little car as close to the entrance as he could get. He stopped under a streetlight and got out of the Subaru. The door creaked when he opened it. *God, what a piece of crap,* he thought. *I feel like someone's grandmother driving this.* It just wasn't manly. Men drove trucks. He slammed the door so hard the side-view mirror fell off and bounced under the car. "Jesus H. Christ!" he swore and decided he was too disgusted to pick it up tonight; he just walked off toward the hotel entrance.

A buzzer sounded as he opened the door to the hotel. He was pretty sure they would have a room. Fishing season was over, and the only people who really visited during the week were retirees who liked to come to the coast on off-season, since it was cheaper and quieter. He was greeted with a big smile from Tom, the front desk clerk. Tom was an overweight, effeminate, harmless thirtysome-thing-year-old kid who had run the hotel for his grandmother since he was eighteen. Nice kid, although not too bright.

"Hi, Tom," Mick said. "I am going to need a room for a few nights, more than likely. My house was broken into, and I am not sure how long it will take to make it livable again."

"Gee, I am sorry to hear that, Mr. Meade," Tom told him as he slowly got out of the desk chair to step up to the counter. "Would you like one bed or two?"

"One would be fine, Tom," Mick said as he got out his driver's license and credit card.

Tom took the cards and entered the information into the computer. "Would you like a view of the parking lot or the slough in the back?" he asked Mick with a little grin.

"Very funny, Tom," he said. Neither one can you call a view. I will take the parking lot, though. After what I have gone through these last few days, I want to be able to leave in a hurry if I have to."

"No problem, Mr. Meade. We got plenty of room. You know how slow it is this time of year." Tom winked at Mick.

What the hell, Mick thought. *What is it with hotel clerks? Do they all wink at you?*

He took the key from the outstretched hand of Tom, who held on to it longer than was necessary, in Mick's opinion. "Whoa, there, Tom," Mick said under his breath. "You are definitely not my type." Mick put the key in his jacket pocket as he walked quickly out of the little office.

He went back to the car to retrieve his bag, then took the key back out as he started across the parking lot. He looked at the key, number 29. Good, it was at the end of the parking lot, away from the road noise. *Maybe I can get a decent night's sleep,* he thought. He decided to just leave the car where he had parked it. He looked around and assessed his surroundings. He didn't see anything out of the ordinary, so he unlocked the door and threw his duffel bag on the bed. Small but clean, although a little musty smelling. It was hard to not have a musty smell here at the coast, especially in an older establishment. Plus, the humidity was usually over 80 percent 99 percent of the time. *Oh well.* He sat down, hard, and bounced a little on the bed. *Not bad.* He lay back for a minute and asked himself why he decided to come here and not to Scottsdale, Arizona, where the sun shines about 85 percent of the time.

He got up and went to use the bathroom. He glanced in the mirror and puffed his chest out and patted his hair. *Well, I may look a little worse for wear, but at least I still got my hair.* He reached up to pat down his colic. He grinned at his reflection and decided he was too hyped up to go to sleep. The Rendezvous bar and grill was only a couple of blocks away. A little walk in the night air would do him good, he thought. He knew he could still grab something to eat there, maybe not one of their killer burgers—that might be a little too heavy this time of night—but he could sure down a couple of their whiskies. It was 9:00 p.m., and he realized he hadn't eaten anything since he had stopped in Rainier, and that had been only a snack. Hopefully, the bartender, Chuck, hadn't been hitting the sauce. Chuck tended to think that rules didn't apply to him, only to his employees, and when he got drunk, he couldn't manage to bake a potato.

As the door closed behind Mick, he hadn't noticed there was a pair of smoldering eyes watching him from a small dark vehicle across the street from the hotel.

Chapter 22

Mick walked in the door and picked a stool at the end of the bar. He looked around the dark bar and saw only one other person who was sitting in front of a flashing video game. He never could understand how anyone could throw their hard-earned money away on those stupid lottery games.

"Hey, Chuck, you cooking tonight, or am I too late?" Mick shouted down the length of the bar.

Chuck looked up and said, "Am now! Slow night, so I sent Carlos home early. I got some roast beef left. Makes a mean hot beef sandwich. Will that work for you?" Chuck finished cleaning the end of the counter and walked down to where Mick sat. Mick ordered a Sierra Nevada Pale Ale and two fingers of Jack Daniel's.

Mick looked at what was on the reader board and said, "Yeah, sounds good to me. I'm starving. Can I get an order of steak fries with that?"

"No problem," Chuck told him and turned to go into the little kitchen in the back.

At least he's sober tonight, Mick thought. He turned around as he heard the bar door shut behind someone. *Hmmm, not usual to have strangers come in rather late on a weeknight.* He nodded at the pretty brunette, who had sat on a stool in the middle of the bar.

Chuck stuck his head from behind the curtain that separated the bar from the kitchen. "Oh! Hiya, Cathleen," he said to her. "Be with you in just a minute."

"No problem, Chuckie. I got a few extra minutes tonight." And she turned to face Mick down at the of the bar.

Chuckie, Mick thought. *Where did that come from? And where did she come from?* She seemed pretty familiar with her surroundings, Mick surmised, so she must have been in here a time or two before. When she turned, she said hello to Mick and introduced herself as Cathleen but then added that he had probably heard that when Chuck called her by name.

"How are you on this miserable, cold, wet night?" She looked at him and smiled.

"Well, all in all, things could be worse, but not sure quite how. Let's just say I have had better days and leave it that," Mick told her and gave her a signs up. She sure had luscious-looking red lips, he thought as he tipped his beer in her direction by means of a greeting.

Just then, Chuck came out of the kitchen with a steaming pile of roast beef, gravy, and steak fries. Mick was pretty sure he started to salivate. "'Scuse me," he said as he picked up his fork. "I haven't had anything to eat since this morning."

"Oh, no problem, sugar. I just come in here to relieve some boredom," she told Mick. "I'll have the usual, Chuckie." She turned back around in her seat and faced Chuck. It looked to Mick like ole Chuckie was a little nervous around Cathleen. He was all thumbs trying to make her drink. It was some foo-foo-looking concoction in a tall frosted glass. Chuck was more of a beer-and-whiskey bartender. He couldn't seem to takes his eyes off Cathleen either. But that could have been because of the three-inch cleavage that was at eyeball level. After all, Chuck was only about five foot five. Her sweater fit her like a vinyl glove, and she was a looker. Not just cute, but classy, beautiful. *What in the hell is she doing in here?* he thought and almost caught himself saying it loud. He gave a little cough to stifle what he had started to ask.

Mick looked at Chuck, who was still looking at Cathleen. "Well, Chuck, that was an awesome sandwich. It sure hit the spot! Could I perhaps bother you for one more beer before I hit the road? I'll take my check too. Thanks."

Chuck finally looked up at Mick. "Excuse me, Cathleen. How is that drink, by the way?"

"Oh, it's perfect, Chuckie." And she pursed her lips into a little kiss. Mick actually saw Chuck turn two shades of red before he managed to get Mick his beer. When he delivered it, he leaned in a little closer to Mick and whispered, "She's new in town. She's recently divorced, has no kids, and she's staying with her mom for now. Her mom lives out Miami Foley way, but she goes to bed early, so Cathleen has been coming in about three times a week, bored, don't you know? She's looking for work. Nice, huh?"

"Very nice, Chuck," Mick said, "but seems a little out of your league."

Chuck looked at Mick and snorted. "Oh, more like yours, huh?" With that little rebuff, Chuck walked back down to the middle of the bar.

Mick's curiosity was definitely piqued at this point, but he was too tired to give it a lot of thought tonight. If she was in town for a while, he would no doubt see her again. He threw some money down on the bar, took one last swallow of his beer, and smiled at Cathleen as he headed for the door. "Nice to have met you, Cathleen. Hope to see you around. Small town, so it's possible." He tipped his ball cap at her on his way out the door. She gave him a beautiful, big smile and a wave with a very manicured hand. Mick walked back to the hotel deep in thought.

He didn't wake up until eight o'clock in the morning, but he felt totally refreshed. It didn't make him feel much better about his situation, though, because it all still remained to be solved, but at least he felt more clearheaded and able to start the day in a better frame of mind. He hit the On button on the little coffee maker and went in to take a shower. He heard his cell phone ring, but he had already stepped under the steaming, hot water. *Man, this feels good!* he thought as he lathered up with soap. In the meantime, he tried to put things in some type of perspective, but there didn't seem to be any perspective.

When he stepped out of the shower, his reflection in the mirror did not a pretty picture make. *Jesus, man, you have got to get back to the gym! Is that a paunch I detect there?* He stood sideways to the mirror and shook his head and thought he would have a hard time picking up a nice-looking woman like Cathleen if he gave in to a beer belly and a slouch. He thought about Cathleen and what a nice woman she seemed to be. Maybe it was time he settled down with someone and thought about having kids before it got too late. His mom would probably roll over in her grave. He smiled as he looked upward. *I will do it one of these days, Mom, I promise.*

He went over to the bed and picked up his cell phone. *Damn.* It was Sheelya already. He decided he was not quite ready for that fate until he met with Colin to see what kind of information he had collected. He quickly dressed, grabbed his keys, and headed out the door. He was deep in thought as he got into the Subaru. He didn't notice the small dark-colored car parked down the street that just happened to pull out behind him as he left the hotel parking lot.

He looked out the window. *Looks like it might clear up.* The sun was actually shining, and there was a blue sky. Unusual for the coast. He fiddled with the radio as he drove into Rockaway. There wasn't much to fiddle with since there was only one radio station that came in clearly. He got a little local news and one hit song before stopping in front of his office. He noticed Colin's car was already there. *Man, I sure hope he can be talked into the cleanup crew,* he thought as he took the steps two at a time. *Nice kid, but he might feel this was a bigger job than he even wanted to tackle.*

Colin was sitting at Mick's desk, with his feet up on the desk, no less. He seemed to be completely engrossed in a conversation of some sort. He hadn't noticed that Mick had come in the door until Mick gave his foot a heavy slap on the bottom. It almost upended the chair and startled the hell out of Colin. He bolted out of the chair, saying, "Whoa, babe, boss here." He quickly hung up and said, "Hey, man. Sorry, I didn't hear you come in."

"Obviously," Mick said. He looked at Colin. He hated standing next to the guy. He was about six foot five, slim, and all muscle. He had to look up at him. "I gathered that since you made yourself at home," he said with sarcasm. "So let's see what you got on Sheelya's little weasel. I can't wait to get her out of my hair."

"Oh, man, I hear ya there," Colin reiterated. He opened a manila envelope and laid out six glossy five-by-seven photos of Sheelya's small plump husband. All were taken with his secretary, or assistant, whatever they liked to be called nowadays. They were all in a slightly compromising position. Kissing, getting felt up, hands under her skirt, and one where she was actually giving him some tongue action in the restaurant booth. *Yuck! Disgusting,* Mick thought. The guy did resemble an overfed weasel.

"Good enough, Colin. Why don't you call her and set up a meeting? Or better yet, I had better do it. She will just give you a hard time. I have a bigger job for you, and you might actually enjoy it more than a meeting with Sheelya. I'm afraid, though, the other job is more physical work, and there is some construction involved. I know you used to help your dad on construction sites before you went to college. I've seen you with a hammer and nails, but this will take some general, major cleanup too. There's probably a week's worth of work just putting the house right again."

Colin didn't hesitate saying yes.

That was what Mick really liked about the kid. He hadn't even seen what he was getting into before he just said he was up for it.

Mick continued, "If you want to ask your sister to help with the cleanup work, I don't mind paying her also. There is laundry and dishes that need to be cleaned and put back where they belong. Plus, it will need a general cleaning after the construction work is done." Colin said she would probably like to do it since she could always use the extra money. "Good, I will take you over to the house and show you how much damage was done, but I have another little job that I just received a message on last night. I want to fill you in on that too."

"Do you know who Wan Ling is?" Mick asked Colin.

"Yeah, isn't he the little dude that owns the Chinese market on the edge of town?"

"Yes, that's the one. He is pretty sure he is getting ripped off, but he's not quite sure who it is. He only has two other employees that work full-time. One is his son, Kai, and the other is just a regular Joe. No kidding, actually his name is Joe, Joe Reynolds. He grew up around here, has never lived anywhere else. So Mr. Ling thinks it is Joe who is ripping him off, and I am sure it's more than likely his son, Kai.

"Before all this shit storm happened, I was able to place a camera in the shop without letting Wan know about it, and then I followed Kai around a couple of different times and actually got a couple of pictures of him fencing his dad's stuff. Now, some of the stuff that I saw him with did not come from the old man's shop. It looked like antiques of some sort, urns and plates and whatnot. His dad carries more Chinese-type stuff, but no antiques. I imagine the kid has a drug problem. He doesn't look like a tweaker. In fact, he always looks clean and put together, but I observed him going into a house out on Birdmont Avenue, and I know those guys that live in that house sell just about anything anybody wants to buy. They will get you high, low, or in between. So unless he is supplying someone else with drugs, he has a problem.

"This is going to break the old guy's heart. He was really planning on retiring soon and giving the business to his son. I was thinking you could follow Kai to the drug house and see if you can sniff out what he is buying or what they are selling.

"I will give Sheelya a call now and get her taken care of. I do need to tell you how much I appreciate what you do. If I didn't have you to depend on, not sure what I would do right now. It's been a rough week, to say the least. Good work, Colin," he said as they pulled up in front of Mick's house.

"Oh, I forgot to tell you one thing," Colin said. "I got a call here at the office from a lady who said her name was Evelyn. She said she knew you and that she knew you had some kind of trouble while you were in Idaho, so she hated to bother you but said she was hoping you would drop by when you got back. She said she thought that someone was following her. Nothing concrete, just a feeling she had whenever she left her house. She also said she had noticed a small maroon-colored car parked behind her on more than one occasion since you left. She said she had never seen the car before and could not describe the driver."

"Jeez, Colin, here I am complimenting you and you were sitting on this little tidbit. When did she call, anyway?"

Colin kind of cocked his head, like that would actually help him remember better. "Well, I think it was just yesterday morning," he said. He looked up at the clock and back at Mick. "Yup, it was yesterday, after I just got into the office, about nine. I remember exactly now because I had set my coffee cup down and some of it splashed onto the desk, and I had my bank statement lying there, when the phone rang."

Mick couldn't help but roll his eyes. "Well, Colin, keep in mind, I don't pay you to check your bank statements while on the job. I will give Evelyn a call. Thanks for remembering to tell me. However, I do appreciate everything you do." He gave Colin a thumbs-up sign.

Oh great, Mick thought. He picked up a pen, and as was his habit when he was thinking, he doodled all over an envelope that was lying on the top of the desk. *Odd how all these things seem to stem from one common denominator, Carla Hardcastle. I guess I should pay more attention to my neighbors.* "Colin, I'm going to go meet with Sheelya. I don't want her coming here. I want to meet her in a more neutral environment, like the café. That way, I can get up and leave if I need to. Then I have to stop in and see my insurance agent. So do you think you could meet me at my house, say, about two o'clock? I will run by Evelyn's on the way back to the house."

Colin looked up from what he was working on. "Sure, no problem, Mick," he said, and he gave him a thumbs-up sign as Mick got up, grabbed his keys, and headed out the door.

Mick had the envelope with the photos in his hand as he got into his car. He tucked them in an inside pocket in his jacket and hoped Sheelya was not in a manic phase this morning. He had enough to deal with without her usual dramatic scenes.

He parked the Subaru in front of Humpy's Café, thinking, *Who names a café Humpy's, anyway? Only here.* It was the only game in town to get breakfast, though, and they were open seven days a week, so it was here or drive into the next little town.

He looked around and didn't see Sheelya's car anywhere.

Chapter 23

He walked into the small café and took the corner booth. He had been there often enough that the waitress automatically set a large brown coffee carafe down in front of him. Just as she walked away, a breathless Sheelya stormed in the door. True to form, it wasn't possible for her to make a quiet entrance; she practically shouted her order at the waitress. Mick whispered an "I'm sorry" as she set down a cup and an herbal tea bag in front of Sheelya and walked quickly away.

"Well, Mick, you snake in the grass! Where have you been hiding yourself for two weeks?"

Mick grimaced and looked at her with raised eyebrows. "For your information, Sheelya, it's only been one week, and it's really none of your business. I do work for a living, as you are aware." He reached into his jacket and pulled out the envelope with the photos of her husband. He slid the envelope across the table to her. "I think this is just what you were looking for," he said as he looked around the café and noted there were only four other people sitting at two tables. Since the grand entrance, they had all been trying to listen and sneak looks over their shoulders at the two of them. "There is probably the evidence you need to get your divorce. It's pretty clear by these photos that he has been having a little dalliance with his secretary, or office assistant, whatever they call themselves these days. Colin did an excellent job, I might add."

Mick could see her demeanor change instantly. From tigress to Cheshire cat. She put both her hands on his and leaned her ample bosom onto the tabletop before saying, "Oh, sweetie, I cannot thank you enough!"

Mick withdrew his hands quickly and put them under the table. He cut into her next sentence. "Sheelya, we are done here. You have managed to finagle your way into three men's lives, and I have helped you defeat the last two financially. You are on your own after this. Let me repeat what I just said: I'm done. We are done. There is no *we* anymore. It's just never enough for you. I will consider what you overpaid me in the past as payment for this time, but don't call me again. Got it?" He had stood up and was looking down at her pouty face. He took some bills out of his wallet and threw them down on the table. "I am not available to you for anything anymore."

By now, of course, all the customers were looking at them, including the ones who had just walked in the door. Two mouths hung open when Sheelya stood up huffily, one boob practically falling out of the top of her blouse. She grabbed ahold of the sleeve of Mick's jacket, and spittle was flying when she hollered, "You can't talk to me that way!"

Mick yanked his arm away from her grasp, which sent her falling sideways back into the booth. He heard a loud "Damn it!" as he continued walking toward the front door. He also heard clapping and whistles from the customers. He couldn't help but walk out the door without a backward glance but a big smile on his face.

He got into the car and drove the twenty-five miles to Seaside Manor, where his insurance agent had his office. He had already made the appointment with Tim while he was in Idaho. *Oh man*, he thought. *Wait until he hears the rest of the story.* It wasn't like he really had to have a face-to-face meeting, but Mick had known Tim prior to his becoming an insurance agent, so Mick was more a friend than a customer. He had known him for about twelve years now. Tim was single when Mick had met him. They used to get together on Friday nights after work and down a few beers. Now Tim was married and had two kids, so they rarely saw each other.

Mick walked into the small insurance office and went right to Tim's door. There were only two agents, Tim and an old friend of Tim's, Harold Lewis. "Where's Linda?" Mick asked. Her desk looked pretty empty.

Tim stood up as Mick entered the office. "Yeah, she's out with her sick kid today. You know how it is, one kid gets sick, we all get sick. Oh yeah, that's right, you don't know." Tim chuckled a little and offered Mick his hand. "Haven't seen you around in a while, pal. So I know, no news is good news. What's up now?"

Mick had given him a partial rundown of the situation in Pine Lake. Now he filled him in on everything else that had happened. He looked at Tim as he ran his hand through his hair. "I just can't help but think that this whole mess is somehow related to my neighbor who was murdered. I don't have anything concrete yet, but there are just too many odd things that kind of relate back to one another." He paused a bit. "I met with Randy Delaney. You know Randy, don't you? A member of our outstanding police department. That being said," Mick said a little sarcastically with that statement. He knew Tim was aware of the fact that he had no respect for the Rockaway Police Department but that he did for his friend Randy. He went on to tell Tim that they were going to check for fingerprints in his house and send some material out for DNA testing, but it could be a while before he got any word back on that. "You would think with a murder involved that it could happen a little quicker, but then we are on the coast," he told Tim. "Of course, our infamous chief of police would like me to mind my own business. You know me though, Tim. Once I get involved, I have to see things through. I was hoping you could hurry things along so I can get money to get another truck. I can't stand driving this little shit car much longer. I feel like it's going to rattle itself apart on the road."

"Well, as far as the truck goes, I have everything in order," Tim said. "I was able to move things along a little quicker, claiming a hardship of sorts." He had a file folder on his desk that he handed to Mick. "We had to take the high mileage into consideration. Plus, the truck was five years old, but with no accidents involved and it being a Ford, which keeps its value pretty well, I managed to get you a check for thirty thousand dollars."

Mick looked at the check and smiled. "That sounds totally fair to me, Tim. What a pain in the ass, though, to have to go buy a new one. I hate shopping for a vehicle."

"Yeah, I know what you mean," Tim said. "I just bought my wife a little Toyota Camry, but the whole experience wasn't as bad as what I thought it would be. You should go talk to Mell O'Conner. He's a mick, just like you." And with that comment, he winked at Mick. Before Mick could retort with a comeback, Tim continued, "He just took over old man Parker's Ford dealership in Tillamook. Nice guy, easy to work with, and he needs the business, so you could probably get a square deal. I just need you to sign on the dotted line here." He slid a form across the desk for Mick to sign and said, "It helped that the body of the truck was recovered with the VIN. It was easier to get the maximum money allowed. Most times it takes a lot longer, and a theft is muddier than an accident. You know how we are. We love to take your money but hate like hell to part with it."

"You got that right," Mick said.

Tim looked at his watch and back at Mick. "I had a cancellation this afternoon, so how about I swing by your house about three thirty before I head for home? I can check the damages and take an inventory. It's mostly just writing stuff up. The adjuster might have to have a look also, but he usually takes the information that I gather. He's really too lazy to double-check on things, and since my dad is in the construction business, he just takes my word for stuff. Does that work for you?"

"Perfect," Mick said. "I will be there, anyway. I am having my assistant come by at two o'clock. He is pretty handy and can start putting stuff back together as soon as I get your okay. My address is 3030 South Coral Street in Rockaway. Weren't you there a few years ago? It's not exactly on your way home."

"No," Tim told him, "but we moved to Nehalem last year. I wanted the kids to go to school in a smaller town than Seaside Manor. We found a small home overlooking the river. Melinda loves it, which is fine by me, but it does have its disadvantages when you need something."

"Yeah, you're telling me," Mick said. "A screw costs twice as much here than it does in Portland."

"It's worth it, though, cleaner air, less traffic, and less homeless," Tim said as Mick patted him on the shoulder and told him he would see him later.

"Don't be surprised at how much damage there is," he told Tim as he went out the door.

"Well, nothing really surprises me in this business anymore," Tim said, but Mick had already closed the door behind him.

Chapter 24

"Crap," Mick swore under his breath. "I barely have enough time to get back home and meet Colin, let alone go by Evelyn's house. I'd better give her a call and let her know."

When he got into the car, his stomach gave a loud, rolling grumble, reminding him he had had nothing but a cup of coffee all day. *It's a Big Jack, then,* he thought. *I don't have time for anything else.* Besides, Jacks was the only fast-food place in town, and you really could not call it fast food. More like not-so-fast food.

He drove through the drive-through window and ordered a Big Jack, apple pie, and large coffee with cream, then pulled ahead to the first window. A sullen, pimply kid took his money with barely a nod and no thank-you. The second window at least offered some semblance of customer service. He was greeted by a young girl with pink hair and pink braces and a big smile. She handed him his order and actually told him to have a great day. He checked the bag before leaving the window. The last time he had been through the drive-through, they had given him someone else's order. The bag was warm in his hand and smelled like old grease. *That's what I get for always being in a hurry.*

He eased back out onto the highway as he sipped on the coffee. "Not half-bad," he said to himself. He drove with one hand on the wheel and put his coffee cup in the console. With his eyes on the road, of course, he reached into the bag for the Big Jack. "Goddamn it!" he swore again as he pulled out a bag of french fries. "I thought that was french fries I was smelling!" He pulled out the Big Jack, but there was no apple pie. *Twice a year I go to Jacks and they can't manage*

151

to get it right either time. I think the last time I went through, I said it would be the last time. This time I mean it. He threw the french fries out the window, knowing it would only be a matter of minutes before either the seagulls or the crows devoured them. He made a face. *Can't stand even the smell of old fry grease!* He looked in the rear-view mirror, and sure enough, three or four seagulls were already on the road, snacking on the french fries. *Well, at least the seagulls like them.* He scowled in the mirror.

He fiddled with the radio on the drive back to his house. This time, the only thing that would come in clearly was NPR. *Hmmmmm, not now,* he thought to himself, and he turned it back off and just looked out the window. You couldn't beat the views on the Oregon coast; that was a sure thing. By the time he got to the edge of town, the burger was gone and he was finishing the last dregs of his coffee. He reached for his cell phone to call Evelyn. On the fourth ring, he heard, "Hello, this is Evelyn. Please leave me a message and I will return your call as soon as possible." So he left a message that he would call her later because he was still engaged in a few things that he couldn't put off. No sense going into detail on a message. He would see her soon enough.

When he drove the car onto his driveway, the Subaru backfired like a great big fart. He saw that Colin's car was already parked on the street. He watched as Colin's lean tall body got out of his Mini Cooper. *Too funny,* he thought. *Why would a man of that size even want to drive a Mini Cooper, let alone own one?* Colin had once told him it got great gas mileage and was a good car for him to start a conversation with the ladies.

Mick got out of the Subaru and, for a second, almost kicked the door like a child. "Piece-of-shit vehicle," he mumbled. But instead he apologized to Colin for being late. "My insurance agent is in Nehalem, and then I realized I hadn't had anything to eat, so I went through the drive-through of Jacks. You ever go in there?" Before Colin could say anything, Mick said with great emphasis, "Well, don't. They screw up every time. That's only the second time I have ever gone through the drive-through, and sure enough, they got it wrong." All in the same breath, he told Colin that his insurance agent would be along in a little while also.

Colin walked up onto the porch with Mick, saying, "No problem. I actually got here a little early and fell asleep listening to music. It's all good."

That was the best thing about Colin's personality, Mick thought. He was always upbeat and easygoing. He could recall a couple of dark, gloomy kind of events that had involved Colin's sister, but Colin just took things in stride. He was just one of those types of people you could depend on in any given situation. Even one as nasty as this. "Well, be prepared. Don't say I didn't warn you." He opened the door and let Colin be the first one through the door.

"Holy shit!" Colin said. Followed by, "'Scuse me. You weren't just a kidding when you said things were a shambles. I thought you might be exaggerating a little bit, but you were not kidding, man. This is a mess! Who did you piss off, anyway?" He gave Mick a little eyebrow action as he walked around, checking all the damage downstairs.

"Honestly, Colin," Mick said, "I really believe this is all related to Carla's murder."

Colin looked at him a little skeptically.

"You remember my neighbor Carla, the gal who I found dead on the floor a week or so ago?" Mick said with some emphasis. Mick just let Colin roam through the house. He couldn't bear to do it again. Mick knew Colin had gotten to the bedroom when he heard a loud noise and a slight retching sound. "Ooops," he said and got up to go into the bedroom. He found Colin standing over the remains of the shit filled linen that was still in the middle of the floor.

"Wow, now that is downright nasty," he said. "That's not dog shit, that's human shit. I can tell the difference."

Mick gave him a sideways glance and wanted to say, "No shit, Sherlock," but thought the better of it. Colin didn't always understand Mick's cynicism.

Colin continued talking, anyway. "My younger sister had a Great Dane once, and that dog could shit like an elephant! Swear to God. You needed a garbage bag practically when you took it for a walk. Which, trust me, was seldom. Never saw anything like it. 'Course, it could have been the hamburger and rice patties she fed him." Colin looked around the room. "Wow, sure stinks in here," he said as he wrinkled his nose. "Whoever you pissed off took that crapper. I can almost guarantee it."

"Well, this is the worst of it," Mick said. "Are you sure you are up for this big of a challenge?"

Colin looked around and went into the bathroom. Mick opened the medicine cabinet and told him that was where he found the little cut-off finger. Colin smiled slightly and looked at Mick. "Well, you know, if the price is right, bro. I can do anything." And he slapped Mick on the back.

Mick looked at him and sighed. "I will pay you fifty dollars an hour if you will start tomorrow. I have to make sure Tim takes a report for the insurance company, though. I don't want you to touch anything until he gets here. That's why I left everything the way it was when I found it. Except for the finger, of course. I let Officer Randy take that with him. Along with a little of the shit." Mick glanced at Colin. "I will give you carte blanche to get whatever supplies you need. I have an account at the Home Depot in Warrenton, but that means going there, so you will need a good supply list before you head out. You can go to the local hardware store if you run out of something, but only if absolutely necessary. You know how much more expensive they are. I know I need a couple of new doors, and make sure that even the bedroom door has a lock on it, maybe a better-quality door. I always lock my door at night when I am home, but it looked like this one kicked in pretty easily, and it wasn't even locked. Obviously, most of this damage was done out of spite or in anger, because I can't find anything of value missing. Not that I really have much of value, anyway. Not sure if this is some kind of a warning or just a psychopath on a rampage, but I want to be better prepared."

"That's pretty creepy about the finger," Colin said. "Do you think it was a man's or a woman's finger?"

Mick glanced at Colin and said, "Definitely a woman's finger. I could detect a little bit of red nail polish on the cuticle, and there was a thin white band where a ring had been. Plus, it was a small finger, too dainty for most men."

"Okay," Colin said. "I will take back what I said about you banging the wrong woman. This looks like some pretty serious stuff. Although, I have a couple of friends that, if you looked sideways at their girlfriends, you might be in a world of hurt. Me, nah. Life is too short to get this pissed off. This took a lot of energy."

Just then, they both turned toward the bedroom door as they heard the doorbell ring. Mick looked at Colin. "Well, at least something works," he said and went down the hallway.

Mick could hear Tim holler, "Anyone in here?"

He and Colin went back into the living area. He introduced the insurance agent to Colin. Tim looked around, taken aback by the mess. Colin told Mick he would come back in the morning with some stuff to start a basic cleanup, and a notepad to write down what he would need to get in the way of supplies. Mick told Colin to go ahead and go. He asked Tim if he would mind giving him a ride back to the office, and Tim told him that would be no problem. Colin said goodbye to both men, and they could hear him whistling as he walked to his car.

Mick shook his head. "Nothing really rattles that kid, I swear to God."

Tim had pretty much the same reaction as Colin but said it more politically correct. "Wow, Mick, you outdid yourself on this one. Who did you say you pissed off?"

Mick shook his head for the third time and asked, "Why does everyone think I pissed somebody off? Maybe there is some other reason that my truck was stolen and my house was ransacked." He observed Tim's rather-skeptical gaze over the top of his glasses. He told him he had no idea but doubted this was related to any woman he had been with recently. He started to show Tim through the house. This was the fourth time he had had to look at his house in shambles.

"Let's get this over with, Tim," Mick said. "I will show you through, and then you can go back through and write what you need to for your report. I am not sure I can handle going over it again. Ya know, I have looked at other people's wrecked places, but this is more personal. It's mine. So now I know what it means when someone says they feel like they were violated. I will be in the kitchen if you need anything."

With that said, Mick felt totally exhausted, and he went to find a clean chair to sit on and a cold beer to sip on while he took a little break and waited for Tim to finish his inspection.

Chapter 25

After Tim had made an assessment of the damages and taken pictures, it was 6:00 p.m. Mick walked with him out onto the porch. Tim looked at Mick with a grim expression. "There is a significant amount of damage in your house, Mick. I'm no expert, but even I can tell there is probably at least forty thousand dollars' worth of damages at a minimum. However, if you have your friend do the work, you might be able to make up the amount you have as a deductible. There is nothing in your policy that states you have to have a licensed contractor. We look at the replacement costs, and the rest is up to you. Like I've said before, we love taking your money, but giving it back is a whole other ball game," Tim said. "Are you going to go back and stay in Tillamook?"

"Yeah," Mick answered. "I can't stay here, that's for sure. I cleaned up the crap by just throwing the whole mess out. At least whoever it was did not get into the garage, so I can use my washer and dryer. I'll let Colin take care of the rest. So it's okay if he gets started tomorrow?"

"Looks like the sooner, the better for you," Tim said. "I will give you a call if anything else comes up. The only thing I can think of is that the company might have a hard time swallowing the fact that you have had two claims in under two weeks. It might look suspicious to them, but I will try to explain the situation. I don't think they will ask for anyone else to come by, and if they do, they can send someone. Doesn't mean you can't get started on the work. They can also check the police record if they have any questions about authenticating the claim."

"Well, thanks for coming by as quickly as you did, Tim. I really appreciate it. I will be staying at the Little Salmon for a few days, I guess," Mick told him.

"Oh, I know something I forgot to mention." Tim turned around as he was walking toward his car. "Save your receipts. The insurance company will actually reimburse you for your hotel stay and a twenty-five-dollar-a-day food cost. I know that's not much, but it's better than nothing. I will try to speed things up, but don't expect any reimbursements for a month or so. These things all take time. Have Colin save all the receipts from anything he purchases as well, and keep track of his time. It all helps in case the amount you spend goes over what the company had figured on. It's all a numbers game, like so much stuff is nowadays."

Mick had left the front door open to air the stench out of the house. He closed the door after Tim left and leaned against the door-frame with a sigh. He looked up at the ceiling. *Why me?* he thought.

As Tim drove away, Mick pulled his cell phone out of his pocket and checked for messages. He had muted the phone while he was showing Tim around the house. Nothing. It was odd that he hadn't heard from Evelyn after the last message he had left, but maybe she had gotten busy or even went out of town. It wasn't like he knew her habits that well. He got into the Subaru, but it took him three key turnovers before the damn thing finally started. *Piece of crap,* he thought as he drove out onto the street. He decided to just drive by her house before he went to get something to eat. He was hoping she was around but maybe just busy and didn't have her phone nearby.

As he drove over to Evelyn's house, he played over in his mind, for the hundredth time, all the recent mishaps and events that had taken place the past couple of weeks. Carla, Tom, Wanda, Mark all had to be involved somehow. The newspaper clippings he had found in Mark's house had at least pointed in that direction. And when he had seen Mark laid out on the floor, albeit a little gray around the gills, he bore a strong resemblance to Wanda. They both had the same wide eyes and small nose, and he would bet money that they had the same hair color, but Wanda just happened to color hers.

Where in the hell was Wanda now, and did she leave before or after Mark died? That was something he was determined to find out.

Mick arrived at Evelyn's house without realizing he had actually driven there. He had been totally lost in thought. He shook his head as he got out of the car. *I have got to get my shit more together,* he thought ruefully. *I never used to have these senior moments. Too much on my plate, I guess.* He stood for a moment and looked up at Evelyn's house. He could make out a dim light coming from what he remembered was her bedroom window. Her car was parked in the driveway. He looked at the time on his cell phone. It was almost seven o'clock, and it was already pitch-black. There was no other light except from the streetlamp, and that was almost a block down the street. There was a dense fog that had descended in the time it had taken him to drive here. *If you don't like wind, rain, fog, and damp, don't move to the Oregon Coast,* he thought. It was now even difficult to see her front steps.

The fog was intimidating. He always felt like something was going to jump out at him. He had felt like that since he was a kid, and his cousin had done that very thing to him. Scared the crap out of him. And he couldn't shake the feeling, even at this age. His mom had taken him and his twelve-year-old cousin, Tommy, to the Oregon coast for a vacation. He had never seen the beach before. He had grown up in the flat wheat filled Midwest. He and Tommy were so excited to go down on the beach and check things out, but his mom was taking her sweet time getting ready. He remembered she had to make some kind of fancy drink in a tall cup with a lid, and then she couldn't find her book or where she had put her sunglasses. He and Tommy were ready to leave her there, but she yelled at them, telling them if they didn't show some patience, they wouldn't be going to the beach at all. So they danced around until she was finally ready. They left her settled on a blanket, with a big rock to lean her back on. She had her drink, her book, some cheese and crackers, and they were dying to go down by the water.

He remembered how the sun had been shining and they were running around, splashing in the waves and tossing the frisbee. They were playing a game of twenty tosses. Whoever caught the most in midair had to buy the other one ice cream. Of course, his mom would be the one buying, but that didn't matter. It was the sport that counted. Tommy was a bit of a porker, and he loved ice cream. All of a sudden, this heavy, damp fog settled all around them. The sun was obliterated, and he could no longer even see his cousin. He called out for him, but there was no answering call. It was like he was the only one left on the beach, and it felt like a foreign land. He turned around but couldn't tell if he was facing the ocean or the rocks, where he had left his mom. He remembered how frightened he had felt. He called for his cousin again, but again there was no answer. He started walking toward the rocks but had miscalculated, and a freezing-cold wave hit him up to his knees. He almost peed his pants, and he started yelling, "Tommy!" and "Where are you?" He turned around again and headed away from the water. He started to run but then heard his mom's voice calling his name.

"Micky, where are you?" she kept hollering, and he walked toward her voice.

He started to relax, knowing his mom was nearby and he would be near her in a matter of minutes. All of a sudden, something jumped out of the fog, with a growl, right in front of him. He let out a bloodcurdling scream, and this time he did pee his pants. He looked up, and there was his cousin, right in front of his face, laughing hysterically. Mick remembered how totally pissed off he was at his cousin, but before he could decide what to do, his mom came up and pulled him to her chest. She was shaking, and all he could do at that moment was bury his face into her warm embrace. He felt some satisfaction when he heard her angry screams at Tommy for scaring him that way.

To this day, he tried to stay away from the fog at all costs.

Mick could feel himself give a shiver. The memory of that day came back like it was yesterday.

Mick opened the car door and reached across the seat. He still had his flashlight, and he had remembered to put new batteries in it on his way back from Pine Lake. Just like a good Boy Scout, always be prepared. He felt under the seat, where he had put his 9mm. He didn't anticipate anything being wrong, but no sense in taking any chances, he thought. Something didn't feel right, but it could be the fog making his mind do tricks and distorting his surroundings.

He made his way up the sidewalk, up the stairs, and onto the front porch. Even the flashlight wasn't a big help in this much fog. He knocked on the door and waited a few seconds before he remembered she had a doorbell. *Duh,* he thought. The doorbell made a long croaking sound, like a bullfrog would make. Only people living at the beach would have their doorbell sound like a wetland creature. He called out Evelyn's name as loudly as he could, but he didn't see any windows open, anyway, where she might be able to hear him. Silence all around. He felt himself shiver again. *Damn creepy,* he thought.

He put his hand on the doorknob, and as he did, the door opened. He hadn't realized in the dark that the door wasn't completely latched. It pushed open easily. He pushed it open further, calling out Evelyn's name as he did so. He walked further into the house, but by this time he had his 9mm out of the back of his pants, safety off and ready to go. He wasn't taking any chances. He called Evelyn's name louder this time.

As he walked slowly, making his way into the living room, he shone the flashlight along the floor and walls as he walked. *Nothing amiss here,* he thought. He shone the light down the short hallway into the kitchen. His first thought was, *Oh no! Not again.* He walked into the kitchen and flicked on the ceiling light. He looked down at the floor at a pair of eyes looking straight at him, but he knew those eyes would never see anything again.

Chapter 26

Mick swore, along with letting out a loud groan. Evelyn was lying neatly on the floor, seeming to have lain down to take a nap. Not unlike the way he had found Carla. He looked around the kitchen. Nothing appeared to be out of place. Her clothes were not rumpled. Her hair was in place. She had makeup and lipstick on. There were no signs of a struggle. He bent down to get a closer look. She really did appear to be looking up at him with a question mark of an expression on her face. Her eyes were wide open. He had not noticed before how they looked violet in color. He had thought it was because she wore a lavender-colored eye shadow, but her eyes were really a violet shade themselves. He could not even make out any signs of trauma. Her hands were at her sides. Even her nail polish was a lavender color. *Poor thing,* he thought. She was such a beautiful lady. Mick felt slightly sick to his stomach. He couldn't help but think, if he hadn't gotten involved with her, maybe this would not have happened.

He got off his knee, stood up, and leaned against the counter. He looked around the room again. Everything looked just like he had seen it the other night when he had been there. Except there were no signs of a meal being prepared or of wine being poured. It looked like a kitchen out of a coastal magazine. Blue and teal colors, eclectic, and cute.

He walked around the kitchen and stopped at the wine bar located around the corner on the way into the living room. *Well, my mistake,* he thought. There had been wine poured. On a silver tray sat a bottle of opened red wine and two glasses. He looked at the label, and it was the same red wine that he had drunk at her house just a few nights ago. It seemed like forever ago, though, he thought. She had told him she liked the red blend best. The bottle was still full. Apparently hadn't gotten past the breathing stage. *She had, though,* he thought glumly as he looked at her again. He wondered if she had gotten his message and had opened the wine in anticipation of his coming by. Now he felt even worse, if that were possible. He didn't really think of himself as a shit heel, but he sure was beginning to. He felt her death was his responsibility somehow.

He slammed his hand down on the counter. If only he had gotten here sooner. He ran his hand through his hair, hoping for some type of epiphany to miraculously appear. *What the hell kind of crazy nonsense is this, anyway?* He felt like it was his fault but also felt like he stumbled into something that was now out of control, like going down the rabbit hole as in *Alice in Wonderland.*

Total déjà vu here, he thought as he got his cell phone to call 911. She was obviously not revivable at this point.

Unlike his house and Carla's house, her house appeared to have nothing out of place. He decided to take a little look around before calling 911. *Could it be three times a charm and I will get this all figured out before something else happens?* He walked to the back of the house, where he knew her bedroom was. He stood by the bed and couldn't help but feel sad at the thought that it wasn't more than a week ago he had actually been in this very bed with a very alive, classy, sexual lady who, at this point, was now no more. He considered himself a hard-core, stoic guy who usually took things in stride, but for some reason, he felt an emotion he couldn't quite comprehend. "Christ," he muttered as he wiped the wetness out of his eyes.

He turned away from the bed, but an open book on the night-stand caught his eye. He looked closer at the book. *Crime and Punishment* by Fyodor Dostoevsky. An odd choice for someone like Evelyn, but they had discussed the book the night he had been at her house. It had been a required reading for him while in the academy. For her, she was trying to "broaden her mind" with things she had never thought or read about before. He picked the book up, and a small piece of paper flittered out onto the floor. Mick bent over to retrieve it and noted his name was at the top of the note. Underneath his name, it read, "Tell Mick about the maroon car following me yesterday," and then underneath that it had the words *couscous*, *celery*, and *maraschino cherries*. He turned the note over in his hand, but there was nothing else written on it. It looked like a partial grocery list with a note reminding her to tell him something.

Mick just remembered that Colin had told him that someone named Evelyn had called and didn't want to bother him but asked to say that she thought someone had been following her. Damn him, he wished he had taken the time to stop in last night instead of going to the hotel. She might still be alive if he had. *What the hell,* he thought again as he reached into his pocket for his cell phone. "This is getting old and very weird." He sighed.

Calling the precinct number was getting old also. He knew they would tell him to call 911, but what was the point? It was obvious she was dead. There was nothing they could do for Evelyn at this point. It was now after 8:00 p.m., and good ole Randy's voice came on the line.

"Randy," Mick said. "You are not going to believe this."

"Whoa, man, you calling me after I just saw you not too long ago? Trust me, I can believe anything you tell me at this point. Who is it this time?"

"Well, that's about the size of it," Mick said with exasperation in his voice. "I came by to see Evelyn, Carla's friend. I told you about her." *Well, not all of it,* he thought. "Anyway, I wanted to see how she was doing, and she's not."

"What do you mean 'she's not'?" Randy asked. "I mean, she's lying on her kitchen floor, no blood, no disarray, no break-in, no muss, no fuss. Like she lay down to take a nap on the floor. Oh, except her eyes are wide open. I was able to walk in the front door. The only light on in the house was from a table lamp in her back bedroom. I can't find anything out of order. It's kind of bizarre, to say the least."

"Christ, Mick, what next? Stay right where you are. I will call the ME and be right there. Text me her address, will ya?"

"Sure thing," Mick answered. "Not sure why you are still on duty, but glad you are, man."

Randy made a snorting sound in the phone as he put on his uniform vest and jacket. "Well, it's like this," he said as he headed out the door. "The chief is on his third vacation this year, and as soon as he left, that lazy ass Phil Patrone called in sick. So here I am on my second night of overtime this week. Not that I can't use the money. I can, ya know. But my wife is pissed. We were supposed to go to a play tonight. Well, see ya in fifteen." With that, Randy hung up and Mick was left looking around the room again, with his eyes resting on Evelyn.

He moved into the living room to wait for Randy.

It actually took Randy less than fifteen minutes to get to Evelyn's house. Mick met him at the door, and he walked him into the kitchen, where Evelyn was lying. Randy had talked to Evelyn at length after Carla's death but hadn't really found anything solid to follow up on except for the information on the stepson, Mark. That turned out to be a dead end. *No pun intended,* he thought wryly. *Coincidental that now Evelyn is dead too?* he wondered. Randy made a cursory examination of the body and did a walk-through of the house but didn't want to touch anything until the medical examiner had arrived. He sat and reviewed everything with Mick while they waited.

It only took the medical examiner a half hour to get to the house. Randy told Mick to go ahead and go on to his hotel. He had called in someone from forensics, but since they were located in Portland, it would take a couple of hours for them to show up. Randy said he had to stay but Mick didn't, so he might as well get some sleep tonight. "I'll let you know if anything unusual shows up, and you do the same, you hear?"

Mick looked a little lost but understood the drill. "Something tells me this is going to lead back to Carla's brother, Thomas Hardcastle. Did you get a chance to check him out?" Mick asked, reluctant to leave.

"No more than what you already had told me," Randy said. "I need to do a little more checking, and I hadn't heard back from the prison warden yet. I was kind of waiting to see what he could tell me before I wasted my time on something that had already been checked out. Don't worry, I will keep you posted. Now, get out of here." Randy practically pushed Mick away.

Mick got back in the Subaru and headed to the hotel. He looked in his rearview mirror when he got out onto 101. He was too preoccupied to notice a pair of headlights that followed him out onto the highway. It only took him about fifteen minutes to get into Tillamook, but just as he turned into the hotel parking lot, he thought better of it. *What the hell,* he thought. *There is no way I can lie down and go to sleep now. I am too wound up!* He parked the car, locked it, and walked to the same tavern he had been in the night before. He had trouble believing it had just been last night that he had been there.

When he walked into the bar, he couldn't help but look for Cathleen, but there were only a couple of local fishermen sitting at the end of the bar. And then a couple of guys playing pool in the back of the bar. Mick sat down and asked Chuck what the special was and if there was anything left. Chuck was engrossed in an episode of *NCIS*. Probably about the third time he had seen it, Mick thought. Chuck didn't take his eyes off the TV as he said, "Special was a Reuben and fries, but it's all gone now. Had a group in after bowling, and they gobbled it all up. I got some chili left from yesterday and some corn bread. Will that work?"

Just then, a commercial came on and Chuck took a Sierra Nevada Pale Ale out of the cooler and sauntered down to Mick's end of the bar. He put the beer down in front of Mick, and Mick answered him, "Yeah, sounds great, but better give me a double shot of Jack Daniel's too. I've had a rough day."

Chuck poured a generous double of Jack and set that in front of Mick also. "Sorry, man," he said. "Want to talk about it?"

Mick looked at him skeptically. He knew whatever he said would be twisted with how Chuck heard it, and then twisted again as the word got around town. "Nah," Mick said. "Better not at this point. You will hear about it soon enough, probably on the local news. Not sure it will make the eleven o'clock, but it will the morning." Mick rested his head in his hands, but not until after he downed the Jack Daniel's. "Whew, I needed that," he said, barely audible.

Chuck went into the little kitchen to heat up the chili as the front door opened. Mick looked over his shoulder, hoping to see Cathleen come into the bar. One bright light in a dark day he could only hope. To his disappointment, it was some guy he had never seen before. Mick took a few seconds to size the guy up. He always liked to know what he might be up against if an opportunity arose that he needed to be aware of. Slightly built older man, probably about sixty. He wore a baseball cap pulled low over his eyes and a fisherman's type of raincoat with a pair of lightweight rubber boots. He had a salt-and-pepper, neatly trimmed beard. *Not a local fisherman,* Mick thought. *They wouldn't be caught dead in a jacket and boots like that. Besides that, the local guys all have scraggly gray beards. Not a one of them knows how to shave.*

He glanced at the two sitting at the end of the bar. They were deep in conversation about the latest episode of *River Monsters.* Now you could tell they were local guys. One wore a sweatshirt two sizes too big, with big lettering saying "Eat Me" on the front, and the other one still had his fishing waders on and his hat had a Garibaldi Marina logo on the bill. They both had long scraggly gray beards. The guy who just came in the door had a long gray/black ponytail pulled through the back of his baseball cap. The two fishermen did not even glance up when the newcomer sat at the opposite end of the bar from Mick.

Just then, Chuck set the chili and corn bread in front of him. The smell immediately got his mouth to watering. Lots of onion and melted cheese. "Yummy," he said to himself and picked up the oversize spoon and started to eat. Before Chuck got very far away, though, he asked him for another Jack Daniel's. *What the hell,* Mick thought to himself. *Might as well be comfortable.* He watched as Chuck approached the newcomer, then brought him the Jack and a Coke. He noted Chuck trying to engage the stranger in small talk, but it looked like the guy just wanted to be left alone, because all Mick could hear were a couple of grunts. Then the guy got up and headed for the men's room.

Chuck ambled back down the bar toward Mick. After all, those *NCIS* shows had a lot of commercials. "Surly bastard," he heard

Chuck say. Mick didn't pay much attention to what Chuck said. He thought half the guys who came into the bar were surly bastards, especially if they didn't want to listen to his blah, blah, blah politics or whatever his choice of conversation was for the day. Chuck had tried to get Mick involved in some of his political discussions, but Mick usually kept pretty quiet. The less people knew how he thought, the better. Chuck was also known for getting pretty worked up over his constitutional rights, as he would often say.

Just then, Mick heard a loud crack and a loud, "You son of a bitch!" He swiveled around on his barstool and watched as the younger of the two guys who had been playing pool swatted the older guy up the side of the head with his cue stick. The cue stick broke in two, and blood started oozing down the older guy's face. He yelled an obscenity that Mick couldn't make out and put his hand up to the side of his face. He was attempting to stop the blood, while the younger kid started screaming all kinds of obscenities along with brandishing the broken end of the cue stick.

Mick jumped off the barstool and started toward the injured man, while Chuck quickly came around the end of the bar with his own weapon in hand. He was brandishing a large metal baseball bat over his head. Mick knew Chuck didn't like to involve the police unless it was absolutely necessary. So nine times out of ten, Chuck would handle the situation himself. Not always in the best interest of the customer, however. When he threatened the kid with the baseball bat, the kid seemed to calm down quickly. He even seemed slightly appalled by his behavior. He looked at the older guy with a look of shock on his face.

In the meantime, Mick had grabbed a bunch of napkins and held them against the guy's face as he led him to the nearest booth to sit down. Chuck sat the kid in another booth and gave him an if-looks-could-kill look, then went into the kitchen to retrieve a couple of clean bar towels to use in place of the napkins, which were not doing a very good job of staunching the flow of blood, anyway. While Mick was mopping up blood and Chuck was having a talk with the kid, the newcomer came out of the bathroom and slouched out the door without anyone noticing he had left.

Chapter 27

Chuck asked the older man if he wanted to have the police called, while the kid, in some kind of remorseful state, started blubbering. "Man, I'm sorry, Uncle Bill. I didn't mean it. You just got me so pissed off. You know how riled up I can get when you just mention Liz's name. She's not a whore, she's just a little mixed up right now."

The man the kid had called Bill was sitting, holding his head in his hands. He looked up and just glared at the kid, while Chuck went to get ice in a bag for Bill to apply to his wounded head.

"Jesus H. Christ, you knothead!" Bill had looked around the ice bag he was holding. "I was just telling you I saw her down off Washington Street with some older guy. When are you going to just let it go?"

"I can't," the kid said with a pained expression as he plopped opposite his uncle in the booth. "I am soooooo sorry, Uncle Bill. I don't know what gets into me, except just the mention of her name with some other guy makes my blood boil and then I just snap."

"You snap, all right. You dumbass, look what you did to me." Bill removed the ice bag and pointed at his head. He then turned toward Mick, who was still standing there, ready to help out if needed. Mick figured the guy was probably about his age. "Do you think I need stitches?" Bill looked up at Mick as he removed the bloody napkins and cloth from his head.

Mick took a closer look at the wound, which was now only producing a trickle of blood. "Well, ya probably have about an inch and half open wound, so it would be a good idea, but it's not like anyone will see a scar there. Your hair will cover it."

Just then, Chuck came back with a couple of clean towels and handed them to Bill, who had closed his eyes and sighed. "Thanks," he told Chuck. "Can you bring me a double bourbon, neat? My head is starting to throb. Anybody got any painkillers?" Bill groaned.

Chuck looked at the wound also and told Bill, "You should probably go get stitches, but if you are determined not to, I have some butterfly Band-Aids in the kitchen. I can probably fix you up with those."

Bill looked up at Chuck. "What the hell are butterflies?" he asked.

"Well, they are sticky strips that are used to hold a laceration together. They work pretty good, and you just wait for them to come off on their own. You might have to just shave a small bit of your hair for them to stick onto your forehead."

Bill agreed with the butterfly idea. He did not want to go to the ER, especially now that he had no medical insurance. So Chuck went back into the kitchen to retrieve his first aid kit.

Mick looked at both of the men and pointed to a scar below his right ear. "See this scar here? Chuck put butterfly Band-Aids on a wound I received from a flying beer bottle about ten years ago. Good as new. Besides, scars give us a little more character. Chuck has bandaged up more than a few men in the past thirty years or so, haven't you, Chuck?" Then Mick went on to say, "Someone like your nephew here had too much to drink one night and started picking on this old man that was having a drink, minding his own business. Well, that didn't sit too well with me, so I started to calmly ask him to leave the old guy alone. Well, his beer bottle came out of nowhere and caught me just below my ear. I was lucky that Chuck was nearby, since I was so taken by surprise he almost got another swing in, but Chuck here managed to sideswipe him first. Then he threw his ass out on the street. He patched me up after that. Good as new too."

"Well, I don't need character," Bill told Mick. "But I don't mind if you help me out and bandage this thing. I would appreciate it." He looked at the kid. "If you weren't my sister's kid, I would beat the living crap out of you. Now, pay our tab and make sure you include enough money to cover the stick you broke. You should be sober enough to drive me home. It will be a cold day in hell before I take you out for a beer again. Good-for-nothing son of a bitch, anyway."

Mick had gone back to sit at the bar but watched as the kid took some money out of his jacket pocket. "Will this be enough to cover everything?" he asked Chuck, holding up some bills.

Chuck was just finishing applying a little Neosporin to the wound. He took the money from the kid. "Yeah," he said. "That was one of my cheaper cue sticks. You need not come back in here for a while, though." He stood up and said to Bill, "The butterflies should hold, but there is nothing that a bandage will stick to, so it will be open. Just keep it clean and it should be fine. You're going to have one hell of a shiner in the morning, though. Your eye is already turning black-and-blue."

The kid went to help his uncle up from the booth, but Bill shook him off disgustedly. As they headed toward the front door, Bill said, "Much obliged to you, Chuck." He cuffed the kid up the side of his head, called him a few more choice names, and then they walked out of the door.

Mick looked at Chuck and told him he missed his calling. Chuck explained that a few years in the Army as a medic had done the trick. "That was nothing."

Mick looked at him with some admiration and said, "Well, I did not know you had been in the service, Chuck." Mick tipped his beer glass and said, "Well, thank you for your service. I think that was enough excitement for me for one night. How about a nightcap and then I will be on my way too? I gotta be up and out early in the morning."

Despite how tired he felt and how much he knew he needed to do, the lonely hotel bed did not entice him that much, so he ended up shooting the breeze with Chuck for another half an hour before he did head for the door. "I guess we pretty much solved the world's problems for one evening, huh, Chuck? See ya in a few days." Mick gave a wave and walked out into the night.

When he was outside, he stood for a minute and looked up at the sky. There were a few stars, and the moon was full, which was a good thing, because there were no other lights in the parking lot.

Jeez, it would be dark as pitch, he thought, *if the moon weren't shining.* He thought about all he needed to do in the next few days as he walked back to the hotel.

As he stepped into the small room, exhaustion hit him like a ton of bricks. His head had no sooner hit the pillow than he was in la-la land. He hadn't even noticed the small dark-colored car in the parking lot. There was a man slunk down in the driver's seat, talking on his cell phone.

Mick slept hard, and when he opened his eyes and glanced at the small clock radio, he practically bolted up out of bed. It was almost nine o'clock. He could only remember a couple of times in his whole life that he had slept that late before. Normally, his inner clock went off and he was up by six. *Well, most days,* he thought as his mind pictured a particular naked woman. He smiled as he swung around and put his feet on the floor. He hit the bedside table, knocking the water bottle onto its side, which started to spill all over his cell phone. "Crap," he said under his breath and reached over to retrieve the phone from the puddle of water. I just upgraded the damn thing. "Why didn't I spend the little extra for a waterproof case? Just like why I didn't spend the extra money for a better security system for the damn truck!" He picked up the phone and dried it on the bedsheet. He turned it on. What he really needed was waterproof, shatterproof, insured phone that it didn't matter what he did with it; he would still have something to use. *Next time,* he thought ruefully as he headed to the bathroom. *No time for a shower this morning, let alone waiting for a cup of coffee. I will just have to grab something later.*

It only took him about five minutes to wash up, brush his teeth, and get dressed in yesterday's clothes. *Oh well, they hadn't really gotten very dirty.* He gave himself a cursory once-over in the mirror, winked at his reflection, and then went out the front door. He looked up at the gray sky. *Looks like rain, as usual,* he thought as he got into the Subaru. This time the car started on the first turn of the key. The windshield was wet from the fog and the drizzle, and he hit the wiper blades' button. Nothing. He tried again. Nothing. He tried different speeds. Nothing again. "Oh, for Christ's sake!" he said, fuming, as he got back out and took his sleeve to wipe down the windshield so he could see to drive to the Ford dealership. He had told his buddy Todd he would be there when they opened. That was nine o'clock, not nine thirty like it was now. He was thinking how he used to always get up without the help of an alarm, but now it seemed harder and harder to get out of bed at all. *Must be getting older.*

He shook his head and turned on the radio even though it was only five miles to the dealership. He drove through the Coffee Hut on the edge of town. It had been in business for years but now advertised a bikini barista. *Hmmm, something new in town,* he thought as he drove up to the window. "I'll have a double almond latte with a few coffee beans sprinkled on top of the whipped cream." All said while he was not looking up but looking at the console, where he had a few one-dollar bills. He found what he wanted and looked up at the open window. "Holy mother," he whispered as he did a double take at the gal looking down on him. She was packed into a bikini. Actually, all 250-plus pounds of her was trying to escape from the bikini. He could have heard the cry, "Let me out of here!" The sight was enough to scare even the most desperate of men. She offered him a wide smile as she leaned even farther out the window to hand him his latte. *Whoa, girl, something is going to fall out there, and I do not want to be here to catch it!* He told her to keep the change as he churned a little gravel leaving the parking lot.

Chapter 28

As he drove the short distance to the Ford dealership, he mused over the sight of all that flesh in that bikini. *Why would Jim do that to himself, or anyone else, for that matter?* He knew Jim Carlson. Not really personally knew him, but he knew who he was. He was a hard-to-miss kind of guy himself. He had owned the coffee drive-through for about eight years, as far as Mick could remember. He was a big, beefy guy, about midforties, and his shirt never seemed to be big enough to cover his gut. He was the kind of guy that you steered clear of if he was in a bar. He tended to like to throw that weight around, and he wasn't very nice to his women. He would have to have a meaty gal, or anything less would be crushed under his weight. *Wonder how many women stop there for their morning coffee,* Mick mused. *I bet not many.* He also wondered how many men that much flesh had scared away from the Coffee Hutch. *Well, this was the Oregon coast, not a little unlike Portland,* he thought. Keep Oregon weird. *Jim must be going a little bit nuts.* He took another sip of the latte and couldn't help but sigh. *They do make the best lattes for twenty miles around, but who wants to see that while they're just trying to wake up and start their day?*

His friend Todd met him at the door of the small dealership, cup of coffee in one hand and an apple fritter in the other. "Hey, Mick, good to see you. Sorry, one of the guys stopped at Loni's bakery on the way into work, and you know me, couldn't resist," he said as he held the fritter up to his mouth and took a big bite. He gave Mick a nod rather than a handshake and proceeded to talk with his mouth full.

Jeez, Mick thought. *Does no one have any class anymore?* Todd was actually bigger and beefier than Jim Carlson. *I wonder if he's met the barista.* Mick shook his head as he followed Todd into his miniscule office. *More like a closet,* he thought.

Todd had to move the chair before he could close the door. "I think I found what you are looking for, Mick," he said as he eased his bulk into the slightly too small chair. He turned on his computer and scrolled through some vehicles until he found what he was looking for. He turned the screen around so Mick could look also. "This baby was in Salem. We had it driven over yesterday. Some guy had wanted it, took it home for forty-eight hours, and decided it was a little too much truck for him. More than likely, his wife said he spent too much money on it and made him take it back. At least that's the story I got from the guy in Salem. It's not black, like you wanted, but a steel-gray color. It has pretty much everything else, though. Supercab, 6 1/2 box, eighteen-inch heavy-duty wheels, four-wheel drive, side rails, backup camera, and it even has the new tailgate step with lift assist. All the bells and whistles you mentioned. I don't think you can beat the price either." Todd finally ran out of salesman steam.

"How much is 'can't beat the price'?" Mick asked him.

"We have this new policy where, with enough money down, someone can take a vehicle home, try it out, and if they don't like it, they can bring it back in forty-eight hours and buy something else. Of course, we can't hold them to another one of our cars, but nine times out of ten, it works. So you can have that one for fifty thousand dollars," Todd said. "The guy put over five hundred miles on it in forty-eight hours. Can you believe that?" Todd licked some sugar off his fingers and reached into his desk for the keys. "Take it for a drive and see if you don't come back to me with your credit card in hand." He held the key out to Mick, who hadn't really said much of anything. With Todd, it was hard to get a word in edgewise, anyway. Mick took the key and stood up. Todd managed to wiggle out of his chair, and they went out to the parking lot together.

Mick spotted the truck immediately. It was a formidable-looking vehicle. He actually liked the steel-gray color, and the wheel rims were macho man, but classy too. He opened the door and stood on the running board, bouncing up and down a time or two. He sat on the seat and breathed in the new leather smell. He checked out the instrument panel. It looked like it had twice as many dials and buttons as his old truck. He put the key in the ignition, and it started with a loud turbocharger sound. *Nice,* he thought as he backed out of the parking lot using the backup camera. His last truck, he decided against the camera for running boards and a bed liner and regretted it after he backed over the neighbor's little Boston terrier. He had always hated the yippy dog, but he certainly hadn't wished it dead. He thought the neighbor was going to come unglued. She had worked herself up into an almost state of hyperventilation that Mick had had to call 911 and let them deal with her. He had tried to muster up the correct amount of contrition, but no amount worked. Needless to say, when she saw him on the street, she looked the other way. He had ended up giving her enough money to buy a dozen of the yappy dogs, but she had settled on another one of the same breed. It even looked like the same dog. He never had understood the whole dog thing. Once he learned that a woman owned a dog, he dropped her like a hot potato. They all treated them like they were their kids or something. They could never spontaneously leave for a weekend without trying to figure out who was going to watch the dog because the dog was not coming with; he always made that clear. He had learned it was just easier to not get involved with women who owned dogs. Simple as that and end of that and end of problem.

He drove the truck around a couple of blocks, then took it for a spin a little farther out of town, where he could get it up to a hundred miles an hour. *Feels good,* he thought. He turned around in the little rest area just south of Tillamook and then headed back toward the dealership. He looked in the rearview mirror and saw a little car turn around in the same spot that he had. *Hmmm.* He watched the car pick up speed but then didn't think any more about it. He was thinking about driving the truck out of the dealership today. He really liked how it drove and how he felt driving it. *A chick magnet,* he was thinking as he drove into the dealership parking lot. He hopped out of the cab with a smile on his face.

Todd was waiting in the lobby with his hands in his pockets and a grin on his face. "Well, how did you like it?" he asked but knew what the answer would be.

What self-respecting man wouldn't like it? he thought. *Well, maybe not the little pussy who brought it back, but his loss.* "I like how it feels, runs great, looks great. Can you do any better on the price?" Mick asked him.

Todd already had some printouts of comparable vehicles, and he handed them to Mick. "No, my boss said fifty thousand dollars or nothing. It's a steal, man, and you know it."

Mick looked at him with eyeballs rolling. "Yeah, a car salesman's famous line. Well, thought I would give it a try. Where do I sign?" Mick said and slapped Todd on the shoulder. "What's the commission on something like that?"

But Todd had already turned away and headed back into his cubicle to print out the paperwork.

The whole process was relatively painless. No bigwig coming to bullshit him. Much easier doing business in a small town, where everyone knew practically everyone else. It was hard to screw your neighbor, although there were those that did. They usually got theirs in the end, though. Mick finished the paperwork in under half an hour and told Todd that he would need to leave the truck at the dealership until he got back from Idaho. Todd said he was going to suggest that, anyway. He wanted the mechanic to put it through a thorough inspection, just to make sure nothing had happened to it in the last forty-eight hours. "You never know what people will do," he told Mick.

"Oh, I probably do," Mick said. "Remember, I was on the narcotic squad once upon a time."

"Oh yeah, that's right. I forgot about that," Todd told him. "Well, it's safe here on the lot until you return."

Mick told him he would probably be about three days. He put three thousand dollars on his credit card, signed over the insurance check, and his loan for the balance had already gone through by the time they were done bullshitting. *Easy-peasy,* Mick thought. *Man, I wish I could figure out a way to get that piece-of-shit Subaru back with-*

out me having to go myself. He scratched his head. He couldn't come up with a better plan at this point. He shook Todd's hand and told him he would be back for the car by the week's end.

As soon as he left, his phone rang, and he looked at the number. It was the local police precinct. "Hello," Mick said and put the phone on speaker.

"Hey, Mick, it's me, Randy. Are you sitting down?"

"Well, yeah," Mick said. "I am in the car, driving, but I have you on speaker now."

"Well, that finger that was in the medicine cabinet, it wasn't hard to figure out whom it belonged to," Randy told him.

"How's that?" Mick asked. He was picturing the finger in his mind as he drove.

Randy started, "Well, the woman Evelyn, who was murdered—"

But he was interrupted by Mick. "Oh no, what about her?" Mick asked. He could feel himself tense up, and his knuckles were turning white as he gripped the steering wheel too hard.

"Well, it was her finger that was left in your medicine cabinet. After you left, we took a closer look at her, and one of her hands was slightly under her clothes and there was very little blood so you wouldn't have noticed it. Anyway, her finger had been cut off."

Mick felt a little shock wave run through his body and found he had to pull over to the side of the road. He leaned his head onto the steering wheel and asked Randy if they had discovered what specifically had killed her.

Chapter 29

Randy told Mick that there was really nothing concrete they had to go on at this point, the whole thing being pretty bizarre. Nothing stolen that they could tell. Nothing amiss. "Why cut her finger off? Unless it was just to send you some weird message. Is there anything you haven't told me that perhaps you should let me in on?" Randy said to Mick. "Whoever killed her managed to cauterize her finger. That was why there was no blood at the scene. It will take us a while to get more information from forensics. You know how those guys are in Portland. Plus, they are up to their earlobes in murder investigations that occur in the city alone. I can tell you, though, that there were no marks on her body that I could detect, and I stayed with the team while they did a pretty thorough investigation at the crime scene. I will keep you posted when I hear something, but you do the same, you hear?" Randy hung up abruptly, causing Mick to just stare at the phone in his hand.

"Thanks, Randy," he said to the dead airspace, thinking, *Evelyn's finger.* That had not been expected. Poor woman. Mick couldn't help but put some blame on himself. Not that it made a tinker's damn. It would not bring her back, but if it hadn't been for his interference, she might still be here. "Damn," he swore as he brought his hand down on the steering wheel. He looked at his speedometer and realized he had slowed to about forty while he had been talking on the phone. He sped up to sixty just as a small maroon car passed him, going about eighty miles an hour.

Mick drove for miles in the quiet car. The fact that he didn't have a radio didn't really bother him. His mind was turning over and over different scenarios, none of which made much sense. What he really needed to do was to see if he could track down Mark's sister, and the only place he knew to do that was to start back in Pine Lake, Idaho. Maybe she left more of a trail than she suspected. In his experience, it never failed to surprise him how stupid people could really be. You could almost count on them to get too cocky and slip up somewhere. He would start at the local precinct there and work his way outward. It was the only way he knew how to do things, anyway. Hopefully, in a small town like that, they wouldn't be wary of strangers with all good intentions. Mick smiled ruefully to himself. He remembered the little post office master. She had been something else, but also friendly and informative. Then again, there was Tammy. She alone would make the trip worthwhile, provided she would see him after the way he left abruptly not that long ago either.

He tried to enjoy the scenery, even though he had seen it before; there were breathtaking views along the way. The mountains were more rugged and majestic than the ones found in Oregon. Mount Hood withstanding, of course. He couldn't concentrate on anything but the repetition of what he had gone over and over already. He would stop in at the post office and see if the little postmaster had any new gossip to feed his imagination. She seemed to be a wealth of information. He had the picture he had taken of Wanda, unbeknownst to her, of course. Maybe he could show it to a few people and see if anyone had seen or heard anything unusual. He wondered why he was bothering, though. Evelyn was dead, and he had pursued Carla's death mostly to try to get some answers for her friend Evelyn. *What really was the point?* he wondered. *Is it that important to me?* He swore quietly and thought that his own stubborn, persistent personality was what usually drove him to do anything he wasn't specifically getting paid for. *If nothing else, I need to take this piece-of-crap car back to Joe's, so I might as well do a little more checking while I am there.* He thought about the time he had been with Evelyn and what a beautiful person she had been. *How terrible,* he thought.

He drove a few more miles and glanced at the gauges on the dash. *Crap!* He realized the gas gauge was below a quarter of a tank. He couldn't remember how far away the closest services were. He looked at his phone. No help there either. No service. He did remember that gas stations were few and far between on this highway. He looked in his rearview mirror and noticed a small dark-colored car that seemed to come up out of nowhere, closing in on his back bumper. "What the hell?" he said out loud. The windows were tinted so dark Mick couldn't see into the windshield, but the car appeared to be driven by someone with a ball cap pulled low over his eyes.

All of a sudden, Mick felt a jolt as the small car hit his rear bumper. Mick felt a slight chill along his spine, wondering what the hell this lunatic was up to. Mick put on his right blinker and started to slow down a little to pull off onto the side of the road. He could see a good-size shoulder up ahead. He would just let this lunatic pass him. Just then, the car behind him ran into his rear bumper again. Mick could hear the impact, along with feeling a slight whiplash this time. Mick looked in his rearview mirror, then leaned across the seat to retrieve his .38 automatic from the glove box. He had only one hand on the steering wheel at this point, and he was trying to break the car as it hit a pothole in the gravel. The small car came at him like a tank this time and hit him with such a force he dropped the gun and started to lose control of the car. He looked in horror as he couldn't right the car, and it started to careen over the embankment. There was little he could do at this point as he grabbed the steering wheel in a valiant attempt to stop its going over. He braced himself for whatever was going to happen next.

"Luck of the Irish," he breathed out as he looked out of the cracked windshield. The car happened to hit a small stand of young fir trees that were growing about twenty to thirty feet down the bank. The car just pointed in that direction, then came to a dead stop up against the trees. Mick retrieved his revolver but couldn't find his cell phone. He was frantically looking under the seat when he heard someone up on the bank calling out something. He found the cell phone wedged under the seat, but he managed a quick jerk and it was released into his hand. It now had a crack from top to bottom, and there was still no service.

He heard someone holler again, "Hey, sonny, can you hear me? Can you get out of the car? I saw that madman run you off the road. Do you need help getting out?"

Mick looked out of the window and saw a gray-haired elderly man standing up, peering down the bank. Mick yelled back up at him, "No, I seem to be okay! I think I can get out. Just give me a minute!" He found he could twist sideways, and he eased himself out of the window. He managed to secure his revolver in his hand. *No sense taking any chances.* And he put his cell phone in his back pocket. He held on to a few bushes here and there and made his way up the bank. He was totally out of breath when the elderly man reached down to grab his hand and help haul him the rest of the way up the bank onto the gravel. He stood next to the elderly man and gave him a quick once-over.

"Did you happen to get a look at whoever was driving that car? Or better yet, did you catch any license plate numbers?" Mick asked. "He seemed to come up behind me out of nowhere and just rammed my rear bumper. I have no idea why or who it was, but I could no longer control the car."

William looked Mick up and down. For injuries, Mick supposed. "Well, that was a close call, I can tell you that. I just happened to be picking up my mail from the end of my driveway when I see this guy going past like a bat out of hell. Hi, my name is William Pryor, by the way." William held out his hand for Mick to take in a handshake. The man didn't slow down as he spoke. "I had a feeling something wasn't right. I had glimpsed your car pass and then that idiot so close behind you I figured I had better follow and just see what was going on. I saw him the first time he nudged your bumper, so I sped up a little bit. Then I saw you start to pull off onto the side of the road, and I watched as he hit you over the bank. I was so shocked I practically forgot everything else. The guy took off as soon as he saw I was going to stop. I might have been able to make out a *66B* on the plate, but I wouldn't place any bets on it. He was going so fast. I am surprised the car could even run after the way he rammed your bumper. I did notice the car was either a Toyota or a small Ford, and it was maroon in color. I have no idea what year. I am no good at much car stuff. Boy, you ask my grandson anything about cars and he can tell you makes, models, and years! Drives me bonkers when I take him anywhere. He's smart as a whip, though. He's going to the University of Oregon next year. Makes me proud, he does." William seemed to finally run out of steam. He gave Mick a sheepish look. "Sorry," he said. "I can go on and on. Gets a bit lonesome after the wife died a couple a years back. Let's get back to you now."

Mick was brushing himself off and checking out his cell phone. He turned it over in his hand and looked at William. "Is there normally cell service here?" he asked William.

William went into a long dialogue about the problems he had had over the years with cell phones and then the internet in general. He ended with the fact that only one service covered this rural of an area, and it didn't happen to be the one Mick had. So he really couldn't tell if his broken phone would have service until he got to a service area that was covered. *Oh well, could be worse,* he thought.

"How far is Pine Lake from here, anyway?" he asked William.

"It's about a two-hour drive from here, and I could take you, but it's almost dark, and I don't do a lot of driving after dark anymore. So how about you come and stay at my place tonight and I will take you on into Pine Lake in the morning? I got a couple of spare bedrooms, always made up in case anyone shows up. You can bunk down for the night. I also got a landline phone. You gotta have one in these parts. So if you need to make any phone calls, you can just use the phone in my office."

Mick looked gratefully at the older man. "I sure would appreciate it," he said. "Not sure what I was going to do out here in the middle of nowhere. Makes me feel a little out of my element. I brought a duffel bag, but it's down in the trunk of the car, and I'm not sure I want to hassle with retrieving it right now."

"Hey, no problem." William stopped him. "Don't worry about it. I've got plenty of different-size clothes at the house also." William patted Mick on the shoulder. "My wife was a wonderful little hostess when she was alive. She loved nothing more than to have family and friends come and stay. She kept something for everyone, trust me. You will be fine without your duffel bag. I know the owner of the only towing company within more than a hunerd miles. I will get you set up in the morning."

Mick couldn't help but chuckle over the thought of Joe's reaction when he saw his Subaru being towed back to his junkyard. *Serves him right,* he thought.

Mick walked with William to William's pickup truck. William sure could talk, and it seemed he hardly ever stopped to take a breath. He heard all about his wife, Emily. The life on the ranch. How she didn't really take to it at first. How, after the first baby, she was a little happier. Mick found himself drifting off and even getting sleepy as William droned on.

"There's a village about an hour northeast of here called Parker. It has essentials at the gas station, but my wife kept purta near everything at the house, just in case. She liked to go to the big-box store in Boise about once a month. We hardly ever ran out of anything. I sure miss her to this day. She was my wife first, then my partner, and then my best friend. She had a stroke a few years back and never made it out of the hospital. Massive, they said it was. She was also the best dang cook in three counties. She even put out a cookbook ten years ago, now it's been. Had all sorts of dishes made with wild game. Fish, fried, flattened, and floundered. Rabbit stew, chicken stew, even squirrel stew. Can't say we ate all of them, though. She did it more for the fun of it. It sold pretty good in town to the tourists. We sure had a good life."

By now Mick couldn't wait to get out of the truck. He wondered how far away the ranch was but didn't want to seem ungrateful by asking.

Just then, they turned onto a gravel road and drove under a massive log archway complete with elk heads on each end and the name "Pryor Ranch" carved into steel. "Wow!" Mick exclaimed as he turned and looked out the window. "Beautiful," he said. "How many acres do you have here, William?"

"Well, I got purt near a thousand, give or take a few." And he turned and winked at Mick. "I bought old man Steven's last fifty acres when he turned ninety a year or so ago. Sometimes I lose track of time, ya know what I mean?" He sighed. Mick told him he knew exactly what he meant. He did too. "Well, Stevens couldn't' keep up with his ranch, and his kids didn't want it, so he went to go live with his daughter in Peoria. Don't know why in the blue blazes I bought them, but I did. Felt sorry for the poor guy. Lived for at least fifty years on that property, and then he has to go live with a daughter. Hell, don't that just beat all?

"I sure as hell ain't getting any younger, and I don't need no more land neither, but I felt I had to do something for him. 'Sides, I didn't want no stranger buying the property and living next to me. He really needed the money. He didn't want to be beholden to his daughter or nothing. I don't know why I don't just sell this place myself. My sons don't want it. Got two of them. One teaches high school in Washington State, and the other is too damn lazy to do any real work. Got five grandkids, though, two boys and three girls. I only got hopes for one of them wanting the ranch, though. Actually taking it over, that is. The one going to the University of Oregon has been studying animal husbandry and will get a degree as an environ-mentalist. He's the one I told ya about. I got my hopes on Joshie. He's twenty-two and graduates in another year. He already works summers and odd weekends when I need him. He loves the horses, and he's a good trainer. He's got to prove himself if he wants to try to run this ranch, though. It's a lot of hard work. More power to him, I say."

Mick looked at William and felt like saying, "Well. you do say a lot, man. Can't remember when I heard such a talker." But he didn't say anything, because just then, they stopped in front of the hug-est log house Mick had ever seen, except maybe in a magazine of expensive homes. Mick got out of the truck and stood awestruck as he viewed the massive log house. "Holy moly, William, this is some spread you've got here! It's huge! How do you find your way around it even?" Mick looked around toward the horse barn and corral and back at the house.

William smiled and said, "It's just a little piece of home." He turned the truck off and jumped out onto the ground.

Chapter 30

Mick was awestruck as he walked into the entryway of the log house. He figured it to be at least five times as big as his house on the coast. The deck spanned the whole width of the front of the house, with a swing hanging at the north end and a set of patio furniture at the south end. The wood columns all had carvings of different animals found in the area. The front doors were enormous and had huge black wrought iron door handles, and there were black bears carved in the middle, surrounded by mountain scenery.

Mick followed William in the front door, into a huge entryway with a staircase on each side. The stairs circled up to a landing encased in a wrought iron and wood railing. When he walked into the open living area, his jaw practically dropped at the size and magnitude of the stone fireplace. The fireplace contained river rock and divided the living area from the kitchen area. The fireplace, including the hearth, looked to be about twenty feet in width. In the front of the fireplace lay a large black bear rug. There were embers glowing in the fire that William must have left when he went to go get his mail and had ended up helping Mick out.

Mick looked around in amazement. "Wow, William, this is some spread you have here. I can safely say I have never seen anything like it in my life." The house was a huge T shape, and everything in it was large, was beautiful, and looked like it had been staged from something he had only seen in a magazine.

William led him to one of the doors off the side of the living area. He opened the door and told Mick that the room was his as long as he needed it. He had plenty of room and no plans for other visitors anytime soon. He pointed directly across to the other side of the massive room and told him that there were two smaller rooms, the size of the bedroom he led Mick into. One was another spare bedroom, and the other one William used as an office/library. The bedroom Mick stood in was beautifully decorated, en suite included. The whole area must have been about five hundred square feet. His view out of the sliding glass doors was of majestic, snowcapped mountain peaks, and the last of the sun was setting behind them.

"Again, wow, William!" Mick exclaimed. "No wonder you don't want to leave here. It's breathtaking, to say the least. If you feel the need to adopt a son, you can count me in."

William just patted Mick on the shoulder and smiled. "I will find you some clothes. You will find just about any toiletries you would require in the bathroom. That was a pretty harrowing experience you just had. You're probably exhausted and in need of a shower. So take your time, and when you are ready, I can heat up some dinner and provide you with a Canadian whiskey that will shake the snakes right out of your socks."

William left Mick standing, looking out of the window, and when he returned, his arms were full of various kinds of clothes, which he threw down on the bed. "There is bound to be something in that pile that will fit you," he said. "I'm going to see what is ready to heat up in the fridge. One of my ranch hands is a damn fine cook, and when he makes something for the guys, he always leaves me a little something too. It's usually enough for at least two people. I'll see you in a bit." William walked out of the room, shutting the door on his way out.

Mick looked through the clothes, then up at the ceiling. Even though he was not a prayerful person, he couldn't help but utter a silent prayer of thanks for William coming along when he did. If it hadn't been for his generosity and kindness, Mick did not know what kind of shape he would be in at this moment. Maybe not even living or breathing. He thought back to the guy who had deliberately run him off the road. *What in the hell was that all about?* He shook his head, found something suitable he could wear, and headed into the bathroom. *Holy crap, this bathroom is as big as my bedroom, if not*

187

bigger! he thought as he looked around at the granite vanity and the immense soaking tub that could definitely fit two people. There was a huge tiled shower with two giant showerheads on each side. He turned on the shower, and the shower area lit up with red heat lamps. It instantly felt warm in there. Mick shucked his clothes off, left them on the floor in a heap, and stepped into the shower, thinking, *This is the life.*

While standing under the hot spray, Mick couldn't help but think about the accident. If that little stand of trees had not been on the bank, he would have ended up in the bottom of the ravine and probably not come out of it alive. Thank God William had come upon him when he did. He could not figure out what was going on, but he sure as hell was going to give it his all to get it figured out. The shower felt wonderful, and he could feel some life snapping back into him. He stepped out and reached for a towel. Like everything else in William's house, it was big and luxurious. Mick took a whiff; it even smelled good, like the pine trees he could see out of the window. He took a pair of well-worn sweatpants out of the pile, and a T-shirt that looked to be about his size. The T-shirt had a logo of *Born to Hunt*, with a picture of a man and a deer head on the front. *Seems appropriate for this country,* he thought as he got dressed. He even found a pair of red plaid boxers in the pile of clothes, and they just happened to be his size also. William was right on about the hygiene products too. There was an assortment of toothbrushes, pastes, lotions, creams, shampoos, and bodywashes. Not to mention some female products that had probably been in the drawer for years. Mick grinned as he finished dressing and then walked out into the living area.

"Boy, you weren't kidding when you said you had about everything anyone would need. You are really set up here. I feel like a million dollars. Well, not quite a million, maybe a few hundred thousand, give or take. I don't know what I would have done if you had not come along when you did. I owe you my life, William," Mick said when he found William sitting in the living room by a now-roaring fire.

William was reclining in an overstuffed brown leather chair. His legs were crossed, and he had a tumbler full of amber liquid.

William turned around as Mick entered the huge room. "I took the liberty of pouring you some of Canada's finest. Whiskey, that is. I discovered this brand when I was on a hunting trip up in Canada a few years back. I thought it was so smooth I had the owner of the liquor store in Pine Lake order me a case at a time. It's a little spendy, but well worth it. Man cannot be without a good whiskey. Especially when you live out here in the middle of no-man's-land like I do. Sit yourself down, man," he said to Mick. "Take a load off." He pointed to a similar amber-filled tumbler on the table by another immense leather chair. "I got some deer meat stew that my cook, Pablo, made, and then there is an apple pie that my neighbor Mable made. Throw in some nice, warm bread that I actually made." William winked at Mick. "Then we're all set." William continued talking as Mick sat down and took a generous swig of the whiskey.

"Wow, you weren't kidding," he said as he held the glass at eye level and looked at the liquid in the tumbler. "This is some smooth stuff. And this chair is big and comfortable enough that I think I could curl up and go to sleep in it! Pretty nice, William."

"Amen to that," William said back, then added that he hadn't really made home-baked bread in the true sense. His wife had a bread maker, and every now and again, William got it out and just threw in a packet of bread mix. "Pretty simple, and you get the benefit of the smell of home-baked bread," he said. "So let's hear your story, Mick. Maybe telling it to someone else can help put things into perspective."

Mick launched into the events of the past couple of weeks. William interjected a couple of times, just asking for a few more details. He was a man of many words and liked everyone to be the same. Mick had thought about the events so often it was easy for him to leave out a few details. William got up twice to refill their glasses, and an hour later, they were still sitting there when Mick finally ran out of words. In the meantime, it had gotten darker in the house, and the only light at all was coming from the fireplace. Mick felt like his throat was parched from talking for so long. William had turned out to be a good listener.

"Wow. Well, that is quite the story, young man," he said to Mick. "Let's get some grub into our bellies and we can digest both while we are eating." He winked at Mick again. "I can hear the wind picking up. And take a look outside. Blacker than black out there, and not a single star in sight. Always scared my wife when she could tell a storm was brewing. Me, don't mind it a bit. Usually means I can hunker down and read or write or something of a quiet nature. Don't think you lead much of a quiet life now, do you, Mick?"

Mick sat down in one of the eight chairs lined up by the long dining room table. "Nah, what fun would that be?" he told William as William placed a bowl of stew, a heavily buttered piece of baked bread, and a slice of apple pie in front of him. Along with that, he asked Mick if he would like a glass of buttermilk. "Buttermilk! Um, no, thank you, William. I will just take a glass of water, if you don't mind." He shook his head at the thought of how that buttermilk would sit in his digestive system with all that whiskey and now this food. William set down a large glass of buttermilk, along with the same food he had set in front of Mick.

"Well, son," William said with a slow, slight drawl.

Mick thought, *Oh, boy, here it comes!*

But instead, William went on to say how his wife had gotten him into drinking buttermilk due to its benefits to your bones, heart, and oral health. She also had told him that a glass a day would significantly lower his blood pressure and keep his cholesterol in check. "And I'll be damned if my blood pressure is as good as my grandson's and my cholesterol is better than my son's, so I guess she wasn't too wrong, off the mark at that. Been drinking a glass a day for years now."

"I wish I could say the same, William," Mick said to him. "My Doc said if I don't learn to relax a little and eat better, he will have to put me on an additional blood pressure medication. And I don't even want to talk about my cholesterol! Last time I had that checked, it was well over two hundred. I know I need to slow down and get back into better shape, but then crap like this crops up and I am right back into the shit of things. I'm telling you, William, I don't know what I would have done if you hadn't been there to help me out tonight. I am truly grateful to you."

William set his glass of buttermilk down. "Well, look at it this way, Mick," he said. "I get purty lonely out here all by myself most of the time. I am sure sorry for your predicament, but I am glad to have you here. That guy obviously pushed you off the road on purpose, and after hearing your story, I realize he somehow must be involved. The local sheriff is a friend of mine, so in the morning we will go in and pay him a visit and let him in on what is going on. That guy is probably long gone by now, but who knows? Maybe the sheriff can help you out."

"Yeah, tomorrow is another day. I don't have anyone who will miss me while I am gone. I will use your phone to call my assistant and just check in with him. He knows I have sketchy cell service or I might have a nonfunctioning phone all together. I will be able to tell better in the morning when we get into town. He's the only one that might worry if he doesn't hear from me. Especially now, with him working on my house and all. I've always been a bit of a loner. I was married once briefly, but it wasn't anything like the relationship you and your wife had, William. My wife was a little on the bitchy side, but in her defense, I guess I was usually the cause of most of her unhappiness. I probably should not have gotten married in the first place, but it seemed like the right thing to do at that time. Thank God we never had any children. I'd probably be one of those dirtbags that skips out on their child support payments and doesn't show up when supposed to. There's not much hope for me in the marriage department."

William stood up and patted Mick on the shoulder, telling him that there is always a new day with new things in store.

William started to clear the dishes off the table. He told Mick to go ahead and use the phone that was on the desk in his office. He waved away Mick's attempts of helping him clear the table. "Nah, nothing to this. You go on ahead and I will be done by the time you are also. We can have a brandy for a nightcap when we are finished. If you don't mind, though, throw a couple more logs on that fire on your way through to the office. It will feel good with the brandy."

Mick settled more wood on the fire and went into the office to call Colin, who didn't answer his phone anyway. Mick left him a lengthy message letting him know what had happened and where he was. He told him he would try again in the morning and just to use his judgment on what was needed for the house.

When Mick walked back into the living area, William was just walking back himself. In his hands he had a bottle and two snifter glasses. "My son gave me this bottle of brandy last Christmas, and I didn't see any reason to open it since I usually just drink the Gibson's. Seems like a good enough time now, don't it?" William said as he looked at Mick with a grin. "Personally, I love a good murder mystery," William told Mick as he set down the brandy. "My wife used to accuse me of reading too much in the evening. She thought I saw plots in normal, everyday circumstances. So this whole story of yours sure does intrigue me. Let's review a few things and dissect a few more of the what, where, and who, and then we had better hit the hay. You will definitely be in for a long day tomorrow. I think I mentioned that the sheriff is a friend of mine. Actually, he is more my son's age, but this being a small town and all, he's my friend too. We can run what I remember of the plates. You never know, we may get a hit of some sort. He could be in the next state also, but it certainly won't hurt to tell the sheriff what you know."

They spent the next hour and a half sipping the delicious brandy and going over the story from beginning to end again. Mick was actually surprised at how helpful William was. He had a way of asking questions that gave Mick a new direction. He ended up going to bed feeling like maybe his theory was right after all. He also felt slightly inebriated by the amount of alcohol he had consumed, and William was right up there with him. *Pretty damn good for a guy his age,* Mick thought. The last thing he thought about before going to never-never land was sitting in his car, leaning against the little stand of fir trees.

Chapter 31

Mick woke up feeling refreshed, if not a little bit hungover and sore as a mother. He looked at himself in the mirror over the dresser. Wow, now that was a shiner! His right eye was totally black-and-blue, and his face was covered in little scratches. He felt the back of his neck, which felt like he had been slugged with a baseball bat. And when he tried to raise his right arm to pat down his unruly hair, he found that he couldn't move it more than about sixty degrees. *I am alive, though,* he thought, *so at the very least I should be able to handle what the day brings.*

As he dressed, he looked out the bay window in the bedroom. Underneath the window was a cushioned bench seat where he could just imagine passing the time of day watching the sun rise. The view was more magnificent than any picture you might have hanging on the wall. Three mountain peaks capped with the first snowfall of the season were majestic in the distance. He could just detect a slight shimmer of water from the reflection of the rising sun. The fields leading up to the base of the mountain were scattered with bovine and an occasional donkey. *No wonder William could not tear himself away from here,* Mick thought. *It's a paradise for sure. Beautiful yet rugged, with a tranquility that fills your soul with peace.* He thought to himself how unsettled he really was at this stage of his life. No true friends. Jumping from bed to bed, unable to find a suitable relationship. *When I put this whole business behind me, I really need to sit and reflect on where the hell I am going.* He took another long look out of the window and zipped up a pair of jeans that was a little long but would work. He opened the door out into the living room.

He caught a whiff of frying bacon and something that smelled like cinnamon. Along with the smell of coffee brewing, it gave him a heady feeling. *More apt would be a slight dehydration from all the alcohol I consumed last night,* he thought with chagrin. With a slight snort, he rearranged his man parts in the jeans. Not only were they a little bit too long, but they were also a little tight on the you-know-whats.

"What's that you said?" William asked him as he walked into the kitchen.

"Oh, nothing," Mick said. "Didn't even know I was talking out loud."

"Well, hell, man, stick with me for a while, and you'll find you talk out loud all of the time. I find I do it all the time, being by myself so much. Pull up a chair. Want some really good coffee?" William pulled out a chair for Mick. "Did you sleep well?"

"The best sleep I have had in nights," Mick answered. "Although I can't help but think that your good booze helped somewhat. Slept like a bear in hibernation."

Mick sat in the captain's chair at the head of the table, and William set down a steaming cup of black coffee in front of him, saying, "There is cream and sugar on the table if you like. I gave up the sugar for my wife but can't help a heavy dollop of real cream. Hmmmmm, delicious. I have this flown in from the big island." William pointed to the coffee bag. "Me and Emily visited Kona one of the times when we managed to get away. Best damn coffee I ever tasted."

"It smells delicious, but that's not the only thing that smells delicious in here. I don't know how I could be hungry after that terrific dinner last night, but I have to admit, my mouth is watering right now. I sure can understand why you love this place." Mick extended his right arm and swept it across the room as he said, "It is so peaceful and beautiful, along with offering a rugged terrain that any man would fall in love with."

William took a swallow of his coffee, and Mick could see his chest swell with pride. He could also see a slight wetness in William's eyes as he said, "Yeah, but I wish Emily were here to enjoy it with me. Taken too soon, she was. She taught me some cooking skills before she passed. Thank goodness! I would be terrible learning on my own. Speaking of cooking, I better get back to those rolls before I reminisce and burn them all." He turned his back on Mick and went back to the oven.

"Well, smells wonderful," Mick said as he sat down with his coffee.

"You just sit and enjoy. Breakfast will be done in two shakes of a lamb's tail!" William said as he took a luscious-looking coffee cake out of the oven. "I have this here coffee cake, believe it or not. It's a frozen concoction that I get from the bakery in town. The owners are two gay gals that spoil me rotten. They make me special desserts and freeze them until I can get in there. Some of the townsfolk gave them a hard time when they first opened their business, but I put a stop to that nonsense. Called a special town hall and gave ever'body a piece of my mind. They been treated okay ever since. There are a couple of old farts that won't go in the place, but who cares? More for the rest of us, I say." All the while William talked, he bustled around the kitchen. He even wore a red plaid apron that gave him a sweet, homey look, which was slightly out of place in this manly atmosphere.

"It sure can't get much better than this," Mick said as he took another swig of the rich, slightly chestnut-flavored coffee. "Again, I can't thank you enough, William. You sure put the emphasis on the word *hospitality*. Don't know where I'd be right now without you."

William came to the table with two plates laden with food. Scrambled eggs with what looked like salsa on top, big rations of bacon, and fried potatoes falling off the sides of the plate. He set these down and then came back with the coffee cake. "I'll just set the whole thing here," he said. "In case you want another piece, I don't have to get up again that way. My damn back has been giving me fits lately. It started a couple of years ago, and if I take it easy, I get by, but I had to take my little filly out yesterday for a ride, and she hadn't been ridden in a while. Took me for a good one, she did. But I sure can feel it today. I love that horse. Don't know how much longer she will be with me, though. I bought her nineteen years ago for Emily. We used to ride the property line together back in the day. When she took sick, she couldn't ride anymore, but she loved it when I took pictures and brought them back to her."

William finally seemed to sit down to enjoy the breakfast he had put together. "Now I have to admit to you, I didn't do this one by myself. As I said, the little gals at the bakery provide me with baked goods. Then I told you about the ranch hand Pablo. He cooks three meals a day for the ranch hands. I don't have only but three hands most of the time, but he acts in both capacities. He was here early, before I even got up and put the scrambled eggs and salsa together. Then he put the bacon in the pan and cut up the potatoes. So all's I had to do was cook everything. Purty good arrangement, don't you think?" And with that, William raised his coffee cup in a salute and took a mouthful of scrambled eggs. He then looked at Mick. "You okay there, son?"

"Oh, I'm sorry, William, a little distracted. I don't mean any disrespect, just thinking ahead about what today will bring. That's all."

"Well, I sure don't blame you there. Relax and eat for now and we'll go into town soon's we're done. I called Joseph, my sheriff friend, as soon as I got up this morning. I know he always gets into the office by 6:00 a.m. sharp. He's been doing that for years. Never one to be a TV sheriff, eating doughnuts at the local café or sitting with his feet up on the desk or strutting around like some bigshot. The man's a wizard when it comes to solving crime. He moved here for the mountains after he had worked as the chief of police in some burg outside of Seattle. He loves it here but takes his job seriously too. My wife always said honesty is the best policy, but you might better think of a spin to your story that leaves out you being in that guy's house and finding him dead, ya know what I mean? That could open a whole new can of worms, and I can almost guarantee you Joseph will sniff it out if it's not reasonable."

They ate the rest of their meal in companionable silence, making the occasional small talk about the weather and ranching in general. Mick was actually interested in what life was really like on a ranch of this size, and it didn't take much to get William to talking and talking and talking. It was a good hour before they actually got up and took their dirty dishes into the kitchen. Mick rubbed his stomach and said to William, "You were right on the money about that coffee cake. That was probably some of the best I ever had! I could have eaten another piece, but then I don't think I could have gotten up from the table."

William told Mick to go get whatever he needed or finish what he needed. William would take care of the cleanup and be ready in fifteen minutes. Mick thanked William for the wonderful breakfast, went in to take a constitution, and brushed his teeth. William was waiting for him by the front door when he came out, phone in hand. "Well, for an ole guy, you sure can get ready quick," Mick told him as they headed out to William's truck.

Chapter 32

"As they say around these parts, 'well, son, let's go get 'er done.'" They walked outside into a clear, crisp, sunny day, and Mick could not help but stop and admire the surroundings. It had been almost dark when he had arrived last night, and he had been so shaken up he hadn't taken the time to admire the mountains thoroughly.

"Again, wow," Mick said to William. "This is absolutely stunning!"

Both med climbed up into William's pickup truck, and they headed into Pine Lake. William owned a new Ford Super Duty truck with a crew cab and an extralong box. Mick had looked at one but found out that was all he could afford, a look. When Mick complimented William on the truck, that was all it took for him to get on another topic that he enjoyed.

"I got this baby last year, and I want to tell you, man, it runs as good as it looks! It can tow over thirty-five thousand pounds of weight. I don't need that much power, though. I usually just pull my horse and trailer out now and again, but this baby will pull up the top of the mountains 'round here like nobody's business." He patted the dash as he said that. He chattered on as they drove, pointing out property lines, fences, cattle, and everything ranch under the sun. Mick only half listened, glad to have William's company but also thinking about his own problems. It seemed to be enough, though, to nod once in a while and offer a yes-or-no response. William wasn't expecting undivided attention, or so it seemed. Mick just leaned back in the passenger seat of the pickup and let William talk. For him, it was actually relaxing, and he let his mind wander from things not related to him. He was very grateful to have found someone like William with a big heart and generosity to help him out.

Mick could identify things that were familiar from when he had come this same way only a week ago. Could so much have happened in that short a time? he thought to himself. He took his cell phone out of the jacket pocket that he had gotten from William. Since he had not gotten a chance to actually talk to Colin yesterday, he figured this would be a good time to try him again. When he looked at the phone, he noticed it was even more cracked than when he had looked at it yesterday. It had what looked like a spiderweb from side to bottom, left to right. He hoped, if nothing else, he could pick up a throwaway phone in Pine Lake until he could get home and get another smartphone. *Man, so different in the days when there were no cell phones at all. You came to depend on the damn things, and if you didn't have one, you were really screwed.*

His mind went over and over the events of the last couple of weeks as William's voice droned on and on. He began to see that they were getting closer to Pine Lake, and it wasn't another ten minutes that the huge "Welcome to Pine Lake" sign was on his right. *Not that welcoming,* he thought, considering the family of bears that were depicted surrounding someone's campsite.

As they came into town, William told Mick that the police department was on the street behind the post office, and maybe that was why Mick hadn't seen it before. It wasn't located on the main drag. William thought it might be more beneficial to Mick if he went in and introduced him to his friend, then he would go down to the café and see what, if anything, Henrietta might know. William explained, since he had lived in the area for so long, the local gals might be willing to open up to him more than they would Mick. If there was even anything to open up about, he said. He might also take a minute to go visit with Marsha, who owned the only beauty salon in town. Between her and Henrietta and the postmaster, it was hard to figure out which one heard the most gossip. Combine all three and there would be no stone unturned, William told Mick.

William walked into the small police station. *Not unlike the one on the coast,* Mick thought. There were two officers sitting at two desks. One had his feet up on the desk, eating a huge powdered jelly doughnut, and the other one was sitting, looking at a huge anti-quated computer screen, with what looked like a pencil sticking out of his ear. He seemed to be twirling the pencil while he was looking at the computer screen. He hoped the guy wasn't trying to get to his brain that way. Mick couldn't help but think, *So much for William's notion of no-doughnuts-or-feet-on-the-desk kind of cop.* He chuckled softly. The officer at the desk closest to the counter quickly took his feet off the desk and stood up when he saw William. Everyone in the area had respect for William. He had the biggest ranch for hundreds of miles around. Mick couldn't help but disguise his laugh as a cough as bits of powdered sugar flew everywhere as the officer stood up, brushing his hands on his uniform before taking William's outstretched hand.

"Howdy, Joseph," William said. "This here is Mick. I talked to you last night about his little predicament. I mentioned I would bring him in so's you could get info on what happened to him last evening. I didn't get into any details last night since it was so late and all, but I saw him get run off the road only a few hundred yards from my driveway. Pretty scary situation, it was. Glad I went to check my mail when I did. Usually, I check it earlier, but I had a cow ready to give birth and I didn't feel right leaving her any earlier. Know what I mean?"

Joseph looked at William like he was quite used to William's lengthy details when he started to talk.

William continued his dialogue. "Well, I could see the car good enough before it took off like a bat out of hell. Pretty sure it was a Ford Focus, dark-maroon color, and I think I caught the letters *66B*, or it was *II8*, on the plate, but it got too far away for me to detect anything else. Hope that helps a bit, anyway."

The officer leaned over to shake Mick's hand and told him to sit on down and start from the beginning.

In the meantime, William was already moving toward the door with a tip of his cowboy hat. "I'll check on back with you all later. I am going on down to the café to see what kind of pie I can rustle up. Mick, check back with me later."

The officer winked at Mick and told William to take his time. He figured it would be a while before Mable got done with him, anyway.

Mick sat across from the officer and began his story again from the beginning to when he arrived in Pine Lake the first time. He briefly mentioned both Carla and Evelyn and their association with him. He explained that he thought if it could be figured out who killed Carla, then everything would just fall into place. Joseph sat the whole time, taking notes occasionally, asking a question or two, and then gave Mick a hard look and asked, "I don't suppose you were in the DeGuard house when he died, were you? We found several different fingerprints, but those take even longer to get results than blood samples, so we haven't received any results yet. It takes quite a while when we are this far away from a lab or forensics or anything remotely police professional. Sometimes it's weeks before we get any answers."

Mick looked at the clock on the wall over the desk and said, "No, but I had looked in the window and could tell something wasn't right, so I called in anonymously to let your department know they had better go take a look."

Joseph's eyes bored into Mick's. "So that was you who called in that tip. Well, we don't know how he died yet either. Those results are not back, but I would almost put my career on him being poisoned. The dog also. I have seen arsenic poisoning before, and they both had the same smell and look of poisoning. Arsenic is fairly easy to come by in these parts. There is a mill not too far from here, and they do a lot of wood preservation, and I am not so sure they are careful with their arsenic storing. At least that is what I have heard. I called to OSHA a few weeks back but don't think anyone has checked up on them yet. Anyway, that is just the most likely possibility. So suppose your story checks out and then I believe you. Why would anyone want to run you off the road?" The officer looked at Mick long and hard, waiting for an explanation.

Mick went on to tell him about the newspaper articles containing stories about a Thomas Hardcastle, who Mick figured had to be Carla's brother. "He should be investigated. That's a shady character if ever I saw one. He has a record of being in jail, and he spent some time in a federal penitentiary. I think that was related to selling drugs or something like that. It was so dark in—I mean the newspaper article I read was really old and hard to read," Mick said. "Carla had once told a friend of hers, who in turn told me, that her father had had a coin collection that she assumed was worth a good deal of money. She had indicated that money was not a problem for her, so she had never bothered with having the collection evaluated until fairly recently. It sounded like she had the collection in her possession, but she never said if it was in her house or a bank vault or what. I am just making assumptions here. I did go online and look up coins. I had found a 1954 coin in her safe in her bedroom, and that intrigued me. I don't know anything about old coins. There are some coins out, it was a few years before, that are worth several hundred thousand dollars. The one that was left in her bedroom safe was only worth about twenty-five dollars, so I think that was a symbolic thing for her to find. Personally, I don't think who robbed her is one and the same person who murdered her. I can't exactly say why, just a hunch I have. When I found her, I could tell she was expecting someone that night, and I don't think that person meant to harm her but, who knows?"

Joseph leaned back in his chair and sighed. "Well, let's say that everything you have reported is accurate. Who in this scenario would want to run you off the road? That was taking a pretty big chance, don't you think? Why didn't he try to run you off the road before you got almost to Pine Lake? Or take you out the same way the other ladies and Mark were taken out? Why would someone trash your house? And why is the other lady—Evelyn, you said her name was— dead also? Things just don't quite add up to me. I will see if I can find out more about this Wanda you met while in Pine Lake. Although if I know William, he's already on that trail. He's a pretty sneaky ole coot himself. Plus, he knows just about everybody in town."

"It sure was lucky for me that he came along when he did. I really don't think I would be sitting here right now if he hadn't." Mick paused and began talking, more to himself than the sheriff. "At first, I thought it was Mark who had killed Carla, but since he is also dead now, I have kind of changed my way of thinking. I never did have a conversation with him, just got to see him up close. That's the reason I went to his house that night. I was hoping I could catch him off guard and he would slip up or something. I was going to flat out confront him about his relationship with Carla. When I saw him outside the post office, he looked a little gray around the gills. He looked totally different from when I had seen him a week previously."

Joseph interrupted Mick. "That's why I think he was being poisoned. He had been in the ER just a couple of days before we found him. He had gone in for vomiting, dehydration, heart palpitations, and a blood alcohol level of 0.32 percent. The ER doc thought he had been on a bender and that was why he was sick. They didn't do any further testing. Now that he's dead, it might be they will look a little further. Maybe he had gone to the ER with some other poisoning besides just alcohol. I will tell you, they found some traces of cyanide in the bottle of merlot that was in the bedroom, but as you know, that can't be conclusive until they find it in him, which I am sure they will. If he was drinking heavily, he probably wouldn't have been able to taste any difference in the wine, since it's a dry wine, anyway."

Joseph went on to tell Mick that he had done some investigating into Mark himself and he had questioned several neighbors and townsfolk. He was surprised by what the neighbors were able to tell him. "Even though the DeGuard house was not in close proximity to their houses, they were generally considered nosy neighbors. People living around these parts look after one another, and my assumption is that everyone thought he was a suspicious character. So apparently, the neighbors were watching him, waiting for a false move. Everybody seemed surprised, though, when I told them that it was Mark that was found dead. They thought he looked like the murdering kind. For all we know, he was and he got what he deserved. I saw his collection of pornography. Now that is a sicko. So maybe he just got what he deserved, but it will be investigated nonetheless," Joseph told Mick. "His sister's name was Marsha McCallister. No record of any kind. That was another thing the neighbors had observed. That a woman was seen coming and going a few times from the house. We don't know if this Marsha was that woman. Like I said, all the fingerprints aren't back yet. They could be the sister's or someone he had living with him. Nothing of any real value was found in the house except maybe his pornography collection. I know some perverts that would love to get their hands on that. We have them locked up in an evidence locker that no one has the key to except me. I called the FBI on that. They can investigate the pornography angle. Who knows, his death could be related to that. Maybe he pissed off the parents or someone else related to one of the girls. I know if that were my daughter in a picture like that, I could easily put a bullet in 'em!"

Just then, the little bell over the door tinkled, and William walked back into the front office. Mick looked at Joseph and asked, "Does every business in town have a bell that tinkles over the door? Has no one heard of security cameras or some other newer technology?"

Joseph gave Mick a wry smile and told him, "When you live in such a small town, everyone knows everyone and watches out for everyone else. So rarely are more sophisticated security systems required. And hey, some businesses have more sophisticated tinkling." He winked at Mick.

William asked how they had made out, and Joseph spoke first, explaining that they had had a great talk but were not any further ahead on who, what, where, or when exactly than they had been before William brought Mick in to see him. "We are looking for Mark's sister as a person of interest, and now we have this Thomas Hardcastle to see what we can dig up on him. At this point, we have some work to do."

Joseph looked at both of the men. Joseph took his coffee cup to the little sink and asked if Ethel had anything new to say.

William told them that Ethel had nothing new but Henrietta said she had seen a stranger in town just last night when she was closing up the café. "The woman works all the time." William said he could not understand how at her age she was able to keep up with everything she did in one day. She had told William that she had stopped at the Minit Mart on her way home because she had remembered she was out of cat food. Mick rolled his eyes and wanted to hurry the story along, but he didn't figure there would be any point. It would just get snagged someplace else in the telling, so he kept quiet. He learned in just twelve hours that there was no such thing as hurrying William in anything. He had his own time and pace. He sure was detail-oriented. William said, "Well, she noticed a car in the parking lot with Ohio plates on it. She always checks license plates whenever she goes out and about. She said she often will ask a person about the state they are from, especially since she has never been anywhere farther from Pine Lake than Boise. She said while she was in the Minit Mart, she didn't see anyone else in there, but while she was trying to decide on the chicken or the tuna cat food—Muffin prefers tuna—she saw a man come out of the restroom. She assumed it was a man because, not like some places nowadays, there were two restrooms in the Minit Mart, one specifically marked for women and one for men. Not those hokey, gender-neutral restrooms they are trying to push everyone into. Bunch of crap, if you ask me. I plan on standing at a urinal until I can't stand anymore!" William made to offer more on how he felt about restrooms, but Mick stopped him.

"William," Mick said, a little louder than he meant to, "can you get on with what Henrietta saw?"

William looked a little startled. "Oh, sorry, yeah, I can get off-track when something just makes my blood boil," he said. "Ethel said the guy had a Chiefs ball cap pulled low over his eyes, and his bomber-type jacket had the collar pulled up high around his neck so you could only see part of his face. Now, the Minit Mart is probably the only place in town that does have security cameras, so's we could probably take a look at them."

Well, you could, anyway, Joseph, Mick thought.

"Henrietta said the guy bought a package of Marlboro cigarettes and one single beer. She didn't get a good look at the kind of beer, because she doesn't know much about beer, but she used to smoke cigarettes once upon a time, so she knew which ones he bought. Anyway, she told me she asked the Chink—her words, not mine—if he had ever seen the guy before, and he had told her no. They both watched him walk out the door, get in his car, and squeal out of the parking lot."

"Did she happen to get a look at the license plate numbers?" Mick piped up.

"All she could remember is that it was an Ohio plate and there were six digits, but she didn't have her glasses on, so they were too blurry for her to see. The Chink—oops, sorry, guys—Mr. Huan hadn't really been paying attention. He didn't see much of anything else but the guy. He was too busy watching an old Jackie Chan movie he had on his little TV behind the counter. Oh yeah, she said it was a small maroon car, she thought a Toyota."

Both Mick and Joseph responded at the same time. Both had questions they wanted clarified from William, but Joseph ended up with the lead, warning both William and Mick that this was a matter for the sheriff's department and he might have to notify the FBI if they found out this Hardcastle guy was some kind of a fugitive. So he asked William and Mick to just let the proper authorities handle everything.

William and Mick looked at each other, and they both looked back at Joseph and nodded. Mick looked down and said, "Hey, Joseph, is that red jelly splatted on the front of your pants?"

Joseph looked down at his pants and turned three shades of pink before he stammered, "You guys get the hell out of here! I have a lot of work to do."

William and Mick laughed as they headed for the door. "And here I told Mick you were not the doughnut-eating kind of sheriff," William said.

They could hear a loud bark of laughter from the other sheriff, who they had forgotten was even there, and then a loud, "Goddamnit!" as the bell tinkled on their way out of the door.

Chapter 33

"Well, William, if you could run me to Joe's Auto, I won't bother you again," Mick told William as they walked back outside. "In fact, you won't have to ever see my sorry ass again," he continued. "Man, you saved my life, though."

William looked at Mick and smiled. "Ya know, I haven't had this much entertainment in well over a year. Since the last time my grandson gave me a visit. I had a blast with him, and this has been as near to a blast as I will probably get. So let's get you over to Joe's. You can square things with him, and then I will take you to the airport in Boise or back to my house, or better yet, I will just take you back to Oregon. I could use a little road trip myself! What did you tell me was the name of that little town you live in?"

"Rockaway," Mick told him. "But I can't let you do that. You've already done more than enough for me."

William looked at Mick with a slight grimace. "Who said anything about letting me? What part of 'I am pretty bored right now' did you not hear, son?" With that, he slapped Mick on the back and got in his truck. "Come on, time's a-wasting!" he said out the truck window.

"Okay, okay, you win," Mick said to him. "Run me to Joe's and then I will meet you back at the café. This may take a while. Something tells me ole Joe might be a little put out that I am showing up without his little beater car."

As they drove into the towing yard, Mick could see Joe working on a wrecked vehicle in the yard. William stopped at the gate for Mick to get out and told him he would see him whenever he was done. He thought he would stop in the post office and have a little chat with the postmaster before he went to the beauty salon. "Just take your time," he told Mick.

Poor ole Joe, Mick thought as he walked through the gate. It was at least an hour and a half to get to where the Subaru was stuck over the embankment, and then trying to get it out of there wouldn't be the easiest job in the world. "Hey, Joe!" he shouted as he walked through the gate.

Joe looked up from under the hood of a wrecked Chevy and hit his head on the hood, which was propped up with a piece of wood. "Goddammit!" he swore and gave Mick a dirty look. "What the hell, man?" He stepped back, rubbing the top of his head as he glared at Mick.

"Well, it's like this," Mick said. "I had a slight problem with the car I rented from you. Not the car itself, although I have driven better, but I got run off the road last night and the car is stuck on some trees over an embankment. It's actually about an hour and a half away from here. The trees saved me and the car from going over the bank, and then this old rancher dude came along and saved my life." Mick noticed how Joe had not let go of the big wrench he had in his hand. He started to slap it against his palm while he eyed Mick suspiciously. "Not sure what I would have done otherwise. The guy who ran me off the road was heading back my way, probably to see if I need finishing off or something. By then it was near dark and old man Pryor actually took me to his place and let me stay the night."

Joe interrupted him at that point and asked, "Ya mean William Pryor?"

"Yeah, that's his name," Mick said. "Do you know him?"

Joe looked at Mick and said, "Hell, not many people in these parts do not not know him. He's got the biggest ranch in the whole state of Idaho, prolly the other surrounding states too. He donates to all sorts of organizations. He and his wife, when she was alive, used to do all sorts of stuff for the town. No one's seen much of him since his wife died, though. More or less stays on the ranch, I guess. He has bought a couple of old cars off me over the years. How's he doing, anyway?"

"Well," Mick said, "seems to be doing just fine, a little lonely sounds like, but he's pretty darn healthy. And what a spread he's got there!"

Joe gave a low whistle. "You're not just a-kidding. I been out that way a time or two through the years. Whooooo-eeee! Beauty of a spread, it is," he said. "Well, how much damage do you reckon the car has got?" Joe eyed Mick over his glasses.

"Well, I know the radiator is shot. I could see a tree branch poking through it. There is damage on the passenger side and the rear end where the guy rammed me twice, and then the front end from hitting the trees. Totaled, I would say, Joe."

"Damn!" Joe swore and took his hat off and hit it on the trunk of the car he was working on. "Well, four thousand dollars should cover it. You gotta fill out an accident report and then let your insurance company know. Shouldn't be a big problem. I got all your info. Listen, don't worry about it. It's not like I don't have any more cars." He took his arm and swept it across the dirty expanse of the junkyard. "In fact, I just got a call not too long ago from a guy who couldn't get his car started. If I am right, he lives pretty close to William's ranch. So's I gotta go out that way, anyway. Since I am the only towing company around these parts, I get covered from Triple A. I will just pick it up then."

Mick was surprised at how easily Joe took in the information, hardly breaking stride, it seemed. He would have sworn there would be more ruffled feathers.

Joe wiped his hands on the rag that was hanging out of the back pocket of his overalls. "Let's just go in the office and fill out a couple more pieces of paperwork. I will need you to go get me one thousand bucks, though. Just like a retainer. And I will recredit you after the insurance company comes through. They are slower than shit."

Mick thanked Joe for being such a good guy about the whole mess. He felt a weight lifted off his shoulders. On the way out the door, Joe had told him that living out in the boondocks like he did, you had to take things in stride. Sometimes there just wasn't anything to make things move any faster or be any different. He had slapped Mick on the back and told him perhaps he should consider a quieter lifestyle himself. Perhaps he should, Mick thought as he walked back to the café. *That was sure easier than I thought it would be.*

He looked up at the sky as he walked and thought about his recent bout of bad luck. *First, my neighbor, then my truck, then my house, then the beater car, and then me, almost getting killed. What next? Man, that was some blue sky. Not a cloud in sight either.* He considered what Joe had said. Perhaps it was time for him to slow down and take some time to smell the roses, so to speak. *This is ridiculous!* he thought. *Smell the roses—what the hell did that really mean, anyway?*

Mick walked slowly back to the little café. He knew William would be gabbing away to someone, or even everyone, with that gift of gab he had.

The waitress gave him a slight smile and a little nod as he walked into the café. "Coffee?" she asked him.

He nodded and looked around the café. The place was deserted except for William, who sat at the small table by the window. He looked lonely without anyone to talk to. The waitress was busy cleaning up after the breakfast rush. Mick went to sit across from William, who looked like he was just finishing the last crumb from a piece of pie.

William patted his slight paunch. "I didn't even ask for it. She just brought it over and set it down. What's an ole guy to do? Makes the best damn marionberry pie in the county! Want to try some?"

Mick looked dubious. "I think I am still eating the huge breakfast you fed me this morning. I couldn't eat a bite of anything right now. I didn't expect you to get this here quickly."

William told Mick that Marsha hadn't been at the beauty salon; she had taken the day off to take her mother to the doctor, and the postmaster had a lobby full of customers, so he wasn't able to talk to her either. "What do you say to hitting the road, then?"

Mick looked at William. "You offered, so I am taking you up on your generosity. To Oregon we go. It's a two-day trip unless you want to marathon through in one day."

William stood up and took his cowboy hat from the hook on the side of the bench. He put it on and reached into his back pocket for his wallet. He threw a hundred-dollar bill down on the table and looked at Mick. "Whoo-ee!" he said. "Let's get 'er done!" He tipped his hat at Henrietta on the way out the door, while Mick followed, thinking, *No wonder he gets free pie when he comes in.* He gave the waitress a small smile and laid down a ten-dollar bill on the counter for the coffee.

"Hold your horses, William. I'm right behind you," Mick told him. He turned on his way out and gave Henrietta a smile, a wave, and a hearty thank-you, letting her know that her hospitality was greatly appreciated.

When they were in the truck and headed back the way they had come, William told Mick that he checked with his son, who assured him the ranch could run for a few days without him. He could check on things at the ranch, and with Gomez there, there was nothing to worry about. Gomez said he could run the ranch in his sleep, and the other guys really respected him. So it all looked good from his perspective. "I've been hankering for a road trip. I told ya that before. So it's all good, as far as I am concerned. You just sit back and relax."

William could not understand quiet time, so Mick was prepared for a lot of conversation on this long trip. "The last time I took a road trip was about five years ago. Emily and I went to the Oregon coast and went on up the whole coastline of Washington. We spent about a week up in the Puget Sound area, checking things out and stopping at little places along the way. That was the last trip she could ever make. She loved it. In fact, we had talked about getting a little house on the coast. She had discovered a second cousin who lived in Astoria, and she fell in love with that area. In fact, we had spent a few days with her, exploring the area. They both had relatives in Norway and had been there a couple of times. Lots of Scandinavian people in Astoria, and many of them were of Norwegian descent. Even went so far as to look at a couple of houses, but we didn't find anything suitable at that time, and she had made a promise to her cousin that she would be back next year. In the meantime, she had contacted a realtor to have information sent to us at the ranch. We had planned on going back the following year and looking more diligently, but that fell through by then."

Mick barely listened as he felt his eyelids drooped. He realized he had probably only slept four hours the night before, and he could feel exhaustion setting in.

Mick woke up with a start when the truck hit a speed bump, and heard William say, "Man, I gotta hit the men's room. This ole truck tank uses a lot of gas, so's I usually fill it up again when I stop for a pee break. You want to grab something to eat here?" William was out of the truck and halfway to the restroom by the time Mick got the cobwebs out of his head.

"No, not here!" he hollered to William's back. "I will cover the gas." Mick got out of the truck to stretch his legs. He ran his credit card through the pump's skimmer, and as he did so, his phone fell out of the truck onto the cement. "Damn it!" he said as he picked it up and looked closer at it. It hadn't looked too good before, but this time it was totally cracked to shit. Even though the battery had died, he was pretty sure the rest of the phone had died as well. He looked at the words "Not Approved" on the pump's screen. "Well, crap," he said and ran the card again. Same two words, "Not Approved." "What the fuck?" he growled and slapped at the pump, like that would really make things happen.

In the meantime, he looked up and saw a little gray-haired old lady giving him an evil eye. She looked like she was dressed for church in her purple flowered ensemble, with matching-colored shoes, no less.

"Sorry," he apologized to her. "Would you like help pumping the gas?" he asked her.

"I can do just fine, young man, but I suggest you watch your language when there are ladies present." She turned away from him in a huff, and he strode off into the gas station to pay for the gas in cash.

William was standing at the register with his hands full of potato chips, candy, and pop. "Just in case we need a little sustenance along the way," he said sheepishly.

"Well, I came in to pay cash for the gas. The damn machine didn't take my credit card. I don't know why. It worked before I left Oregon."

William told him not to worry. He had to pay for the junk he had in his hands; he would just get the gas at the same time. Mick tried to protest, but it didn't really do him any good. *Just as well,* he thought as he went back outside to pump the gas. He only had about twenty bucks left on him. *What the hell else?* he thought as he finished with the gas then headed for the men's room himself.

When he returned, William had replaced the gas nozzle and was already climbing back in the truck. Mick asked him if he wanted to take a break from the driving, and then he backed back out and agreed. "Yeah, thanks. I guess that is a good idea." He climbed into the passenger side while Mick adjusted mirrors, messed with the seat, and checked all the gauges on the dash.

"Want a root beer?" William asked him.

"Hey, thanks, but no, thanks," Mick said as he held up a bottle of water that he had picked up in the station. "Watching my figure." He glanced over at William. "There is a small town I remember passing through on the way here. Can't remember the name of it, but I do remember seeing a hotel with a restaurant and lounge. It was too early when I passed through before, but it's easy off, easy back onto the freeway. It's another four hours or so from here, but I figure it's about the halfway mark to Rockaway. So now it's your turn to sit back and relax and leave the driving to me. We can stay there and get an early start in the morning."

As Mick drove away from the gas station and back onto the freeway, he looked in his rearview mirror. He noticed a black Ford Ranger pickup speed behind him. It looked like the guy could barely see over the steering wheel. *I'm getting paranoid now,* he thought to himself. He glanced over at William, who was sipping his root beer, looking out the window. *No sense causing a stir when I don't even know if there is a reason.* But he had a slight uneasy feeling. He put his eyes on the road and the pedal to the metal and turned on the radio to a country Western station. *Smooth sailing from here,* he thought.

Chapter 34

They reached the Riverside Hotel right on the dot of 7:00 p.m., and it didn't take long to check into two separate rooms and unload their bags. Mick hated to share a room with anyone but a brunette or a blonde, maybe even a redhead, but definitely not an old man who would surely fart and snore in his sleep. Mick remembered when his last girlfriend kicked him out of her bed because he snored too loud and she needed to get to work the next morning. William had already informed him of his nightly idiosyncrasies, one of which including his having to get up about three times to take a leak. He told Mick that his wife often just slept in the spare bedroom, making it easier for her to sleep the night through.

"See you in the bar in about fifteen minutes or so," Mick told William as he stepped through the door of number 69. *Hmmm,* he thought, *lucky number.*

Mick pulled his cell phone out of his pocket and glared at the broken screen. "Well, I'll be damned," he said to himself. It looked like the phone might work. At least it looked like there was service available. He could see a couple of new messages. He clicked on the message list and saw one from Colin, and the other from his insurance agent. He decided to call Colin. The insurance agent could wait, and he wasn't ready for any more depressing news.

The phone only rang once, and Mick heard Colin's deep voice on the other end. "Man, where the heck are you?" Colin actually sounded a little huffy, which was totally out of character for him. "I have been trying to reach you for two days now. Are you all right?"

Before Mick could answer, though, Colin continued, "I could really use some advice about now."

Mick went on to reassure Colin that he was basically okay but that it was a rather-long story and he would rather not go into it until he got back home. He did let Colin know that he did not have reliable cell service or a reliable phone at this point. Since his phone had been damaged in the car accident.

"Wait a minute," Colin said. "What about a car accident?"

Mick stopped him from further questions. "I said I am okay and will fill you in when I get home. I am beat and haven't eaten for hours, so I will hang up if you don't get to the point."

"The house is actually coming along just fine. A little slow since it is only me working on it, but moving along. I got all the cleanup done and all the debris and crap discarded. I had to rent one of those big dumpsters but figured you wouldn't mind footing the bill for that. Some stuff that was thrown around, I was pretty sure you wouldn't want to try to salvage. So it just ended up in the trash. I am working on the doors. I had to get three. Then there is some Sheetrock repair and paint. The cleanup took the most time, but hey, that wasn't the main reason I wanted to talk to you," Colin said. "Sheelya the witch called, screaming and all freaked out. She really laid it on me when I told her you were not available. She called me every name in the book. She is worse than the Wicked Witch of the West! She finally just cursed and hung up on me. So just to let you know, I don't think she heard a word of you-don't-want-her-business."

Mick could hear Colin take a deep breath, then he lowered his voice and said, "I had a really odd phone call yesterday, right after Sheelya hung up, as a matter of fact. A lady called, asking for you, but I could barely hear her. She was more whispering than talking in a coherent voice. I told her you were not available but would be back in a day or two. I asked if I could help or take a message. She said no, but again, I could barely hear her. She told me it was confidential and she could only talk to you. I tried one more time, telling her that I could be trusted, that I work for you, etc., but she wouldn't talk to me. She seemed a little breathless too, ya know what I mean?"

Mick rolled his eyes upward and sighed. "Yes, Colin, I do know what *breathless* means. As a matter of fact, women that don't want their husbands to hear what they are saying talk like that too. Do you know what I mean?" If Mick could see Colin through the phone lines, he would know he was blushing. The kid was rather naive, after all. "Did you get the number she was calling from?" Mick asked Colin.

"No, it was blocked somehow and didn't register. I asked if I could have the number, and she kind of freaked out. She just said to never mind and she would try to call back again, and then she hung up. Never gave me her name either."

Mick looked at the time and realized thirty minutes had gone by when he told William he would see him in fifteen. "Well, it's not like I have been playing around much lately." He looked up at the ceiling. *Not anything he would count as such, anyway.* He said, "Well, sorry you had to deal with Sheelya. I will have to reiterate our last conversation when I get back. In the meantime, do you think I will be able to stay in the house when I get there tomorrow evening? I am bringing someone with me."

Now he could hear Colin chuckle. "Well, you don't waste any time, do you? As long as she doesn't mind the smell of paint, it should be okay."

"I don't have a woman with me, you knucklehead," Mick told him. "I have with me an elderly gentleman who, by the grace of God, literally saved my life. I don't want him to have to stay in a hotel, that's all. I am sure he can handle a little paint smell."

"Well, this sounds like quite the story," Colin said. "I can't wait to hear all about it."

"You can wait until tomorrow, though," Mick said. "I need to get off the phone now and go meet William for something to eat. See you tomorrow." And with that, he hung up before Colin could think of something else he just had to tell him.

Mick put his phone back in his pocket and flexed his wrist. The swelling had gone down somewhat, but it was really black-and-blue and sore as hell. The bruising now extended from his wrist up to the back of his elbow. He considered himself lucky, though. At least it wasn't broken. Lately, he felt like some kind of cat with nine lives.

He looked at the little bedside clock, and now he was more than half an hour late. He couldn't help but wonder who the woman who had called was. He was kind of hoping whoever it was, maybe she was some type of clue to what had been going on. This was getting weirder by the day. He turned to look around the room, surveying the way in which things were situated. He learned from his instincts, and especially from recent events. Never feel too confident. He looked at his reflection in the mirror over the dresser. He shook his head at his reflection and said, "Man, you sure have let me down lately."

His grin was more of a grimace. His right eye was still puffy, and it hurt to smile. He tried flexing his arm, but that hurt too much too. *Man oh man, I am not what I used to be. An old cliché, but so true,* he thought as de decided to leave both the light and the TV on when he left the room. People wouldn't know if he was in there or not. Those Beer Nuts William bought were long gone by now, and his stomach gave a low growl as he walked out the door. *Man, a Jack and Coke would go down pretty smooth right now.* The front desk gal had said they stopped serving dinner at eight but they always served burgers and some sandwiches. *A juicy cheeseburger would go just fine with a Jack and Coke.* He locked the door and headed for the bar.

Mick walked into the bar and had to adjust his eyes to the dim lighting. He could actually hear William before he could see him—it was that dark. *How does a person eat in here?* Mick wondered. He spotted William near the end of the bar talking to a couple that could easily have been Roy Rogers and Dale Evans. He took a step and almost fell off the threshold on the outside of the doorway. *Jesus, could it be any darker? What are they thinking here?* He quickly looked around to see if anyone noticed that he practically fell on the floor. At least the dark covered just about everything, he guessed. *I would hate to meet a woman in here,* he thought. *I wouldn't be able to tell what she looked like till I got her outside.* He grinned to himself as he walked toward William and the couple at the bar.

He stood by William a good two minutes before William paused for a breath from his story and actually realized Mick was standing there. When he turned to look at him, Mick slapped him lightly on the shoulder. "Man, you sure do have some stories, don't you?" The couple barely turned to see who was standing next to William; they seemed so engrossed in his story.

William grinned and said, "I am glad to see you could finally make it." He turned to the couple and made introductions. They were older even than they appeared from the doorway, but they sure in hell still looked like Roy Rogers and Dale Evans. Mick shook hands with both of them, and William went on to say that the two had just gotten married the day before yesterday. They were on their honeymoon and on their way to Nashville, Tennessee, where they had tickets to the Grand Ole Opry. Mick could see the possibilities there, that was for sure. They were dressed for the Ole Opry twenty years ago, but he wasn't sure about today. William went on to relay everything he had recently learned about the newly married couple. It included their age, where they were from, what kind of a wedding they had had, etc.

Mick held up his hand. "William, I don't know about you, but I am famished and thirsty on top of that. I am going to sit in that booth by the window. The one with the light over it, so I can see what I am drinking. You can join me if you wish." With that, Mick said, "Nice to meet you, folks. Good luck. Good cheer." And he waved as he walked to go sit down. He hadn't wanted to be rude to William or the older couple. *But sometimes you just have to do what you have to do,* Mick thought. He sat down and tried to make eye contact with the barmaid.

When the barmaid finally noticed him and made it over to his booth, she actually sat down across from him to take his order. Gratefully, she gave him her undivided attention. He said Jack and Coke, a double, and then he looked her in the eyes. *Man, if she weren't a hottie. With a capital* H, he thought. She had the hugest deep-brown eyes. Kind of like a deer in the headlights. Her eyelashes were superlong and thick and couldn't possibly be real, but he could feel something stirring when she looked directly at him. Her lips were hot pink, thick, and luscious-looking. Her little sweater, which showed just the right amount of cleavage, was the same color as her lips. He swallowed before he said, "Could I also get a cheeseburger and fries?"

"Sugar," she said, "you sure can, and it will only take a few minutes." With that, she eased herself out of the booth and sauntered back to the bar.

Yum-yum, he thought. *I know I could dive into that!* He shook his head at himself in disgust. Why couldn't he just concentrate on work? She brought him his Jack and Coke and leaned over when she set it down. She gave him a big smile and knew what effect she was having on him. Probably a big tease, he thought, but he couldn't help admire her tight ass and long legs in the little formfitting black skirt that barely covered her rear end. She knew how she looked and the effect she could have on a man. He couldn't help a chuckle as he watched her.

He continued to watch her behind the bar while he waited for his burger. He looked around at the interior of the bar—what he could see of it, anyway, in the blackness. There wasn't anything else better to watch. She was reaching up to get a bottle of Black Velvet off a shelf that she could barely reach. "Come on, girl, you can do it," he muttered under his breath as her skirt met the bottom of some black lace panties. She managed to maneuver the bottle toward the end of the shelf, and he caught his breath when he watched it start to fall. "Good reflexes!" he shouted at her as she grabbed the bottle with both hands before it hit the back of the bar.

She turned around and smiled at him. "Haven't broken anything in two years," she said as she put the bottle down and adjusted her skirt. "The owner of this bar can be a mean son of a bitch when he wants to be, so I have learned to be careful." She mixed two Black Velvet and Cokes and took them down to the end of the bar, where the cowboy couple were still enraptured by what William was saying. She spoke to them for a few minutes before she went back to the kitchen to get his cheeseburger and fries.

He could feel his mouth water as he waited for her to come back to his booth. Of course, she had to lean down to set the plate in front of him. Not that he minded. She had a beautiful cleavage. She was all tanned a golden brown, and in the middle of her breasts hung a small gold heart necklace covered in rubies and diamonds. All Mick could think to say was, "Hey, how about another one of these?" He held up his empty glass.

"Why, of course, sugar," she said and walked back to the bar.

In the meantime, some idiot was knocking his empty glass on the top of the bar like she wasn't paying any attention. His glass couldn't have been empty more than two minutes. *Some people have no class,* he thought. Just then, she turned toward the man and shouted, "If you don't cut that out right now, Stanley, you can go to the next town and have your next drink!" She made what looked like a vodka martini and set it down roughly in front of him, spilling a little bit as she did so. He pouted but didn't say another thing.

Mick started to eat his burger and watched as William took the hands of the couple between his own and said some blessing or some-thing—Mick couldn't hear at that point. William was all smiles, and so was the couple, although Mick thought theirs was a little on the sloppy side. They could have downed three or four drinks as long as William had been talking, Mick thought. He watched as the old gal ran her hand up the thigh of her new husband, and William asked the barmaid for a cold turkey sandwich. He then came to sit down opposite of Mick. He probably still had the same beer he had ordered when he got in here.

"Nice couple," William told Mick as he sat down. "They are planning on making their way clear across the old US of A and then back to Texas to live on a ranch in the middle of nowhere."

"Well, they sure are dressed the part for Texas," Mick said to William. "Not so sure about Idaho, though, but glad you enjoyed yourself."

Just then, the barmaid set an amber-colored drink on ice in front of William. She gave William a wink and said his sandwich would be out in just a minute. William gave her a sheepish grin and turned toward Mick. "What I wouldn't give to be a little younger," he said with a sigh.

It only took two more stories and another drink for Mick before he realized how tired he felt. Now he could barely keep his eyes open, let alone look at the barmaid. "Man, I am beat," he told William. "I am ready to go get some shut-eye. What about you?"

William agreed with the idea of hitting the hay, as he said it. Mick went up to the bar, and with one last look at that beautiful cleavage, he paid the bill, which included a generous tip.

Chapter 35

Both William and Mick had set their alarms for 5:00 a.m. to get an early start. Mick set the alarm on his cell phone to see if it would actually work. He had very little charge left when he realized he had left his charger plugged into the outlet at William's house. He had forgotten about it. William did not trust technology and had set the little alarm clock in the hotel room. Mick woke up to hearing William banging on his door, saying, "Get up, sleepyhead! Time's a-wasting!" *Well, so much for the cell working,* he thought groggily. Just one other thing he had to deal with when he got back home.

Mick rushed through his daily routine in record time and met William out in the parking lot. "Well, good morning," William said as he watched Mick approach the truck. "How did you sleep? I slept like a newborn calf."

Really, Mick thought. For an old guy, he sure did look chipper. He smelled fresh as a daisy. *How in the hell does he do it at that age?* Mick acknowledged William with a nod and said, "Well, I have slept better. Man, that bed was hard. But with a good, strong cuppa joe, I will be ready to hit the road. How about you? Do you want me to drive?"

William took him up on it, preferring to be able to just look out the window. He handed Mick his truck keys. While Mick settled the hotel bill, William went to the little buffet that was set up with some breakfast items to go. He put two cups of black coffee, some type of dry pastry, and a banana for each of them in a little caddy. *That should hold us over for a while,* he thought to himself. Plus, he still had peanuts and a couple of candy bars left from yesterday.

William could overhear Mick talking to the gal at the desk. She looked like she might have been interrupted during the middle of some type of religious ceremony. She was dressed in full Sikhism attire—at least William thought that was what it was. He knew Mick was asking a question about a charge or tax or something on the bill but was having trouble understanding her strong Indian accent. William went out the door with the small cardboard tray of stuff. He got in and pulled the truck up to the front door to wait for Mick, then he settled comfortably into the passenger seat.

It seemed like it was another five minutes before Mick walked out of the door. Mick could hear Waylon Jennings railing away on the radio. Crooning *might be a better term,* he thought. He climbed into the driver's seat and asked if William wouldn't mind listening to a little news first. "No problem," William said. "Was there something wrong with the bill? That seemed to take quite a while, and I know you well enough by now to know it wasn't her looks or personality. I don't know about you, but I couldn't understand a word she said."

Mick interjected. "I was starting to get pissed off," he said. "There was some crazy tax I had never heard of at the end of the bill, and I just wanted to know what it was for, but I gave up after a couple of tries. I think she does that on purpose. It was only about nine dollars, but with me, there is a principle involved."

"Oh, I get that," William said. He handed Mick the pastry as he took a sip of his coffee. "I am not sure how well this will wake you up either. Tastes pretty weak to me, and this pastry will really stick in your craw. It's dry as an old dog bone."

Mick looked over at William and couldn't help but smile at his choice of words. He really did live in the backwoods, he thought.

While Mick drove, William rambled on about his growing up—when, where, and how—and then about his parents. Mick could only half listen. Personally, he never could understand what people got out of talking about their dreams. He didn't believe there was anything to trying to interpret or analyze a dream, but he guessed William did by the way he was talking in-depth about it. "He was a short scruffy-looking guy with a salt-and-pepper beard and a ball cap pulled low over his forehead," William went on. "He wanted to start a fight with me. I'm a lover, not a fighter." He looked at Mick and winked. "I bet you can't say the same."

"What's that?" Mick said. His mind had not been on William's dream; he was thinking about what Colin had said about the woman who had called him. He did not mean Sheelya. God, he really thought she had understood what he meant by "Don't call me. I'll call you." But she was a hardened witch, he knew. It might take more than words to finally get rid of her.

He drove along, trying to conjure up the face of a woman that might have been the one who called him.

William began talking about a dream he had had in the night that had woke him up in a fright. Mick listened with only half an ear, thinking about who had called. If it had been Wanda and if she had killed Mark, she would be long gone by now and not apt to drop him a line or anything like that. But if she hadn't killed him, maybe she was afraid of who had and was reaching out for someone who could possibly help her. She had seemed pretty self-assured when he met her. Bitchy with an edge, but pretty smart also, like she wouldn't have any problem handling herself in most circumstances. He wondered what her involvement was. He felt there was something fishy about her. Maybe she had figured out he was following Mark, trying to understand his relationship with Carla. "Oh, what the hell," he murmured. "This is getting me nowhere."

Just then, he spotted a gas station / café, and he pulled off the highway. "Time we got something real to eat, old man." He nudged at William, who had started to doze. *No wonder I hadn't heard him talking for a while,* Mick thought to himself. "Let's get some gas while we are here too, even though there is still almost half a tank. If I remember correctly, the next gas station is over a hundred miles from here."

He got out of the truck to stretch his legs and got his credit card out of his wallet to stick in the slot on the gas pump. William said he would go and get a table, and hopefully they could get a decent cup of coffee. He really felt like he needed it. This time he had no problem running his credit card. *Thank God,* he thought. He couldn't handle another problem right now.

"Sounds good, William. I will be right behind you." *Man, his truck has one big fuel tank. Even almost half-full, it took seventy-five dollars' worth of gas. I sure like how this baby runs, but man, that's a hole in the pocket for the gas!*

William was sitting at a small table in the middle of the café, drinking his coffee and chatting with some gray-haired gal at the table next to his. He had to hand it to the old guy; he sure was friendly, and this gal was a looker for her age. Mick smiled at her as he sat down opposite of William. William introduced Mrs. Splender to him, then went on to say that she was on her way to visit her sister in Southern California and just happened to blah, blah, blah. He smiled at the both of them but looked at the modest menu. *Oh, good, they serve breakfast all day.* He asked William if he would like for him to order for the two of them since he had to go up to the counter and place the order. William said he would have whatever Mick was having and then turned his attention back to Mrs. Splender. Mick shook his head slightly as he headed up to the counter. He ordered two orders of eggs over easy, hash browns, sourdough toast, and a side of ham. He looked back at William, who was still deep in conversation. *Hope that would suit.* Mick probably could have ordered dry cereal for all William would be paying attention to his breakfast.

Mick gave their order to a surly-looking kid with a face full of acne. *Poor kid,* he thought as he went back to sit by William. He had been lucky to never have to deal with acne as a kid.

This time William did not even glance up at him; he was so deep in conversation. Mick heard his name and went up to pick up their order. When he set the plate down in front of William, he still barely noticed him. "A-hem," Mick said. "Don't mean to interrupt a scintillating conversation, but eat up, mister. We have to get back on the road if we want to make it to my house by two."

William took his eyes off the lady and looked at him like he was an intruder. Then he smiled and said, "Sure thing." Then he added, "It was nice to meet you" and all that jazz to the lovely Mrs. Splender. Mick did note that she passed him a piece of paper on their way out the door. *The old dog,* he thought to himself. *Well, more power to him.*

The breakfast had actually been decent, considering it was almost fast food.

They were back on the road in half an hour, and this time William was at the wheel. Mick found himself lost in thought again for the hundredth time, if not more than that. He knew Sheelya would have gotten what she wanted from that measly husband of hers. Unless he was smarter than he looked. Mick didn't know how much the guy was worth, but he did know how good Sheelya was at getting what she wanted. He could not remember her ever mentioning it, anyway, and that wasn't like her. She usually bragged about how much someone was worth, but she probably didn't knowing that he might not have helped her otherwise. That would have served her right, he thought. After all, she had a bit of a reputation that ran up and down the coast. She just couldn't seem to help herself. Mick hoped her next husband would live in the Portland area, and then maybe he would never have to set eyes on her again. Just one more thorn in his side that he would have to deal with when he got home. He was beginning to consider a harassment charge, although he had never done anything like that in his life. All these women running around in his brain was giving him more than a headache. He gave up and started to tell William about a few things he should consider seeing while on the coast

He talked about some of the best places to eat at on the coast while William drove. William was pretty keen on having some fresh fish and chips. He remembered a place he and Emily had stopped at while they were passing through. He had trouble recalling the name of the little place, but then something Emily had said reminded him that the town was named Garibaldi and the little restaurant was right in the middle of the marina, it seemed. "The Porter House or Port House. No, it was the Portside." He asked if it was still there. Mick told him he didn't think it was the same place but that it had been taken over by a younger couple who had remodeled it and they more or less specialized in pulled pork and tritip stuff. They did have fish and chips, but it wasn't their specialty, because the little restaurant right across the pavement from them was known for their fish and chips, so they tried something else. Both were very good, though.

Mick went on to tell William a few idiosyncrasies about some of the people he knew who lived there. Also, how hard it was to find anyone who would actually do a day's work for a day's pay. "Gets damned frustrating when you actually find someone that has to come from the Portland area just to change out the plumbing in your bathroom. I can do a lot of handyman stuff, but who the hell has time anymore?" He scowled at William. "I get up, go to work to scratch out a few bucks, and before you know it, I go to bed and get up to do it all over again. Ya know what I mean?" He looked at William, who literally had not taken one eye off the road. "Well, there is the occasional fling that necessitates some attention." Mick grinned, and at that point, William did look over at him and grinned back.

Mick fiddled with the radio dial and settled on a classic rock / country type of music. Something they both seemed to enjoy. At least the music kept William's prattle at a scaled-down pace, which Mick was grateful for. He could remember how he could tune his wife out when she started in on him. ("When are you going to clean out the garage?" "I need my oil changed on my car." "That back hedge is getting so tall it is starting to bend over the fence. Joan was over here two weeks ago, complaining about it.") No wonder he hadn't been able to stay married. There was no free time for hiking or biking or bowling or much of anything but the yard and shopping and the occasional movie. He didn't know how other men did it. Although his dad managed to settle down nicely with a new woman. Maybe there was hope for Mick yet, he thought, and on that note, he drifted off to sleep.

Chapter 36

It was 3:00 p.m. by the time Mick and William pulled into Rockaway. Mick's right leg was screaming to get out of the car. He had torn the meniscus in that knee the previous winter, and whenever he drove a long distance, it gave him fits. Even using the cruise control didn't always help. Thank goodness this time he had William to help him with the driving. The last trip, it had taken a couple of days for the pain and swelling to subside. He stood by the car door a full minute before he thought he could take a few steps. It was getting dark, but not nighttime yet. Colin had left the front porch light on, anyway, so that helped. Mick turned to see how William was faring; after all, he had a good twenty years on Mick. They hadn't been out of the car since their last bathroom break more than four hours ago.

"How's it going there, old boy?" Mick came around the car to see if William needed any help. *The old guy is probably doing better than me,* he thought to himself.

"Right as rain, Mick," said William. "Although I don't think I could have stood it much longer in the ole truck. My back tends to get a kink in it, and my left leg went to sleep." William opened the back door on the passenger side and lifted his suitcase onto the ground. He stood surveying his new surroundings. Clean, quiet small residential neighborhood not far from the ocean, he could tell by the smell and the sound of the surf. He was surprised he could hear it that clearly; he figured they were at least five or six blocks from the ocean. "How far away is the beach, Mick? That's quite a loud sound coming from the surf."

Mick was walking up onto the porch with his bag. He turned around to tell William it was only three. "I will show you one of my favorite walks in the morning. The reason you can hear the surf so well is that it reverberates off the mountain to the east. The hill is only a little farther than what I am from the ocean. I sleep with the windows open in the summer, and the sound will lull me to sleep. I love the smell too. It seems to seep clean air to me."

Mick had told Colin to leave the door unlocked since he wasn't sure if he had replaced it yet or not. *Looks like not,* Mick thought. He turned around to say to William, "It's not much, but it's home to me." He hit the light switch and put his bag down on the floor by the door. He couldn't help but have a cautious glance around, considering the last time he had come home, what he had found then. He let his breath out slowly, not realizing he had been holding it. He could tell that all looked as it should. Colin had made a fast track to get it cleaned up. Mick knew he would not have been able to do anything that quickly. He was always getting sidetracked. Mick couldn't even see any dust or debris at this point. He walked into the kitchen and laid William's truck keys on the counter. William followed him in, while Mick told him the house was really more of a bungalow than a house. "Just drop your bag by that bookcase for now. The bathroom is right down the hall, next to the spare bedroom, and I have a little office space in between my bedroom and the spare bedroom. I have another bathroom in my bedroom. It's small, but comfortable, and meets my needs, anyway," Mick said.

William dropped his bag in the armchair by the window and went to use the bathroom while Mick went to see if any progress had been made in his bedroom. He slowly opened the door with some trepidation but found everything to be about the same as the living room and kitchen. It smelled like fresh paint. The bed was even made. *Wow! Got to hand it to Colin,* he thought. He went to open the bathroom door, and that was where the neat and clean ended. *Holy crap,* he thought. The bathroom was still in a shamble. There was dust everywhere, tools lying about, no medicine cabinet on the wall. Oh well, he was just glad Colin had gotten as much done as he had. He and William would just have to share a bathroom. It had been done before. For a minute he thought back to his wife and remembered how she had hated to share a bathroom with anyone, including him, most of the time. The couple of times they had gone somewhere with another couple, he had always had to make sure there would be two bathrooms available so she wouldn't have to share.

As he closed the door on the mess in the bathroom, he figured Colin must have gotten his nephew to help him; otherwise, he never would have gotten as much done as he did. His nephew was only fifteen, but he looked up to his uncle Colin and he was probably pleased to be able to give him a hand and end up with a little pocket change. *Not like most kids today,* Mick thought. *Sense of entitlement. Colin's nephew was an all-around good kid. Hopefully, the influences of today's world would have little effect on him and he would remain the all-around good kid that he seems to be.*

Mick walked out of the bedroom as William was coming out of the bathroom. He told William that things weren't quite all put together so they would have to share the bathroom. He hoped that William didn't have a problem with that. "No problem for me, Mick. Like I said, I am just glad to be out of Dodge and on a little adventure." He gave Mick a little, good old boy clap on the back as they walked into the kitchen together.

"So, William, would you like a beer or a whiskey or both?" Mick gave him a grin. "I got a couple of cold ones, and I got some Canadian whiskey. That's probably all I've got. Last time I looked, there was about half a bottle of OJ and some sour milk. I hadn't had time to go to the store before the shitstorm hit. Although I gotta admit to you, I am not much on grocery shopping." He opened the refrigerator door and reached in for a beer. "Well, will you look at that! Colin must have figured I'd be too tired from the drive to think about groceries. Look at this." Mick waved his hand toward the refrigerator and stood aside to show William. There were cheeses, a loaf of bread, a package of turkey meat, two different salads, eggs, creamer, coffee, butter, pickles but the best part, was a six pack of Sierra Nevada Pale Ale. Man, this was what he would call going above and beyond. But in reality, he thought, this was probably more like his sister, not Colin. They were both good people.

He took out the two beers but couldn't find where the opener was. He reached in his pocket and took out his keys. He just happened to have a little opener attached to the key holder. He snapped off the top and handed one of the beers to William. They clinked the bottles together in unison. "Take a seat, William, not that we haven't sat enough today, but those chairs are more comfortable than a truck's."

"Hey, are you putting down my truck?" William asked Mick with a sideways glance and a smile.

"Hell no, man, but you know a truck is a truck. We need to put our feet up a few minutes. I want to check out the news, then I will rustle us up something to eat." They both sat in Mick's overstuffed chairs, but then he couldn't find the remote control to turn the TV on. "Oh crap," he said and got back up to search for the remote. He ended up finding it in the kitchen on the counter.

When he sat back down, William had his shoes off and he was rubbing his feet with his hands. "Whew, don't know about you, but my feet do swell up a bit if I've been riding in the car for very long. And today was a long day. Hope you don't mind if I took my shoes off. My feet don't smell too bad, at least. This beer is going down awfully good too." William smiled at Mick. "I usually drink a German beer when I do drink a beer. Got a hankering for 'em after I was over in Germany, but that was many years ago. This is a good-tasting beer." He pointed at the beer in his hand as Mick was trying to adjust the volume of the TV.

Mick, being a typical bachelor, had few furnishings in the house. He never went in for knickknacks or had much of anything lying around. He was much more of a minimalist before minimalism, if that was even a word, became popular, he thought.

He had acquired a few nice pieces of artwork and a few good books and that was about it. At least the asshole who had broken in hadn't destroyed his furniture. He had just purchased it last year, and it had taken him almost another year before that to decide on what he wanted. One brown leather recliner and one brown leather chair that matched it. A love seat that had a small armrest/cupholder, two beautiful zebra wood end tables, and matching coffee table. He had settled on an ocean scene watercolor for over the small fireplace and two matching sconces on each side of the fireplace. That was about it. He had one other piece of artwork, but that was in the hallway. It had been his mom's, and he couldn't part with it. It was a huge ocean scene with the sun about to set behind the mountains. It looked like it could have been painted around here, but the artist's name had faded over time, just as the painting seemed to have also. He didn't have much left that had been his mom's. The painting and a few pieces of jewelry. She had given him the jewelry in hopes that he would give it to a daughter someday.

"Sorry, Mom," he said out loud and lifted his beer bottle toward the ceiling.

"What's that, Mick?" William asked as he looked at him.

"Oh, nothing important, kind of reminiscing is all. Was just thinking about my mom and how well the two of you would have gotten along. She was the nicest woman. I can't help but think she would be a little disappointed in the path I seem to have taken. Not exactly moving forward very quickly. Ya know what I mean?"

William thought a moment before he looked at Mick and spoke in a subdued voice. "Sometimes we have to step back and reflect a little on where we've been and where we are going. I wasn't on such a positive path once upon a time either, until I got out of the Navy and met Emily. Now, there was a smart lady. She was the one that encouraged me to buy the ranch. My dad had left me a little money when he had passed away, but I was already four years in the Navy by then. Thought I might just as well make a career of it, and I did. Got a good pension when I got out, and I was only thirty-eight years old. Felt like I had a lifetime still ahead of me. If it hadn't been for Emily, I might not have a pot to piss in today. I had been sent to Fort Collins once, and I fell in love with the mountains and lakes there. Figured Idaho wasn't much different. I didn't buy the ranch until I had gotten out of the service, but it was at her prodding that I did so. It sure worked out well for us." He smiled. "Don't be so hard on yourself, Mick. You still have a few good years left in you." He winked at Mick and tipped the now-empty bottle toward him.

"Well, thanks for that, William. I sure don't know, though. What I do know is that I am now famished. How about you? You want another beer while I put together something to eat?"

"Don't mind if I do, but I can help in the kitchen too."

"No, it's okay," Mick told him. "But I do have something you could do for me, if you don't mind. Would you walk to the end of the street and get my mail? It's a multiple-person mailbox, and I am in number 9. I would really appreciate it, and I will be done by the time you get back."

"No problem. I could use a stretch of the old legs, anyway," William told him.

Mick got him the mailbox keys from the hook by the door, and while William was gone, Mick put together two turkey sandwiches with cheese and some wilted lettuce that had been left in the crisper. He added the two different salads to the plate, tossed in a pickle, and found two forks in the drawer. He set them on the little counter just as William returned with the mail.

They ate pretty much in silence with the news on the TV in the background. When they finished eating, William rubbed his stomach and said, "Man, that was good. I hadn't realized how hungry I was." He got up and took his and Mick's plates to the sink. He put the food stuff in the refrigerator while Mick was perusing his mail.

Mick was mumbling while he sorted. "Bill, bill, political crap, WWAF wanting a donation, *Reader's Digest…*" Why he still got that, he wasn't sure. "Hmmm, what's this?" He was more or less talking to himself, holding up a legal-size envelope with no return address on it. He tried to read the postmark, but that was smudged, like it had gotten wet. *Damn.* He had been meaning to talk to the neighborhood association. It wasn't the first time his mail had been damp. By the looks of the boxes, they appeared like they were not all made correctly. He could see a slight gap in some of them. He turned the envelope over to open it. He pulled out a single piece of white paper. There were a few splotches of red on the paper. It wasn't really a letter but just the words "You Will Get Yours Soon!" Written in capital letters boldly in the middle of the paper. Mick looked closer at the red splotches. They sure looked like blood to him, he thought.

"What the hell?" he said out loud and looked to William. "Does this look like blood to you?" Mick held up the piece of paper, and William bent down to scrutinize the splotches or rusty-red color.

"Well, you are more of an expert on these things than I am, Mick, but it looks like blood to me. What do you think it means? Obviously, the words themselves are menacing. What are you going to do?"

Mick looked up at William and said, "Ya know, I don't freaking know. Wait for the next episode, I guess." With that being said, the two men bade each other a good night and went to bed with their own separate thoughts.

Mick figured he needed to get up and get into the office early, anyway. Might as well try to get a good sleep, but he knew that wasn't going to happen very easily. He had asked Colin to be at the office by 9:00 a.m., but he knew Colin was always there earlier than Mick, so that would not be a problem. William had told him that there were a few things he wanted to check out in the area. He had Googled them on his phone while Mick had been driving. He also told him he wanted to stay a few nights as long as that was okay with Mick. He wanted to be available if Mick needed any help with anything. Mick figured two heads were better than one, and he had really taken a liking to the old rancher and was delighted that William wanted to stay and continue to help him. They agreed that William could stay as long as he wanted and they would have coffee in the morning and decide the next steps. At the very least, Mick would need a ride to the office since he was without a vehicle at the time.

Chapter 37

Both Mick and William were up and dressed and in the kitchen by 7:00 a.m. Mick told William he always got the coffee ready the night before and let the program take its course, which was usually by 7:00 a.m. "I find myself in a fog in the morning until after my first cup of coffee clears some of the cobwebs, so it's just easier if it's all ready to go."

"Amen, there," William said. "Emily was up at six every morning, and sometimes I just could not get out of bed until I could smell that coffee aroma. Yum, just something about that smell that makes you want to sit, savor, and read the paper or do the crossword puzzle. Do you ever do any crossword puzzles?" William asked Mick.

"As a matter of fact, I was just going to go out and get the paper. Our local paper is only a weekly paper, but I just can't get out of the habit of reading the paper while I drink a cup of coffee, so I get the paper from Portland. Most of that is trash, but there is something about starting your day with your coffee and the local news. Not to say I don't do the crossword and word jumble."

William gave Mick a sidelong glance. "Hey, how much entertainment do you think there is in a small town, anyway?"

"The local paper is usually comprised of DUIs, domestic violence, and the local community gossip column. Oh, and don't forget the weekend garage sales and business opportunities. Whoo-ee, a lot going on here!" He looked sardonically at William.

"It takes me about half an hour to read the paper and another half an hour to do the word puzzle."

Mick went out to pick up the local paper from his sidewalk. He was in time to see Billy pedaling his bike to the end of the street. Mick couldn't help but admire the kid for his stamina. He remembered when he had to deliver the paper, and it wasn't for pocket money; he had to help out with buying groceries. His mom was not going to be beholden to anyone, even if she had a right to certain services. Mick shook his head, as he always did when he thought about the hard life his mom had had. She had been such a good woman, and she had gone in such a bad way. It just wasn't fair.

When Mick went out the front door, William stood at the kitchen counter, doctoring up his coffee. Three tablespoons of sugar and a dollop of half-and-half, all in a large coffee mug with a whale's tail for a handle. He turned the coffee mug upside down before filling it with coffee. He was smiling as he doctored his coffee.

"Something amusing you this morning?" Mick asked when he had returned with the paper folded in his hand.

"No, not really," William said. "I was just trying to remember how many coffee mugs my wife had purchased as souvenirs. Any trip we took, she came home with a coffee mug." He smiled at the whale's tail as he sat at the table and reflected on the good life he and Emily had had. "I probably have one whole cupboard filled with coffee cups, and I use the same one day after day. She bought it for me when she went to visit her sister in Las Vegas. Got a set of Hooters on it." He gave Mick a wink and took a of gulp of his sweetened mixture.

Mick was actually whistling as he sat down opposite William, opened the paper, and handed William the two pages that contained the puzzle section. "Figured I would give you crack at the puzzle first." He smiled at William as he took a gulp of his coffee. He then proceeded to spread the rest of the paper across the table, blocking William's access to any part of the paper, anyway. It took Mick a good three minutes before he looked over the top of the paper that he was reading, and he said, "Oh, crap, William. I am sorry. I am so used to sitting by myself in the morning. Why don't we go sit in the dining room? At least there is more space for both of us and our papers."

William told Mick that his wife always picked up the local paper from wherever they traveled and she would read it from page 1 to the end, and that included doing the puzzles. She had always enjoyed reading what other communities were doing. Sometimes she took new ideas home to the local Lions Club, which they both belonged to. William started on down memory lane as they drank their coffee.

Mick separated the sections of the paper and gave William the classified section. A lot of retirement-age people lived in the area, so there were still a lot of things posted for sale in the classified section of the paper. Plus, there was always the crossword, find the difference, and word scramble. *That should keep him quiet for a little while, anyway. Well, if not quiet, at least maybe busy.* Mick smiled to himself and read the headlines.

Just then, his cell phone rang. He looked at the cracked screen, thinking he still needed to get a new cell phone. It said, "Blocked number." He debated just putting it down on the table. Not like he didn't have enough to deal with at this point. *Oh, what the hell,* he thought. "Hello," he said into the phone. William looked up from the paper at him with a quizzical expression.

Mick had to strain to hear a barely audible, "Hello."

Mick said hello again, followed by, "Hey, I can't hear you. Who is this?" He could just barely make out the voice saying his name, but he took a stab at who he thought it might be. "Wanda, is that you? Where are you? What is going on, anyway?"

He heard the whispered voice again. "Mick, I can't talk any louder. I am afraid he will hear me. I haven't been able to get away from him since I left Mark's house."

Mick had to strain to hear her. It sounded like she was in a tunnel or something; there was some kind of an echo or a vibration or something he could hear in the background. "Where are you?" he asked her again.

"I don't know," she said. "I was blindfolded when I was brought here. I only had the blindfold off once, and that was just after we crossed the border into Oregon. I saw a sign when he let me out to use the bathroom, but I wasn't able to get very far away from him. He took my cell phone, but he didn't realize that it was actually Mark's cell phone. I had mine tucked into my bra, and I had your number on my call records."

Mick told her if she had her cell phone, she should be able to bring up the location of where she was.

"I thought so too, and I tried that, but I think that was disabled by Mark, because it doesn't show anything. I know I am in a dark, musty, cold cellar. There are no windows and no lights, and I am scared for my life. I think I am near the ocean, though, because I can hear seagulls and the sound of the surf seems to be pretty close by."

Mick took another stab at it. "Can you estimate about how long you were in the car?"

"Well, I usually can't go more than five hours without going to the bathroom, and I really had to go by the time he let me stop and get a break. I had my hands tied behind my back, so I couldn't check the phone. All the way through Idaho he had me in the trunk of his car. The only reason he let me into the back seat after the potty stop was that it had gotten dark outside and he figured no one could see me and I wouldn't try to pull anything at night. Oh, shit," she said.

"What is it?" Mick asked her.

"I hear something above me, footsteps, I am sure."

With that, Mick didn't hear another word. He looked at his phone, willing it to say something. She had never gotten to the *he* part. Who the hell was he? Either she was a good actress or she really was in a dark cellar, probably scared half out of her mind.

He noticed William looking intently at him. Mick realized he was gripping the paper with the opposite hand from which he held his cell phone. He looked up at William. "Well, that was interesting. It seems that the caller was Wanda, the woman I told you about that I thought was the sister of Mark DeGuard. I met her in Pine Lake. It seems she is being held like a hostage in some dark, dank cellar. She did not know where she was. Or so she claimed. Something seems kind of fishy to me. I don't know if she's telling the truth or not. I didn't pay too much attention to the postmark on that little threatening note I got last night. Maybe it hadn't even gone through the postal service but was hand-delivered into my box. It's all just a little bizarre that she had my number. I do not remember giving her my phone number, and I also do not remember having if off my person while I was with her. So how do you explain that?"

IT ALL STARTED WITH MY NEIGHBOR

Suddenly, Mick stood up and pushed his chair behind him. The table moved, and some of William's coffee splashed out onto the crossword puzzle he had been attempting to do. Mick went to check under his sink and pulled out the garbage container. He lifted up the remains of last night's dinner and found the envelope the letter had come in. It was only slightly damp, but he took it and held it under the brighter light in the kitchen. He also put on his reading glasses. It always amazed him how much clearer he could see with them on. "Novel thought," he murmured as he shook his head. He could tell there had been no postmark. It looked more like some kind of a stamp with a date, to make it look like it was postmarked. It was a pretty good facsimile, though, he thought. He laid the envelope on the counter and went back into the dining area.

William was still nonchalantly bent over the paper. "Well, seems like that letter had not been mailed to me but stuck in my mailbox. So whoever put it there was near the house at some point in time yesterday, and if there is any connection between Wanda and whomever she is talking about, it might be that she is also nearby. I think I told you that I was pretty sure there was a relationship between Mark and the woman who called herself Wanda. I had seen some old newspaper clippings when I was in his house. She says she is pretty sure she is locked up someplace near the ocean. She can hear seagulls and the sound of the surf. I think there is some connection between her and whoever dropped that letter off to me yesterday. Either she is lying to me to try to see if she can lure me into finding her or she really is in danger. We know whoever ran me off the road is dangerous. He wanted me dead, and I am not. But I can't help but think he thinks I know way more than I do or that I have something he wants. Either way, I don't know what the hell it is." Mick stood there looking puzzled.

William folded the paper and laid it down on the table. "Well, I suggest we get you to your office and I will check out a couple of things, then you can call me when you are ready for a ride, or I will just head back to your office. Whatever works best for you." William said he would just go brush his teeth and be ready to leave in two shakes of a cow's tail.

239

Mick looked at him and couldn't help but smile. Kind of corny, he thought, but he sure was glad William was there. He didn't think he could deal with everything by himself. William picked up his coffee cup to take another sip, but while he had been listening to Mick, it had grown cold. He gave a sigh and dumped the remains in the sink. Mick told him he would be ready to leave the house in about ten minutes. William went back to use the bathroom to brush his teeth before they headed out the door. "Not bad for an ole fart," he said to his reflection and tipped his cowboy hat at the mirror. "Besides, I am beginning to take a liking to all this espionage stuff!" And he smiled at himself.

Chapter 38

Mick figured he should go back to the sheriff's office and have another chat with Randy. Maybe he could do some checking to see if any old coins had turned up locally yet or not. Mick thought he would make a half-hearted effort to check with the local pawnshops, just in case someone was desperate enough to drop a coin collection off in one. Highly unlikely, though, he thought. He could show Randy the pictures he had taken on his phone. He pulled the cell phone out of his back pocket and brought up the picture section. Well, then again, maybe not. They were definitely not easy to make out, what with the cracked screen and all. He tried enlarging them, but that actually made them harder to decipher. Hopefully, if he got a new phone, they would be easier to view.

Mick was standing on the sidewalk by William's truck when William walked out of the house. "I guess, before I do anything, I will need to stop at Verizon and see about getting a new phone. The screen is too damaged to be able to make out what the newsprint says in the picture, and I was hoping I could show them to Randy. What do you want to do first, William?"

William looked at Mick and smiled. "Well, as I said before, I don't mind just tagging along. Two heads are better than one, I always say."

Mick looked at him and told him what a weary old cliché that was but he thought it was true and Mick would be glad to have someone to talk to anyway.

Mick went around to the driver's side before remembering it wasn't even his truck. He hit the side of the truck and swore. "Damn it. I forgot I don't even have a vehicle to drive right now. Thanks, William. Sure glad you are here. I should have called the dealership first thing to see if my truck is ready for me to pick up."

William got into the driver's side. He had to take off his Stetson in order to be able to see over the steering wheel.

"Hey, I am going to stop by the office first. On second thought, why don't I go on to Verizon while you chat with Colin? No one wants to go to a cell phone store unless you really have to buy a cell phone. Colin is an interesting fellow to chat with. He traveled extensively before I met him. Seems his mom had left him a little money, and he, being young yet, spent most of it seeing the world. He has lots of stories to tell. You could probably entertain each other for a long time, but I will probably only be about an hour. Will that do?"

William was game for almost anything. He was enjoying this little adventure. "Anything you want, Mick, ole boy. Just tell me which way to go." He gave him a sideways glance and stepped on the gas.

When they arrived at the office, Mick noted an unfamiliar car at the curb. It was parked in the parking lot where the sign clearly said, "Reserved for Owner." Mick looked at the car. *Hmmmm, pretty nice,* he thought as William had to circle the block to try to find a parking spot for his oversize truck. The car looked brand-new. It was a Porsche. A deep-burgundy color, with tinted windows, black interior, and some fancy kind of wheels Mick had never seen before, not on any car around these parts, anyway. As he walked around the car, he saw a pink poodle emblem on the rear bumper. "Hmmm, it's gotta be hers," he said under his breath. He stopped on the sidewalk and took out his phone and hit Colin. William stopped alongside of him and looked up and down the street as he heard Mick speak into the phone. William could tell by the look of frustration on Mick's face and his body language that something was sure pissing him off.

"Well, yes, Mom. I am working today. In fact, I am in the office with a client as we speak." Colin was talking to Mick.

"Colin, is Sheelya in the office with you now?"

Mick could hear her voice in the background. "Yes, that's correct, Mom," Colin responded.

"Well, I am sorry, Colin. I happen to be right outside the office, but I am not coming in right now. I have enough crap to deal with today, and I don't want to have another altercation with her."

"No, that's fine, Mom. I gotta go. Talk to you later."

Mick looked at the phone in his hand and then turned to William. "Well, I was planning on you having a nice, interesting conversation with my assistant, but I think he may actually need your expertise, ole buddy." Mick winked at William. "Seems he is dealing with an extremely pesky client that we are trying to get rid of. I think your gift of gab might just be what he needs at this point. Would you mind going in and trying to rescue the young man, William? That woman is way out of his league. He will not know how to handle her, and as you know, I have things that I have to get done today," he said. "Let Colin know we have met and you need our services but then steer the conversation wherever you want to. Sheelya will get bored and eventually get tired of waiting for me too."

William agreed that the plan was okay with him, telling Mick he could have some fun with it.

"Well, then, good luck." Mick patted William on the shoulder and watched as William reached in the back of the truck and took out his rather-large Stetson Horizon cowboy hat. He put it on his head, adjusted the brim, then adjusted the wide silver-and-turquoise belt buckle he wore around his waist. "I have a job to do," he said and handed Mick his truck keys as he walked up the stairs into the building. Mick couldn't help but smile as he pulled away from the curb, throwing a few pebbles onto the sidewalk in his haste to get away.

Mick drove to the Verizon store first. Fortunately, Meredith was on duty for the day. Being a small store, they only had about four employees, and Meredith happened to be his favorite. It had nothing to do with her petite, perfectly proportioned figure, nor her perfect, pearly teeth, not even how she always leaned into him when she was taking an order or explaining something. It was her bubbling personality that he enjoyed the most. *Yeah, right,* he thought as he walked in the door. *Who am I kidding?*

"Mick, nice to see you," Meredith said as soon as she saw him. "Haven't seen you in a while. In fact, this must be the longest time you have not been in the store. Phone broke, I take it?" She gave him a big smile full of those beautiful white teeth.

"Well, yes," Mick said, "and I am in kind of a hurry, so how about I let you decide which phone I should get this time and I will succumb to the waterproof, protective case and the stupid thing that hooks it on your belt? I need all the help I can get at this point. Three broken phones in one year is even a little too much for me."

Meredith picked out one of the new Samsungs and then brought one out from the back room with all the equipment Mick would need. She set everything on the counter and then took his phone out of his hands. Not without a little suggestive squeeze of his hand, though, he thought. He watched her as she deftly transferred all his old information and pictures to the new phone. Man, she was a cutie, but too young for him, he thought sadly. They discussed a few things about the new programs the phone had and some incidental small talk, and then Mick said he had to be on his way. She gave him a little pout and told him not to stay away so long next time. His reply was, he hoped he wouldn't be back in the next two years at least. He looked at the time on his new phone and knew he couldn't have gotten in and out of there in less than an hour. And he hadn't. *Oh well,* he thought. *Everything always takes longer than you think it will. I hope Randy hasn't gone to lunch yet.* He then pulled away from the curb. He did not notice the small dark car that pulled out behind him.

He pulled up in front of the police station and could see Randy sitting behind the counter as he went in. It looked like he was in the middle of booking someone. There was a scruffy-looking young man sitting across from Randy at his desk. The kid looked higher than a kite, so it probably wouldn't take Randy too long to finish with him. Mick decided to sit on the bench in the front office and wait. Randy was having some difficulty keeping the kid awake long enough to answer his questions. It would have been comical if not for being more sad than funny. The kid almost fell out of the chair, but Randy leaned over and kind of pulled him up and over to the right and he was able to sit up again. Although it looked like his eyes were closed. *Man,* Mick thought, *I am grateful I never had kids. There is just too much unhealthy stuff for them to get themselves into these days.* You would think it would be better in a small rural town, but it really wasn't. Fewer people, fewer cases, just a matter of numbers. Mick couldn't help but overhear what they were saying. Kid got hooked on heroin because his dad left drugs and paraphernalia in places he thought the kid wouldn't find. *Yeah, right,* Mick thought. *Kids are not stupid.* The kid mumbled that he had seen his dad shoot up before, so it didn't seem such a bad idea. If his dad did it, then why shouldn't he? *Poor kid.* Apparently, his mom had overdosed on Oxy and alcohol over a year ago, and she had been a really good mom until her dad had passed away from lung cancer. Randy was being very gentle with the kid. Probably knew what he had been going through. He could hear the lecturing tone in Randy's voice but could tell he felt sorry for the kid too. Might get off with a hand slap if he agreed to go into a treatment program. *Sounds reasonable,* Mick thought. The kid didn't even look twenty-one, so if he got into treatment, there might be hope for him. Mick hoped so, anyway.

Mick got off the bench and walked down the small hallway to the restroom, thinking, *I can't listen to that any longer.* He shook his head, thinking back, when his dad had left his mom, how heartbroken he was. He looked at the two doors in front of him. The last time he had used the restroom in here, there had been a man figure on the door on the right and a woman figure on the door on the left. *What the hell,* he thought. Now the door on the right had a sign that stated, "Staff Only," and the door on the left had a sign of both a man and a woman. He tried the doorknob on the door that had the Staff Only sign on it, but it was locked. He figured the department finally got tired of using the same bathroom as the public. He remembered when he was working, they had to have a calendar made up monthly with whose turn it was to clean the restrooms. No one ever volunteered, that was for sure; he remembered they used to get downright nasty. He liked separate bathrooms for men and women, none of the horseshit you saw in Portland now. Most places had gender-neutral bathrooms. Mick shook his head as he opened the gender-neutral door, thinking, *What in the hell is the world coming to?*

When he got out of the restroom, the kid was not sitting in the chair any longer. Randy was filling out paperwork. Mick walked behind the counter and sat in the chair the kid had vacated. "Where did the kid end up?" he asked Randy.

Randy looked up at him with a sadness in his expression. "Oh, I had him go lie down in the back room. He can sleep it off. I told him if he shows he can stay in a program, I will let him off this time. I feel sorry for the kid. His dad is a piece of crap. Maybe the apple doesn't fall far from the tree, but if I believed that, I couldn't work at this job any longer."

"More paperwork than ever, isn't there?" Mick said.

"Oh, man, you are not just kidding. All Ts crossed, all Is dotted preciously, or we get called on the carpet and have to come in, even on our days off, if something isn't correct. And our current, illustrious chief enjoys calling us in, the prick," Randy said.

Mick shook his head. "Well, I for one, am glad not to have to deal with all the bureaucratic bullshit. Although I must admit, the steady paycheck was not too bad. I never know what I will be doing next," he said. "I brought some pictures I wanted you to take a look at. Do you have time now, or should I come back?" he asked him.

Randy shoved the pile of papers further down the desk, where they merged with other piles of papers. "The hell with this!" he said. "Let's see what ya got."

Mick thought his friend looked more harassed and tired than usual. *Poor guy.* He spread the pictures out in the bare spot where all the other, more official-looking papers had been.

He assembled them in some sense of order and went on to explain to Randy where he had found them. Randy looked at the pictures and scanned through the articles. It took him a while because they hadn't really come out very clear. He stopped at the picture of Thomas Hardcastle. "Kind of a nasty-looking piece of work, isn't he?" Randy said to Mick. He turned in his chair and fired up his computer. He pulled up the name Thomas Hardcastle on the criminal site they had access to. He found an extensive rap sheet. He read off the criminal activity while Mick watched. "He's been at it a long time," he told Mick. "Starting with petty thievery at sixteen, which sent him to juvie. Doesn't appear like he learned much there, because he stole a car and robbed a convenience store after he got out at twenty-one years old. That got him a couple of years in prison. Which taught him nothing again. There are smaller infractions in between. Looks like he laid it low for a while, anyway. He went on to bigger and better things after that. Armed robbery when he was about thirty. That sent him away for a long time. It looks like he was in the Snake River Correctional Facility here in Oregon. They gave him fifteen years for the armed robbery. Should have only gotten ten, but it looks like one of the guards was injured during the robbery, and neither he nor his buddy would admit to who shot the guard, so they both got fifteen years. Then due to his long rap sheet, they gave him some extra time. That would put him around forty-seven or so," Randy concluded. "It looks like the buddy got in some kind of fight while in prison. He's now permanently disabled from a knife wound that took a chunk out of his shoulder. He got transferred to another prison, and then Hardcastle got out of Snake River a month and a half ago." Randy fiddled on the internet for a while longer but couldn't find any more information of interest.

"I could give the warden a call and see if he will tell me where Hardcastle was supposed to be going to. He's on parole, so he has to report in, and he is supposed to stay in one place because he will have a parole officer to follow up with. I know the warden. I met him a couple of years ago at a conference in Nevada. Seemed like a decent guy. Man, that's one job I would not take for a million dollars. Warden of all those inmates. No, thank you." Randy looked up at Mick for confirmation.

Mick said he would appreciate any help Randy could give him. Randy let him fiddle with the computer while he went to the front desk to use the phone to call the warden.

Carter Flag was his name. Randy remembered how he was a walking, talking justice system book. He could quote passages of prison rules and often did for the fun of it. He would mimic the prisoners, too, changing his voice, sounding like a dozen different ones. The guy had kept several of the conference attendees at the bar long past the time they should have been, but he was so good at the

247

imitations, like a comedian onstage. They were in stitches and hadn't realized what time it was until the bartender hollered out, "Last call!" Randy remembered also how they had all looked the last morning of the conference. Like something an old cat had dragged in. All of them bleary-eyed and reeking of stale alcohol. Randy was surprised they were all able to make it to the first conference and stay awake. Although when he thought back on it, one of the guys hadn't made it and had spent his night over the porcelain throne. He was a mess when Randy had seen him later in the day, waiting to board the plane. Randy shook his head, thinking back on it.

Mick brought up the most recent picture he could find of Hardcastle. It was taken way back when he had been booked, so he was now several years older than back then. *Wouldn't want to meet up with him in the dark, that's for sure,* Mick thought. He could see tattoo lines on his neck creeping up onto the back of his head. He had three dots by his left eye, and then the outlines of two teardrops underneath the dots. Apparently, he hadn't killed anyone, but maybe he had made an attempt. The guard being a near miss. Mick had some knowledge of prison tattoos. He had been assigned to follow one of the guards around the Oregon State Penitentiary when he was in the academy. It was part of his internship. Boy, that had been a scary time! That place was full of psychos. They canceled that part of the program after one of the internees had gotten stabbed with a piece of glass from a broken pickle jar. He had died before anyone could get to him. That would have been a memorable obituary, Mick couldn't help but think. Death due to pickle jar shard in the chest. *Poor man.* He had had a wife and two little kids. *I digress,* Mick thought to himself. *Why in the hell do I always feel compelled to trip on down memory lane at the oddest times?* He shook his head to himself.

Back to the tattoos. He chastised himself. He had been told to "learn up" on the meaning of them. It would give him a better understanding of what type of prisoner or outlaw on the street he was dealing with. A prisoner could have any type of tattoo put on himself while in prison; there was a kind of honesty code among prisoners, and they did not elaborate on their types of tattoos. If the teardrop was solid, then there was a good chance that the prisoner had killed someone. And the more teardrops they had, the more people they had killed and gotten away with it, so to speak. People you did not want to mess around with, generally speaking.

Mick hunted for any more information he could find on Hardcastle and on Mark DeGuard, for that matter. He could hear Randy talking to someone, so he assumed he had connected with the warden. He heard him say, "Yeah, Thomas Hardcastle, number 1523491. Yeah, when exactly was he released? September 25 of this year? Where did he go? Do you know?" There was a long pause before Randy spoke again. And then he could hear him say, "Really? Well, that is interesting. I really appreciate you giving me that information, Carter. We may have a problem on our hands here. Yeah, you too. Thanks for the help. Goodbye."

Randy came back and sat down across from Mick at the cluttered desk. "Well, sounds like the warden knew that Hardcastle's sister had been murdered. How he found that out so quickly is beyond me, but Carter said he is an internet/news junkie, so maybe that's it. He knew the sister's friend had been killed also. Seems like he— meaning Carter—took a personal interest in Hardcastle since one of the inmates had been injured and would not divulge who had injured him, but Carter was pretty sure it had been Hardcastle. He seemed to prey on the physically challenged, so to speak. Carter told me, if there had been any way he could have kept him in prison, he would have. He said he was a vicious little son of a bitch and to watch your back," Randy said. "So here's the interesting part: Guess where he said he was going to go and live? You got it, Tillamook, Oregon."

"No shit," Mick said and sat leaning back in the chair, deep in thought.

Chapter 39

Mick sat with Randy for a while longer, discussing Mick's would-be theories and scenarios. Of course, Randy cautioned him about his no longer being in uniform, and therefore, he had no right to pursue anything that had to do with Thomas Hardcastle. He made sure he lectured him that if Hardcastle really did have something to do with the murder of both the women, then it would be the police who needed to pursue him, not Mick. "If he has indeed killed possibly three people, then he is more than a little dangerous. For all you know, you could be his next target," Randy said and gave Mick the sternest look he could muster. What Mick really heard, though, was, "Blah, blah, blah," thinking to himself, *There is no way I could just let this guy go now, especially if he's the one who ran me off the road.*

"Thanks a lot, Randy," Mick told him. "You know I respect you, and I will take your advice into consideration, but not exactly to heart, if you get my drift." He stood up and, with his fist, pounded on his chest in the vicinity of his heart and winked at Randy as he walked out the door.

Now what? he thought to himself. *What in the hell does the guy want from me?* Mick got in the truck and started back to his office, thinking, *The she-witch should be done by now.* Two hours or more had passed by. He knew her well enough to know how easily she could get bored. He saw his empty parking lot as he turned the corner toward his office. "Thank God," he said to himself. "How in the hell can I get rid of the woman once in for all?" He eased the truck into the small parking space. He got out and walked up the sidewalk and into the office. He found Colin and William deep in conversation. In fact, so much so they had not even heard Mick until he was right up next to them.

When he said, "Hey, you two," they both looked up with startled expressions.

William spoke first. "Well, you were sure enough right about this young man." He gave Colin a slap on the shoulder as he spoke. "He has two stories to my one, and he ain't half my age yet! Now, don't that beat all? Thank you, Mick. It has been a very interesting couple of hours. After we got rid of that dang cantankerous woman, anyway. Whooo-eee, she is something else, ain't she? Colin here was real patient with her, I must say. Treated her like she could be his mama, and we know that ain't so, don't we?"

"I can't thank you enough, William," Mick told him. "If you can figure out how I can get rid of her once and for all, I am all ears. She sure doesn't take no for an answer."

William looked at the two men and smiled. "Well, I can imagine you two have some talking to do, so I think I will head to that little café you mentioned to me. What was the name of it? The Crow's Nest, I think you said. I will get myself a Coke. I will be all ears and quiet as a mouse."

Mick looked at William and smiled skeptically. "Somehow, I don't quite see that, William, but you go ahead and I will meet you there after I talk to Colin for a bit. Or if you get bored before I get there, you can always head back this way. Tell Kathy you want to try the blackberry pie. It is their specialty, and it comes with vanilla ice cream."

William said that sounded good to him and gave a wave as he went out the door. Mick saw a big shit-eating grin on his face as he did so. He could tell he had thoroughly enjoyed his time with Colin.

Mick looked at the pile of crap on his desk. He usually went through all the mail himself, not trusting it to anyone else, even Colin, just in case there happened to be something incriminating in the correspondence. He wasn't exactly a bad boy, he thought to himself, but not exactly a good one either. *Oh hell, this has to wait a bit.* He turned toward Colin and said with a chuckle, "I am sorry about Sheelya, Colin, but I figured you were already stuck with her, so why should I add myself in the mix when it wasn't going to solve anything, anyway? What did she want this time?"

Colin proceeded to tell him she was madder than hell and figured that Mick was avoiding her and that he, Colin, had something to do with it.

"Do with what?" Mick asked, exasperated. "She knows that I play by the book when it comes to her and her situations. Not that I haven't reaped my share of the rewards where she is concerned, but as an investigator, I have been aboveboard on everything. Were you able to convince her not to come?"

Colin took a deep breath and said, "Well, what she had to say could have easily been said in ten minutes, but you know that is not her style. So I patiently listened to how wronged she has been, harassed and harangued, etc. Apparently, her weaselly husband might have caught on to what she had in mind, so he had most of his money transferred to offshore accounts that she apparently cannot touch. He's got the house in Oceanside, which she thinks is only worth about a million dollars, but he is willing to give that to her. She claims they were in the process of building a bigger house on a bigger piece of property, with a better view, of course, but then she found out that the property was in his son's name, not his. She was practically going to explode while she was screaming at me. She thinks you knew all about it and that is why you have been avoiding her. She called you every name in the book, and then some. Actually, then she started to scream in Spanish. I just sat and let her go on. I figured she would get tired of screaming before too long, but then William stepped in and turned on his country charm, and he got her to calm down. Kind of like a tigress that found her cub, so to speak. He started asking her all kinds of questions in a concerned, fatherly manner. Then she started asking him all sorts of questions. I think she was sizing him up as her next conquest. He carried himself really well. He answered her questions calmly, giving her his undivided attention. I think she really would have carried it further, but he told her his wife had just died and he was still in mourning, and then he started talking about his wife. I am sure you have already heard some of it." Colin looked at Mick.

"Oh yeah, he's quite the talker, our William is," Mick said. "Nonstop practically from Idaho to here."

Colin said that his charm seemed to work on her, though. "She said she wasn't done with you yet, but at least she left. I tried to convince her that you knew nothing about her husband's oversees operations, or his financials, for that matter, but I don't think she believed me. Not sure you are done with her yet, boss."

"Well, what can I say? But thanks for doing your part. I owe you one. Actually, more than one, if you count the mess my house was in." He looked at Colin, who was making a motion with his fingers, representing it was going to cost him something extra. "Oh, good grief, Colin! I am indebted to you. How is that? I haven't forgotten you, trust me. I will give a substantial down payment and the rest when the house is finished. My next stop will be the bank to get out some cash. How will that be?"

Colin looked at him and smiled. "I know you are good for it, boss. Just giving you a little shit, that's all. You deserve it after leaving me with that witch. And that is a nice word for her."

"On another note," Mick said. "What you have done so far in the house looks great. I really appreciate what a fast worker you are. I know I could not have done what you have in the amount of time you have. The bathroom was a surprise, but I realize you couldn't have gotten everything done. What are you thinking about the rest of the time? Do you have an idea about how much more time you might need?"

Colin cocked his head, as Mick had seen him do before when he was concentrating on something. "Well, I reckon it will take about two more full days to get the bathroom done and the rest cleaned up. Can you pay me in cash for the work I have done so far on the house? I am a little strapped for cash at the moment. The rest, just the usual payroll check will do. I promised my sister I would help her out with a house payment this month."

"Totally understand what you are talking about. Man, I have been hemorrhaging money this past month. This Hardcastle guy has a real hard-on for me, and I wish I knew why. I now think that it was probably him who ran me off the road and probably destroyed my house. Thank God for William, who saved my life, and for you, Colin, for being in a position to be able to help me. Don't know what I would have done without the both of you."

Colin looked lost in thought, then told Mick, "Just say the word and I will help you find the scumbag and put him away for good. Between the two of us, we know a fair number of people around here. We should be able to find him without too much difficulty. You know how small an area this is and how much people look out for one another, and oh yeah, they love to stick their noses in where they might not belong too. I can put some feelers out, anyway."

"Sounds good to me, Colin. In the meantime, I think that gal who called herself Wanda is, or was, I should say, Mark DeGuard's sister. I got a new phone today, but I kept the old number, so if she calls back, I will be on the lookout for her. If by any chance she calls the office, try to get her to stay on hold. Maybe we can even trace her call. If nothing else, tell her to call the cell phone, that I am watching for her to call. I don't remember giving her my office number, but then I am pretty sure I never gave her my cell phone number either, but somehow, she has called both numbers. Pretty cagey of her, don't you think? I wish I knew whose side she was on, anyway."

Mick went back to the business at hand. "So back to the house. Is there anything pressing you have to take care of here? Or I can take care of and you can get back on the bathroom detail?" Colin told Mick that he needed to make a couple of phone calls and pay a couple of bills, nothing for Mick to deal with, more like a housekeeping detail. But there was one call that Mick might want to return sooner than later. He went on to explain that a man by the name of Allen Wilson had called yesterday. "He said it was important. He wanted to hire an investigator to check into his business dealings. He feels like he is being ripped off, but he can't put his finger on who it is. Said it was not much money at a time but seems it was happening more frequently the past couple of months. Here is his name and number," Colin said as he passed Mick a business card.

Mick looked at the card and then told Colin he was pretty sure he knew who it was, the man who owned the little convenience store on Washington Street. "Jeez, why the hell doesn't he just retire? He looks a hundred years old. I will give him a call. Do me a favor, though. You know how bad I am with misplacing things. Text me his name and number, will ya? At least then I won't lose the number. Unless I lose my damn phone, which I wouldn't put past me either." He handed the card back to Colin. Then Mick told him to knock off as soon as he could and get back to the house. That was more important to him at this point.

Colin said he would lock up the office, but he wanted to order a big dumpster from the waste management company. He had been so busy he had forgotten to do that, and he had put a lot of crap in the backyard that Mick hadn't seen yet. "So don't look, man. I will get it out of there before you have to go in the backyard."

Mick looked at Colin over the top of the sunglasses he had just put on his face. "Forget the bills. They can wait. You have more important things to deal with." He gave a slight wave and headed out the door.

Chapter 40

Mick got in the truck and headed east toward the Crow's Nest, which William said he was going to. Mick felt a little guilty leaving him on his own for that long. More than likely, though, with his gift of gab, he had found an audience by now. There was never any lack of people in this little town who wouldn't love to talk to a guy like William.

He parked the truck and went into the little café. He looked around, and there were only a couple of booths filled, but no William. He saw that the Nelson sisters were sitting together at a table for four by the window. As soon as he looked at them, they both flung their hands up in the air, waving for him to come over to the table. *Talk about identical twins,* he thought. Even though they were now in their seventies, he couldn't tell Evelyn from Evaline. They both had curly gray hair. *More like frizz balls,* he thought. Same length, same style. They wore the same square black glasses, and they still usually dressed in the same outfits. Good grief, like two peas in a wrinkly old pod. He couldn't help but smile at them, though.

"Hello, ladies," he said.

They beamed up at him. They both were wearing lime-green sweaters with sequin collars and matching white hats. He was surprised they didn't have white gloves on too, but he guessed those were reserved for Sundays.

"What kind of trouble have you been into lately?" he asked them.

They both looked up at him at the same time and giggled.

"I was looking for a friend of mine. He said he was going to the Crow's Nest, and since this is the only one in town, I figured he

IT ALL STARTED WITH MY NEIGHBOR

would be here. Nice-looking older man wearing a big Stetson cowboy hat."

They looked at each other and smiled conspiratorially. "Why, as a matter of fact," Evelyn said, if it was Evelyn. And then the other sister said, "He's in the restroom. Too much coffee."

They both giggled again.

Just then, William appeared from around the corner. "My, how time flies when one is being so raptly entertained!" He smiled and winked at the sisters, who not only giggled but also blushed this time.

Mick rolled his eyes toward the ceiling, afraid he would laugh out loud if he didn't look in another direction. He began to think he had stepped into another time zone, what with William's big Stetson, oversize inlaid-turquoise silver belt buckle, and alligator cowboy boots. Not to overlook the twin sisters in their 1950s retro outfits.

William made to introduce the sisters to Mick when one of them said, "Oh, William, you don't need to introduce us to Mick. We have known him for years. Since he was knee-high to a grasshopper. We knew his mom too. We met the both of them when they first vacationed here. We also remember that nasty little cousin of his. Right, Mick, the one that scared you half to death that summer?" She looked at William over the top of her glasses. "They rented the house next to ours on the beach for a whole month that summer. Then Mick would come every summer and stay with his aunt. We would even babysit him a time or two when his aunt got sick of the two boys and their noise. Whoo-ee, those boys could get riled up sometimes! We had a lot of fun with them, though, didn't we, Evaline?" Evelyn finally wound down enough to take a breath. She looked up at William and fluttered her eyes at him.

"Well, then," William said. "No introductions are needed, are there?"

Mick put his hand on William's shoulder, indicating with a little pressure that it was okay if they made a quick exit. William looked at the women and took the hint. He placed his Stetson back on his head, smiled at them, and said, "It was delightful meeting you, ladies, this afternoon. I hope I might meet up with you again before I leave these parts." Mick watched as he theatrically removed the big hat and

RONELLE HERRICK

swept it to the side in a grandiose movement of goodbye. This time Mick could not help but laugh out loud as he made his way toward the door. He saw that the twins' expressions went from delighted to crestfallen in a matter of a second.

They both said at the same time, "Oh, please do stop by before you leave, Mr. Pryor. We would love to have you in for a cuppa tea!"

"That sounds wonderful, ladies. I'll be sure and come around." He turned and followed Mick out the door. Mick watched as he shrugged his shoulders and whispered to Mick, "Well, I might, anyway."

When they got outside and into the truck, William looked at Mick and said, "I was beginning to feel like I was the one going to be their lunch. I did find out some very useful information, however." William fastened his seat belt as Mick left a little gravel in the wake of leaving.

Mick looked over at William. "How's that?" he asked him.

William had turned around in his seat and watched as the twins stood at the café window and were waving at him.

"Wow, you sure made their day. Most probably their week and month also." He laughed as William turned back around with a silly grin on his face.

"I must say, Mick, I can't remember when two ladies tried to outflirt each other for my sake! That was a world of fun. But in all seriousness, I did learn that they have seen a stranger in town. They live in that next little town over, Oceanside, I think they said it was. They sure could talk, and they kept trying to talk over each other or get the last word in. Anyway, apparently, there are few tourists this time of year, so it's easy to spot a stranger in town. Sounds like they do their fair share of the busybody business. They have seen someone that matches the description you mentioned at the gas station and then again in the convenience store. They said he is of medium build, grungy kind of appearance, grayish beard, and covered with tattoos, even on his face. Which made them shudder as they described that." William smiled, then continued, "One of them said that the guy always wore a baseball cap pulled low over his face so that you could barely see anything but his beard. They told me they witnessed him

258

being extremely rude to the owner of the convenience store. And when she asked him to leave, he started to verbally abuse her. He stopped when he saw the twins staring at him with their cell phone in hand, like they were going to call someone, so he abruptly left the store. They said he didn't pay for the cigarettes he had asked for, just sulked his way out, giving them a dirty look as he went. I guess he made a rather-menacing impression on both of them."

"Well, that's more information than we had before, anyway," Mick said. "I'm sorry you got subjected to the twins. They are quite the pair. Live in a different era. Neither one was ever married, although they seem to like men."

William interjected, "Oh, I picked up on that right away. Most likely, they chased any potential suitor away. They look and think exactly alike, so how could any man pick one from the other? They look like they come as a pair."

"Yeah," Mick said. "I do remember when I was a kid and visited my aunt, they practically smothered me. They were harmless but overwhelming at my age. And they kept wanting to ruffle my hair. I do remember I hated that. Did they say anything else that you think would be significant?"

William was silent for a moment, which caused Mick to look over at him. William was hardly ever silent. "Well, apparently, this guy the twins had seen has been asking questions about you. That was a red flag in itself. The locals don't take kindly to any stranger asking about one of their own, so to speak. It sounds like he is not being very discreet with his questions either. So Evelyn or Evaline—I never did figure out who was who—followed the guy in her car. The other sister was at a dental appointment, so she did not say anything to her but followed him at a distance so he would not notice. She said he turned off at Trask Road and she followed him a little farther at a distance and watched him turn onto a smaller gravel road. She had never been down the road before so wasn't sure if she would even be able to turn around safely or not. She went past the gravel road, turned around at the end, and then went back to the dental office. She said the guy had tattoos on his neck, face, and arms and he was pretty scary-looking to her. So she didn't dare do anything but turn around. She was going to go to the police and report him as a potential problem, but by then her sister was done with her dental appointment and by the time they went to the grocery store and got home she had forgotten. Blamed it on old age. Which makes total sense to me, anyway," William said. "God, they look ninety at least, so probably doesn't take much for them to forget either."

They had driven a little farther down the road when Mick's phone rang. He picked it up and looked at the number: Caller Unknown. He let it ring to go to voice mail, forgetting that he was looking for Wanda to call him. The caller did not leave a message.

"Shit," Mick said as he slapped his forehead with the palm of his hand. "Talk about old age. I already forgot that I was going to answer any call, in the event that it is her. Goddamn it, anyway."

Just as they passed the sign for Oceanside, the phone rang again. It had only been about fifteen minutes from the last time it rang. Mick picked it up and noted the number. It was Colin this time. He answered. "Hey, Colin. What's up?"

Colin explained that he went ahead and paid the bills since there were not many and he had been on his way out of the office when he answered the phone. "It sounded like the same gal I had told you about that called but wouldn't leave a message or her name."

Mick took the phone away from his ear and looked at it. Sometimes Colin was a little less than astute. "Colin, I think it was just yesterday that you told me that, so yes, I do remember." He shook his head as William looked at him and smiled.

Colin continued to talk so missed Mick's sarcasm. "Well, I am pretty sure it was the same woman, but she still would not leave her name. She sounded breathless again, and her voice was shaky, like she was scared or trying not to cry. She talked really fast and low and said that she had tried to call your cell phone but it went to voice mail and she didn't dare leave a message."

"Colin!" Mick said. "Slow down. Did she leave a number this time? I had a call about ten minutes ago from an unknown number, but I didn't answer it, like a dummy."

Colin explained, a little slower this time, that yes, she did give him a number this time. He tried to talk to her for a little longer, but then she suddenly hung up on him. He was actually still asking questions without realizing she had hung up. She had said that she was afraid for her life. That this guy had her locked up in some dark, dank basement. She did not reveal the guy's name, just that she was being held prisoner. "She did sound really scared," Colin told Mick. "Oh, and she said she could hear seagulls squawking or screeching. She knew they were seagulls because she had lived at the beach once upon a time. That's about it," Colin repeated.

Mick told Colin not to get too excited. She had told him pretty much the same thing when he had talked to her. He still wasn't sure that the woman was indeed Wanda or if she was on the up and up. He would go with the assumption that she was telling the truth, and he asked for Colin to text him the phone number she had given him. He would see what happened when he texted it. Mick filled Colin in on what the twins had told William since he had another ten minutes before he reached the convenience store in Oceanside.

"Well, I will let you know if I hear anything else, but I have left the office, and I just pulled up in front of your house. Hopefully, I can get everything back in order and cleaned up before you get back here. Can't promise, though," Colin said. "Oh, hey. Did you remember to call that Allen guy?"

Mick slapped his forehead again. "Well, goddamn it, it's a good thing your brain is younger that mine. I have so much crap going on I forgot that too." When he hung up the phone, he looked over at William. "Jeez, I can't remember shit anymore. I hope it's just 'cause there is so much going on, not that I am getting early dementia." He sighed. "Sounds like the same woman called, and I am going to assume it was Wanda. I should have answered the phone before, but I was thinking about the damn Hardcastle guy. I need to make this other phone call before I forget again. I need to keep reminding myself I do have a business to run in order to continue to pay the bills, so I had better make myself useful."

Mick pulled into Oceanside, and he parked on the street near the post office. William got out to stretch his legs and told Mick he was going to walk to the end of the street. The phone call took longer than he thought it would. Allen Wilson not only wanted to find someone to help him expose his greedy partner, who he was certain was stealing from him, but he also wanted to talk about his construction business and how long he had been in business. He stated he had had the same partner for over ten years but that he was so pissed at him he didn't care if the guy was thrown in prison or not. He had married a gal about a year ago, and she was always on him for bigger and better, so Allen figured the guy just threw caution to the wind and got greedy.

Mick ended up actually having to cut him short with an apology that he had another call he needed to take, but he reassured him he would be able to help him and he would be able to expose the partner. They set a date for three days later in the week to meet with the guy and collect a retainer.

Mick got out of the truck and looked down the road for William but didn't see him anywhere. *He can't have gotten far,* Mick thought. *This little burg is only about three whole blocks long.* Mick got back in the truck and drove the three blocks to the end of the street, where there was a parking lot that he could turn around in. There was William, standing at the edge of the parking lot where the cement ended and the sand began. Actually, that wasn't entirely true; this parking lot always had dunes of sand that would blow up on it, at times so high the city utility crew had to bring in a little dozer and push the sand back onto the beach. William raised his hand in a wave when he saw Mick's truck, but he kept on talking to a young woman who was trying to control her black Lab, who was almost pulling her over.

Mick got out of the truck and walked over to them, saying, "You sure manage to keep entertained, don't you, William?"

William turned to Mick and said, "William, meet Melissa. And this is her dog, Eeeka. Eeeka is a little anxious since she hasn't had her walk yet. Sorry, Eeeka." With that being said, William bent over to pet the dog, who then jumped up on him and practically knocked him ass over teakettle. He managed to right himself by grabbing onto Mick. Which was just what Melissa had done about five minutes ago to William. "Whoa, there, boy," William said. "We'll all be in the sand in a minute."

Melissa looked at him apologetically. "Sorry, William. He is a handful. He's only two, and Labs tend to be a little high-strung, anyway. He didn't hurt you, did he?" Melissa asked him while she looked at Mick.

Mick looked back, thinking, *Wow, she is adorable. How does William manage to do it?* Melissa told Mick that she usually walked Eeeka down the beach away from any people or dogs. She would then let him off the leash so he could really get a run in. He always walked back quieter after that.

"Well, he sure looks like a handful for a little gal like yourself," Mick told her and then thought, *What a knothead! Little gal? How rude!* She was petite, with bright-green eyes and curly auburn-colored hair. She had a smattering of freckles across her nose and cheeks. He could see where she could be very distracting. *Damn.* He wished he had more time to chat, but instead he said, "Well, you enjoy your walk. I have to get this gentleman on home for his nap." He winked at Melissa and smiled at William, who scowled back at him. Mick took William's arm and steered him back toward the truck.

When they got out of Melissa's earshot, William yanked his arm back and told Mick in no uncertain terms what he thought about that remark. Mick apologized but reminded him they were on a mission, and as much as he would have liked to stay and chat, they had work to do.

William had been headed to the post office and still planned on continuing in that direction. Mick told him to try to not get distracted this time. He was going to Roxanne's. She was the owner of the little restaurant just a block down the street. The place had been there forever and a day, and Roxanne knew everything and everyone. "They have the best clam chowder and crab cakes for miles around too, not to mention their desserts, which are to die for!"

Mick opened the screen door of the restaurant. No little bell signaling an arrival. Wasn't necessary either. The door screeched on its hinges, and then when he let it go, it slammed with a bang. Only one couple looked up, though. The view from the windows of the restaurant was breathtaking. It sat up on a knoll over the ocean almost on top of some magnificent rocks with blowholes that, when it was stormy, would shoot water up over the roof onto the sidewalk. There were only six people total in the place. It was between lunch and dinner, so a good time to try to talk to Roxanne, he thought. Just then, she came out from the kitchen area and had started to ask him where he would like to sit when she recognized who it was.

"Mick, so, so good to see you! Where have you been, anyway? I haven't seen you in months!"

Mick smiled and gave her a little hug. "I know, I know. I have been pretty busy with work and all, but I sure have missed you and your cooking. I think I will just sit at the counter. Is that okay?"

"Of course, silly. Sit wherever you like. I am just glad to see you," she told him. "Would you like a menu?"

Mick looked at his watch. "Well, to be honest, I really only have time for a piece of your chocolate cake. Do you have some of that today?"

"Sure do," she told him. "And for you, I will add a little side of our homemade French vanilla ice cream. I will be back in a jiffy." She turned and went back into the kitchen.

Mick took a moment to look at the view. It sure was beautiful. Roxanne sure had the perfect spot. She worked very hard, six days a week, and did most of the cooking herself. Her mom had left her the restaurant when she passed away a few years ago. Roxanne had been working in it since she was about twelve years old. He had dated her for a while a couple of years ago, but like most of his relationships, it hadn't lasted long. Mostly because Roxanne was too busy for a relationship. She not only worked six days, but they were also usually twelve-hour days. She didn't seem to mind it, though. They had remained friends, and that was more important to the both of them. If he needed a date for a special occasion, he knew he could count on her to go with him. She was a good-looking woman, and her appearance was important to her, but more from a customer service standpoint than to attract a man. She was always so busy working that she didn't have time for a serious relationship.

He watched as she delivered two steaming plates of seafood over rice to the couple by the window. Then she went back and delivered the family of four, of four clam chowder and bread that filled the air with the smell of garlic. Mick heard his stomach growl. It had been a while since he had eaten breakfast. His mouth started to water. When she came out next, she had a plate filled with chocolate cake and a heap of vanilla ice cream. She set it down in front of him and sat in the center stool next to him.

"So tell me what's been keeping you so busy. I can take a minute and hear your story." She gave him an encouraging smile.

He looked at her and lowered his voice to just above a whisper. He didn't want to say *murder* in front of young kids. "Well, it's like this: I have been about maxed out and gotten myself all worked up over my neighbor who was murdered."

Roxanne looked at him. "You mean, Carla was your neighbor?"

"Yeah, did you know her?" Mick asked her.

"Well, not personally," she said, "but she would come in here with a lady friend every so often. They would have dinner and drinks and be totally absorbed in what each other was saying. In fact, I thought they were lesbians. They would spend at least a couple of hours whenever they did come in. What happened to her?"

"Well, I went over to her house to check on her because her screen door was banging in the wind. She didn't answer to my knock, and I figured she was probably home, because she always had a friend stop by on Wednesday mornings. When I went in, I found her lying on her kitchen floor deader than a doornail."

"Oh, wow, how awful!" Roxanne looked at him with sympathy. "Were you very close to her?"

"No, not that close. In fact, I am sorry now I didn't know her better. She was a very nice person, and we had started to talk more the past few months, and now I am finding out things about her that I had no idea about. It makes me sad that someone can live next door to you for a couple of years and all you pretty much say is, 'Hello,' 'How ya doing?' That was pretty much it. Then boom she is murdered, and now I have been finding out who some of her family is."

Roxanne looked at him. "She would often come to Oceanside. We were shocked to hear about her being murdered. The gal she came in here with lives here in town. Her name was Evelyn. I can't remember her last name."

Mick interrupted her. "Evelyn! That was who Carla was waiting for on Wednesday morning. That was her Wednesday-morning tea date. Did you know that she was murdered too?"

Roxanne looked at him with a shocked expression. "Oh my god, no. I don't think anyone in town knows that yet. Evelyn lived down a tree-lined road, and you couldn't see her house from the main road. She didn't really come into town that often, except when she went to the post office or to meet Carla. She was kind of reclusive, bookish-like. When did this all happen?"

"It's only been a couple of days. That is the main reason I wanted to stop and see you. You know so many people here. I thought maybe you could tell me something, which you have, actually, in that Carla and Evelyn came in here together once in a while."

Roxanne looked at him and started to say something, but then the couple with the kids caught her eye, so she told Mick she would be back in a minute. "Duty calls," she told him.

Mick watched as she went to the family and then back to the kitchen and brought out some more pop in two more glasses. *Well, those kids will be bouncing off the walls,* he thought to himself as he watched the one kid kick the other one under the table. Just then, the kicked kid spilled the pop that Roxanne had just set in front of him, and then the noise began. "Really? Thank God I never did have kids," he mumbled to himself. Roxanne had to go back into the kitchen and get some rags, and when she came back out, she had another pop in her hand. The mom was attempting to quiet the kids down, but it didn't seem to be working very well.

Just then, there was a bang when the dad slapped his hand down on the table and sternly told them both to straighten up or there would be no movie tonight. Both kids shut up immediately and sipped quietly on their pop. *Good for you, Dad,* Mick thought.

Roxanne came back and sat back down, telling him she really only had another minute or two. He thanked her and took the faded picture of Thomas Hardcastle out of his back pocket. "Have you seen anyone like this in town lately?" he asked her.

"Well, it's kind of hard to make out. Is that the only picture you have? He looks a little familiar."

Mick dug out his cell phone and scrolled through some pictures. "Not sure this one is any better, but it's not a newspaper clipping, so you might be able to make it out a little clearer." He showed her the picture he had taken from Randy's computer. The mug shot of Hardcastle. "This one is pretty hard-core," he told her.

"Boy, wouldn't want to meet him in the dark," she said. "He's a mean-looking bugger. Ya know, Mick, I think I might have seen someone that looks rather like that. Some scrawny, kind of unkempt guy came in here two days ago. He wanted a cup of coffee and a cinnamon bun to go. His jacket was zipped up to his neck, and his ball cap was pulled low over his face. He gave me the creeps because all I could see of his face were his beady eyes. He was very abrupt, but you know me. I am friendly with everyone who comes in here, scruffy or not. He was not taken in with my customer service skills. As soon as I handed him the coffee and the bun in a bag, he just slammed some money down on the counter and stalked off. Not letting the door close behind him but literally slamming it. It made poor little Mrs. Chambers jump in her chair. I just figured, 'What the hell, short man syndrome.' But I did go to the window to see which way he went, and I watched him get into a small maroon-colored vehicle. I am not good with makes and models, and he was too far away for me to catch a license plate number. I can tell you, though, he was nasty-looking. Like the guy wouldn't have a problem knocking his own mother on the head. He slammed on the gas and squealed off down the streets. I asked myself where the lazy-ass cops are when you need them. In fact, Charlie had just been in about an hour ago, for his daily coffee and doughnut, which he thinks he should get every day for free. One of these days, I need to let him know that nothing is free. He's so arrogant, though, he wouldn't think that I was talking about him."

Mick looked at his plate. *Damn, I wish I had actually taken the time to taste what I was eating.* His plate was clean, and he couldn't even remember what it tasted like. "Thanks a lot, Roxanne. That is helpful. The old twins were in Tillamook this morning, and they said they had seen someone matching the description also. Although, you never know with them. William was entertaining them, so they could have said about anything for him to continue."

"Who's William?" she asked him.

"Oh, just an interesting old guy I picked up on the way back home. He is probably waiting for me, so I had better get going." He got up and put some dollar bills on the table.

Roxanne got up at the same time. She leaned over to give him a little peck on the cheek. He leaned in for the kiss, then slapped her on the bottom. She slapped him lightly on the cheek and told him to come back when he could stay longer. With that, she bounced back into the kitchen. He smiled as the ancient screen door slammed shut behind him.

Chapter 41

Mick stepped outside into the blinding sunlight, put his sunglasses on, and looked up the street to see if he could spot William. *Son of a gun, if he wasn't just standing on the corner, rocking back and forth on those cowboy boots, talking to another woman. What's with that guy? An elderly chick magnet, for God's sake.* Mick couldn't help but chuckle, thinking the guy had it better off than he did. William did not even notice as Mick approached, what with the gal he was talking to and the stunning ocean view he was facing.

"Well, I have got to hand it to you, William, you sure know how to make friends."

William turned toward the sound of Mick's voice but still didn't exactly acknowledge him.

"What's up, old buddy? Never have seen when the ole cat got your tongue," Mick said.

William turned from the gal he was talking to and said, "This has got to be the most mesmerizing view I have ever seen. I wish Emily could have seen this view. The sun is shining on top of the water, looking like sparkly diamonds, and that huge rock with the hole in it is unbelievable! I bet there are magnificent sunsets here. I really thought there was nothing that could surpass the mountain views I have from the ranch, but I believe I may be wrong about that. This is more than beautiful!"

"Well, it is damn hard to beat, William, but again, different geography. Where you live is beautiful too, just a different kind of beautiful. I must admit, it would be hard to pick one over the other."

William seemed to collect his thoughts and remember what his goal was. He turned toward Mick and said, "Mick, let me introduce you to Connie. She is an interim post office employee. She has only been here in Oceanside for a month. She has been filling in for the postmaster, who had to have a total knee surgery, and needless to say, it has not gone so well. So Connie may be here a couple of more months. She is one of those people who minds her own business but always keeps her eyes and ears open, so to speak. Connie, tell Mick what you have seen in the time you have been here."

With that, Mick observed William laying on the fatherly charm and touching Connie gently on the shoulder. She smiled up at him. Mick rolled his eyes upward but smiled at Connie and held out his hand in introduction. "Connie, so glad to meet you. Any information you might have will be helpful. I am sure William already informed you about our interests, and I don't want you to waste your time repeating anything you have already told him, so we will be on our way now."

William stopped him from walking away. "Connie does have some information, Mick, that you might want to hear. Even though she hasn't been here for very long, she is very observant."

Connie looked at Mick and smiled tentatively. "Well, I did see a man fitting the description William mentioned. He came into the post office about two days ago. He said he was having something sent to him while he was on vacation, but he did not give his name as Hardcastle. He said his name was Mark DeGuard."

Mick looked at the gal and asked her what was sent to him.

"Well, I have worked for the post office for about twelve years now, and I am considered a traveler. I don't mind going to different post offices when they have staffing needs, because it gives me an opportunity to see different places. So in other words, I adapt but usually keep my mouth shut about internal politics and just crap in general. This guy that sounds like the same person who William described was asking for mail for a Mark DeGuard. He had some kind of official-looking paperwork with Mark DeGuard's signature on it, so we gave him the mail we had for Mark DeGuard. It all looked aboveboard."

Mick asked her what kind of mail it was, and she said it was all kind of secretive-looking stuff, a nine-by-twelve black plastic envelope that she had only seen a couple of times before in the twelve years she had worked at the post office. She told Mick she had always covered for employees who were going on vacation or other medical leave, and usually in rural areas, so she really didn't pay attention to people's mail like a regular employee might. "I'm sorry if I can't be more helpful." She looked up at Mick with big doe brown eyes.

Mick looked at her in turn and thanked her for her help. He told her he was a private investigator investigating a murder in a nearby town and asked her if she minded giving him her name and number. She, of course, did not mind, and Mick tucked a little card in the pocket of his jacket with her name and number on it. Mick asked her to call him if anything else came up that she thought might be helpful. She gave him a big smile as she took his card and put it in her purse. They all gave a friendly wave as they turned and went in opposite directions.

"Well, that was interesting," he said to William. "And I found out more interesting information at Roxanne's café too. I think we should see if we can find the roads the old twin said she followed the maroon car down on. What do you think, William?" Mick looked at William, and for the first time since he had met him, he seemed to hesitate.

"Well, Mick, not so sure this is the best idea. Don't you think you might have taken this as far as you should go and now leave it up to the police?"

Mick looked at William with about the most stubborn look William had ever seen. "No, William, I don't think so. When I have a mission, I have a mission, and I am about the most stubborn son of a bitch around. Besides, I know the drill. The police will have excuses because they are too damn lazy to do their job, so basically someone has to do it for them."

William shook his head. "Well, I had to put my two cents in so in case something happens, I can say I told you so."

Mick looked at William and gave some thought before he said, "Ya know, William, you don't have to stay here. You have a son and grandson. I don't have any family ties, not even a dog that will care if I am not around, so I really think you would be better off heading home now. I really appreciate all you were able to do for me."

William turned toward Mick with a determined look on his face. "No, Mick. I have come this far. I really want to see this through with you. I haven't felt this energized in years, before Emily died, anyway. So let's get 'er done, man!" William slapped Mick on the shoulder and started walking toward the truck.

Both men got into the truck and gave each other the thumbs-up.

"I sure hope you won't regret this, William. I reckon I can find the road Evelyn—or was it Evaline?—found but didn't dare drive down on."

William told him that he would have some interesting stories to relay to his grandson, provided he made it back home, and he gave Mick a wink on that comment. Mick scowled at him. "Don't make me regret that I didn't send you home, old man." He put the truck in reverse and headed out of town. Mick told William he figured he knew pretty much every back road around the county. He did like to do some fishing when he had any free time. He found it was one thing he could rely on to unwind and relax a little bit. These rivers weren't that challenging, but just being outside in the peace and quiet helped him unwind and gave him a new perspective on things.

He drove about five miles down Bay Ocean Road, where there were a few scattered trailers and small run-down cottages. The road paralleled the Trask River, which meandered its way through some lush green woods. Mick explained to William that most of the places were either boarded up or falling down, not inhabited by anyone anymore that he was aware of. The Trask was not a very big river, but when it rained for days on end, it could overflow its banks, and it did so big-time five years ago. Everybody was evacuated, and most people in this area were less than poverty level and did not have insurance, so it was pretty much vacant now. "If I remember correctly, there were only two or three driveways off this road, and only one leads toward the river. The other two are on the opposite side. Here is the first one. Hold on to your Stetson, William." Mick could feel his hands tense on the steering wheel as he drove the truck slowly down the overgrown driveway.

The drive was so overgrown with wildflowers and weeds he couldn't tell if anyone had been down this way or not. There were some signs of trampled grass and a pop can or two, but nothing else. *Maybe just kids getting a few jollies,* thought Mick. He looked over at William. "We do have some homeless camps scattered around town. You generally find them out in areas like this, because the sheriff's department runs them out of town or throws them in jail if they try to camp in the city parks. They don't take to any kind of riffraff here like they do in the big cities."

As they neared the end of the driveway, they could see a small trailer with a caved-in front deck and a rotted, sagging roof. There were no signs of any habitation except for some very large mole mounds in the long grass. Mick stopped the truck by the sagging deck and turned toward William. "I don't think I have ever seen mole mounds quite that big before, have you?"

"Ummm, can't say that I have. Maybe they grow bigger when they live by the water." Just then, William pointed to a huge gray heron that had taken flight from the edge of the river. "Wow, now that is not something I see every day. Not any day, actually. That one must have had a wingspread of at least six feet!" William was in awe at the size of the bird.

Mick had hardly noticed it since he saw them all the time. He said, "They are pretty magnificent, all right. Wait until you see the pelicans and white egrets. They both started coming back a couple of years ago. Not sure why they weren't here for a few years, but I am glad to see them back."

"This looks like a dead end, anyway," Mick said. "I don't think anyone has been here for years, except maybe kids, by the looks of the rusty beer cans and firepit." He paused. "Let's go see what else we can find." He went to turn the truck around but had some difficulty, what with the length of the eelgrass and blackberry bushes. The ground was wet also. He ended up churning up some earth and making a rut at least ten inches deep. "Shit," he said. "Guess I will see what she's made of." He put it in four-wheel drive and stepped on the gas. It moved like a monster truck, and he was back out onto some gravel in a heartbeat. "Well, at least I know the four-wheel drive works." He inched on down the road toward the next driveway.

The second driveway seemed to be more overgrown than the first one. It was almost completely hidden by overgrown blackberry bushes and Scotch broom, but it looked like someone had tried to clear a narrow path through the brush. Mick decided that due to the overgrowth of brush, that was probably not the driveway anyone would have found their way down on, unless they had cut a path through the woods. It was obvious that no vehicle had been down it for years. Mick decided to pass and kept on driving slowly to see if there were other driveways more approachable.

They drove another couple of hundred feet or so, and Mick could see a dilapidated shed off to the left. It had a blackened cement firepit in the yard where the grass had been trampled all around it. Beer cans littered the area, along with old McDonald bags and wrappers. There were a couple of rusted, ripped old camp chairs lying on top of a tattered gray tarp. Mick looked at the shed, but with the sun's rays at the angle they were, he could barely see, so he got out of the truck to take a closer look. The shed had a wooden pole with an electric box attached. Looked like the kind you would hook up an RV to. There were a lot of people in the county that lived permanently in their RVs, but by the looks of this place, it had been abandoned some time ago. Probably kids again, camping out, or possibly a homeless camp that got deserted when the weather got bad.

Mick looked at William, who was still sitting in the truck. "I'm going to take a look in the shed!" he hollered at him. William gave him the thumbs-up but made no move to get out of the truck, so Mick turned and went tentatively up the rickety front steps. The door was fastened with only one hinge; the other one had rusted through. He peeked around the door and was surprised at how dry it appeared inside. Dirty, for sure, but no dank, moldy air assailed his nostrils. He stepped into the small area. There was a small metal table and two folding chairs, one of which the seat had caved in. The other one looked intact. There was also a small bed built into the wall underneath the only window in the place. There was a dirty mattress on the bed and an old Army blanket, both of which had been chewed on by critters, mostly likely rats, he thought. Mick looked up at the low ceiling and almost gave a scream. He caught himself and shuddered instead. There were two bats hanging from one of the exposed beams. Neither of which made a move for him, but they sure gave him goose bumps. He looked around one more time, then stepped outside and almost bumped into William, who stood there, chuckling.

"What do you think is so damn funny?" Mick asked him.

"Well, I caught the look on your face and thought maybe you had seen a ghost or something. What was it?"

"Hell, worse than a ghost, if you ask me," Mick said. "There were two bats hanging from the rafters, and there is nothing that gives me the creeps more than bats! That terror of a cousin of mine I told you about, he got bitten by a rabid bat when he was about fifteen. They thought he wasn't going to make it. He was sick forever, it seemed like. The only good thing was, he missed a couple of months of school. They are nasty, nasty in my book." He shivered again. "Someone stayed here, but it looks like it was a long time ago."

William told Mick that he had walked around toward the back of the shed and didn't see anything but a hole in the ground. "Looks like it was used for a shitter. Toilet paper and rags lying around it." He hadn't seen anything else of interest.

"Whew, let's get out of here," Mick told him.

They both got back in the truck, and Mick sat there a moment before starting the engine. "To my recollection, there are only two more driveways left before you get to the bay. This could just be a wild-goose chase, for all we know."

William looked at him and said, "What the hell, man. Then I can just chalk it up to a little sightseeing adventure. Nothing ventured, nothing gained, I guess. Let's just go check out what's left to check out. I have certainly never seen this kind of country before. So it's not a waste of my time, anyway."

Mick started the truck and drove cautiously down the drive. They came out onto what was left of the gravel road. He looked at William and smiled. "Well, they say third time's the charm, so let's go, then." Another five hundred feet or so, and this time they saw a small house off to the right. It appeared closer to the road than the other sites they had checked out. "I think I will keep the truck parked out here and walk into this one. What do you think, William?"

"Well, by the looks of things, someone has used this driveway recently. The brush is trampled flat. So if we really are sleuthing, as you insist on doing, I would say yes, then. Let's walk to check out what is down there."

Mick drove another few feet down the road and parked the truck under a huge cedar tree. He was able to get it off the road so that if someone came down that way, which he doubted, they would be able to get past. He supposed a fisherman might use the road to get to the bay. He remembered a great little fishing hole down that way. At least he thought it was down that way. Before he got out of the truck, he leaned across William and retrieved his .45 handgun from the glove box. He gave William a serious look and told him he thought that William should remain in the truck. "I might find something this time, William. By the looks of the driveway, someone has been here recently. I would feel better if you stayed here. If there is trouble, you at least can call the police."

William started to protest, but Mick held up his hand and said, "William, I'm sorry, but I insist. I can't have the possibility of you getting hurt on my conscience. Besides, if I am not back in fifteen minutes or so, then call 911 and let them check things out. Deal?"

William did not look very happy, but he took the keys Mick handed him and told Mick to be careful. "Holler if anything looks dangerous and I will call 911, anyway." With that, he gave Mick a thumbs-up and Mick loped down the path.

This time Mick came upon a run-down cottage, and he slowed his pace to a cautious walk and then stood behind a stand of cotton-wood trees to get a better picture of what was there. He could see that someone had recently been there. There was what looked like a green bag of garbage on the front porch, and it was intact. If it had been there for very long, something would have gotten into it and scattered it everywhere. Crows, seagulls, or racoons were all over the place. They loved garbage.

Mick stood there for almost five minutes, then decided he had better make a move or William would be calling the police. He hadn't seen any movement or heard any noises, so he figured it was safe to go forward. He wasn't feeling secure enough to just go up to the front door, so he made his way through the trees to the back of the cottage. He approached the back step quietly. He could see a small dirty window to the right of the back door. He walked toward it in hopes he might be able to see in the window. He was over six feet tall but could barely see anything through the window—it was so covered in dirt and caked-on salt spray. He tried using his hand to scrape at some of the grime, but it was pretty well packed on there. When he reached his hand up to shield the reflection from the sun, he heard a slight rustle behind him. He turned toward the sound and saw a big stick headed right for his face.

Chapter 42

When Mick woke up, he tried to touch his head but was unable to move his hands or arms. His head was screaming painfully, and he realized his hands were bound tightly together around a thick wooden post. As he opened his eyes, or tried to, one of the them was swollen shut. He let out a groan. "Jesus H. Christ. What the hell hit me?" he muttered out loud.

He looked around at his surroundings and found he was propped up on a cold, damp dirt floor. It felt like he had been dropped down the rabbit hole. It was musty and dank. With his good eye, he could see a small streak of light coming through the one clear spot of a small dirty window. He could feel the cold and damp coming through the material of his jeans. The walls were made of rock, and they were lined with shelves containing old wooden crates. He figured he was in an old root cellar, trussed up like an old chicken or something. Man, he felt like an idiot. Good thing he had insisted William stay in the truck. Hopefully, he was okay. Mick could not figure out how much time had passed, but it was still light outside. He couldn't have been there very long. His hands were still warm, although starting to ache. He could wiggle his fingers even though the rope was pretty tight. He could move his legs enough to bend them a little, but he couldn't move his feet. *Oh hell,* he thought. They were bound together also. He stopped and tried to think, but his head was throbbing so bad it made common sense unrealistic.

"Shit," he said out loud. He always carried a Swiss Army knife in his pocket, but he was pretty sure he would not be able to get to it, trussed up as he was. He thought about the guy who had slugged him. At least he had gotten a look at him first. *Although who knows,* he thought. Might not do him any good to have seen the bastard if he couldn't get out of here. He tried to readjust his position and discovered his back hurt in places he didn't know he had. He figured he might have been dragged down the stairs. He was beginning to figure it served him right for not just letting the police handle things. If he hadn't been so damn stubborn, he probably would not be here right now.

The damp floor was starting to chill him, and he thought he might just pass out; his head was hurting so bad. He was beginning to think that William might have fallen asleep in the truck or, worse yet, that Hardcastle got to him too. He felt like hours had gone by, but it was probably not as long as he thought.

Just then, he heard a gunshot, followed by another one, then a short volley of gunfire ensued. Mick felt himself tense, hoping it was "good guy meets bad guy and good guy wins." *When I go up shit's creek, I sure do it right,* he thought to himself.

Just then, he heard his name being called. It sounded like William, and the shouting had a note of desperation in its tone. Mick held his head up and yelled as loud as he could, which caused about the worst spasm of pain he had ever imagined. It made his body shake. *Good old William,* he thought. *That is one tough old bird.* With that thought, he passed out.

William came down the dark cellar stairs just as he saw Mick slump on his side. Boy, he was a mess, he thought. He had bits of dried blood everywhere. He went over to examine him and gently put his hand on Mick's head. With the touch, Mick opened his one good eye and looked askance at William. "Boy, am I glad to see you," he said, barely audible. William told Mick that it was a good thing he got conked on the head; anyplace else, he might not have survived.

"Thanks a lot, old man," Mick told him. "Can you help me out of these damn ties and tell me what in the hell happened out there?"

William took out a pocketknife and sliced through the ropes. Mick sat up a little straighter and rubbed his arms and wrists while William undid the ties that bound his feet. "Oh god, my head aches like you would not believe," he told William.

"Well, I guess I would tell you that I do believe it. You look like crap and should go to the hospital to rule out a concussion and get a couple of stitches. You took a nasty one on the head. There's a baseball growing there too."

Mick reached up and gently touched his eye and the top of his head, then grimaced and almost lost it again. He took a deep breath and asked William to just help him the hell up. "I ain't no sissy, ya know." William leaned down to give Mick a hand up, and Mick winced and moaned with the effort. "So who fired the shots, William?" Mick asked him.

William led Mick over to the stairs, where he could sit in a more comfortable position before trying to get up the stairs. He grinned and patted his chest. "Well, I have always carried a piece in a shoulder holster under my shirt for more on forty years. Ever since I went hunting once and dropped my rifle in the river when I slipped. When I regained my balance, I spotted this cougar just watching me. Scared me to death. My rifle was gone, and all I had was my hunting knife. Turns out the cougar wasn't much interested in me since he happened to be gnawing on a dead female deer he must have just come upon. It was still pretty fresh, so fortunately, I was able to high-tail it out of there before he changed his mind. Then one other time, I surprised a bear cub while I was walking my fence line, looking for things needing repairs. I was—"

Mick interrupted him. "Please, William, would love to hear it, but how about another time? I would love to get out of this damn cellar and into some fresh air."

"Oops, sorry, Mick. Guess I still got a little adrenaline going on. Come on, I will help you up the stairs. I shot that bastard dead. Then I called 911. Couldn't help myself. Figured that where we were located, it would take them too long to get here, and I knew you were taking longer than you were supposed to, so I started to check things out myself. I startled him coming down the road, and he fired first, so I took a shot and he went down. His car was parked a little farther down the road from where you left your truck. I walked down and spotted it and figured there would be trouble. Sure enough was. I am sure he is that Hardcastle fella. Looks just like your description.

Lousy shot, I must say. Once he did see me, he just started firing away. I don't think he could hit the broad side of a barn. Nailed him square in the chest. Probably died instantly."

Just then, they could hear sirens and the gravel and brush scrunching and flying. They looked at each other and gave a high five. "Leave it to the boys in blue, probably having a doughnut," William said.

Just then, they passed the prone man lying in the dirt in a pool of his blood. Mick was tempted to turn him over and get a better look. If his head hadn't hurt so bad, he might have. As it was, he could barely stand upright, even with William's help. They reached the truck at the same time as the police, along with a fire truck and an ambulance. Officer Randy got out of the police car first and ran over to Mick.

"Jesus, Mick. What the hell happened to you? I tried to tell you to mind your own business, but you just couldn't, could you?"

"Well, it's like this," Mick said, and on that note, he collapsed to the ground.

When Mick came to, he was lying on a gurney in the ambulance and they were buckling him in and cleaning up some of the blood. He could hear William telling his side of the story. *Well, better him than me, anyway,* Mick thought. *He has a much better gift of gab.* The EMT was shining a little penlight in his eyes and asking him all kinds of questions. He was trying to hear what William was saying, but there was too much other noise going on. So he just closed his eyes and answered the questions. The way he was feeling, he figured it probably would be the safest thing to go on in and get checked out. He could hardly move his head without seeing stars, and he could only see out of one eye.

The next time he woke up, he was lying on clean sheets, with a clean nightgown on, and in a clean hospital room. *Whew, how long have I been out?* he wondered. He opened his eyes, and William was still there, although in a much better environment than when he last saw him. He started to rise up on one arm but winced and lay back down.

"Don't start getting all riled up, young man," William told him. "The doc said you suffered a concussion and cracked two ribs, so they want to keep you at least overnight for observation, just to make sure you don't have a subdural or something like that."

"Oh crap," Mick replied. "Never fails. When you get in here, they don't want to let you go."

"Well, from what I have seen, it's probably a dang good idea. You were knocked a good one. Probably lucky to be alive," William told him. William looked at Mick's one open eye and said, "There is a little detail I left out of the exciting events."

"What's that?" Mick asked him.

"Well…" William looked a little sheepish when he said, "In my rush, I forgot to tell you that there was a woman coming down the road with Hardcastle. She looked like she might have been a reluctant participant in the events, but it was hard to tell and everything happened so fast. He was struggling with her, practically dragging her behind him. When she broke loose, I fired and he went down. I saw her take off like a bat out of hell. She did not run toward me like you would have thought she might if she was frightened or he had hurt her, but she ran right through the bushes. I know she had no weapon. I was kind of concentrating on not getting myself killed, and when he went down, I was too shaken up to follow her. Besides, I am an old man, ya know. Not like I could have caught up with her. She was outa sight way before the sirens started."

Mick looked out of the hospital window before he said, "What did she look like?"

William said she had auburn-colored hair. She was probably about five feet, four inches or so, kind of petite. Very determined look on her face, from what he could make out. Maybe a few freckles. She seemed pretty fair-skinned. "I told Officer Randy about her and where she ended up going through the brush. He took a bunch of notes and was going to send out a bulletin notifying other departments in the area to be on the lookout for her. Look what I found." William held up a gold bracelet with some red stones. "I don't know why I didn't turn it over to Randy, but I just couldn't help myself, knowing how you wanted to solve this case for yourself. Looks like the clasp broke and it caught up on a small branch. Ever see that gal you were telling me about wear it?"

Chapter 43

Mick's overnight hospital stay turned into a forty-eight-hour stay, and he was biting the bullet for the hospitalist to show up and discharge him before noon. His concussion turned out to be pretty serious, and every time he moved, he had a shooting pain in his ribs. He was told in no uncertain terms that he needed to take it easy for a few days. "Don't get excited, don't drive, don't do anything strenuous." Well, that was a laugh. He could barely move, but he was determined to do what he could.

William took Mick back to the police station when he got out of the hospital. The good news was that Colin had finished the house and got everything all cleaned up. William had taken Mick's hospital stay to heart and had managed to do some sightseeing for a couple of days, so he was feeling pretty chipper. William pulled up to the door of the police station and helped Mick get out of the truck. Mick felt like a pussy having William help him, but at this point he hated to admit it: he needed the help. He winced as he stepped off the side bar of the pickup. "Thanks, William. I don't need to tell you again and again how grateful I am for your help. Couldn't have done it without you." They walked into the police station together. William had already been there and pretty much told his whole story more than once and could not think of anything else significant that he could tell. Randy had a few questions for Mick that he surmised he had not been so forthcoming with before.

Mick gave Randy any and all information he had. Randy assured him that William was aboveboard and honest and his gun was legal, although he was out of state, so there was a slight problem there, but Randy was going to overlook that. Randy went on to say that he had asked the Portland team to put a rush on all the fingerprints they were still waiting for verification on. That included the DNA samples that had been sent in. "I am sure we are going to find that all these murders are going to tie up into one neat little package, but with the way things go these days, we may still be looking at a week or more before we find out anything conclusive." He went onto to explain that they did get evidence that a Wanda Carlisle had been in Mark DeGuard's house. She matched the description that Mick had given, and she was the same age as Mark's sister would have been. "She is probably also the woman that William had seen head through the bushes. So a few more things to check and hopefully we can wrap all this up. How are you holding up, Mick? You sure took a beating." He looked at William and said, "You know that normally you would be in a jail cell while we sort all this out, but because you have been so helpful, we are not doing that. Killing someone is a serious offense, but it was obvious he fired on you first. So don't either the two of you leave town, and I will get back to you with any results that come forward." Randy looked at Mick rather sternly. "Mick, mind your Ps and Qs and lie low, okay? I know that is what the doc told you, anyway, so just listen for once in your life."

Mick and William got in the truck, and Mick asked William to drive to the end of town to a burger joint he said had the only decent burgers in town. The burger joint was basically empty, so it only took a few minutes to get something to go. Brenda, the counter girl, actually had to ask Mick if he was all right. She looked forward to his flirtations whenever he stopped by, but she could tell he wasn't himself, so she just handed him the burgers with a smile.

Mick looked over at William, who looked like he had aged about ten years. He told him, "Hey, man, don't beat yourself up over this. If anyone needs a beating, it's me, for getting you into all this, and hey, I got my beating, so we are fair and square. I figured Hardcastle had some type of mission and then he was planning on coming back and finishing me off, so again, I owe you my life."

William looked over at Mick and said, rather sardonically, in Mick's opinion, "Just keep in mind, Mick, you are not a cat. Might be good to do what the doc said and take it easy."

They drove back to Mick's in silence, each lost in their own thoughts. When they got in the door, Mick let William get some plates down from the cupboard, and Mick took a quick walk through the house. "Wow, Colin sure did a bang-up job. Don't know how he got so much done in that short amount of time. It's great. I just took a look at myself in the mirror for the first time. I didn't dare when I was in the hospital. I sure look like I was dragged down a flight of stairs. I could use a Jack. What about you, old man?"

William told him it sounded like a great idea, and he brought the bags of food and plates into the small dining room.

Mick practically fell onto a dining room chair. "I am beyond exhausted. You go into the hospital because you need the care, but then they wake you up every few hours and stick you, prick you, or get your temperature. Does not make for a very restful night." Mick poured William a double-plus Jack.

The poor guy still looked upset. He turned to Mick when he set the drink down in front of him and said, "Ya know, I have killed my fair share of animals in my life, but I sure as hell have never killed another human being. It just kind of don't sit right in my craw. It feels pretty bad."

Mick told him that he could totally understand. He remembered the first time he had killed someone in the line of duty. He had been a rookie at that time, but he knew if the shoe had been on the other foot, it would have been him killed. He took his leave with pay and was back to work in a month. Taught him to be a little more cautious, though. "Let's see what's on the tube. Maybe all the bad news will distract us a little." They sat and watched the news in silence, sipping on Jack and slowly eating the burgers.

Mick woke up feeling like a great weight had been lifted from his shoulders. He hadn't even remembered getting himself to bed. He didn't have that maniac to worry about anymore, and he was pretty certain that was the guy that had killed Carla, Evelyn, and Mark. He could concentrate on his own business again. He owed Colin, not only money, but also a lot of gratitude. The kid had mentioned how he wasn't that enamored with what he was studying in school; maybe he would go into business with him. There was no shortage of investigative work on the coast. Mick could branch out a little farther north and south if he had the right help. *Should I really do that, though?* Mick wondered. *Things so far where jobs were concerned were pretty steady. I had better give that some serious thought before I open my big mouth, though.*

Mick looked at William's door, which was still closed. *Poor guy must have been out of it. I need to figure out something special I can do for him.* He walked into the kitchen to put on a pot of coffee. He put some fake sugar and a good helping of half-and-half in a cup and went outside to get the paper off the front deck. Not there, of course. He looked down his walkway and saw it sitting on the median by an azalea bush. *God dang, that kid.* That was the third time in less than a month that he couldn't manage to heave it onto the porch. He was going to have to give Paul, the manager of the gazette, a call. He felt sorry for the kid. He knew his money went to help his mom out, but come on, he just needed to throw it with a little better aim.

He took the paper to the table and went to pour his coffee when he heard a little ping from his back pants pocket. He looked at the screen but didn't recognize the number. Hoping it was something simple, he said, "Hello, this is Mick, of Meade and Associates. How can I help you?"

There was a long pause, and Mick thought no one was there and had started to hit the End button.

"Hello, Mick," a female's voice said.

Mick looked at the phone like he was expecting some great revelation.

"I see some nasty business got taken care of."

Mick sat down with a loud thump on a kitchen chair, and his heart beat a little faster. "Wanda?" he asked. "Is that you?"

THE END

About the Author

Ronelle Herrick grew up in small-town rural America, where reading and writing became her favorite pastimes. After a long carreer spent in healthcare, she and her husband were able to retire to the Oregon coast. Here she was able to fulfill a dream and put her energy into writing a novel.

CPSIA information can be obtained
at www.ICGtesting.com
Printed in the USA
LVHW101731120722
723335LV00005B/88